D0289420

The
King's Agent

BOOKS BY DONNA RUSSO MORIN

The Courtier's Secret

The Secret of the Glass

To Serve a King

The King's Agent

The King's Agent

Donna Russo Morin

KENSINGTON BOOKS
www.kensingtonbooks.com

KENSINGTON BOOKS are published by

Kensington Publishing Corp.
119 West 40th Street
New York, NY 10018

All Kensington titles, imprints, and distributed lines are available at special quantity discounts for bulk purchases for sales promotion, premiums, fund-raising, educational, or institutional use.

Special book excerpts or customized printings can also be created to fit specific needs. For details, write or phone the office of the Kensington Special Sales Manager: Attn. Special Sales Department. Kensington Publishing Corp., 119 West 40th Street, New York, NY 10018. Phone: 1-800-221-2647.

Kensington and the K logo Reg. U.S. Pat. & TM Off.

ISBN-13: 978-0-7582-4682-0
ISBN-10: 0-7582-4682-X

First Kensington Trade Paperback Printing: March 2012
10 9 8 7 6 5 4 3 2 1

Printed in the United States of America

To Princess Zelda,
and all who love her as I do

Personaggi

*denotes historical character

***Battista della Palla:** born in Florence in 1489; served as the art agent to the French king François I.

Battista's men:

Ascanio, antiquities expert;
Barnabeo, dealer of Battista's excess items;
Ercole, a jack-of-all-trades, assists as needed;
Frado, Battista's longtime companion and most trusted friend, excursion logistics manager;
Giovanni, a linguistic expert and scribe;
Lucagnolo, paintings expert;
Pompeo, once apprenticed to Cellini; inventory keeper.

***Federico II of Gonzaga:** born 1500; marquess of Mantua.

Lady Aurelia: noblewoman, ward of the marquess of Mantua.

***Pope Clement VII:** born 1478 as Giulio di Giuliano de' Medici; served as a cardinal from 1513 to 1523, as pope from 1523 to 1534.

***Baldassare del Milanese:** an art dealer of nefarious repute; a rival of Battista della Palla.

***Michelangelo di Lodovico Buonarroti Simoni:** born 1475; sculptor, painter, architect, poet.

***Company of the Cauldron:** a group of Florentine artists who gathered on a regular basis over the course of more than fifty years; the company included the likes of Giovanni Francesco Rustici, Leonardo da Vinci, Michelangelo Buonarroti, Andrea del Sarto, and many others.

You are my master and my author,
You—the only one from whom my writing drew the noble style
For which I have been honored.

—Dante Alighieri (1265–1321)
Divina Commedia

One

Here one must leave behind all hesitation;
Here every cowardice must meet its death.

—Inferno

His hands quivered ever so slightly. Not with fear—he scoffed silently at the very notion—but with the exhilaration thrumming through his veins. His moment of triumph, of victorious possession, came upon him and he would not deny its power.

Battista della Palla stood before the carved door, shoulders hunched, broad body curled inward, as he jimmied the miniscule, well-worn silver rod into the small, square lock well. Dark eyes stole a quick, sidelong glance down each end of the empty corridor. A few flicks of his leather-cuffed wrist and . . . *click*.

He hummed a contented sigh, pushed back the swath of wavy black hair from his face, and pushed over the arched swing shackle of the padlock. The heavy, intricately scrolled device dropped into his hands and he palmed it into his satchel; such locks were a treasure worth filching. For Battista, their value lay far beyond the monetary; they were trophies of a hunt well served. With a last glance to the empty passageway, a waggle of dark, thick brows, and a twitch of a smile, he took a bow to an imaginary audience and slipped in.

Stepping into the largest private room of the palazzo, he tucked his small tool back into its pouch on his cuff. One lone candle burned low in the far corner, its pale yellow light outshone by that of the three-quarter moon. The gray glow streamed through the four tall leaded windows on the opposite wall, checkering the room with squares of muted incandescence.

He had seen the inside of many a nobleman's bedchamber, spent more than a little time in them, for here the privileged kept their valuables. Here Battista did much of his work.

The fire burned low in the grate to his left, meek blaze sparking upon the gold cloth of the pastoral tapestries covering the inside wall beside him. There, in front of him, at the foot of the curtained bed, stood the mahogany strongbox, rugged and rigid with its thick steel bands, incongruous against the flowing cerulean bed draperies.

Battista grumbled an irritated chuckle. Two more padlocks bound each band, ones equally as intricate and as valued as the first. He knelt before the large chest, knees cracking, leather braces stretching against flexing calf muscles, nettled mumblings unchecked. The duca di Carcaci guarded his treasures well.

What a shame I must steal one.

The passing thought came and went in Battista's mind, one tinted with pale regret, brushed away with the impatient hand of his oft-thought though transitory vacillations. He had attempted to acquire the piece through diplomatic and pecuniary methods, had offered the duke a handsome purse—more than generous—and with it offered the nobleman a chance to assist Firenze. But both opportunities had been summarily denied, and now Battista must do what he must, whatever it took for his beloved Florence. If such efforts brought him a princely income in the doing, then so be it.

He dealt with these locks—round, bulbous, and brass—as easily as the first, and tossed open the heavy cover of the chest, cringing at the grating creak of the hinges. His glance tripped up and about sheepishly, as if waiting for the door to be thrown open and incarceration to commence. But with no true cause. The stillness continued unabated, as did his thievery. Only his gaze faltered, fixed upon the massive portrait crowning the large bed.

Four people gazed back at him, their happiness in the moment and in one another captured and undeniable. The *duca*, a middle-aged man but with youthful countenance, his wife still pretty, a full figure enhanced by the attentions of a loving husband and the births of their two children. Two girls played at their feet, perhaps two years apart in age, yet identical in their dark-haired beauty and mischievous smiles.

Battista recognized his feelings of respect and longing, measured out in equal parts, for he respected a man who loved his family, as his own father had, and desired to see himself the anchor of such a portrait, the patriarch of such a family. The yearning grew with each passing year.

Not likely, he chided himself with a surrendering shrug and a quirk of his lips, *and not now.*

Florence needed him now; it could not wait while he found love or conceived children.

Battista turned his almost-black brown eyes back into the cavernous strongbox, deep-dimpled chin tucked into his chest. His face bloomed at the treasures found within, so many of them made his hand tingle as it passed over them. But he came for only one, and rummaged quietly amidst the costly rubble within until he found it.

He stood the small statuette on the palm of his hand and studied every portion of the foot-length carving. There was no mistaking the Gothic style of Nicola Pisano, nor that this piece was a model created more than two hundred years ago as a basis for one portion of the artist's monumental work on the pulpit of the Siena Cathedral. Few knew this miniature existed, and its anonymity compounded its value tenfold. How Battista's patron knew of it was not for him to question.

Drawing out a thick cloth from his sack, Battista efficiently wrapped the piece, and placed it vertically in the leather satchel resting on his hip—worn, smooth, and shiny, curved to his back where it had rested for years, as if it were an organic extremity born with him.

Battista closed the strongbox, reattached the locks, and—with a tip of his head in gratitude to the man in the portrait—exited the room with the same ease with which he had entered.

Quiet hugged the palazzo in its nightly embrace as Battista made his way unremarked and unnoticed to the ground floor—where Frado waited, impatiently, with their horses, just outside the kitchen door at the rear of the building as agreed—and through a statue-guarded foyer and down a west-facing corridor. It had cost Battista little to get the pretty scullery maid to explain the layout of the palazzo: a good dinner, some time in his bed—which he enjoyed as much as she, bless her feisty heart—and she'd told him of every corridor and door in the palace.

Turning left, he did little to muffle the clack of his boot heels on the ochre marble tile, or contain the strut swinging his hips. Though many locks held the treasure of the house, Battista's thievery had been far too easily done; a man with such little a mind for security as this nobleman deserved to be robbed. Battista quickened his step as he neared the end of the corridor and the two doors on either side.

A few more steps, into the door on the left, and he'd be in the kitchen and on his way out. He grinned, lifted the pronged latch, and pulled the door open.

All air left his lungs with a wheeze. His eyes protruded almost painfully from his head.

The four armed and armor-clad men lounging about the room—polishing swords and playing at dice—stared at him with the same bewildered gape . . . but only for a fleeting moment.

"*Arresto!* Stop!"

"Get him!"

The cries erupted as the guards jumped to their feet, overturning chairs, upending tables, in their rush toward the intruder. Battista jumped backward out of the room as leather-clad fists and sword tips stretched out at him.

"*Porca vacca*. Damn it! The *right* door is the *right* door!" Battista cursed himself, slamming the door shut in their faces.

Shoulder bolstered against the portal, his whole body trembled as hard warrior bodies crashed against the other side, jarring the door violently in its cradle. With one hand, he set the latch. The other seized the handle of the largest of the three daggers tucked into his belt. He planted one foot back, stretched his arm high and taut above his head, arching his back, stretching like a bow about to launch its arrow.

With a propulsive growl, he slammed the dagger into the wood of the door at its edge, penetrating through it and into the jamb surrounding it.

Seconds, the thought rushed at him as rushed across the hall. *It gives me seconds, no more.*

Barging through the opposite door, he almost fell into the nearly abandoned kitchen. The house fire embers glowed red in the two large stone alcoves at either end of the massive room, the blood-colored gloom festering in every corner.

Three servants, two boys and a woman—those on night duty should the master return and call for anything—flinched back, already roused by the screaming and banging from across the hall. They stared openmouthed as Battista ran through the room, pulling down copper pots and cauldrons with a deafening clatter as he went, anything to throw between him and the angered guards soon to follow.

"*Scusi.*" He ducked his head sheepishly to the older woman as he rushed by her, seeing his mother's condemnation in her wrinkled face and narrowed eyes. His steps faltered, his head swung back, and he swiped a biscotto off the counter between them. "*Grazie, donna mia*. Thank you, my lady."

The woman rolled her eyes, but not without a hint of a grin.

With a raucous splintering of wood, the door across the hall ruptured open and the four men burst out, a rushing ocean hurling through a broken dam, tripping over one another to get out and get at him.

"*Sbrigari!* Hurry!" The old woman flapped her apron at Battista, pointing him to the wide double door in the east corner of the room with one fleshy finger.

Battista spared her no more pleasantries, running for escape as the guards jumped and tumbled over the obstacles thrown down in their path.

He burst through the doors, gasping at the cool night air as with his last breath. If he didn't move quickly, it would be.

In the shadowy courtyard, two horses whinnied in alarm; a male voice squeaked in almost-feminine surprise. Battista turned to the sound, finding his horse and his accomplice waiting, just as they planned, on the cobbles below the portico, the small, round man no more than a perched ball on the smaller of the two powerful steeds.

"We must away!" Battista shouted, running full tilt now, hurtling himself from the top of the five steps, leaping across the beast's derriere with a two-handed launch, and landing directly, if painfully—with a gruesome groan at the jolt to his groin—on his horse's saddle.

"They are on to us, *amico mio,*" he hissed at the flustered man bouncing on the horse beside him, grabbing the reins and taking control of his mount. "The chase is afoot, my friend. Hiiya!"

The leather straps snapped at his will and his horse leaped forward, Frado's following, impelled by the panic now thick in the air.

The horses' metal shoes clopped noisily against the stones and into the quiet of the night, thudding onto grass-covered field, an ever-increasing thrumming of urgency. In those seconds Battista had foretold, cries of protest rang out behind them and galloping pursuit exploded, muffling the men's bellows.

"*Dio mio.*"

Battista spared a quick look at his praying friend, the urge to laugh barely contained at the sight of the flabby man hanging on to his reins and the saddle's pommel for dear life, bereft of even the pretense of control over his horse as he bounded up and down, grunting with each downward slam on the hard seat.

The sound of pursuit grew ever closer. Battista dared a look and saw their pursuers had taken form, if only as ghostly shadows intent upon malice. Were they close enough for his dagger to find them? He couldn't be sure. No matter, only two blades remained and at least four men came for them, if not more, as the alarm most surely had brought others to the chase.

He tugged his horse closer to Frado's, close enough to see the look of sheer panic upon the man's round, red-splotched face.

"We have no choice." Battista raised his deep voice over the thunder of the hooves. "We must throw them."

Frado answered with a pitiful look of pleading, but Battista shook his head.

"Do it, Frado. You know you can."

With a curled lip of anger, Frado reached into the saddlebag behind him, drawing out a moist goatskin sack, one of a perfect size to fit into his palm. Without looking backward, tilting precariously as he lifted his right arm, he threw the dripping ball, quickly reaching in for another, then another again.

The sound of splitting skin and splashing liquid pop, pop, popped behind them and within seconds a screeching of horses followed, answered by painful, frustrated human cries and a rumbling as bone and flesh—of horse and man—tumbled hard upon the ground.

The sounds of pursuit faded behind them, dissipating into the dominion of night's stillness, returning it to tranquility once more.

With more than a modicum of disgust, Frado shook the residual drops of wolf urine off his hand, casting a worried glance toward Battista.

"I hope the horses are all right."

Battista's brows jumped up his forehead as he turned, catching the glint of amusement in his friend's winking eye. He threw back his head then, howls of laughter ringing out through the starlit sky, bursting with peals of relief and triumph.

"To home, my friend," he hooted.

"*Sì*, home." Frado chuckled, round head bobbing in relieved agreement.

They turned their horses south, no one behind them close enough to see, and made for Florence.

Two

And just as he who, with exhausted breath,
having escaped from the sea to shore,
turns to the perilous waters and gazes.

—*Inferno*

"Ack, you son of a dog. You cheated!"

The outrage scaled the stairs, penetrated the door, and trounced upon Battista, waking him from his deep slumber, be it midday or not.

Battista pulled a pillow over his head, his arms dropping back to the silk-covered ticking with a plop. His exhaustion permeated every bone and muscle in his laden body. He wanted no more than to sleep a few more hours; not even the thought of gloating over his prizes could rouse him or his spirit.

"I didn't, I swear, Giovanni."

An answering yelp soon followed and Battista sighed, hoping it punctuated the end of the fracas. Such nonsense could not last long; such nonsense would not dare keep him from his rest.

"You lie like you smell . . . badly!" The next salvo launched, the battle ensued.

Men barked at one another; chairs thrown out scraped across stone floor. Someone threw a punch and it landed with a riotous thwack.

"*Basta!*" Battista roared, flinging the pillow off and to the floor in one fluid motion of frustration, jumping out of bed, and kicking it as if it were the men who woke him. Stumbling and tripping to his door, his unsteadiness adding fuel to the flames of his fury, he leaned out the door to scream once again. "Enough!"

Despite himself and his ire, he bit back a smile as silence doused the tomfoolery below, as hissing whispers took the place of childish braying.

Battista walked back into his room and stood in the midst of the chaos. He could not remember what time he and Frado had arrived home. They had traveled hard all through the night, not knowing for sure if di Carcaci's men had regrouped and resumed their chase. Not daring to slow and find out.

They had arrived at Battista's three-story home on the Street of St. Proculus in the shadow of the Palazzo dei Pazzi as only a smudge of the next day's light appeared on the horizon; not a soul had been stirring in the quietest of hours, save for those spirits haunting this ancient city.

As he stood with the afternoon sun streaming through his southern windows, he looked down at himself, shiny black hair falling in two large, soft waves to his chin.

He still wore his thick hose, though the laces fell loose, the long ties hanging down to his knees. He wore neither boots nor stockings, satchel nor jerkin; his ecru linen undershirt hung out on one side only, as if he had fallen asleep while trying to dispatch it, and the whole of it was a mass of wrinkles, wounded by the crush of his hard sleep. The night's antics had exhausted him, not an easy task on a man of his prowess, of his eight and thirty years. Oh, but what a night it was.

The sculpture! The thought of it lurched into his mind. He kicked at the piles of clothing and linens covering the floor, searching for the satchel.

With a rejoicing cry, he spied it, rushed to it, and flopped to the floor beside it. Throwing the flap of the bag wide, he took the wrapped bundle in his hands and tenderly unfurled its covers with a cautious grace as if he unclothed a beautiful woman. It had been his night's conquest and he caressed it with the respect such a distinction deserved.

Rising slowly, he laid it lovingly upon his mattress as he headed for the corner chamber pot. Opening his breeches, taking his stance, he took his aim, and—

"Take that back, you scurrilous mongrel!"

He jumped at the screech rising up from below, and turned to yell back.

"*Merda!*" He cursed, realizing with disgust that his release had already begun. Battista stared down at the mess he'd created—censuring his own slovenliness. What would it require to cure him of the excesses of his maleness?

"Nuntio!" he called down for his servant, certain the abiding man never strayed far. "Your assistance, if you please."

"*Sì,* Messere Battista." The answering cry came but two seconds later and Battista smiled at its cheerfulness. "I'm coming."

The scene below was no improvement from the one left behind.

With one sharp and critical glance, Battista could see all, for better and worse. The open design revealed every corner of the ground floor; no walls stood to hide the offenses. One bricked corner served as kitchen, another bookshelf cubby as a study, while the entire street front half of the modest home functioned as a catchall of settees, feather mattresses, tables, books, cards, dice, bottles, and men. Upon every surface treasures sat, painted tables overflowing with glass vases, antique bronzes, ancient illuminated manuscripts, and around them the crates, boxes of every shape and size, stood like sentinels, some full, others empty, tops off, waiting with open hungry mouths for their own treasures to be packed in. The wooden-slat boxes commanded the room above all else.

If he had the family he imagined in the portrait, it would be here, in this part of the house, that they would take their leisure together, read together in the quiet of the evenings, and entertain their families in the sacredness of a Sunday afternoon. But that portrait lived only in his mind. In truth, this room belonged to his band of men as much as to him; here they congregated—day, night, and every moment in between. Battista refused to complain, though a part of him longed to, and far too often these days, for without these men he could not do his work.

"There he is. He will tell you the truth of it." Frado's call greeted him first, though Battista had not yet taken the last step off the stairs.

"Battista!" another man cried. "Frado jabbers that he saved you from near death. Tell us this is but another of his vividly imagined tales."

A trunk-legged older man jumped to Battista's side, his high-pitched squeak incongruent to his boulderlike build. "I have news, Battista, such that will please you well, I'm thinking."

Others rose from their lounging positions, chattering away as they gathered round him. Battista stood in the heart of the maelstrom, not knowing whom to answer, which to turn to first, like the mother bird who has brought but one worm back to a crowded nest.

He answered none of them, merely held up a long, lean hand as he made his way to the kitchen and the warmth of its ever-burning fire. An early spring had come to call, long before the pending late April Easter, but here and there a chilly day made a surprise visit, a day such as this.

With slow nonchalance, he placed the sculpture in the center of the large, round cherrywood table in the center of the area, took his time to pour a mug of spiced hot water and to grab a sweet bun from the still-warm pan. Sauntering toward a vacant settee, he plopped himself onto it and bit off a large bite.

"I am most sorry to tell you, Ercole"—Battista chewed on the sweet bread along with his words, wide jaw muscles bulging with the effort—"but it's true. If not for Frado, I would be in the clutches of the duca di Carcaci and his guards at this very moment."

Battista smiled over the rim of the terra-cotta cup as he sipped from it, watching Frado swagger away, his age-imposed monk's tonsure of black hair and round circle of baldness hidden beneath a royal blue *beretto*. Ercole and another followed grudgingly behind. Battista held his tongue as his portly friend carried on about his audacious exploits in last night's adventure. Frado tortured them with a performance worthy of the stage, pudgy arms mimicking as if he himself had scaled the palazzo walls, taken on twelve guards single-handedly, and come away with every treasure the duke possessed. Battista allowed the man his glory gratefully. Indeed, if not for Frado, he would have felt the noose about his neck years ago; it was his pleasure to share every moment of réclame and profit with the man.

"Speaking of profit," Battista announced to the room as if they had been privy to his thoughts, "have you sold any of the extra items from the Fénis Castle?"

"Ah, it is of this I longed to tell you." The stocky Barnabeo sat beside him, gap-toothed grin spreading at the opportunity to share his news at last, voice squeaking higher with pleasure. "Del Nero has taken both pieces, the painting and the bronze, at a most generous price."

As he spoke, Barnabeo took from his waist a large purse, which he handed to Battista with a noted flair, pride in a job well done in the flourish.

The jangling of heavy coins brought them all to attention, and every man drew near, once more the baby birds looking for a morsel from their mother.

"*Sì*, Francesco, I should have known." Battista nodded happily, well pleased. He called Francesco del Nero a true friend, as he did only a few. The support of his fellow Florentine patriot del Nero kept them all fed, and del Nero's recommendations to Filippo

Strozzi brought Battista entrée to those who held the greatest art in all of the Republic. "When you drink these florins away, and I know you will," Battista told the men with a wink, handing each one a heavy gold piece, "be sure to raise your tankard to del Nero."

"Del Nero!" the men sang in chorus, laughing at the prospect Battista so easily foretold.

Battista called Frado to him, leaned over the back of the small sofa, and handed the man the purse and the coins left within it. "You know what needs to be done with these, my friend. But take an extra for yourself. You've earned it."

Frado pulled two coins from the purse and tucked them into a barely visible flap on his well-stretched jerkin, but not without a smug smirk in Ercole's direction. All knew of Ercole's desire to take Frado's place, of his longing to accompany Battista on his expeditions and not be a part of those who worked in either their preparation or conclusion. For all that Ercole and Frado had much in common . . . same age, same build, and same quiet disposition . . . all knew what Ercole would do he would do for the glory of it. What Frado did he did in loyalty to Battista and to benefit others. True purpose is the gauge by which all lives are judged.

"Now, my friends, to the matters at hand." Battista rubbed his hands together, then brushed the trunk hose covering his thighs, ridding himself of crumbs, knocking them to the gray stone floor without thought. "Giovanni, write to King François and tell him of our latest acquisition on his behalf, would you? He will be overjoyed, I am quite sure."

The young fair-haired man nodded. "*Sì*, as sure as I am that Pompeo cheats."

"*Dio mio*, Giovanni, let it go. I do not cheat." Pompeo ran in from the kitchen where he studied the newly acquired statuette quietly. As he ran his hands through his hair, the thick black spikes stood out like a porcupine's quills while his smooth and youthful cheeks turned scarlet, nose still swollen and red from the impact of Giovanni's fist. "How often must we have this same argument?"

"As often as you cheat." Giovanni jumped to his feet, sticking out his chest as he thundered toward Pompeo.

"You are sh—"

"*Basta!*"

Once more Battista put a halt to the bickering, jumping between the infuriated men with a strong hand toward each. Unlike most Tuscan men—typically lean and small, unremarkable and unintimidating—Battista rose to an impressive height, and few had the nerve to test the brawn accompanying the breadth.

He sighed with exasperation, eyeing both with paternal impatience. "Pompeo, I do not know if you cheat. I know only that you win at cards far too often. Giovanni, you stink at cards, which is why Pompeo always plays against you and why he always wins."

The others in the room howled with laughter, both combatants possessing the grace to grin as they stepped apart, leaving their argument for the next time the cards were dealt.

"I will send the missive, Battista, this very day," Giovanni said contritely, returning to the subject of his work.

"*Sì, bene.*" Battista sat once more, stretching his long legs out before him, propping his feet upon the ottoman, and wiggling his long, still-uncovered toes. "Have we received any more requests from France?"

"Nothing yet," Giovanni replied. "But there are a few old requests we've yet to fill."

Battista turned a scowling brow to the man in the chair beside him. "Make me a list, Gio? *Per favore?*"

"Of course." The young man stood at once.

These fellows to a one were dedicated to Battista, to his work for Florence and for the food, clothing, and comfortable lives their work provided. He ruled them with a loving but firm hand and they responded with affectionate and devoted diligence. They were his *famiglia*, as much as his mother and widowed sister, who lived but a stone's throw away.

"Pompeo, have you added this piece to the list?" Battista called to the man behind him as he stared out the window. He marveled at the glass coverings so recently installed on this floor of the house; cloudy and cluttered with lead, they were difficult to see out of, or, by the same token, into. And for the latter he was most grateful. He willingly gave up the view of the passersby on the street for the privacy and seclusion the barriers afforded.

"I have." Now calm, his veracity no longer questioned, the youngest of the group came to sit with Battista. "I may look at it a bit more before packing it away, if I may. It is quite beautiful."

Battista beamed at the man more than a decade younger than he. Pompeo's deep admiration for art and antiquities made him ideal for his work. He had spent his childhood apprenticed in the *bottega* of the great Cellini, and had learned much at the master's hands. When Pompeo admitted knowledge to be his gift, more so than ability, he had found his way to Battista.

"Of course. But by the end of this day, *sì?*"

"*Sì,* Battista, *grazie.* Someday I hope to travel to the cathedral and see it for myself. If it is anything like this, it must be brea—"

The door flung open with a slam, whumping away Pompeo's words, and a thin, lavishly dressed man of Battista's age rushed in.

"I have news. Oomph!" the man cried, tripping over one of the dozens of crates strewn about the room, bringing forth a curse before the tidings. "*Merda!* Is it not yet time to send these things on their way?"

Battista chuckled at the comical picture Ascanio created as he stumbled, arms windmilling, struggling to gain his balance. "There is not enough yet to fill a quarter of a cargo hold. Transport costs a fortune. Unless we fill the entire ship, most of our profit will sail away with it."

"I understand, but can we not . . . not"—Ascanio swirled his jeweled hands about as if stirring two big cauldrons of soup—"not organize it better?"

As if he heard his name called by a thought, the stooped Nuntio wandered down the stairs, yellowed rags bound for the garbage heap in hand. "I will work on it today, signore."

"*Grazie*, Nuntio. You are—"

"Enough of your housekeeper's cares, Ascanio. What is your news?" Battista barked.

Ascanio stood in the middle of the room, hands to hips, jaunty grin upon his ruddy face.

"France and Spain are at war . . . again!"

Three

Necessity brings him here, not pleasure.

—*Inferno*

The small orchestra—nothing more than a *chitarra*, a harpsichord, and a viola—in the shell-shaped niche played a lively saltarello. A smattering of couples kicked and hopped, merrily displaying their grace and virtuosity, their costly costumes and glittering gems. Amidst this intimate gathering in a small *sala* of the Mantua palazzo, cheerful voices, smiling faces, and bubbling laughter filled the quick hollows between songs . . . a cheery night indeed.

Jolly for all save the two growling at each other over their chair arms.

The master of the house did little to disguise his impatience with his ward, who sat beside him, each slumped into the exquisitely upholstered chairs, each falsely convinced of their anonymity in the far corner of the spacious green marble salon. She burned with her own ire, the crimson stain painting her pale face as no cosmetic ever dared.

"I have no immediate plans to travel, Madonna Aurelia, and therefore neither do you." Federico II of Gonzaga, the marquess of Mantua, made the pronouncement through his small, clenched teeth, looking much like a dark version of his favored bichon frise kept forever by his side, though not nearly as amiable as that tail-wagging creature.

"I am not suggesting you travel, *Zio*." Though the nobleman was not her uncle, the Lady Aurelia called him by the title—for the sake of explanation—as she had the men who came before him.

The chestnut-haired woman clamped her hands in her lap, wringing them almost painfully, as if she could stifle their angry quiver. How she loathed it when he spoke to her as if she were a child, when he used the formal form of her title, as if to badger her with his serious intent. This man, to whom she must forever answer, had become lazy of late, as those who judged him turned their gaze to other sights.

Inheriting his title from his father while too young to wield it, Federico had lived under the regency of his mother, Isabelle d'Este, for many years. In the hopes of escape, the headstrong adolescent had launched upon a military career that ended with middling success, and returned as a man to take his rightful place as lord of Mantua. His mother, still spry and intellectually curious at fifty-three, had taken to travel, leaving her son free to do as he chose. And he chose to do little. With no wife, an accommodating mistress, and a rich court, Federico rarely stirred from the confines of his palazzo, his one niggling duty the protection of the Lady Aurelia.

"I hoped to do some traveling on my own." Aurelia leaned toward the marquess, willing him to turn his gaze back.

She would not, by nature, raise her voice, only if she must. She respected the power of this man, of the nobility represented in this room. These courts of the Italian city-states retained the military and political influence of the previous age, when families gained position by protecting their rulers. They then in turn became dependent upon these lords for their hospitality and largesse. It was a vicious circle, and she lived in its center. But she comprehended her own power and, more importantly, her value, and it gave a determined lilt to her voice.

"Not alone, of course," she continued when the marquess deigned to look at her, round brown eyes skeptical beneath raised bushy brows. "There is a group of women about to set off on a journey to Venice, and I long to accompany them. Your mother is there and we would join her. There will be chaperones and servants by the score. Surely such protected travel would not be remiss."

"This is a question asked and answered, Aurelia." Federico raised his voice, punctuating his admonition with a pounding fist on the padded chair arm. Jumping to his feet, he tugged down on the skirt of his fitted velvet doublet, throwing his lace-encircled hands up into her face. "I will not entertain it further."

The music squeaked to a close, strangled upon the grip of his anger, and the courtiers hushed in the empty wake of it. The marquess stomped away, parting the dancers upon the veined stone floor, to take a seat with a group of men at the distant corner, as removed from her as possible without leaving altogether.

Aurelia cringed, teeth scraping together, eyes raised to the portrait above her and the condemning faces of Luis Gonzaga and his three sons, Guy, Fillippino, and Feltrino, the branch of the House of Gonzaga that had begun the family's control of Mantua two centuries ago. As they looked down, their descendant denied and humiliated her; she wanted nothing more than to disappear. Each hand moved to a chair arm, gripping it till the knuckles shone white, and she started to rise.

"Dear Aurelia, you must tell us who made your gown!" The woman sitting to her left grabbed one of her hands, her congenial comportment camouflaging the hard pull nailing Aurelia in her seat.

"Perhaps you could call for us, when next they come to fit you. We would all wish to be so wonderfully costumed. Is that not right, ladies?" Another woman gathered close, giving Aurelia no time to answer, nor did the bevy of female courtiers flocking around her like geese to the tossed crumb. They prattled on, asking questions for which they expected no answers, as the musicians struck their instruments once more and the dancing and laughter recommenced.

Aurelia smiled obsequiously, not ignorant of the worried glances these women exchanged, untouched by their pretty words and sympathetic simpering; they had seen such scenes between her and the marquess before, but they seemed to be occurring more and more frequently—and urgently—than ever. His harsh and cruel behavior appeared at times inexplicable.

No one knew much about Aurelia, only that she came to be the ward of the Gonzaga family some years ago. Aurelia was not a young woman, not a rosebud about to burst, but a flower in full bloom, a solitary, well-simmered beauty. Though she was kind, charitable, and most always affable, a loneliness lived within her, wrapped in the deeply pale skin of one forever shielded. But a feisty vein thrummed through her, one not intimidated by the noble personage who held her fate in his hands, and for that the women of the court admired—and pitied—her.

Their trilling created a vortex in which Aurelia's anger and embarrassment subsided, in which she retreated and disappeared, and their conversation turned with distracting grace to other things . . . parties attended, palaces visited, remarkable personages encountered. Words meant to divert her now poured salt into her open wound. She could bear the taunting of it no longer.

"Signore, *buonanotte.*" In the rousing beginning of a *piva,* in the rustle of activity as couples rushed to take positions on the floor, Aurelia flashed onto her feet, stepping away with a quick curtsy before her feminine guard could prevent it.

"Good night, Aurelia," the ladies called after her, offering nothing more to raise the woman's spirits.

* * *

Escaping from the noise, the eyes, and the ears of the *sala*, Aurelia slowed her pace, in no hurry to return to her own suite of rooms but aimless and bereft of any other possible destination.

The palazzo of the Gonzaga family was nearly three hundred years old, and among its many buildings it boasted more than three hundred rooms, so many places to wander and be lost. But after all the years among them, she saw nothing unique in any of them; Aurelia's eyes were blind to the beauty of the castle's architecture and that of its surrounding buildings, and the breathtaking frescoes, paintings, and sculptures enhancing every room and cubby. Her feet faltered just steps beyond the salon's threshold and her mind emptied; she lost her way upon paths she had walked for so many years.

"Aurelia."

He whispered her name before he stepped out of the shadows behind her. She didn't need to turn to know who spoke.

She should have known he would follow her; Federico hated for anger to fester between them for very long, but neither could he appear reticent before his courtiers. The marquess approached her with contrition clear on his dark features and the hesitance of it in his faltering step, as if she may not accept it and turn him away.

"I am sorry for my outburst, *donna mia*, my lady. It was not well done of me."

Aurelia did turn then, how could she not, and it gave him all the encouragement he needed. He crossed the short expanse between them. He gave her a slow, graceful bow as he often did when they were alone, no matter how frequently she reminded him the gesture was not required.

"You know from whence my stubbornness arises." The young man took her hands in his, giving them a soft, affectionate squeeze. He still looked young to her eyes, far younger than his seven-and-twenty years, and at no time more so than when he was repentant. "I do not take my duty to you lightly, my lady."

He laughed a little and turned, as if to study one of the mammoth sculptures forming a gilded picket line along the barrel-vaulted hall; a long-fingered hand worried the hilt of the bejeweled ornamental sword hanging by his side, the tinkling of the metal in its sheaf echoing softly in the cavernous corridor.

"I know," she whispered, and in the wisp of words she breathed all the genuine fondness she felt for him.

Federico jerked back, a cynical smirk upon his face. "You are probably the only thing in my life I do not take lightly."

"I do know," Aurelia said again, stepping to him, resting a hand gently upon his velvet-covered forearm. "Nor do I take my own duty lightly. But I am not a child."

They both laughed then, at the enormity of her jest, and it dispelled further any ill will between them.

"And I do understand that you are most happy when at home," she continued softly. "But if I do not see something other than these walls, and soon, I will surely lose my mind."

The marquess waggled his pointy, beard-covered chin, brows pinching together. "I cannot imagine what it must be like for you."

In his eyes Aurelia saw his sympathy and his devotion, but it did little to assuage her need.

"But there is nothing, save my own death, that would convince me to let you travel without me. Perhaps the . . . others . . . have allowed it, but I cannot."

Aurelia hung her head, chestnut hair catching the light of the torches above them with a fiery glint, changeable eyes grasping the shades of deep brown sadness. Any hope she may have kindled in her heart extinguished in that moment.

Federico bent his head to hers, lips curving down at her blatant disappointment. "But let me think about a journey. Perhaps something in the near future, *sì?*"

His hopeful petition, offered like a child gaining good graces, she found incontestable. She would not put aside what she owed this man, this family of honorable men.

"*Sì*," she told him, with a pale imitation of a smile. "I will look forward to it."

But as they said their good nights and parted ways, she knew there was nothing to look forward to, only more days without end in this most magnificent prison.

She turned toward her rooms then, surrendering to the exhaustion nipping at her, fatigue a small, hungry creature, its sharp teeth voracious for a feeding.

As soon as Aurelia entered the outer chamber of her apartments, three young women flocked around her, ready to do her bidding, no matter how simple, as if she herself were incapable of her own care.

She stood resolute within the hub of the whirlpool, allowing the wimple-clad young women to do their duty, answering their questions, delighting—despite herself—in their giggles as she described the men, the women, the clothes, and the food of the lavish night of entertainments. Aurelia allowed a degree of familiarity to burgeon between her and those who lived to serve her, for theirs were often the most intimate relationships she experienced.

"Now have a care, Teofila," Aurelia chided as the young women rushed through their duties, removing the many layers of her evening clothes, placing her jewels in the strongbox, turning down the linens on the bed in the adjacent chamber. All the young girls were eager to be gone; on a night such as this, there was plenty of food, drink, and men left over to satisfy even the servants of the household. "Do not give your heart to the first cavalier who pretends to deserve it. There are far too many to choose from this night. You must make them earn your attention."

Aurelia bit her heavy top lip, confining the grin brought out by Teofila's embarrassed laughter. She felt an affinity toward the young girl, for she looked much as Aurelia did, chestnut hair of deep waves, eyes hinting of both greens and earthy hues, depending on her mood. It was how a sister might look; it was how Aurelia imagined her sisters did look.

Once Aurelia was in her nightgown and robe, hair unpinned and brushed out, a small fire sizzling in the grate in the bedchamber, all her cares were met and still the women hovered near, though their eyes looked to one another and the door with more and more frequency.

"Be gone, you old women." Aurelia corralled them, shooing them with her hands as a farmer's wife urged the chickens back to the coop. "I have had more than enough of your pestering."

Her words chided them warmly. With grateful bobs, her attendants took their leave, giggles slipping along on the promises of the night that lay before them.

Aurelia once more stood alone, and she both embraced the solitude and despised it.

Like these twittering young girls, like the noblewomen still making merry in the grand ballroom below, Aurelia enjoyed the beauty this life offered, a life fit for a queen. The finest gowns, the most exquisite jewels, they were all hers at the flick of a finger. But as if cursed, things so easily come by meant little.

When she looked behind her, the endless sameness stretched back further than she could remember, and only more of the same lay ahead, the same stretch of road to be traveled day in and day out. The words she had spoken to Federico echoed in her mind; yes, she was dedicated to her duty, body and soul, to her one and true purpose. But when she heard the other women talking of their lives, their families, and their entertainments, it compounded the weight of emptiness she must bear.

Aurelia flopped down upon the floor at the foot of her bed, legs atangle in the silk linen, head hung in the cradle of her hands.

She never had any fun.

Four

And when, with gladness in his face,
he placed his hand upon my own,
to comfort me,
he drew me in among the hidden things.

—Inferno

Fifty-two men, naked to the waist save for the sweat of their efforts, ran in the massive, hard-packed sand pit of the Piazza di Santa Croce, flashing in and out of the shadow of its grand Basilica.

"To me, Pompeo, to me!" Battista screamed to his teammate, catching the glimpse of an opening ahead.

The young man obliged, hurling the heavy ball of *giuoco del calcio fiorentino* across the distance between them. Rushing to Battista's side, Pompeo launched his body between Battista and the opposing team coming at him from all sides, intent on stopping him from nearing the goal line running the width of each end of the piazza. All around them, the mayhem of the melee continued as men head-butted, punched, elbowed, and choked one another, anything to keep the other team from besting them, each capitalizing on the sport-shrouded opportunity to make another pay for besting him in either love or dice.

Great guffaws of triumph rang out, groans of pain and frustration rumbled, as the players closest glimpsed who now possessed the ball. Equally as deadly with either hands or feet, Battista could hurl or kick the ball across the goal line to score a *cacce*, whichever method presented the best opportunity.

Never as happy as when in the midst of *calcio*, Battista sneered merrily as he rampaged across the field. He had grown up playing the Florentine kick game, and he hoped he died an old man, staggering about the grounds. Few upon the field were as tall or as sturdy as he, and many a team fell to his agility.

Battista lowered his head, put his shoulders to the oncoming rush, and barreled forward with a roar. The low wall delineating the goal line stood but meters away, and so did a row of the angriest, most determined players he had seen yet today. Their eyes burned red, their lips formed gruesome snarls.

He cupped the red and white ball in the crook of his arm, and pulled his arm overhead, poised to launch. From his right, at the farthest tip of his vision, he saw them . . . two red-breeched players hurtling toward him.

With the graceful twirl of a court dancer, Battista lowered his poised arm behind him, turning with the movement to come round full circle. Dropping the ball to both hands, dropping both hands to his knee, he took one step forward with his left leg, and impelled his right forward, his foot smacking the ball, launching it over snarling men and goal wall alike.

"Vittoria! Fantastico!" The whoops and cries of victory filled the square, colliding with the stone buildings lining all four sides, rebounding again and again into the air. Spectators cheered or jeered, congratulating or commiserating with their favored team as money exchanged hands from the losing to the winning wagerers.

The pile of victorious players jumping on top of Battista was as dangerous as the opposing team had been, and he struggled to free himself of the crazed horde, but not without his own cries of delight and triumph. Pompeo found him and they embraced in the shared conquest, strutting across the piazza together, enfolded once more into the arms of their most dedicated fans.

"*Bèn fatto!*" Frado saluted as he threw each man a cloth to wipe away the dirt and sweat coating his skin. "Very well done indeed."

"You have won us a fortune this day," Ercole joined in, still accepting the mix of coins, large and small, from the swirl of grumbling men who shoved them into his hand. "A celebration is in order."

"Agreed!" Battista cried with enthusiasm, tossing aside the now-dirty rag and accepting his shirt and doublet from Giovanni's hands.

Beside him, Ascanio assisted Pompeo with his own clothing, as the tall, thin Lucagnolo leaned down and kissed a fey woman softly on her cheek, handing her over to another woman, similar of face but of a much heartier disposition.

"How is she?" Battista stepped to the only married man among them.

"Fine, *grazie*," Lucagnolo responded, eyes following the two women as they made their way through the tumultuous crowd just beginning to abate.

Battista studied Lucagnolo's face, handsome in that very Roman way, the strong, straight nose, the high, protruding cheekbones, a face much like Battista's, though far narrower. The concise response did not worry Battista overmuch; for the quiet Lucagnolo, such was a typical rejoinder. The worry in the man's piercing blue eyes concerned Battista far more.

Lucagnolo's young wife had been ill off and on for many months, and though the devoted husband retained many a skilled and expensive physician with the income derived as both an artist and adviser to Battista on painted artwork, none seemed able to find a cause, nor a cure.

"Her beauty is as breathtaking as ever," Battista whispered with a squeeze of the man's bony shoulder.

Lucagnolo nodded, a wisp of a smile touching his thin lips.

"Come, let us away to the trattoria. I've a need for much wine." Battista gave him another squeeze and together they turned to the waiting band of men, the group trouncing off to the southwest corner of the piazza as if they had taken possession of it through their victory.

Just beyond the long Palazzo dell'Antella, patrons encircled every round, scarred wood table running along the front of the Angelo di Fuoco, some drinking toasts, others drowning their sorrows. The still-rising midday sun found the piazza, and its springlike warmth raised the heat of the festivities.

"Come, come." The small, spry owner of the trattoria spied the approach of Battista and his men. "Marco, a table, chairs, *presto!*"

"*Grazie*, Pasquale." Battista accepted the man's hospitality, well earned through years of patronage. Without request the table thus placed, the correct number of chairs along its perimeter, soon filled with flagons of white Frascati wine and dozens of trays of food filled with *salame* and other sliced meats, chunks of *parmigiano* and sharply flavored cheeses, and breads.

"For you." Pasquale himself brought over the tray of stuffed eggs, Battista's favorite.

"Ah, *grazie*, Pasquale. *Grazie mille.*" Battista eyed the treats with unfettered delight. Boiled, their yolks removed and mixed with raisins, cheese, and spices, the eggs were stuffed and closed once more, then fried to a golden brown.

The men said little as they stuffed their mouths, gulped heartily of their wine, and watched the throngs of people coming and going through the square. Battista's eyes wandered to the Basilica, its many white stone peaks and ornamented spires. His gaze moseyed to the palazzo above his head and the varying shapes of the windows. From this vantage point, one perceived their differences, though from the Basilica they somehow all looked the same. His thoughts languished upon little else but the delicious flavors assaulting his mouth and the moment of triumph still as fresh as the thin sheen of sweat upon his brow, accepting the nods and smiles of congratulation tossed his way by passersby.

"Did you see Alberto?" Pompeo asked him with a hearty belch, sitting back from the table, having consumed more than his share of the victuals.

Battista threw back his head and laughed, brushing dampened locks off his forehead. "I did. He does not enjoy losing. Not that he has to do it often. When you tur—"

"May we join you?" The deep-voiced request came from behind Battista.

Turning in his chair, Battista acknowledged the two well-dressed men, cheerfulness watered away like cheap wine.

Cecchino Bracci accompanied Bernardino Altoviti, as always, dressed similarly in short velvet *farsetti,* voluminous cloaks of camlet trimmed in miniver over these doublets, and high-crowned hats, costumes as befitted their stature as representatives of two of the leading families of Florence. The Altoviti men had been great soldiers for centuries, bestowed with the imperial knighthood, now ambassadors of great distinction. Minor nobles themselves, the Bracci family owned one of the largest banks here in Florence and in Rome as well.

Yes, they were two of the finest members of the Florentine community, but they were serious men, far too serious for a day such as this.

Battista reached for a *damigiana* of wine, pouring each newcomer a great dose of white liquid from the short, narrow neck of the large bottle, hoping to lighten their natural dourness with the spirits. But it was not to be.

"You have heard France and Spain battle once more for control of Italian lands?" Bernardino leaned his horselike face toward Battista, urgency in his hushed question.

Battista smacked his lips, removing with his tongue a piece of food stuck between his teeth. "Of course I have, Bernardino. It is all anyone has spoken of for days."

"It is a sign, do you not think?" Cecchino asked the table at large, round puppy eyes blinking rapidly, not as reluctant as his companion to tender his words publicly. "The Medici days are numbered, I tell you. This action portends it for certain."

The other men at the table greeted his pronouncement with hopeful nods and grunts of agreement. None here backed the Medici, including Battista. He, and his family of apothecaries, had been loyal to the Medici, but after the death of Giovanni de' Medici—who had died as Pope Leo X—and the influence of the teachings of Savonarola, the Dominican friar outspoken against moral corruption, Battista's beliefs and loyalties had shifted, like most in Florence.

All here were old enough to remember the benevolent rule of a *signori*, a republican body of government, functioning with the complete support and endorsement of its citizens. The taste of the returned *Signore*, a ruling family—one whose concerns did not often align with its citizenry—had turned bitter indeed over the last decade.

The glory of the Medici rule had reached its peak half a century ago, under the administration of banker Cosimo and his grandson, Lorenzo, Il Magnifico. Though they took no title, their furtively wielded power bestowed them with despotic power, authority equal to that of the *gonfaloniere*, the head executive office of the *signori*. Cosimo had expanded their reach to Rome, Milan, Venice, and beyond. Under Lorenzo's diplomacy, Florence dismantled dangerous alliances, creating his own and ensuring the peace of the land.

But everything had changed under the rule of Piero, Lorenzo's son, a feckless man who had fled when Charles VIII of France marched on Florence. The Republic rule that followed lasted only eight years—but few Florentines had forgotten the sweetness of it—before the Medici returned, under the power of Giulio, Lorenzo's nephew. The man who was now Pope Clement VII had appointed Cardinal Passerini of Cortona as his administrator, and with him the citizens' dissatisfaction grew sharper with each passing day.

"Passerini is a crude and greedy foreigner," Cecchino spat, "with no respect for our elected officials."

"You speak the truth there," Battista joined in, as always pushed to anger at the mention of the contemptuous man. "Florence should be ruled by Florentines."

The grumbling of agreement whirled about the table, an opinion festering throughout the city.

"I have heard he sends part of our taxes back to Arezzo, that sewer he crawled out from," Ercole sniped.

"I wouldn't doubt it," Bernardino agreed. "But Clement does not seem to care. We have appealed to him over and over to replace the man, but every request has been dismissed or ignored."

"And the bastard, Ippolito," Frado grumbled in his cup, cursing the sixteen-year-old illegitimate nephew of the pope. "Already he swaggers with obnoxious cruel power. They are born to their evil."

"And the pope allows it," Bernardino quipped.

"He is leaving us no choice," Cecchino riled them all further.

"And now a French king comes once more." Bernardino clasped his hands together as if in prayer and leaned forward. Every man at the table focused upon the message he had come to deliver. "A French king has freed us from tyranny once before. I believe with all my heart he will do it again."

Battista held firm to that hope, ever more resolute as François I had made the same intimation himself when last they had been together, when the king had made it clear that Battista, and Florence, could count on his support in return for the great works of art Battista provided him.

"That is why you must continue your work, Battista," Cecchino chimed in. "Intensify it if you must. For the time is upon us and your work might well be the key to our freedom."

Battista nodded his head, throwing back a last gulp of his wine. He scanned the faces of his men as he wiped his mouth with the back of his hand. Seeing the same burning passion in their eyes that pulsed in his heart, he banged his empty cup upon the table. "*Sì*. The time is now."

Nuntio rushed at him the moment Battista opened the door. Behind the bowed man's back, he spied the stranger sitting upon his settee, and his hand eased toward the daggers at his waist.

"He comes with a message. I tried to make him leave it . . . I tried to keep him beyond the door . . . but he pushed his way in." Nuntio's rheumy eyes drooped at the corners, flicking back and forth between Battista and the stranger.

The strange visitor stood but did not move, drawing out no weapon, no look of fear or concern upon his unfamiliar features. Battista recognized no threat and concerned himself more for Nuntio's fretting.

He gently took the older man's gnarled hands—the skilled fingers that had once picked more locks than Battista might see in a lifetime—in his, led Nuntio to the large table, and poured him a glass of whatever lay in the bottle perched upon it.

"All is well, Nuntio. Have no fear." Battista put the metal cup of red, fragrantly fruity liquid in the man's quivering hands. "I know you did your best. You always do."

Nuntio graced him with a silent, grateful glance before lowering his lips to the wine.

Battista turned back to the stranger, the soft sheen of patience and caring upon his face disappearing behind a stony countenance.

"You have entered my home when you were not made welcome. I can only hope, for your sake, you have good cause."

The man's right hand reached to the pouch at his waist.

With a clamorous clanging and the sharp *shing* of steel upon steel, four swords and three daggers promptly pointed at his chest, the only missing weapon belonging to Lucagnolo, now returned to his wife.

The man's dark-avised face paled, and he swiftly raised both hands in the air.

"A message, signore. One I was instructed to put into your hands and your hands alone."

Battista took in the measure of the man through narrowed eyes. With a flick of his head and the tip of his dagger, Battista gave the man permission to continue. With the weapons leveled at him, he'd be a fool to attempt anything else.

Wary gaze remaining cautiously upon the circle of men surrounding him, the stranger pulled out a thick fold of parchments. At once, Battista recognized the seal of the French king. He replaced the dagger to its rightful place with his usual reverse twirl flourish and stepped forward, accepting the message. François had never sent a communication directly to Battista before; he didn't know what to expect or what this man knew, but Battista would reveal nothing to him in the ignorance.

Drawing out two large coins from his purse, Battista placed them in the man's hand. "A pleasant journey to you, *messere*. I am saddened we will not see you here again."

The man reached out tentatively and accepted the coinage; there was no mistaking Battista's cryptic salutation, nor the profundity of it in his pointed glare. "*Arrivederci*, signore."

With a tilted tip of his *beretto*, the courier took his leave. With a tick of Battista's chin, the bald and bull-like Barnabeo stepped out behind him; he would award the man a safe, if covert, escort out of the city.

Battista watched their shadowy images pass the glazed windows, swiftly retreating to the table, breaking the red wax fleur-de-lis seal with a snap, and unfurling the folded golden parchment with a crackle. As he sat, his men gathered round him, their silence thick with curiosity and the scraping of chair legs across stone floor.

His wide-eyed expectancy sagged, mouth pursing. "It is in Latin."

Without a word, Giovanni raised himself up and reached across the wide expanse of polished cherrywood, pulling the pages from Battista's hand and his reluctant grasp.

With deep sighs of disappointment, the others stood and set themselves away . . . some to cards, some to more drink . . . leaving Giovanni to his work. All save Battista.

"I can't do this if you keep hovering," Giovanni grumbled without looking at the man pacing behind him.

Battista's broad shoulders slumped as he raised his dark eyes heavenward. "But you are taking so very long."

"Well, it is a very long message." Giovanni did turn then, his own impatience in the set of his jaw. "And it is strangely wrought. Please, a few moments of stillness and it will be done."

Battista looked as if he would argue, but thought better of it. Stomping to a chair in the front room, he flounced into it like a denied child on the cusp of a tantrum. His thoughts churned in turmoil, tossed about on the turbulent ocean of this message. The king must be riled indeed, to send a message directly. Only something so grave or of such dire consequence would impel him to forgo their usual and multibranched routes of communication. Battista envisaged plans to capture Florence or perhaps the imperative for Battista to return to France.

The years he had spent at the French court were some of the dearest in Battista's memory, especially the time in the company of the king's sister, Marguerite of Navarre. Their discussions on the fanatical friar Savonarola and his teachings were among the most stimulating of the young man's life. If not for Marguerite and her brother, he would be dead by now, at the least imprisoned. When first he'd arrived in France, when his name or allegedly words by his hand were linked with an assassination attempt on the then Cardinal Giulio de' Medici, it was only by the protection of François that he had been spared prosecution. In a printed declaration, the king of France had placed the property of the della Palla family, and those of other families indicted as rebels, under the official protection of the French Crown. Such aegis included

Battista himself and, with the act, the king had secured the young man's lifelong loyalty.

Battista did not know his own mind should the missive call him once more to the king's side. He would do whatever François asked, except, perhaps, turn his back on Florence when she needed him most.

The anxiety of his thoughts propelled him to his feet once more. He spun toward Giovanni, only to flinch away again for fear of halting the man's progress.

"I believe I have it now."

The call found him like a beacon through a dense fog, and Battista clung to it, rushing to Giovanni's side.

"As I said, it was strangely formed. My translation is but the gist of it, as opposed to word for word." Giovanni offered the parchment filled on two sides with his own pretty hand, and Battista grabbed it.

A deep furrow formed on his smooth ruddy brow as he read it, sat, and read it again. The men around the table inched closer, each looking for the opportunity to grab the missive from his hands.

"Tell us, Battista," Frado encouraged with soft persistence.

"It is bad news." Ercole's fatality revealed itself, refuted quickly by a shake of Battista's head.

"Not bad news, no. A request." He spoke with a peculiar inflection, confusion and hesitance in the indistinct diction. "But it is very strange indeed."

Frado snatched at the paper, the others crushing around him to spy the words over his round pate and around his chubby form. Battista watched their faces, saw their bewilderment dawn.

"There is a dire insistence in his words, if I am reading this correctly." Frado spoke first, looking to Giovanni for consensus.

"*Sì, sì.* It is there. But I couldn't be certain if I conveyed it properly," Giovanni replied.

"You did, Gio, most distinctly," Battista assured him of a job well done. "But why is he so insistent? And what is this piece he speaks of?"

Pompeo leaned forward, hands braced upon the table. "He gives us very little information. His reference to Praxiteles is clear, but then he confuses the point with the next line." The young man turned his intense black eyes to Giovanni. "You are sure of it?"

Giovanni took up both parchments once more, dedicated, not defensive. "Ah, *sì.* That section was quite clear. 'By Praxiteles's hand it was wrought, but which Praxiteles I do not know.' "

"This means something to you?" Battista asked of Pompeo.

"It does. Praxiteles was a remarkable Greek sculptor, in the days long before the birth of our Lord. But he is the only Praxiteles I know of."

"A child of his by the same name?"

Pompeo shook his head vehemently, spiky hair tossed with the motion. "Praxiteles never married. It is rather interesting, in truth. It is oft told that he loved the same woman for all his life, modeled many of his works after her in fact, but they never married nor had children. Marriage may not have been necessary, but the insistence to procreate was deeply ingrained."

"A child by another woman, perhaps?"

"Perhaps, though his unwavering fealty to the woman was well known and often remarked upon."

"Knowing who made it is but a small part of this mystery," Frado grumbled, pointing to the pages on the table with unfettered accusation. "Finding it with this . . . this . . . bizarre information will be quite another." His round face scrunched and reddened at the thought of the effort lying before them, much of it upon his rounded shoulders.

Battista waved a hand back and forth before his face as if to scatter an aggravating fly.

"What do we know?" Reaching across the table, he pulled the translation closer. "It is a sculpture, not very large, almost dagger-like but with more purpose to it, and wrought by the hand of a man named Praxiteles." He raised one long finger from a fist for each item mentioned.

"Well, then," Frado mumbled, "we know everything."

Battista slammed his palms upon the table and each man jumped at the slap.

"It is enough to begin, yes?" It was a puzzle, and he had never met one that did not excite him.

Few of the mumbled acknowledgments were enthusiastic.

Battista stared at Frado, a narrow-eyed, twinkling glare, the slightest upward tilt on his full lips. "Enough. *Sì,* Frado?"

Frado looked hard at the man, at the youngster who had insisted Frado's skin be saved as if it were his own. Long ago, Frado had thrown the lot of his life in with this patriot disguised as a scoundrel; he would not—could not—change anything now.

"Yes, yes, yes. Enough. Come now." Frado pushed his rotund form away from the table and stomped away, heading for the study and the shelf upon shelf of books. Ascanio, the most learned on sculptures and antiquities, followed close.

With his satisfied smirk full blown, Battista rose to join them, brought up short by the hand on his arm. He looked up to the face and found Giovanni and his apprehension.

"Are you not concerned by the last line? That I did translate word for word."

Battista looked down at the closing words of the translation.

It is said to possess the strength I need to reign victorious.

The two men exchanged a glance over the paper; each reflected the same worry and hesitation, the same struggle with the perplexing allusion.

"A victory for François is a victory for Florence. We must not forget." Battista gave Giovanni's shoulder a squeeze. "The path to victory is never without peril."

Giovanni offered but a hesitant nod, mouth stretched in a grim line across his face, and said no more of it.

* * *

With the setting of the sun, Nuntio gathered every candle and candlestick and set them about the study, on every small table, on every opened shelf, until the cubby glowed. The three men, heads bent over thick leather-bound books and unrolled sheets of parchment, offered silent thanks, rubbing their tired eyes and creaking necks.

"How are we to see the dice?" Giovanni called across the expanse.

"Perhaps it is a sign from God that you should cease your wicked gambling," Nuntio mumbled back, but even he smiled at the ludicrous sentiment.

"Take thee off, all of you," Battista called to Giovanni, Ercole, and Pompeo. "We are in for many hours, you—"

"Days," Frado sniped, curmudgeon's nose stuck in his book.

Battista glowered at him but gave no response to his interruption. "Make for your beds, all of you. We'll send Nuntio round if we find anything."

Pompeo rose and took a few staggering steps toward them, mouth opening with a cavernous yawn, a lion's silent roar. "Are you sure, Battista?"

"Quite sure. I will need you when we—"

"If we—" Frado again, with a fling of a page.

"*When* we find something. We can handle it for now." Battista smiled snidely. "Frado is most happy in his work."

Pompeo suppressed his laughter between clamped lips and scurried out with the others, before Frado directed any more of his frustration toward the retreating men.

The blanket of silence tucked in about them. Ascanio stood and stretched, back popping with the change in position, and removed his green doublet, revealing the bright yellow, puffed-sleeved *camicia* beneath, a blazing color that matched the lined and stuffed bombast hose.

Battista raised one eyebrow at him, always amused but never

surprised by the flair of Ascanio's clothing, though this flouncy, heavily embroidered shirt was one of the more elaborate ones he had seen in some time.

"Venice," Ascanio said with a grin, as if that explained it all.

Battista shook his head with a chuckle and bent his back to the book in his hands. It pressed heavily on his knees and his feet tingled from the pressure. In the stillness, his eyes grew dry, stuck on the same words on the same page, he ac—

"Aha!" Frado jumped up, sending his chair flying out behind him. "Come, come, you must see this."

Battista and Ascanio were already on their feet and jumping to his side, keen study following his stabbing finger to the book on the table before them.

"It was written by Pliny the Elder of Rome, sometime in the first century . . . 64, 70 . . ." His tongue stumbled over the words as he rushed them out.

" 'And Praxiteles created it, but no man looked upon it and no man looked away, such was its power. Wars were fought over it. Wars were won and lost because of it. Praxiteles begged for it to be hidden away. He died knowing it was.' "

Frado finished reading, voice fading, excitement draining away, lost on the forceful tide of the words. The three men barely breathed in the wake.

"What the hell is this thing?" Ascanio croaked, two hands rifling in his wavy brown hair, their confounded stares the only reply.

Battista turned away, from the question and all it implied. He fell back into the wing chair, its wooden clawed feet creaking with the sudden weight.

Frado stood before him. "I have a very bad feeling about this, Battista." He rubbed circles around the globe of belly hanging in perfect roundness over his leather belt.

"You ate too much." Battista tried to joke his trepidation away, but it was a sorry attempt at best. "You know of the absurd superstitions of the pagans as well as I, so much based in the fanciful. I am sure this is but another example."

"You are sure, are you?" Frado used his sarcasm with a heavy hand, hammering home the one thing they could be sure of . . . that they could be sure of nothing.

"We must continue our investigation." Battista's eyes scurried from the scathing implication and he reached for another giant tome. "Of that I am sure."

They set back to their reading, not a one of them sleepy any longer, not a one ready to entertain the thought of sleep, leery of things that walked in the night.

"Phryne," Frado mumbled, head still bent over his book.

"*Scusi?*" Battista asked.

"He loved a woman named Phryne, a courtesan it seems, but one renowned not only for incredible beauty but for her daring and intelligence as well." Frado barked a laugh, one filled with respect. "It seems her magnificence inspired Praxiteles so, he is celebrated as the first to sculpt a life-sized nude female form." Frado's jowls quivered as he shook his head with lusty reverence. "That must have been some heavenly body indeed."

Battista snickered silently, glad Frado had found something to inspire him, and they settled back to silent study. But it was not long until Ascanio, this time, once more broke their reverie.

"Do either of you recognize the name of di Bone?"

"Giotto." Battista and Frado said the word together, an assured chorus.

"Ah, of course." Ascanio flipped a page backward, then forward again. Not a word more required to explain the identity belonging to the nickname.

Giotto di Bondone was most often called simply Giotto, though a few, very few, referred to him by the intimate moniker of di Bone. Many credited the Florentine painter and architect with the renewed vigor for the arts that had captured the entire peninsula in its fervor. The Florentines considered him one of the land's most cherished sons.

"What of Giotto? What have you found?" Battista put a hand to his chin, pulling on the small tuft of hair growing from the upward curve in the middle of his full bottom lip. Frado closed the book in front of him with a snap.

Without raising his eyes, Ascanio paraphrased the text before him. "This passage talks of a painting by Giotto, a triptych in fact. And in the same portion, both the names are mentioned." Ascanio held the book aloft before his handsome face. " 'Praxiteles created it, Pliny warned of it, and Giotto's *Legatus Praxiteles Canonicus* pieces will show the way to it.' " Ascanio looked up, mind working furiously on the Latin phraseology behind an unfocused gaze. "The Legend of Praxiteles's Legacy."

"*Dio mio!*" Frado slapped his forehead with his hand and threw himself back in the chair. "We do not have to find one piece! We have to find three pieces to find the one piece! *Bafa—*"

"Wait, wait, there's more!" Ascanio yelped over Frado's cursing, holding up a halting hand as he read aloud again.

" 'With Dante's words to lead across the land and Giotto's images to guide through the cities, only the truly selfless may find the glory.' "

"Dante and Giotto, *Dio mio, sì.*" Battista covered his face with his hands, pulling them away, tugging at the skin as he dropped them to his lap. "If it is a triptych by Giotto, the words must be those of Dante's *Commedia*. Threes," he mumbled to himself, but neither of his companions refuted the obvious conclusion.

Try as he might, Battista could avoid Frado's piercing stare no longer, nor deny the consternation of it. But neither would Battista back down from his appointed task. He slipped forward on his chair, perched on its edge, elbows on knees, hands clamped together.

"We have been preparing for this all our lives, *amico mio*. Do you not feel it?"

Frado shook his head back and forth, as if to deny it, but not a word against it did he speak. Ascanio's gaze volleyed between them, the air thick and heavy with the harbingers unearthed.

"Across the lands, through the cities," Frado intoned, repeating the words with a grisly condemnation. "How far will this take us, Battista?"

It seemed a simple question, yet both knew it spoke not just to geography.

"From city to city, from state to state, until we find it." Battista sat back, crossing his thick arms over his chest with determined finality, daring either to contradict him.

Frado threw his hands up into the air, beseeching the heavens, face comically twisted with sarcastic amusement. He surrendered, but it would not be categorical.

"From city to city, from state to state . . . would that include those at war?"

❧ Five ❧

This miserable state is borne
by the wretched souls of those
who lived without disgrace and without praise.

—*Inferno*

The pink blush of the setting sun dappled her skin as she strolled through the tunnel of tall cypress trees. In the near distance, the statue awaited her, the three women so finely wrought, their faces so similar, their hands posed in the exact same position. Within the circle marking the end of the path, their long arms crossed before their bodies at the wrists, slender fingers delicately positioned, creating a cage or a basket around which something invisible rested between their arms and their breasts, something captured and protected.

Aurelia refuted them. Turning sharply to the left, she chose a different path through the ornamental garden of the palazzo, making for the isolation of the mock grotto full of dangling mosses and the calm tinkling of its fountain.

She entered the secluded space, a raised hand forbidding her two maids—her constant shadows and companions—to follow. It was not the first time she had halted them thus, and they stopped at the edge of the stone path, turning their backs and closing the circle around her.

Blocking out their presence in her mind, Aurelia sat on the stone bench with her back to them, closed eyes facing the furry green wall. She drew in her breath, and released. With each pass through her lungs, it slowed. She heard nothing but its soft, rhythmic shush, and she sunk into the space it created. Time ceased, as did her physicality, and her essence moved free.

But not for long.

"Monna Aurelia?"

The niggling call pulled at her.

"*Per favore*, my lady?"

Aurelia opened her eyes to narrow slits. This was not Teofila's first attempt to pry Aurelia back to earth; she saw it in the tight lines about her maid's pink mouth.

"It is time?" Aurelia asked dourly.

Teofila nodded, daring to step into the grotto as Aurelia stood.

With a critical eye, the maid scanned her mistress's appearance. With gentle hands, Teofila brushed the back of the full pleated skirt of gray damask and gave a small tug on the wide belt of matching fabric trimmed with garnet jewels. She scrutinized the position of the almost-off-the-shoulder neckline, which revealed, as did the slashings of the puffed sleeves, the maroon lace *camicia* beneath. The straight line of the damask rose high on Aurelia's chest; Federico would not allow her to lower it as fashion prescribed.

Teofila tucked an errant chestnut curl into the dark red net *scuffia* that held Aurelia's abundance of hair, the heavy, loose bunch resting upon the back of Aurelia's neck.

"We will need to pluck you soon," Teofila murmured, and Aurelia huffed, forever annoyed at the painful custom that raised a woman's hairline high upon her head.

She had had enough of her maid's nitpicking. With an impatient gesture, Aurelia stepped around Teofila. "Let us away. The sooner the evening begins, the sooner it will end."

* * *

Aurelia stepped into the glowing dining room, surprised at the long line of people perched on each side of the endless banquet; faces sparkled in the trio of multibranched candelabra posted at even intervals along the table's length. Beneath their glow, sterling and gold platters covered every inch of the thick gold cloth, filled with a wide array of offerings . . . salted trout, roast capon, sweet rice cooked in milk of almonds . . . game, meat, fruits, salads . . . it was all there, more than even this horde could consume.

She took a step forward, spying the young women and men with whom she most often sat, and faltered. No empty chair awaited her among them. She beckoned to them with a quizzical stare, but their sheepish and puzzled glances skipped away like stones thrown along a pond's smooth surface.

"Come, my lady." Federico appeared at her side and she turned, silent and skeptical, placing her hand upon the embroidered arm he offered.

Passing her companions, she spared them no glance, fearing it would reveal their concern and intensify her own. The marquess brought her closer and closer to the far right corner of the table, and Aurelia's free hand fisted, nails digging crescents into her palm.

The empty chair sat in the middle of the most revered women among the company . . . the grandmothers, the widows . . . the oldest. She took her seat, looking slight amidst their buxom fullness, tall to their stooped, bright amidst their gray.

"Signore, *buonaserra, come stai?*" Aurelia greeted the women on each side of her, plastered smile set as firm upon her face as able. "Good evening, ladies. How are you?"

They twittered at her, clearly delighted to have her among them, blind to any truth behind her darkened eyes.

She nodded, offering polite responses without thought. But as if of its own volition, her piercing glare found Federico and stabbed him, jaw jumping as she bit back the harsh reproof with which she longed to whip him.

The nobleman, perched at the head of the table, had the decency to look contrite, gaze skittering to the man on his left, blatting a laugh, holding up the forced jocularity as a shield against her.

Aurelia twigged his game. She had never underestimated his intelligence or his intuition. The festive lives of the younger courtiers goaded her, true, inciting her to badger him for more of her own freedom, but to remove her from their company . . .

"My physician assures me the swelling will abate soon." The warble came from her left and the shrunken woman beside her. The elderly ladies about them all leaned forward as the woman opened her mouth, revealing a wide gap on the bottom of her mouth, a swollen, red gum filling the hole.

The sight served as a catalyst, the conversation erupted, and every woman among them launched into a detailed account of her latest illnesses and miseries.

Aurelia dropped her knife onto her plate and it clanged angrily, an earsplitting echo of her emotion.

I must be appeased. Aurelia's thoughts rooted in her mind. *If he will not do it, I will do it myself.*

Six

Worldly renown is naught but a breath of wind,
Which now comes this way and now comes that,
And changes name because it changes quarter.

—*Purgatorio*

He stared out the four storied windows, small in the grasp of the domineering architecture of the Apostolic Palace. The pope's gaze wandered over the manicured gardens spreading out on the ground below, a profusion of the pale greens, yellows, and pinks of spring in bloom, yet all he saw were the blemishes of his own bad decisions, counted them as if they were nothing more than barren and scarred patches of earth amidst the splendor.

In his moments of human weakness, he indulged in delusion, convinced himself that what he had done, he had done for the benefit of the papacy, for the strength of the Catholic Church. With the benevolent eye God had bestowed upon him, he saw the truth even as it taunted him; more than a small measure of his efforts were for his own glory, and that of the Medici. And now . . . now righteous punishment beckoned.

Clement heard the remote clip of slipper heels upon the marble, the distant ticking of a condemning clock. The sound grew louder, more insistent and urgent, as it neared, but the pope did not turn to it, keeping his deeply lined face upon the leaded glass and the vista beyond.

"Do you truly believe in redemption, Marcello, no matter what the sin?"

The clipping skidded to a halt with a jagged screech. The pope's young secretary froze, hand bearing a sealed parchment outstretched to the air, mouth working soundlessly.

"It is a question you, above all, need never ask." The young man found his tongue and bowed to the pontiff, though the man still did not see him. A fellow Florentine, a devoted subject, the young man rose, eyes wide with fervent adoration. "You spoke as God wished. There is naught in that to be redeemed."

Clement sniffed a sardonic chuckle at the young man's reverence; he had once been like him, once believed he could do no wrong as long as he invoked God's name in the doing.

Pope Clement turned deep-set eyes upon his faithful servant, long wiry beard—long turned gray in a life stretching across half a century—hanging low upon his barrel chest.

"I am more confused than ever, my friend." He sat then, and the mammoth walnut desk dwarfed him as few things could. He slumped over its carved polished edge and hung his head in his hands, the top of his scarlet cap pointing out to the room. "When François defeated Charles at Pavia, I saw my path so clearly. To give France my support served the Church best. I knew it to be true."

"*Certamente*, Your Holiness." Marcello inched slowly forward.

"The Spanish ruler cannot regain his power. His grasp would exceed his reach. We all worried upon it. But it has all turned sour."

Clement spoke of the other Italian princes, those of Venice, Milan, and of course Florence, who had joined him, the king of France, and the king of England in the formation of the League of Cognac. The official act had turned a cold, harsh papal shoulder to the king of Spain.

"You could not foresee the acts of the barons," Marcello offered hopefully.

"No!" Clement slapped the hard surface before him. "But should I have turned so quickly back to Spain? Could I not have trusted François a little longer? I would not then have to turn back."

The memories ravaged the man's lined face, casting dark shadows in its many crevices. Not a month after he tossed his support to the French, Spain countered and regained the upper hand, taking Milan. As the Italian barons turned on Clement with dissatisfaction, he had had no choice but to turn to Spain for mediation. But it was not a sincere coupling, and the instant Charles released François from his prison the pope had realigned himself once more with his French ally.

"He called me a wolf then, Charles did," Clement mumbled. "No longer the shepherd he had once followed."

"He is not a man of his word, Holy Father. He is intent upon power, naught else."

The pope looked up then, to the righteous young man before him. The urge to tell Marcello to run almost overwhelmed him. Instead, Clement crooked his finger at his secretary, who leaned forward with blatant vacillation.

"Days of hard reckoning are upon us, the Church and I. France and Spain are once again at war. And we are harassed more every day by the heretics screaming at us from the north."

Marcello crossed himself at the vague mention of the German princes who allied themselves with Luther and the thousands of Catholics there and in Holland who abandoned their faith, more with each passing day that Clement refused to consider any of Luther's ninety-five theses of reform.

Clement saw the revulsion upon his servant's features and it brought him up sharply.

"I am sorry, Marcello." The pope rubbed his long face, washing himself clean of his own angst. "You have brought me a message and I have long delayed you from your duty."

Marcello's brows knit and he did nothing to deliver the folded parchment into his master's hands.

Clement swallowed; he recognized that face, the long moodiness of it forewarned dire news.

He reached forward and snatched at the missive, damning his own hands that shook the rattling paper.

Without looking up, he read the succinct yet stunning communication: " 'Charles and his troops have taken Piacenza.' "

He discharged the paper to the desk as if it burned him to touch it, and though he glared at it—willed it away—it would not depart.

Clement stood slowly, pain evident in the sluggish unbending of the long body, and turned back to the wall of glass, mumbling to it as if to find wisdom in its transparency. "*Sì*, the day of reckoning. When you are trapped in the middle, either way may lead to peril." Without turning, he gave his decree. "It is time we send a letter, Marcello."

"Yes, Holy Father." Marcello fairly ran to the diminutive desk in the corner, to draw out parchment, quill, and ink pot. Dipping the quill in the tiny glass vial, tinking it against the rim, he poised it over the paper. "To Spain, Your Holiness?"

With a grimace of fatality, Pope Clement shook his head. "No, Marcello, to France."

Seven

In that book which is my memory,
On the first page of the chapter that is the day when I first met you,
Appear the words, "Here beginneth a new life."

—*La Vita Nuova*

The growl came at them through the thick forest on either side, though from which side neither could tell. Battista and Frado pulled in the slack on their reins as the horses whinnied and shied at the bellow of the unseen bear.

"He is waking up from a long winter's nap, naught more." Battista calmed Frado with his words, leaning forward, caressing the silk of his pitch-black stallion's mane, soothing the beast's head-jerking protestations with each stroke.

But Frado was not as easily mollified; his protruding gaze scoured the woods surrounding them, shadowed though the sun shone upon it, shafts of light pinched between thick-trunked trees. The woods, too, came to life after the cold-weather dreariness; maple and oak were fuzzy with bright green and maroon sprouts and curled fern tips sprung up from beneath the bed of fallen, dried pine needles. The forest of Casentino, just north of Florence, had always been rife with bears, and Frado had always done his best to steer clear of it.

"Are you sure we must tread this path?" His voice trembled

with his unease, but whether he spoke of their travel on this particular day or the quest itself Battista could not fathom. He chose to deal with the question only in the present.

"I was convinced of this nobleman's involvement before Pompeo's report, but upon hearing of it, no one could deny the assertion. Not even you, my doubting friend. He is widely known as an art connoisseur. It makes perfect sense," Battista cajoled, but Frado would have none of it.

He made a vague unhappy noise deep in his throat, a wordless objection, his gaze refusing to meet Battista's as it continued to search for brown fur among spring green. "If you are successful, if you acquire the triptych without getting yourself killed, word of its disappearance will spread far and fast." Frado said nothing Battista had not already thought of. "Such attention we do not need."

Battista mulled Frado's warning, offered for at least the tenth time since their destination had been determined a few days ago. It echoed the warning in King François's letter, dire predictions of threats not only to their lives if it were known what they were after but to many others as well, especially if more war ensued.

An artifact to cause war; one powerful enough to end it.

The words—the sensation they caused—plagued him, an apprehension swaddling him with a cloak of fretfulness, and though he pushed at both contemplation and consternation, each returned with agonizing repetition.

He shook it off yet again, but with a parting of certain return, and flashed a jaunty smirk upon his companion.

"The sun is high, the air is warm and sweet, and we are on an adventure, *amico mio*." Battista pulled on the reins and his horse trotted closer to Frado's. "Let us make the best of it, *sì?*"

Digging his heels into the glossy flanks of his horse, Battista lurched forward, breaking from a trot to a gallop, a desire to launch the escapade or perhaps to outrun the pursuing thought.

Frado rolled round eyes heavenward, annoyance at his friend's exuberance clear on his already-stubble-shadowed face, but slapped his reins, urging his steed to join Battista as he galloped off.

Not another bear call greeted them, nor that of any human, as the pair kept to the woods and fields, avoiding any towns or villages along the trail northward. Late afternoon of the second day arrived with a light drizzle, and as they crested a small rise the magnificent palazzo rose up on the next hill, greeting them with its splendor.

Neither spoke, neither moved, far too assailed by the sight before them to do either. In all of his travels, Battista had never visited the Palazzo of Mantua, had never seen for himself the architectural beauty of the cluster of buildings comprising the compound, its cornerstone laid two hundred years ago in the fourteenth century.

The grouping of structures spread across the horizon, abutting the supporting village gathered at its feet to the west, the lace edge of the magnificent gown. Battista surveyed the cream and terra-cotta stone edifices rising into the violet crepuscular sky with respectful regard for artistic beauty. A mixture of military stronghold and noble palace, the spiky turrets sat atop the Gothic arched loggias, fusing the strong with the delicate. Battista beamed at its splendor.

Revelation quickly forgotten, his heart skipped a beat, catching up quick, thudding arrhythmically against the walls of his chest, for only the palace's impenetrability rivaled its beauty, and yet he must penetrate it. Battista sucked in his breath, willing the burst of oxygen to still the unsteady beating.

"We are in time," he said, as if to distract Frado from the flash of fear exposed for an instant across his features, forcing the muscles in his face to relax.

Though they advanced from the west, ignoring the main approach from the south, skirting the large thoroughfare leading up to the palazzo, they could see the entrance from the edge of the forest, watched as the opulently outfitted horses and gaily festooned conveyances delivered the guests invited to the evening's gala. It was this very event—the celebration of the marquess's birth—that had brought the pair to this door in a rush, knowing a well-attended occasion such as this would provide the perfect camouflage for their roguery.

With a cluck of his tongue, Battista urged his horse forward into a slow canter, Frado quick to follow.

They circled the palazzo, lost and invisible amidst the comings and goings of the palace and the festivities taking place in the village in honor of the lord. Taking turns, their backs to the palace, one spoke gaily of nothing, while the other surveyed the field, noting every egress and every guard. When each assured the other with a silent signal, one of many created over their years together, they left the grounds as casually as they had approached, making once more for the seclusion of the forest.

Within the curtain of the trees, they dismounted and studied the palazzo yet again.

"You will not be able to exit as you enter," Frado said with little inflection; only someone who had known him as long as Battista would recognize the thin pitch of skepticism in his tone. "Especially not carrying a triptych of paintings, rolled or not."

"This we knew." Battista pointed to the columned loggia on the mezzanine level of the western wall. "It is just as the plans showed us. From there I will descend, three from the right."

Their intelligence had assured them Battista would find the paintings in the marquess's trophy room. And though the location seemed far too obvious, it had come to them from a number of reliable sources. What their sources could not tell them was if the paintings hung on the wall or were otherwise kept, but all conveyed the sure sense that their placement in the room would be obvious. The trophy room was on the eastern side of the palace, inconveniently so, for escape from that side, with its main entrance and thickly populated portion of the village, would be impossible.

Frado's gaze followed the digit to the third opening in the long row of arches. "Then from there I will wait."

Battista clapped him on his shoulder, leaving the hand resting for a moment. There was no more to say, no more to do, but for Battista to change his clothes and to wait . . . wait for full dark to descend and the party to become fully engaged.

"You should eat, Frado." He laughed the suggestion, tying his horse loosely to a budding birch.

Frado tossed up his hands, shrugged, and began to gather small twigs for kindling. He could always eat. Not so Battista.

"Two hours, no more, Frado." Battista pierced him with his dark stare. "Upon your honor."

Since their acquaintance began, these two had run roughshod over the Italian countryside. Since then, the agreement between them had stood, though never had it been tested. Long ago they had made the pact, should one or the other not return in the appointed time, the man left behind would flee, taking the other's disappearance as a sign of capture, taking themselves to safety.

Frado's thin upper lip curled with blatant disagreement. "Upon my word, Battista."

He made the vow without pleasure, but he would keep it nonetheless.

Battista smiled with bitter sweetness, accepting the affection offered through Frado's discontentment.

"How do I look?"

He preened then, twirling round so Frado might enjoy the full impact of the purple silk doublet embroidered with green leaves, black trunk hose, and a gold-trimmed hip-length cloak. A bright peacock feather adorned the ribbed cap worn on the side of his head, and his flat black leather shoes were slashed lengthwise at the toes, allowing the green of his stockings to show through.

"Ascanio would be very proud." Frado smiled, but it soon faded away, lost in the darkness surrounding them and the meager light of the small fire between.

He stood then, crossed to Battista, and without word or preamble wrapped his pudgy arms around his friend, round head resting upon Battista's chest.

Battista stumbled back a step with the force of his friend's embrace, hands shocked into the air with the surprise of it. With a sniff of a laugh and a shake of his head, he returned the hug, kissing the top of Frado's bald pate.

"Get off me, you silly man," Battista chided without genuine rebuke.

Disentangling himself from his friend's arms, he mounted his horse, and, with a last glance at the dear face, set off.

Battista sat tall in his saddle, one now caparisoned with a gold-tasseled blanket, as he approached the guards at the gate; he had played parts before, this one merely unfolded upon a grander stage.

"*Buonanotte*," he called out with not the slightest hint of hesitation, handing down the forged invitation to the closest guard.

The helmeted soldier unfurled the small scroll, eyes squinting in the dim light of the three torches at his back, and studied Battista with an equally acute stare.

"*Benvenuto*, signore," the guard at last decreed with a bow, and his fellow soldiers followed with equally unenthusiastic murmurs of welcome.

Battista ignored the lackluster greetings, as the minor nobleman he pretended to be undoubtedly would, and led his horse into the cobbled courtyard, one so vast another impressive palazzo could easily fit within its confines.

The yellow and cream stone walls rose up around him on all four sides as the fountains in its center gurgled with water and wine, the liquid sparkling with a brilliant profusion of torchlight, a glow turning night into day, revealing the details of the wrought-iron-railed balconies and twirling Solomonic columns. He took himself to a fountain, accepting a large chalice of deep red liquid from the posted servant, and tossed it back for one long gulp of liquid courage.

Battista had more than a little knowledge of the palazzo and its layout, having studied the plans for hours in the days preceding the trip, but he had no idea where the gala might take place and could but follow the horde of brilliantly attired guests, a helpless fish in a fast-running, overpopulated stream. He paid keen attention to his whereabouts, drawing a red line on the image of the palace's layout etched indelibly into his mind as he made his way through arched entries and barrel-vaulted corridors.

No smile touched his face, no greeting passed his lips; Battista walked with his shoulders slumped in an attempt to mitigate his height, refusing interaction with any of the other guests, to keep himself as unnoticed as possible. More than a few women—women of all ages—turned admiring glances his way, and more than a few men appraised him with a mixture of admiration and envy, but he ignored them all.

He arrived in the massive ballroom, his teeth grinding together as he struggled to keep from gaping at the intense beauty of his surroundings. Clearly meant, by size and style, as a main chamber for entertainments, it served as well as a shrine to one of the Gonzaga family's greatest loves . . . horses.

With almost-dimensional rendering, the regal beasts appeared set against the lush landscape background, six of them in all, as if they jutted out into the living space. Alternating with the majestic beasts, statues of classical deities stood in alcoves designed in the Corinthian order. Above each horse, the six ordeals of Hercules were painted in a manner to imitate bronze bas-reliefs. Above them, a sumptuous frieze of acanthus leaf volutes accentuated by the golden Gonzaga eagles in each corner.

With justifiable veneration, Battista took himself off to the far back corner with almost leaping strides, taking himself out of the milling horde and their crush to see and be seen.

In this dimly lit, almost forgotten place, he became a part of the scenery, blending in as inconspicuously as he might. If curious eyes assailed him, he ignored them; if any greetings came to him, he responded with almost-rude dismissal. He hovered on the fringes of the gathering, waiting.

Long ago Battista had learned that in every situation an opportunity always presented itself; the stronger his belief, the more it became truth. Tonight would not be the occasion to change that conviction.

But tonight, conviction seemed incapable enough to hurry events along. He busied himself, sipping watered wine and avoiding any interaction, but the tedium became annoying.

Battista paced the room as time vanished, lost intangibly forever. He strode about with purpose, as if aiming for a destination rather than dispelling impatience.

A bevy of bashful beauties approached from the left. Battista smiled thinly, holding up a finger in the other direction, as if hailing someone on the far side of the room, and took himself off—away from the crestfallen lovelies—losing himself in the miasma of the milling crowd.

But his concern clung to him like the scent of a pinewood fire; to stay too long in a place he meant to pillage was folly. He could not divest himself of Frado's image, sitting at the base of the western wall, bottle in hand as he played the part of an inebriated villager, watching the sliver of the moon shift in the sky and growing more fearful with every inch it moved.

The last notion settled Battista's mind; he would have to make his move, diversion or no. Grabbing a small tumbler of grappa from a passing tray, he tossed back the rough liquid, felt it burn a path down his gullet, and aimed for the door.

The sudden blare of the heralds' horns frightened him; one foot faltered, the other skidded. As each anxious gaze looked beyond him, Battista shook his head at the irony, the quirks of fate that forever brought him what he needed, but not necessarily in the form he imagined. With elegance and splendor, the marquess of Mantua made his entrance, his beautiful mistress on his arm, a gaggle of equally splendid followers trailing behind.

In the distraction of the grand arrival—in the hubbub of the blaring trumpets, the marquess's rousing greeting, and the applauding assemblage—Battista slipped from the room, invisible to anyone's notice . . . save one.

The ease with which he passed through the corridors frightened him. Though quiet, the hallway was not completely devoid of inhabitants; Battista passed a swaggering group of young men, clearly drunk and looking for trouble . . . a coupling of lovers, the rustling fabric and deep-throated moans revealing what the darkness of the alcove did not. But not a single guard did he spy, nor a suspicious servant did he stumble upon.

He entered a long, window-walled corridor and took a quick moment to scan the sky; the moon was no longer visible in the east, where it had been rising when he entered the palazzo. He had little time left, half an hour perhaps, and he would lose his accomplice and Frado's assistance in escape.

Battista trod the fine line between a walk and a run, long legs gobbling the floor with determined strides. He made it to the northeast corner of the palace and the circular stairway tucked away within its spiral. He dared to run up them, safe in the seclusion of the dark stone walls.

At the top, he turned left—corrected himself—turned right.

The passageway was not as wide on this floor as the one below. Along each side, doors alternated positions with wall sconces, each fixture resembling a sword pointing at the floor with the flame flickering from the cupped pommel, each door closed and gilded with gold.

Battista's breath quickened as the moment of acquisition at last arrived. He counted the doors on his left, grateful he needed the third and not another of the many stretching down the long corridor before him.

He came up short at the portal, imbalanced by the lack of padlock. A brief, scourging warning of entrapment crossed his thoughts and he erased it with logic, if a trifle convoluted. A man such as the marquess of Mantua would be secure with the efficiency of his guards; he would feel no need to lock away his treasures.

Sheer folly. Battista smirked at the inferiority of the man supposedly superior by birth.

He opened the door, entered the room, and closed it behind him with the silence and grace of a dancer. With his back to the portal, he surveyed the room, one lit by three sconces lined up along the far wall, a chamber unlike any he had imagined or expected.

At first glance, the most singular item within these walls appeared to be the Persian carpet covering a gleaming dark wood floor, its maroon background the host for the thick green tree and the golden fruit hanging from its curled branches. The walls were bare save for the round, brass sconces.

There were no trophies in the trophy room. Battista took two steps farther in, thrusting fisted hands onto hips in agitation.

That's when he saw it.

The chest was made of wood, of that he was sure, but of such a dark cast he could not deduce its variety. This very darkness kept it almost hidden from view, immersed in the shadows beneath the three light fixtures hanging above, tossing their light foolishly upward to the beamed ceiling overhead. Battista gloated with a satisfaction about to be met.

He rushed across the expanse of the room, steps silent upon the resplendent rug, and sunk to his knees before the mammoth trunk. The paintings he sought must still be in frames, he surmised from the vast breadth of the chest, and he cursed the time it would take to pry them from their casings.

He set to work on the padlocks securing the three encompassing steel bands. The locks were not as intricately formed as he expected, but were merely basic shapes, a circle, a cloverleaf, and an inverted triangle, but the mechanisms proved far more difficult than their simplistic construction foretold. He worked his small pin in each hole, the clicking of metal upon metal drowned out by the clock ticking dangerously in his mind.

"Finally!" He grunted with exasperation to the empty room as the third lock fell away beneath his fingers. He flicked at each one, sending them dropping into a waiting palm, placing them quietly on the floor at his knees. With two hands, he hefted open the heavy domed cover and looked in.

"What the devil . . . ?"

Battista's clipped words echoed in the almost-empty trunk, one large enough to hold two men. He sat back on his haunches, hands on his thighs, as he studied the one item within with ill-disguised disgust.

At the bottom of the otherwise empty chest lay a scroll, a curled and beribboned length of golden parchment no larger than his hand. He shook his head as if to deny its very existence, leaned forward as if to chastise it, but stopped—squinted and held. Lengthwise along the outside of the parchment had been inscribed two words, *Giotto's Triptych.*

This scroll was not the triptych, he groused silently with a petulant purse of his lips. It was, however, most assuredly some piece of the escalating conundrum surrounding the painting. Raising himself up, Battista tipped his head into the cavernous box. With a scrunch of his nose, he sniffed . . . then sniffed again. It smelled caustic, as though the wood had been recently painted, but with a most toxic-smelling lacquer.

He brushed away the worry of the stench. He had to leave; he had pushed all boundaries of safety having stayed as long as he had. He was quite sure Frado neared panic, as the moment of Battista's agreed time to retreat must surely be upon them.

In the same movement that brought him to his feet, Battista

bent over and snatched the parchment from the bottom of the chest.

Less than a second passed, less than one step away did he take, when the sharp click rang out.

From beneath the trunk it came, the grating noise disturbing in its own right.

Battista swiveled back. Before his eyes, the impossible happened.

As if released by the detraction of the parchment, the bottom of the trunk fell away, splashing into some sort of liquid-filled basin waiting the few inches below, visible only when he bent all the way over, cheek skimming the floor as he spied the container hidden behind the stubby claw footing of the chest. Instantly smoke belched up and out, great funnels of dark gray vapors streaming out of the chest and filling the room.

Battista jumped up and back as if to avoid it, but the rancid billow enveloped him, as it did the chamber. His eyes watered; his throat closed against the harsh air. He staggered around trying to regain his bearings, one thought louder than any other.

A trap.

He had known deep in his being that accessibility had been far too easy. He cursed himself for his stupidity. The Gonzaga family had been powerful for centuries; they did not do so by being naïve. He had to get out—he had to escape before the smoke escaped from beneath the crack of the door, before the noxious odor and thick gray fumes alerted the guards to his nefarious actions.

Battista spied the door. Stashing the scroll safely in his satchel, he stepped toward it.

And then things grew worse . . . much worse.

The flames ignited and swooshed through the room as if to devour it with one lick of their destructive tongue. The propulsion of heat tossed Battista against the wall. He held his hands to his ears as if to prevent the ringing from bursting in his head.

But the explosion did not clang, but a bell . . . three bells in fact.

One hidden within each sconce on the wall behind the chest, each sent into motion by the waves of heat-propelled air. The riotous clash was as loud as the bells atop Florence's churches, those that filled the entire city when calling the faithful to service.

Move! The thought seared his brain as the flames seared the wooden floor. Finding nothing to grasp upon the stone walls, it spread its destruction along the planks beneath his feet. If he didn't move now he would surely fall through, to the guard and the prison waiting, no doubt, on the floor below.

Battista jumped through the door, slamming it closed behind him, hoping to keep as much of the vapors trapped within as possible. He turned right, the spiral staircase the intended goal.

Too late.

From out of the stone stairwell guards rushed at him, armored, sword-toting guards, bearing rapidly down upon him.

He spun away, reversing direction and tearing down the corridor, shoulders hunched, head down, as if he ran upon the *calcio* field. Daring to sneak a look over his shoulder, Battista saw one of the three guards enter the room—perhaps to douse the flames, though Battista recalled nothing he had seen to use—the other two giving chase . . . fast.

"*Stunad,*" he cursed himself for his stupidity, for failing to plan for a different path of escape. He suffered now for his own arrogance. He had no time to slow his pace and find the right room, the correct door to lead to the chamber that would lead to the loggia, and Frado beneath it. Battista ran, ran and prayed his exertions would lead him out.

He turned, turned, and turned again, somehow finding himself back at a circular staircase, though if this was the same that had brought him up he could not be sure. Heading down might mean a better chance for finding the way out. Three steps down . . .

. . . and the guards rushed up at him from below.

With a growl of anger, Battista reeled, running back up. But instead of heading down the corridor, he ascended the next circle of stairs rising upward, hoping the third floor provided a more apparent egress. The clang of armor and sword, the pounding of boot heel on stone, impelled him faster and faster. But not fast enough.

His gaze rose above the ledge of the next floor, his right foot gained the top step, when the pain seared through his left calf.

With an outraged bellow, Battista fell, top step colliding with his gut, purging the air from his lungs. He swiveled round, looked down. The dagger penetrating his flesh hung from his leg; the guard who had engorged him stood just inches below.

Battista kicked out his good leg, heel colliding with the guard's face. The guard pinwheeled his arms, to no effect. Eyes closed in pain, blood spurting from his nose and mouth, he fell backward, falling on another guard, who fell on yet another.

There was no time to bask in the comedy of the triumph; trained soldiers would be back on their feet—back at him—in seconds. Battista reached down and before his thoughts stopped him, he pulled the dagger from his calf with a grimace. Blood spurted from the wound, staining the dusty gray stone with its red wretchedness.

He jumped to his feet, brushing impatiently at the strands of sweat-soaked black hair hanging in his face, teeth gnashing at the pain exploding in his leg. A few steps into the corridor and it widened to a large alcove on his right, one filled with two wing chairs and a table set before a cold fireplace, a gathering space for a small, intimate party.

Battista grabbed one chair and hurled it down the stairs. The crashing of wood and stone met with the cries of pain and protest. He grabbed the other chair and did the same, then again with the table, knowing the three pieces would create a bountiful bottleneck in the curved stairwell.

With a hobble, he set off again, no time to waste.

Another long corridor stretched before him with only a turn at the end. He could not engage in another footrace; the wound slowed him far too much. Battista lurched into the first door on the right. If he had kept his head at all, if his unfailing sense of direction had not failed him, the room would be located along the eastern wall.

The starlit sky beyond leaded glass was the first sight he glimpsed within the room, the lack of balcony was the heartbreaking second. He limped to the windows, threw open the sash, and looked down. Battista wondered, with more than a dollop of derision, how many people he would kill along with himself when he hurtled his body out.

"Stop, you fool!"

The harsh feminine cry froze his hand upon the sill, his knee halfway up. He hopped on his good leg, turning round, pulling two daggers out of his belt, one for each hand.

She stood in a dark recess, a door with no frame, a hidden aperture he had not seen or fathomed. The quick impression of her beauty took a backseat to the certainty of her ill-concealed impatience.

"You'll never walk away from that drop. This way." She gestured a beckoning hand. "I'll get you out."

Battista appraised her, seeing more than just the petulant look of annoyance on her porcelain-skinned face. She held no weapon, nor anything to impede or wound him, and she wore an exquisite brocade gown, a noblewoman . . . a hothouse, defenseless flower.

Battista stole another quick glance to the ground far below. She was right, of course, and he knew it. She had called him a fool. With a shrug, he took the first step on what might well be a fool's errand. He followed her.

She led him through the dark room behind her, straight for another door. Stopping before it, she hissed at him, "Grab my arm."

Battista blanched. "What?"

She grabbed his hand, placed it on her opposite arm, and squeezed his fingers round it.

"Keep hold."

Without another word of explanation, she opened the door, out onto another corridor, one narrow and ill lit.

A cry of alarm rang out, but the woman did nothing to acknowledge it.

Battista spun to their right, saw the two guards at the far end, and opened his mouth. Before a sound escaped his throat, his savior opened another door directly opposite the one they had left behind. On the other side of it, the woman flung a bolt, locking the guards out, but for how long Battista could not guess.

The room inside was softly lit, aglow from candlelight and fireplace flame. Pink and green lace festooned every piece of fabric. Battista almost laughed at the frivolous absurdity of it.

"You have an affinity for lace," he managed as she rushed him diagonally through the large, luxuriant chamber.

She doused his sarcasm with a withering look. "It is not my room. It is Isabella's, the mistress. She is still downstairs, well enough for you. Now hurry."

In the far corner, she pushed at the wall, and once more a hidden door revealed itself. He stepped through quickly, right behind her, and looked back as the partition slowly closed of its own volition. Upon the wood floor, across the matching pink and green carpet, he had left a red-splotched trail of blood, an arrow pointing directly to their means of escape.

"There's nothing for it," she hissed. "They will figure it out quickly enough when greeted by the emptiness of the room."

Battista nodded grudgingly at her astute reflection and turned to follow. Instead of finding another chamber as he expected, he found himself standing close beside her in a narrow, almost pitch-dark stairwell, the steps heading in a straight line downward.

With each bend of his leg, the wound in his calf throbbed, alleviated only by the knowledge that at last he headed in the right direction.

Light shone in a rectangle around the cracks of a closed door at the bottom of the stairs. His guide pushed at it and it gave way with ease. Battista lunged behind her . . . and stopped.

The sight he beheld was no less brilliant than the one he imagined awaited him in Heaven, if, by some miracle, he should earn his way there.

A masterpiece covered every inch of the walls and ceilings . . . the room was the painting . . . the room was the art. He had heard of this chamber, as so many had, as any lover of Italian artistry must, and had been saddened his mission would not allow him to see it.

The Camera degli Sposi, the famous Bridal Chamber. So I am able to see it after all, distressing though the visitation may be.

He permitted his gaze to take in every inch of the frescoed room. Crafted by the brush of the genius Andrea Mantegna, it was the definitive example of illusionist painting, a technique allowing the art to share space and physicality with the people viewing it. To his right, a life-sized lord sat within a lush portico surrounded by a simpering court. A great meeting took place before him on the north wall, one filled with many and varied noblemen—one no doubt a prestigious Gonzaga family member—greeting one another with amiability. He raised his besotted gaze upward to the oculus that offered the illusion of blue sky and his breath caught, as if he did, in fact, glimpse Heaven.

"You really are a fool," the woman railed at him, pulling him toward the north wall, reaching out as if to shake the hand of a nobleman upon it. She pushed and a rectangle of partition gave way, Battista stumbling behind.

The rush of cold air sobered him, bringing clarity to his pain-muddled mind. With a great gasp, he filled his lungs with the pure air and the taste of freedom.

He bent over, bracing his arms upon his thighs as he caught his breath, as he willed the throbbing in his leg to subside. They stood in a small, intimate courtyard circled with a white-filigreed wooden wall overgrown with vines, an enclosure not unlike the one depicted upon the wall of the Camera degli Sposi. His breathing returned to something resembling normal; he straightened and stepped toward her.

Lifting her hand to his lips, he brushed his mouth across the smooth flesh, a dashing countenance attempting to shine beyond the sheen of pain-induced sweat upon his brow.

"I can never thank you enough, *monna cara*, you have saved my life." With the gallant gesture and obsequious salutation, he stepped away.

"Where do you think you're going?" her sharp tongue snapped at his back.

Battista did not slow his already-lethargic stagger, one noticeably off-kilter were he to stop and make an assessment, but pointed to the elaborate gate at the far end of the courtyard.

"That is the way out, is it not?"

"Well, yes." Her words sounded very far away now, long sounds slithering at him, and Battista wanted to congratulate himself on a quick and painless parting. He turned to look at her, and found her only two steps away. Confusion possessed him; his head began to hum, stars burst in his eyes, and the ground rose up to meet him.

Eight

To run over better waters
the little vessel of my genius now hoists her sails,
as she leaves behind her a sea so cruel.

—*Purgatorio*

Aurelia stared at the man lying prostrate on the checkered gray and beige stone of the courtyard. What had impelled her to assist this thief she could not say. She had watched him in the ballroom, his beauty catching her eye, the gleaming black hair, the soft though nearly black brown eyes. But she had seen beautiful men before, many in fact.

His manner had enticed her. Try though he might, there was something suspicious in his movement, to her eye at least. A devilish charm, an edgy allure of danger, accompanied his suave flippancy, and it beguiled her.

Thankfully, the marquess's speech had been short, and while the words still echoed on the roll of applause she had rushed from the room to find this man. Her curiosity—as forewarned through the ages—had brought her to this fine mess.

Aurelia took a few steps forward and stood over the man. He breathed still, his chest rose and fell, but the puddle of blood below his left leg spread with a dastardly ooze, staining the stone beneath. The loss of more blood may soon prove fatal.

She pulled at the short cloak bunched beneath him and, one end in each hand, she braced her arms across her chest, ripped the gold ribbing along the edge, tearing away a swath of fabric with it. With an economy of movement, she wrapped the cloth around his injured limb, the sinew hard beneath her hands. Within seconds, the material darkened with the tarnish of blood, but it did not flood through and quickly slowed.

"Well, that's that at least," Aurelia said to the night, for it was her only alert companion. The implied silent question followed the words: *What next?*

She straightened her legs, gaze reaching out to the horizon beyond the palace confines, heart trembling at the panorama, at the infinite, unknown vista stretching out before her. With a peek at the man at her feet, her glance turned to the building at her back, traveling all the way up the cold stone walls, walls that had forever hemmed her in. She bit her heavy upper lip, but it did little to stem the salacious grin spreading her mouth wide.

Aurelia curtsied, to the palace and the unseen lord within. "May strength, faith, and wisdom be my companions."

Stepping to the man's head, she lifted it, bracing it against her now-bent knees, decision defined and accepted, her swift actions reflected her resolve.

"Wake up. You must wake now." She slapped his cheek gently, then again with more tenacity, his sharp cheekbones pronounced beneath her palm. She was a strong woman, vigorous from hours and hours of riding and walking the palazzo grounds, but he was a large man, tall and dense with muscle. Aurelia did not think she could drag him to safety. She leaned over, her lips so close to his ear she could smell the tang of male sweat and fire in his hair, and closed her eyes.

"Now is the time." She hissed a ferocious whisper from between the tips of her teeth.

His eyes fluttered. His lips parted in a moan. It was enough.

Aurelia pushed against his shoulders, bracing her unfurling legs, their bodies forming an inverted V as she used the leverage to raise them both to their feet. Further roused, the man's head lifted from his chest and his blinking eyes took in his surroundings.

"Still here?" he spat incredulously at the discovery of his lot.

"Not for long." As the sounds of armored guards clanged just beyond the palace door, Aurelia stepped to his left, his injured side, and threw his arm over her shoulder, shoving her body in the crook of his arm and hefting as much of his weight onto her back as she could abide.

"No," the man grumbled. "Stay. I . . . can . . . go on alone."

He took a step and faltered, dumping more of himself upon her.

"You will get nowhere without me," she hissed.

Aurelia half-carried the stumbling man, turning them right with a lumbering though spritely step.

"The gate," he muttered, dimpled chin jutting toward the double-doored exit they left behind.

"The guards are upon us in an instant. They will know a stranger would use that exit."

After but a few gangly paces, she brought them to a much smaller gate, no wider than a single person, tucked away in the vines in the east wall, near the palazzo itself.

"A servant's door," she told him, but only out of a need to flaunt her own knowledge. "As I said, you need me."

Slipping them sideways through the narrow egress, she took a quick moment to shut the gate behind them and, with his body relying on hers more with every step, rushed them across the meadow abutting the village and into the forest just beyond.

Aurelia saw little in the glow of the half-moon hanging in the western sky; the troupe of tree trunks above blocked out even that meager light, allowing no more than inky blotches to gleam through. She brought them but a few paces into the foliage and smuggled them into a tight brace of evergreens, thick enough to keep them hidden, not so far as to lose their way.

Battista slipped out of her embrace the instant she loosened it, slumping to the forest floor, leaves and twigs crackling beneath the burden of his weight. She arched her back, stretching against the feel of the burden relieved.

Leaning his back against the bole of an evergreen, he reached down and patted his cloth-wrapped leg, hand coming away with no more than a few dabs of blood.

"I am in your debt, Signora . . . ?"

"Aurelia," she responded, prying her gaze from its study of the palazzo, scanning the space between for any guards who may have picked up their trail. But the small expanse of farmland was empty of all save the budding shoots of spring growth and the packs of scavenging guards headed out along the roads, not into this forest that would lead a stranger to naught but a cliff and a fatal drop to the river below.

His thick brows rose on his smooth forehead. "Aurelia? It is just . . . Aurelia?"

"The Lady Aurelia." She sat down beside him, offering as skeptical a glance as she received. "It is enough."

He laughed then, a low, sultry purring. "Very well then, Madonna Aurelia. I am Battista della Palla, and I owe you my life."

Battista lifted her hand off her lap and brushed his lips across it. She smiled at him as she would at a mischievous yet indulged child.

"Yes, you do." Aurelia longed to laugh as well, at him and his devilish charm, at what she had done, at the thrill of the unknown stretching before her. Her wishes had come true and she would suffuse herself in every serving of it like a fat man at a feast.

With keen observation, she took in their position, the activity visible at the palazzo, and the condition of the man beside her.

"Where is your horse? Where are your men? You have not come to this errand alone?" She frowned at him, at such a ridiculous notion.

Battista stared up at the sky above and smacked his lips. "No, I did not come on this journey alone. But my companion, with my horse, is long gone by now, I presume. Or he had better be."

It was her turn to raise a skeptical brow and he capitulated beneath it.

"I'm not sure if the agreed-to time has passed, or if he heard the alarm." He shrugged as if his situation were of no great consequence. "In either case, he would have taken himself away, saved himself as it were. It has been our agreement for the whole of our lives."

"Oh, I see," Aurelia stated with biting succinctness. "Then you are a habitual thief?"

"How dare you, woman!" Battista blustered with outrage, but one only slightly sincere. She saw his amusement in the smile that narrowed his eyes. He tipped his body closer to hers, slipping sideways along the trunk holding their backs. "I am an art dealer, and a highly res . . . ected one at that."

She smiled at his slurred protest. His handsome face, now no more than inches from hers, revealed his fatigue and weakness and her amusement faded.

"If I am forced . . . into thievery . . ."—his head slumped farther still, until it came to rest upon her shoulder, his words slithering through lips no longer moving—". . . then I do . . . whatever . . . God will forgive me."

His last argument—prayer—uttered, Battista lost consciousness, full weight once more falling upon her.

Aurelia shook her head in wonder. A penitent thief, a religious rogue . . . of all the men to encounter, of all the creatures on the earth to indulge her capricious desire, she had to choose such an irresoluble person.

With a gentle touch, she lifted his head, shimmied out from under him, and laid him down upon the soft pine needles, bunching his cape beneath his head. She scurried on her knees to his legs, squinting in the dimness at his wound. The dark stain of the makeshift bandage had become moist; the wound still bled and required another wrapping. Her appraising gaze latched onto his satchel, and she snatched at it, sitting back off her knees as she pulled it onto her lap.

Aurelia's groping hand found smooth metal first, and she pulled out an engraved, finely wrought flask. She shook it and received the heavy gurgle of a full flagon. She pulled out the cork with a pop and touched the opening to her lips, nose curling, shivering at the strength of the libations dripping down her throat. She put the stopper back in the container, but kept it out of the sack; she would use more to clean his wound.

A bundle of rope, a pouch of metal rods—tools of some sort—and two pieces of well-worn flint; the man was indeed prepared for anything. His vigilance served him well. In the meager light, Aurelia unwrapped Battista's wounded leg and dribbled some of the powerful liquid onto the raw, bloody slash about two inches in length. The man flinched and thrashed a bit, but didn't regain consciousness and Aurelia rewrapped the leg with a linen also found in the sack, its unknown dried meat removed and set aside. The ministrations had an instant effect; Battista calmed, breath growing deeper as he lapsed into a heavier rest.

Aurelia sat back down, resting once more against the curved trunk. In the distance, she heard the refrains of orchestral music; the party carried on, as she knew it would. The marquess's guards would have done their jobs well, containing the alarm, dousing the fire, secreting the search so as not to disturb or inform his guests. Only the nobleman would know of the intrusion. The pine needles beneath her pricked her skin as did her guilt for the worry she caused.

The man beside her snuffled in his sleep and Aurelia smiled at the silliness of it, the expression feeling peculiar but pleasing.

They dare not dally too much longer, for night would soon make its way to day. But if he didn't rest a bit, he might not make the journey to . . . wherever they might be bound. The thought of sleep impossible, every nerve in her body tingled with heightened alert; she hummed with the adventure in her grasp, unable to temper the mix of joy and fear thrumming through her.

Reaching out, Aurelia pulled his satchel close once more. True, she had found all she needed, but perhaps there were other items of value, or so she told herself, arguing against her own chiding conscience.

Her fingers curled around a parchment and she pulled it out. Aurelia could see the slanted lines and twirls inscribed on it, but not the words themselves. Her head tilted as she studied it, at the oddly familiar curve of the letters. She had seen this hand before.

Aurelia held the parchment out, then up, searching for a patch of unfiltered moonlight. She stood, saw the beam of illumination wafting upon the patch of forest a few steps to the left, and with another tinge of guilt untied the bow as she made quickly for it.

In the pale gray light, the unfurled parchment revealed its secrets.

Aurelia wanted nothing as much as to deny them with a scream. She read the words, now convinced of which hand had wrought them, and read them again. Not one to welter in anger for all she may be constantly piqued at the marquess, but in this she found a wealth of the disturbing emotion. How could he not have told her that this revelation, and what it led to, still existed? How could no one have told her? How could nothing have been done?

Aurelia's hand, and the parchment in it, fell to her side.

Battista groaned in his sleep, her head snapped toward the forgotten man. Who was he and what was he doing with this? She wavered between the thought that the parchment changed everything and her much-believed conviction that nothing happened without a reason. She could destroy the parchment, but it would only be an impermanent repair.

No, she shook her head, vehemence tossing her now-scattered chestnut curls further asunder. No, she had arrived at this moment for a purpose; the fates had brought her exactly where she needed to be. How many wars were won by those who kept their enemies close?

Aurelia returned to the man's side, rewound the scroll, tucked it into her palm, and sat down to wait.

He awoke of his own accord, though just moments before she meant to wake him. Pink dawn light hugged the horizon beyond the woods; it would only be a matter of an hour or so before it touched them.

Palm heels to swollen eyes, Battista rubbed at them as he sat up slowly, flexing and unflexing his left foot, testing the strength of his injured calf, satisfied, if not elated, at the results. Battista looked at her sheepishly.

"Aurelia, is it?"

She smiled slightly, not blaming him for the pain and loss of blood that rendered his recollection fuzzy.

"Indeed." She nodded. "I am Aurelia. You are Battista della Palla. And this . . ."—with a flourish she revealed the scroll hidden in her hand—". . . is what you were after."

Battista's dark glare jumped from her, to the parchment, and back. He opened his mouth, said nothing, and closed it again. He pushed against the ground, as if to stand, but had not the strength for it. He could deny her question no longer.

"*Sì*, it is," he grumbled with more than a tinge of exasperation. "Well, actually it isn't. I thought I would . . . acquire a . . . a sculpture, yes, a sculpture. But—"

"You mean a triptych, *sì?*"

The man's square jaw sagged an inch, though he tried his best not to allow it, and she kept him pinned to the moment with a narrowed stare.

"A triptych, yes." He shrugged, throwing up a hand toward her and the parchment, upper lip curled with dissatisfaction. "But all I found for my troubles was this parchment, though the label implies it may be of value yet."

So he hadn't read the parchment, she thought, all the better.

"I know much of this piece, of Giotto himself, for I am a student of art and have been for a long while." She inched closer, tapping the air between them with the parchment to drive home each contention.

Battista tried to snatch it, but his reactions were too slow and with a flick of her wrist she denied him the prize.

"He painted it for Scrovegni, you know, or at least that is the most prevalent theory. It is because of their mutual admiration for il Poeta."

The names she tossed so casually at him—that of Giotto's last and perhaps greatest benefactor, the moniker by which so many Italians referred to Dante—had the hoped-for effect. Battista looked at her greedily, as if she were the next masterpiece he must filch.

"I know more, much more," she assured him with a cock of her head. "And I will share all I know . . . if you take me with you."

Battista's hopeful, wide-eyed expression closed like a slammed shutter.

"What a ridiculous notion." He shook his head and winced with pain, continuing to argue as he rubbed between his eyes. "You are a member of the marquess's household, the same I have just pillaged."

"Pillaged?" she scoffed at him with a tilt of her head, brows rising high upon her smooth forehead. "Truly? If that sorry escapade is what you call pillaging—"

He waved her impudence away with a long-fingered hand. "I have made off with an obviously invaluable item. Why would I take you with me?"

She rose and his gaze rose with her.

"Because you are intrigued by my knowledge and want more of it. Because you are seriously injured and weak, and won't make it ten feet from here without my help. And because . . ."—she held out the parchment before his face, taunting him with it—". . . because I have already read this, could just as easily destroy it, and never reveal its message to you."

Battista smiled and in it she glimpsed one of his most powerful weapons, his malignant magnetism. She tried not to quiver as his gaze combed over her. "You are correct, my lady, those are all good reasons for taking you, but how do I know I can trust you?"

Aurelia chewed on her lip; a sign of her veracity would seal their bargain, her lust for adventure indulged, her purpose respected.

Without another word, she held out the scroll and released it into his hesitant grasp without vacillation. Aurelia watched him as he read it, observed the curtain of curiosity—one she had worn since her first reading—muddy his assured gaze. Aurelia squatted down beside him, perusing the words yet again.

They bent together over the parchment, able to read it in the growing light, their heads brushing up against each other. He finished a second reading before she did, and she felt his stare upon her face.

"It is clear and yet it isn't, though I have read it more than a few times." She stepped away but not without a twitch to throw off the shiver upon her shoulders. "It is apparent the pieces of the triptych are no longer together."

"Agreed." Battista nodded. "But there is nothing said of where they are."

"Only the reference to the one painting and Dante's words—"

"Which I knew," Battista rushed to reveal, not to be outdone by her knowledge.

"—that will show us the way. But to which painting?"

Battista shook his head, eyes rolling heavenward. "One painting to find three, to find—" He broke off his thought with a forced laugh. "Frado will wail with the angst of it."

But Aurelia had stopped her musings, head tilted to the sky.

"The morning birds are beginning to call. We must away."

Battista pushed against the ground, fighting against the weakness, and she jumped to his side, helping him up. But once on his feet, he swayed before taking a step, and she quickly helped him back down.

"You cannot travel on foot," she mumbled, gaze jumping from him to the palazzo and back again. "Wait here," she ordered, and set off along the faint deer path pointing toward the palace.

Battista chuckled, tossing his hands weakly upward in helpless surrender. "How and where would I go?"

She spared him not a response as she ran through the field, running with her back bent, hidden in the tall grass until she reached the stables. The young groomsmen were still asleep, thank the fates, and the horses left behind by the frenzied guards knew her scent, did not rankle at her appearance. She often indulged in an early morning ride, and the beasts knew her well. She saddled a great white charger—the perfect pale beast to balance the dark man waiting for her in the woods—along with her favorite stallion, the steed's black, moist nose nuzzling her neck with familiar affection, as doubts crowded and nudged against Aurelia, but she refused to give them sway. She kept her mind on only what she need do in that moment, all else be damned.

But as Aurelia scurried the outfitted horses out the rear door of the stable, as she grabbed a satchel and filled it with feed, as she rushed through the meadow with them, praying not to be seen, one thought etched itself in her thoughts and she greeted it with a mixture of pain and fiendish delight.

Now I am the thief.

Nine

The more perfect a thing is,
the more susceptible to good and bad treatment it is.

—*Inferno*

He recognized the slant of nebulous light through the translucent wood-framed oilcloths. Battista blinked against it, eyes adjusting with prickly slowness. He lay in his room, he distinguished it without another glance, but how could it be possible?. . . He was in the woods. Yes, in the woods in the early morning, with a woman, a very beautiful woman, and they were looking at . . .

Battista flung himself up, linens falling away to expose his unclothed body, skin warm as a balmy afternoon breeze fluttered upon it.

Where was the woman and, more important, where was the parchment? He raked back the waves of dark hair from his face and closed his eyes, willing himself to remember. With painstaking deliberation, the images revealed themselves.

Aurelia had returned with two horses and somehow he had gotten himself upon one. Though he did seem to remember her pushing at his behind with a strength and a curse he had not expected from one so seemingly dainty and demure. He remembered musing on her depths, far more than a lovely face and a curvaceous figure. She had led them away, along the edge of the forest and away from the palazzo. He had told her to head south for Florence, told her the name of the street this house sat upon.

But there were no memories beyond that moment, and what could have taken place between then and now frightened him.

Battista clamped a hand over his mouth, squeezing his face as he tried—to no avail—to remember more. He crawled sheepishly from his skin and studied the events earlier in the night through an outsider's critical eye. To launch such an attempt alone was arrogance of grotesque proportion. Were his father alive he would cuff Battista sharply on the back of his head, and all too well deserved it would be, too. He could not confuse his success with who he was, but keep it only as what he had achieved. Battista flinched these thoughts away with painful aversion.

A puzzled frown creased his face as he allowed his fingers to investigate his skin; the thick growth of hair upon his cheeks told yet another discouraging tale, one he had no desire to hear. At least two days had passed since his last memory, an abundance of time for mischief to run amok.

Tossing back the bed sheet with an impatient hand, Battista surveyed his leg. The dull throb radiating from his calf reacquainted him with his wound, but upon inspection he found but a small wrapping. Peeling it away gently, he revealed more crude stitches than he dared to count, but no spreading redness, no oozing pus, to indicate infection. His leg and the binding reeked of earthy odors; he scrunched his nose at the malodorous mixture of sharp mint, dirt, and lavender. A physician had attended him; the chopped herbs speckling both his leg and the bandage testified to it.

Battista replaced the dressing and swung his legs out of bed, steeling himself at the true test of his health.

With a deferential hesitance, he planted his bare feet on the smooth, dark wood and eased his weight onto his legs. He stood unaided without overwhelming pain, but he could not step fully upon his left foot without the deep throb of discomfort, a soreness testifying to muscle trauma, not of raw, tearing flesh. Encouraged, Battista took a few steps. He could not walk without favoring the leg with a heavy limp.

He grabbed at his satchel hanging on one of the tall carved posts of his bed. Rifling through it, tossing aside the items intrinsic to his trade, his frantic search was futile. No parchment lay within its confines.

"*Merda!*" Battista flung the bag away, cursing at the parchment's absence, for he held clearly the memory of their returning it to the satchel; he had put it back in there himself, along with Aurelia's heavy veil that she had tossed off her head, as well as the half-full flask of brandy she had used to treat his wound. The parchment's disappearance incited his fear to panic.

Unconscious of his nakedness, he shuffled to the door as fast as he could and threw it open.

From below, the sounds that were the chorus of his life rose up: male voices, raucous laughter, coins clattering upon tabletops, men chewing and slurping with little heed of good table manners.

Many, if not all, of the men he considered family were below. He prayed Aurelia was among them and that she still had the parchment.

She wished she could wash away her wide-eyed expression, the smile of childish delight, but it was a fruitless struggle. Aurelia had never walked alone—anywhere—she had never seen a city as magnificent as Florence, and her solitary experience of it produced an almost-unconscionable thrill.

It had taken two days to convince Battista's man to allow her the expedition. The man who called himself Frado had been so grateful to her for returning Battista to them—his relief no doubt a direct equal to his guilt for leaving him in the first place—his caution gave way to his gratitude.

It had taken her all her efforts to find her way from Mantua to Florence, asking only other fellow travelers for direction, and only those with women among them, refusing to enter any village or town not gated as Florence, for fear of miscreants or discovery. Her own fearless audacity had surprised her, though she knew she had been born for more than her life had asked of her thus far.

Frado had been so frantic with caring for Battista, bringing a physician, and fetching whatever medicinals the man required, he had nearly forgotten her. His attention finally swung her way, as he expressed his gratitude once more, with the assurance of Battista's survival. No questions did Frado ask; no information did she offer. Aurelia thought he awaited word from Battista before deciding how to deal with her.

But after two days of her pecking at him, Frado had procured a simple dress she could don without aid of maid, hired a simple village girl for an afternoon to help relieve her of the heavy formal gown and to bathe. And now she found herself strolling the grand avenues of the city, no chaperone shadowing her every move, no one denying her the freedom she had craved for so long.

Aurelia circled around the unknown fairways without fear of becoming lost, certain the resplendent palazzo that had greeted her just outside Battista's door would lead her back to it once more.

Beyond the blue door of Battista's *casa*, she had stood before the palace, immobilized by the beautiful architecture, features she would easily recall and return to . . . the contrast between the rustic brick of the first floor and the white plaster of the two above it. The elegant mullioned windows and toothed cornices were but the first course of the splendid banquet served by the city of Florence.

She strolled at leisure beneath the blurred anonymity of her thick lace veil, smiling at the pagan symbols festooning the entire city . . . the statues of gods and goddesses, the simplistic hieroglyphics used in signs and business names. And alongside them, as comfortable with each other as the birch and the oak, were the plethora of churches and cathedrals. She felt more at home and more welcome with each step she took into this intriguing, bustling, dichotomous city.

The palaces rose above the modest homes that circled them in clusters, gold spires pierced the sky, red and white domes jeweled the landscape, and a turreted, tower-studded wall girdled it all. And most lovely of all . . . the gracious Florentines.

At the side of the marquess of Mantua, the Lady Aurelia had traveled to many a splendid palace, met and hobnobbed with a surfeit of nobles, but always she had entered their compounds within a sheltered conveyance, always had she been treated with utmost deference. Never had she walked among so many so anonymously, yet she treasured every unfamiliar smile and greeting offered, offered with nothing more than the courtesy of one fellow citizen to another.

And everywhere there was something for sale, from beneath the merchants' shutters and their jutting benches heavy with wares, or from the shaded loggias at the foot of the grand palazzo; if one desired it, one could find it.

Aurelia cursed her lack of money; she possessed a heavy purse full of gold florins. Unfortunately, she had had neither the time nor the opportunity to extract it from her rooms in Mantua. How she longed for a treat, an olive oil–dripping slab of fresh *panini*, its warm, yeasty aroma dispelling any remnant of unwashed body or the livestock that rushed intermittently through the streets, harried, raggedly dressed men with their sticks hurrying behind.

She surprised herself when she came upon it, not knowing how she had made her way through the twisting streets to this vast piazza as the sun bid good-bye to the slight chill of morning and rose to the warmth of afternoon. But there the statue rose before her. Aurelia had heard of it, of course, all of Italy knew of Michelangelo's Giant, but she never dared imagine she would see it, and yet her feet had led her to it as if they had known where it stood all along.

At the end of a long gallery running in a straight line between matching buildings with rows of square arches, the fortresslike structure rose up as a sentinel standing watch over the city. Square, brick, and turreted, a tall, pink-stoned campanile topped the building, clearly one of importance, as cloaked and robed men came and went from its door, their own significance leading them in a rush.

And there, just to the left of the enormous black wood door, stood the famous statue.

Aurelia climbed the five stone steps to bring her directly beside its base; her eyes—green with the light of the sun—rose slowly over the finely sculpted statue.

It was indeed a giant; Aurelia guessed it to be taller than three men. She did not shy away from the barbarous vulgarity of his nakedness, but found her perplexity over its formation equally as tantalizing. When she studied the face, all her uncertainties were answered, all of David's mysteries were revealed. The face was, as she had heard, a bit large for the size of the head, but upon his features she saw all of the fear, tension, and aggression the real David must have felt when attacked by the colossal Goliath. Wrinkles perforated David's forehead, thick brows drawn together, with a scornful twist to his full lips, fearful, yes, but with an inner assuredness that all evil could be felled. There was great nobility to the man etched into immortality, a beautiful determination astounding the eye as well as the soul.

Lost in her reverie, she sensed the man before she saw him, having intuitively known for some minutes that she was no longer alone in her intimate study of the statue. Aurelia turned then, in the shared experience lingering in the air between them, and smiled at the slight man beside her.

He was short, with spiky salt-and-pepper hair, the lines of a hard life etched the man's face, and yet his amber eyes glowed with an uncanny illumination radiating from within. He smiled at her, thin lips spreading within the camouflage of untended facial hair.

"Have you never seen it before?" he asked her with a voice full of gravel.

Aurelia shook her head, a mirroring smile offered in return. "No, never. Though I have dreamt of it. Can you tell?"

The man chuckled low with wise amusement. "It is in the wonder in your eyes."

"And you, signore? You have seen it, many times, I think, *sì?* It is in the pride of your smile."

"Oh yes." He laughed aloud then, a baritone's cheerful song. "I know it very well. But it is good for me to visit it now and again."

Aurelia turned her admiring gaze back to the sculpture. "I would look upon it every day, were I able," she said, her hushed voice full of her wonder.

He put a soft hand upon her shoulder, but his touch provoked no fear.

"*Buongiorno, cara.*" He bid her farewell with similar familiarity, a strange bond having formed over such an astounding achievement.

"Good day to you, sir." Aurelia dipped him a curtsy and watched him walk away, back a bit bowed, gait a bit slow.

She indulged in a few more minutes of luxuriant appraisal, dipping another curtsy before departing from the Giant's side, as if she offered her respects to the artist, wherever he may be.

With the satiated stroll of the well pleased, she made her way back to the palazzo she recognized and the *casa* with the blue door across from it.

She entered the house without a knock, for indeed, those within had barely taken note of her during her stay, but the raucous, rude salutation stopped her in her tracks.

"Where the devil have you been and where is the parchment?"

Ten

A great flame follows a little spark.

—*Paradiso*

Battista stood in the middle of the vast chamber, arms akimbo, greeting her with a baleful glare; his air of frustrated impatience he served to himself as well as his houseguest. If he had taken a moment's pause, a second to think, he may have grasped the obvious.

He may not know what lay in the heart of this woman, but surely if she had purloined the parchment she would not be returning to his home; a woman who had saved him from the Mantua palazzo, kept him alive, and brought them successfully to his door would not be dim-witted enough to deceive him and then return. But he had stewed in the juices of fear for too many hours, and he needed the release of it as the nonsensical boiled over.

The Lady Aurelia seemed unable to move, but only for a vacuous moment.

As she rushed to meet him across the expanse, she yanked her veil away, thick chestnut curls falling to disarray. Brown-green eyes burned with ire, full mouth stretched in a grimace.

"I do not know these . . . people . . . who inhabit your home." She stood toe-to-toe with him, flapping a hand at the men perched about the room, those struck dumb by the force of the energy between the two before them. "Or whether or not you trusted them. How could I?"

Battista relaxed his stern posture, but stood his ground.

"Perhaps it was unwise to have disappeared for a whole day?" He refused to acknowledge the truth of her words, grasping for some other point, no matter how obscure, with which to counter. He lifted a finger, aiming it at her heaving chest. "And you could have left the parchment with me."

"Parchment? What parchment?" Giovanni quipped, pale eyes beseeching the men beside him.

"No idea," Ascanio mumbled, petting his well-manicured mustache as Pompeo raised his shoulders to his ears in silent ignorance.

"Of what parchment do you speak?" Frado jumped into the fray, entering the circle of the engaged combatants, only to be denied by Aurelia's vehemence.

"I did not know if you would survive, you lost so much blood, nor was I allowed into your room." She edged forward, hands cutting the air with a hard slash. "Did you want me to just place it in the middle of the table here and hope for the best?"

His mouth opened, empty of any worthy reply, and he closed it with a click of teeth. Battista tugged on the tuft of hair below his lip, mouth spreading in sardonic amusement. She was right, on all counts, and he had no cause to question or disparage her. He was not a man too proud for apologies, but looked upon them as the honorable thing to do if they would be genuine and heartfelt.

"I am sorry, Monna Aurelia. Please forgive the dishonor of my reproach."

He saw the smile she struggled with and it encouraged his own to grow wider.

"You may thank me now, for saving your life . . . again." Her head tilted sideways, brows flung skyward, nipping at him with the sarcastic quip.

Battista threw back his head and burst out laughing; the rowdy, masculine hilarity filled the house, catching them all with its contagion.

Who is this woman? he wondered in delight as he stepped forward and bowed low before her. "For your assistance, and my life, I thank you . . . again."

"What parchment, Battista?" Frado commanded, booted feet stomping on stone, his cutting query severing the jovial sparring.

Battista rose from his bow, placing a calming hand upon the insistent man's shoulder.

"May I have it, *per favore*, my Lady Aurelia?" he asked with a low creamy hum, all smooth kindness now, strong face tender with respectful petition.

Aurelia rolled her eyes, as if she saw right through him and his courtesy, and tossed her response to Frado.

"If you take four steps from the bed in my chamber, a board will creak beneath your feet. Beneath the creak you will find the parchment."

Frado ran off as if the devil himself raced him to the quarry.

"Are you hungry, signorina?" Nuntio appeared by Aurelia's side, one arm raised gallantly to her as the other gestured to the table and the food spread upon it.

She took his arm, a pleased smug smile offered to Battista, one criticizing him for allowing his servant to be more of a gentleman than he.

Battista followed behind with an incredulous, if amused, waggle of his head. He joined her at the table and in the meal, having found his lost appetite upon her return. But they had barely sat when Frado rushed back into the room, incautiously clearing some room on the polished banquet table with a flailing arm and flattening the parchment upon the empty space as the men in attendance gathered round him.

As Battista shared a look with his dinner companion, the words upon the scroll returned to his recollection, as did the puzzle they offered.

"Would you fetch Lucagnolo, Ercole? But only if his wife can spare him." Battista made the request between bites of wine-soaked veal, the tender meat melting on his tongue. He had learned soon upon waking that the young's man wife still suffered from her illness, one that had, in fact, worsened in the last few days.

"And Barnabeo? Do we have need of him?" the rough-and-tumble man asked of the only other not among them as he headed for the door.

Battista shook his head. "His expertise could not help us with this."

Over his plate, he watched as the four remaining men read the confounding message, each following Frado's finger as it brushed across the parchment, the scratching coming in fits and starts as he balked over the bewildering words.

Battista lowered his gaze quickly as Frado's rushed up to his face, the feel of his colleague's scathing look sufficient to reproach him, but averting his eyes would not save him from the tirade surely on its way. Frado flung himself into the closest chair, the wooden legs screeching against the stone.

"First one and *then* three? Tell me this is a joke, Battista. Tell me it is some kind of cruel jest or I may just throttle the lif—"

"I know, Frado, I know, *amico mio*. But what can we do, eh?" He raised his hands up and out as he shrugged his shoulders to his ears. "We know a piece such as this, one of such import, would not . . . could not . . . be gotten easily. That which is most cherished in life is often the most difficult to attain."

Frado offered no argument, but his cynical gaze flicked from Battista's face to Aurelia's.

Battista heard the thought behind the glance and spoke to it without further prodding. "She saved my life, not once, but twice."

They spoke of her as if she were not there, but she seemed to derive no insult from it, continuing to eat with graceful movements, cutting small pieces of her meat and savoring each bite, one at a time.

"I think we can trust her. I am fairly certain she can help us."

Aurelia did respond then. "I told you I could. And I will."

This last she directed to Battista, who accepted the pledge with a lukewarm nod.

"But we do not even know where to begin. This . . . this . . ." Frado waved an impatient, stubby hand at the parchment. "If these words were any more cryptic they could be the clues to the Holy Grail itself. I can make no sense of it. Can you?"

Battista floundered for some appeasement, but Pompeo delivered it.

"Here, this passage is the most important and the most intriguing, I think." He lowered his eyes to the parchment, a finger tapping the words about a third of the way along the message. "The painting we seek was rendered by the same who painted a Madonna and Child with St. John, an—"

"Oh, *sì*," Frado blundered over Pompeo's words with his sarcasm. "There are only hundreds of those about, as if it were not one of the most popular subjects of the moment."

"True, Frado, true. But here, these words, 'the air ship will point the way.' Those are the most peculiar of all."

"All of this is peculiar," Frado mumbled under his breath, the low growl of a guard dog as danger approached.

"It is illogical." Ascanio took a chair at the table, pouring them all a glass of *vino da tavola,* the dark red liquid releasing its heavy aroma as it splashed in their tankards. "Whatever is an air ship and where would you find one?"

"Air ship?" The soft voice of Lucagnolo entered as he did, thus summoned, on the heels of Ercole, and any polite greetings were lost in the inauspicious subject matter.

Battista ignored it and rose, as pleased to see Lucagnolo as the young man was relieved to see him, returned and recovered.

"Bettaccia?" Battista said the single name in question as the two men separated and his throat tightened over a hard swallow at the helpless look Lucagnolo offered in explanation.

Battista enfolded the man back in his arms, a rough embrace the only support he could think to offer.

"Did I hear correctly?" Lucagnolo asked, narrow, slanted eyes blinking with curiosity, falling on Aurelia with undisguised speculation.

"You did, Luca," Battista told him, turning with a gesturing hand to the woman among them. "Please make the acquaintance of the Lady Aurelia. She is . . ." Words failed him, and Battista realized he knew little of the woman, or how to explain her. He must correct this lack of knowledge, and quickly. ". . . She alone is to be thanked for my survival and my return."

Lucagnolo bowed low. "Then it is with great gratitude that I welcome you, madonna," he bade her greeting with the formal salutation in his shy, sincere manner.

"*E tu*, signore." Aurelia tipped her head graciously.

"Read this, Luca." Ascanio pulled out the chair beside him and pulled the parchment toward him as Lucagnolo filled the seat.

The soft-spoken man puzzled them all as he read the last of the words, a wan grin tickling his thin lips. "I may know of what this speaks."

"*Cazzata*," Ercole barked the vulgarity calling Lucagnolo's knowledge into question.

The others laughed uncomfortably at the unflattering skepticism; Ercole may have said it in too harsh a manner, but it spoke of a shared uncertainty.

Lucagnolo playfully cuffed the older man's shoulder as he rose and made his way to the corner bookshelves, running a searching finger along the spines. "I would not lie to you, Ercole, you are far too fearsome. It is a phenomenon more than a few are starting to speak of openly, though many fear retribution from the Church."

At this last, any light amusement among them scurried away to the dark corners of the room, as if to hide from the judging eyes of the religious fanatics, those in a long line of reformists since the Dominican friar Savonarola first brought the idea to Florence a few decades ago.

No one spoke as the painting connoisseur made his search; Aurelia pushed away her plate, either too full or too curious to eat another bite.

"Yes, yes, of course," Lucagnolo at last announced with an edge of impatience directed inward, pulling out a square, heavy tome from a lower shelf.

Shuffling through the pages of the large book, the young man crossed the room, plopped the heavy volume upon the table with a bang, and pointed a knowing finger upon the open page.

"Look at this and you will know almost exactly what the words speak of."

The painting sketched in the book was a combination of hard-angled buildings and gracefully rounded people. It projected a vanishing perspective, with Mary glimpsed in the foreground just through an open door, two men in the gallery beside the building, and others in the background, the success of the dimensions depicted, a function of the perfect spatial and size balance of each person and object rendered.

Ascanio clucked his tongue in recognition. "Carlo Crivelli?"

"Crivelli, *sì*. You cannot see the brilliance of the man's colors here." Lucagnolo nodded, with a nigh on reverential whisper. "The brilliant reds of the men's robes, the vibrant golds of the building's stone, or the cream of Mary's skin. But this is what we need look at the most."

At this, his finger rose to the top portion of the picture and the fluffy clouds infesting it. The men hunched forward, as did Aurelia, each vying for a closer look at the odd shape appearing, at first glance, camouflaged by the waves of scuttling clouds.

Perfectly round and vibrantly white, the circular apparition emitted a beam of light through the sky and into the room where Mary stood.

"*Dio mio*," Ercole whispered harshly, crossing himself with a vigorous gesture.

"What in all creation is that?" Frado snipped.

"Exactly." Lucagnolo nodded, using the other man's question as his answer.

"But, but that is not a ship, at least not one like any I have ever seen. Where are the sails, and the masts?" Frado's unease over their situation clanged in every clipped word.

"*Sì*," Ercole rushed to agree. "This is some sort of circle, like the tiny dishes my mother uses to serve biscotti to the priest."

"Only the priest?" Ascanio raised one brow, smoothing his perfectly trimmed mustache with lithe fingers.

Ercole nodded his boxy head with a shrug. "*Sì*. My brothers and I are too brutish, she says."

"True, on both counts," Lucagnolo acknowledged with a half smile, turning back to the page before him. "But there are other paintings with these . . . these objects floating in the air. Some are calling them air ships."

Beside Battista, Aurelia shivered noticeably, but he believed her chilled, not cold. It had become rather warm in the house, truth be told, though the fire had burned low and Nuntio had opened the back doors to the small, night-filled courtyard, tree frogs peeping languidly with their song of early spring.

"This is not of the Madonna and Child." Battista turned back to the unsettling painting and Lucagnolo.

The young man shook his head. "No, it isn't. But there are many others like this. I am almost certain I have seen the very one in question, but I cannot remember the artist's name."

"Then there is but one thing for us to do," Battista said, and without need for further explanation, the men stood, the maunderings and exasperated sighs rising with them.

As the majority of the men set themselves once more to the study and the books and parchments filling it, Aurelia took herself away from the table and set about the room, rubbing her arms as she walked among the crates and boxes.

Battista limped behind, tired, yes, but concerned, for them all.

"Are you well, my lady?"

She found him just over her shoulder and offered a pale imitation of an assuring smile. "Yes, fine."

He thought she had more to say, thought he saw it in her eyes, but her lips closed upon silence. "It is . . . disturbing, *sì?*"

Her smile became more heartfelt. "Yes, disturbing indeed."

She crossed to one of the largest crates, pushed into the front northern corner of the room.

"These boxes, they are full of . . ." Her words faded, but her raised brow implied she would accept nothing but the truth, as if she already knew his answer.

"Gifts. For the king of France." He laughed as he answered her, as he offered her the transparent sophistry. But she didn't join in the jocularity.

Rubbing one hand along the rough wood of the crate, she condemned him, "You really are a thief then."

His jaw flinched as a surge of anger rifled through him. He narrowed his eyes at her, a pretense of charming civility clinging to his sharp features. "I offer money, lots of money, as well as the opportunity to support Firenze . . . our homeland. The king of France asks for masterpieces. In return, he pledges his support and military protection, if the need should arise. No one has a right to deny such offers." The devotion to his city resounded thickly in every fanaticism-laced word.

She stepped away from the crates and, with slow consideration, took in every magnificent painting covering the walls mounted in a haphazard array, every lush tapestry spread upon the floors, and the dazzling bronze and gold statues glittering in the candlelight, all displayed for the enjoyment of no one save their owner.

Aurelia turned her gaze on him then and her silent study reached deep in his soul, scorching him with its heat. It violated him . . . as if she looked beyond his physical being.

"Your passion is true, as is your inspiration. But your eagerness for personal property muddies it."

He shrugged a broad shoulder, dark eyes twinkling. "A man has to eat."

"True," she conceded, harsh, judgmental shadows fading from her features, though no answering smile did she extend, "but not a gourmet meal every night."

By the end of the third day, the house became a festering mess of dirty dishes, unwashed men, and books and parchments discarded and piled everywhere. Nuntio did his best, but age and infirmity slowed him and the demands outweighed his ability. Ascanio, Pompeo, and Giovanni had not returned to their own homes since the searching had begun; perhaps the eeriness of the material disturbed them too greatly to find comfort in any form of solitude. Ercole came every morning, leaving only late at night, and Lucagnolo came as often as possible.

Aurelia closed the book on her lap—rubbing her dry, tired eyes with the heels of her palms—another endless tome detailing artists and their work, another few hundred pages of lookng at painting sketches without finding the desired one. As she stared vacantly out at the wreckage all around her, she did not know what to feel, relief or disappointment. Her stomach grumbled and she clasped onto the normal feeling, anchoring her to reality; she was hungry and needed to eat.

Placing the heavy digest aside, she rose, took a step toward the kitchen . . . and tripped, stumbling over something—or things—hidden by her full skirts.

Her head tipped forward as her feet remained stuck behind, the off-kilter balance of her body propelling her onward without control. In a split second of panic, she saw the small, round table between chair and settee, the protruding sharp points of the sculptures upon it, as her face careened wildly toward them, an arrow intent upon its target. She threw her hands out, praying they would catch her bef—

The arms grabbed her at the waist, expelling the air from her lungs with a yelp.

Aurelia opened her eyes, not remembering when she had closed them, to find herself sitting in Pompeo's lap, both of them panting with their efforts, fear, and relief of the moment.

She blinked at the young face so close to her own and swallowed away the bitter taste of alarm. "*Grazie,* signore."

"*Prego,*" Pompeo replied, a wide-eyed smile of surprise on his face. But as if he suddenly realized their intimate posture, his smile turned rascally, his arms remaining firmly wrapped about her. "My pleasure to be of service."

The laughter broke Aurelia from the clutch of her distress, and she turned to the other, forgotten men enjoying the moment at her expense.

"Be careful, signorina," Giovanni twittered behind a cupped hand like a silly adolescent. "Pompeo likes older women."

The men guffawed at the jest. Aurelia did not know what offended her more, the lewd implication or that Giovanni thought her old. Granted she was not emerging from adolescence as Pompeo and Giovanni obviously were, but neither was she decrepit with age. She believed herself to be near the same age as Battista, quite sure, as well, that they did not consider him to be old, but men were not judged by the same harsh criteria as women.

Aurelia turned her narrow gaze at Battista, as if he were the parent able to bring these children to heel, but he wore an equally amused smirk, avoiding her glance.

She pushed herself from Pompeo's all too eager grasp and straightened her skirts with an indignant flapping of her hands. Aurelia searched the floor between her chair and her landing point, grimacing at the pile of empty wine bottles littering the floor. With all the control she could muster, she pointed at them in accusation.

"Someone has to help Nuntio clean this place up. Look at that," she demanded they give attention to the mess upon the floor, "and that, and that." The finger spun round the room, at the food-crusted plates growing fuzzy with mold, at the piles of books blocking almost every inch of space, at the discarded doublets and boots rank with their owners' stench.

Silence met her tirade; the men stared at her. Aurelia wondered if she startled them with her outburst, quickly realizing—with ever-increasing anger—that their glances were those of expectation.

Thrusting a finger at her own chest, she almost laughed at their ill-informed estimations. "You imagine *I* would do it?"

"Well, you are the only woman here," Ercole groused, saying what they all thought.

Aurelia raised a derisive glance heavenward, shaking her head and the mass of unkempt chestnut waves upon it. "And I have been waited on all my life. I know nothing of cleaning or cooking. Look at me." She flung her hands up into the air, performing an ungainly pirouette, displaying her disheveled and wrinkled appearance without shame. "I know not even how to care for myself."

Her confession hung bitterly in the air. Would they think ill of her for flaunting her station? But with a scathing flash of insight she realized such preeminence would be the least of her words' offense.

"Were you the marquess's mistress?" Battista ventured the question, the same she saw in each of their intrusive stares.

She could have bitten off her tongue with her teeth and spat it out for its crime. Her own words had brought her to this moment, one she had been avoiding for days. Aurelia thought Battista would have asked her to explain herself far sooner than this and she had been formulating the story for some days. But she had underestimated the power of gratitude.

With a sigh of capitulation, she plunked herself down upon the couch beside Pompeo. Perhaps it was better to tell them all at once; it would eliminate the need for duplicating the tale with each telling.

"No, I was never the marquess's mistress." She shook her head, clasping her hands primly upon her lap. "I have been the ward of the lord of Mantua since just after my birth."

They had gathered around her, slowly, as if afraid to spook a fretful bird.

"Are your parents . . . dead?" Battista asked, wedging himself into the small space on the cushion to her left.

Touched by the gentle sympathy in his voice, Aurelia still could not allow it to hinder her response. "I never knew my parents." She offered the rehearsed answer, took a deep breath, and continued. "My life has been a very privileged one, it is true, but by its very nature, it has been overly sheltered and sequestered. There were directives left, by those who created me, putting stern prohibitions on my activities. It was always meant for me to live a very pious, devoted life, though without the need for vows."

It was a story so very close to the facts and yet so vacant of any meaningful truth, but she gleaned, by the sympathetic faces gathering around her, that it was enough.

Not a word did the gathering offer to such a tale, for what could they say? Battista patted the ball of her hands and Aurelia had to fight the urge to fling off the embrace. She had no need for sympathy. Understanding, yes . . . a relief from the mundane existence, most definitely. But pity without action was useless to the extreme.

"Come, Monna Aurelia, your supper awaits," Nuntio offered from his perch behind the settee, and she turned a grateful smile to the supplicating man.

"Wonderful idea, Nuntio," Battista praised him. "And on the morrow you will make for the lower village, near the Ponte Vecchio, use whatever funds you need to hire a maid, or perhaps two," he continued with a shamefaced smile and a wary glance about the house. "Your dedication should not be a burden, my friend."

Nuntio gave a gratified bob of his head and led them to the kitchen.

Aurelia had not seen day turn to night, had forgotten her hunger in the anxiety of the last few moments, but the mention of food brought the basic instinct rushing back.

As the men gathered about the table and the steaming platters of food Nuntio had set upon it, the conversation turned back to their search.

"Did I show you the work by da Panicale?" Ascanio asked of Battista, who nodded. "Frightening, is it not?"

They all nodded in agreement, including Aurelia. She had not known such works existed and their very reality frightened her. Those who guarded her life had taken great pains to guard her education as well, from her.

Da Panicale's was a crude rendering to be sure, wrought sometime early in the fifteenth century, but the anomaly of the picture could not be denied. Akin to the piece by Crivelli, the circular object dominated da Panicale's painting, but in this work there were hundreds of them, arranged in almost precise rows, as if they were lines of an attacking army.

"A Florentine, da Panicale," Giovanni said, as if the fact made the reality of the image that much harder to bear.

"Lucagnolo was correct," Battista murmured. "There are many paintings with such . . . things . . . in them."

The thought set more than one man pushing his plate away, sending a few back to the search, but whether to resolve the issue or to avoid it, Aurelia could not tell.

Before very long, only Battista and Aurelia remained at the table, each batting the last forgotten morsel of food around on their plates, but neither taking another bite. Try as she might, her gaze returned to him again and again; for all equal efforts, she could not deny the beauty of the rugged face. Yet it was not the splendor of the man enthralling her, but his reality.

He looked up at her then, as if the inquisition of her gaze poked at him, and smiled in question, rich brown eyes, so deep they reflected points of light with equal brilliance, crinkling up at the corners.

"Why you?" She placed her knife on the table and leaned forward, hands splayed in front of her hunched shoulders.

He wrinkled his brow at her. "*Scusi?*"

"Why have you chosen this as your path? Why do you trade your morality for the sake of Florence?" She understood the depth of what she asked him, cudgeled her brain to make the query simpler, but she could not, she could but repeat the first question, "Why you?"

He laughed then, leaning back, resting his elbow on the arm of his chair, and tipped his head upon his hand. "Why do any of us do what we do?"

It was an evasive answer and she would not let it serve. She kept the question upon him with a piercing stare.

Battista smiled with a capitulating shake of his head. "I could tell you how my father was killed when I was still young, also in defense of Firenze. Or I could tell you of King François's kindness and charity to me and my family, for that would indeed explain a great deal as well." He leaned forward then, and their faces were no more than inches from each other; she could smell the wine's nuttiness upon his breath. "But they are all merely pieces of the puzzle. Who knows why we do the things we do. Do you?"

He turned the tables on her, sultry stare studying every inch of her face. Aurelia backed away, from him and his probing, uncertain how to deal with either.

They sat bound in the expectant silence and she struggled for a way out of it, only too thankful when the distraction came.

"I have it! Sweet holy Mother of God, I have it!"

They all began to talk and yelp at once, turning to Giovanni as he jumped from his chair, holding a slim volume high over his head as he pranced about in victory, yellow curls falling in his crinkled, pale eyes.

"The painting? You found it?" Battista wheeled round.

"Give it here." Ascanio tried to pluck the book from Giovanni's hands.

"Show me," Frado barked.

But Giovanni would not have the moment—or the book—snatched from his grasp. He rushed to the table and shoved the book upon it, resting it between Battista and Aurelia, the other men tumbling over one another to get a look.

It was round in shape, the painting was, a unique characteristic alone, but at first glance there appeared to be nothing else unusual about the work. Perched over a haloed cherubic St. John, the baby Jesus in his loving embrace, the Virgin's large prayerful presence dominated the center of the piece. Over her right shoulder, the majority of the background depicted a shoreline and rolling hills on the opposite side. But the small portion of setting behind her left shoulder had them all straining for a better view.

Beyond the trees, just behind Mary, were more gently sloping hilltops. Upon the highest one, a man stood, gaze raised to the sky, hand shading his eyes as if he struggled to see. At the apex of the man's gaze, the undeniable object hovered, for it satisfied even Frado's conception of a ship, with a pointed prow and rounded bottom. And yet it hung in the sky as if it flew like a bird.

"An air ship," Ercole whispered, and each one of them heard the quiver in his voice.

"But . . . it doesn't point to anything," Ascanio spat a frustrated sputter.

Giovanni answered with a smirk, "It points to nothing in the painting, but who knows what it points to on the wall upon which it sits. Look." With a tick of his chin, he redirected their attention to the words beneath the etching.

They had all been so preoccupied with the rendering itself, they had not bothered to read the caption accompanying it. The work was attributed to the great Florentine painter Sebastiano Mainardi and its current locale was no more than a few paces from this very house.

"*Dio mio,* it hangs in the Palazzo Vecchio." Pompeo's voice cracked, a telltale sign of a puberty not long discharged.

As if goaded into action by a cattle prod, more than one man rushed for the door, corralled back by Battista's loud call.

"Where are you going? Have you forgotten the time?"

Giovanni, Pompeo, and Ercole came up sharply, laughing with embarrassment; they had lost track of the hour—of the day—truth be told.

"We will all go," Battista promised them, "first thing on the morrow. For now, make to your beds. We have all earned a good night's rest."

They bid one another good night, those who lived elsewhere at last taking their leave of the *casa,* every face set in the same mask of turbidity, the same fear of the unknown and the ship that flew in the sky.

Eleven

Do not rest in so profound a doubt except she tell it thee,
who shall be a light between truth and intellect.

—Purgatorio

"You are quite anxious to be off," Battista greeted Aurelia as he entered the room, amused by her fidgety waiting.

As she hovered impatiently by the door, stepping toward it and away as if in a dance, Aurelia's fingers fluttered on the sides of her gown, her gaze plied upon the portal as if she might open it with her will. She had taken great pains to improve her appearance—the simple daffodil gown she'd worn since arriving was far less wrinkled than it had been yesterday and her hair was pinned up in a simple, if neat and flattering, coif.

She answered him with a wide smile irradiating her beauty from within and it took him aback; despite all the thoughts he chewed upon concerning her during the last few days—and there were indeed many—he continually tried to ignore her comely countenance. Green eyes glowing, full lips moist, porcelain cheeks flushed with excitement . . . features too striking for any to disregard.

"Very anxious, *sì*," Aurelia tittered. "I am most impressed by your beautiful city, at least what I have seen of it, and long to see more."

Battista enjoyed this side of her immensely, had always seen it lying just beneath her stoic surface. By her own description, she had led a serious life, one bereft of many joys; it explained why she had helped him with so little consideration, had left Mantua with him so quickly. And though she tried perpetually to don the grave mien that was most probably her usual aspect, a feisty spirit longing to be unleashed lay just below, a spunky sprite hiding in the foliage of a magical garden, waiting to spring loose upon the world. He glimpsed the nymph now and again, though she tried to keep her impish smile a secret. If walking the streets of Florence appeased such mettle, Battista was only too pleased to be her guide.

"Have you broken your fast?" he asked, making for the kitchen and whatever fresh bread and jam might be available.

But she shook her head, pacing between the door and the window once more, peering out. "No, I haven't. I'm not hungry just now."

Battista laughed and changed direction; he would not allow his own peevishness to delay her one moment more. "We will have something to eat along the way, yes?"

"Oh yes. That would be wonderful."

Before he could say another word, she tossed up the latch and pulled open the door, stepping out into the bright spring morning, thrusting herself into the stream of activity flowing just outside. Dawn's rain had hurried away, leaving only small puddles in the ruts of the hard-packed dirt street, tiny blotches of water that caught the sun and sent it sparkling back upward.

"We're leaving, Frado," Battista called out over his shoulder, joining Aurelia on the busy street. Frado bounded gracelessly down the stairs, pulling up fast on their heels.

They had traversed barely a few paces when Battista's men caught them up, Lucagnolo among the group, but not Pompeo, who saw to other work for Battista, an errand of little importance in comparison, but one needing doing no matter. Every face wore the same almost-childish zeal—albeit one tempered with trepidation—as that shared by Aurelia and, were he to be honest, Battista himself. Even Barnabeo's boulderlike bald head and scarred face could not disguise his cautious curiosity.

The troupe turned left from Battista's house and then quickly left again, away from the grand palazzo. They took up almost the entire width of the avenue, forcing others upon the fairway to step aside and make way; their legion could not have been more ostentatious were they to blare trumpets as they marched in military formation.

"This will not do." Battista stopped, as did the group around him, now a clogging cluster of confusion.

"If we enter the Palazzo Vecchio all together, the soldiers will be upon us in an instant. We must go separately or at least in smaller groups."

They met his pronouncement with relenting grunts of agreement, yet not a one of them volunteered to let others go first.

"Who has had their breakfast?"

Slowly, and with shared perplexity, Ascanio, Barnabeo, and Ercole raised their hands, fearing punishment for having started the day with a meal, as did most people.

"*Bene, bene,*" Battista said with a decisive tick of his head. "Then you three shall be the first. Go, now. The rest of us will have a bite."

The three men needed no further encouragement, rushing away with satisfied smirks, turning a closed ear to the grumbles of disappointment chasing them away.

"Have no fear," Battista assured those peevishly left behind. "Giovanni, you and Lucagnolo will follow in a very short while. Aurelia, Frado, and I will make our way there last."

The plan seemed to pacify his companions and they continued on, enthusiasm only slightly dampened by the delay. Turning left yet again, Battista led them onto a broad avenue, the Tiber River just visible at the end of the slight curve of the Via del Proconsolo.

As if in unspoken agreement, the men swerved to the east side of the avenue and a cozy, casual *osteria* with but a few patrons and more than a few empty tables.

"Will this serve?" Battista turned to Aurelia as she followed along behind, almost hesitantly. "Would you prefer a trattoria or perhaps a *ristorante?* There is one I—"

"No, no, this is fine. Just fine, it's just . . ." Aurelia caught up quickly with a shy, almost-silly smile, shoulders hitching up. "Well . . . I have never eaten in a public establishment before."

The men skidded to an abrupt halt, astonishment clear in their wide-eyed, drop-jawed expressions. Battista wondered again at the strange existence of this woman.

"I, well, of course, I have taken meals at various inns," Aurelia sputtered with some need to explain. "But I would be served in my chamber, not in the common room."

"Well then, you are in for a real treat. I will order some of my favorites for you, shall I?" Battista pulled out a chair and tucked her in, dispelling any hesitation in her demeanor with his guidance. She seemed to be a woman choking on a man's domination, but the unknown served as a powerful suppressant.

In the shade of the vine-covered latticework arching over their heads, the group soon munched on a variety of sweet buns served with spiced hot water.

Battista watched Aurelia watch the comings and goings of the busy street, her smile never fading even as she munched enthusiastically upon her treats.

"If we were to turn at the next corner, we would make our way onto the circular Via dei Bentaccordi. It was built on the site of the old Roman coliseum." He licked the thick sugar off his fingers and gestured over his shoulder. "Just on the other side of that is the Piazza di Santa Croce. It is one of the most beautiful places in all of Florence."

He boasted, assuredly, but it was a proprietary immodesty, and easily forgiven.

"Ah, *sì*," Giovanni joined in. "It is where Battista and I play *cal-*

cio. You should come and watch, Aurelia, if you are still with us next Sunday."

Aurelia nodded, mouth full but spread in a grin, silent with her noncommittal. A peculiar anxiousness assailed him, as if by contagion. This quest had put a bizarre shroud over any thoughts of the future, and the details of her peculiar life had only added to the oddity of it all. He had not asked her, or himself, what would become of her after they found the triptych and the longed-for antiquity. Would she return to Mantua, return to that life without an explanation; would she be able to? And what of his involvement, how would she explain that to the marquess?

Battista flung away the thoughts as he took a long quaff of warm brew; jarring questions of his assignment cudgeled his brain, he had no need to add more.

"In the Piazza della Signoria, where we will find the Palazzo Vecchio, you will see Michelangelo's *David*." He continued his description of his fair city, resuming his role of guide.

"Oh, but I have seen it!" Aurelia cried with excitement, almost tottering her cup as she fluttered her hands about. "I do not know how I found it, nor do I believe I came this way." Her head swiveled back and forth, her eyes searching for anything familiar. "But there it was, so magnificent, so breathtaking. I spent the most glorious minutes with it and this lovely man."

"A lovely man?" More than one of her companions pestered her with a cautious query.

"*Sì*. We were both enraptured by the statue. We just stood before it in silence for the longest time."

"Beware, Aurelia," Battista chided her, any amusement at her wonder dissipating on the wings of responsibility. "Florence is a beautiful city, full of great sites, but like any city, it is replete with those who would do you harm. Many a dangerous rogue walks these streets."

"No, no, he was not that kind of man." Aurelia shook her head with a wistful smile. "He was older than I, of a kindly disposition, and had the most extraordinary eyes. They were the color of honey."

"Ah, I see." Battista's smug tone said he clearly did see, but he would not taunt Aurelia with his knowledge. He turned to the two youngsters at the table. "I believe we have waited long enough, be on your way."

Giovanni and Lucagnolo needed not another word to set their feet upon the dirt, any remaining sustenance quickly forgotten.

"And Lucagnolo?" Battista called, and the young man turned, shielding his eyes with a hand against the sun rising in the east.

"Sketch," was all Battista said, and Lucagnolo's knowing wink confirmed the assignment.

"As for us"—Battista turned to the two remaining by his side—"I believe Aurelia is in need of another day gown, or perhaps two."

"A fine idea." Frado waggled his turkey-throated head and got to his feet. Battista was pleased to see his longtime companion warming to the newcomer among them; it had been a gradual change in the face of Frado's initial suspicion, but it now crept toward the endearing, especially after hearing Aurelia's story. Frado had reached almost fifty years of age without a wife or children, and Battista knew he missed both. Perhaps he looked upon Aurelia as the daughter he never had.

"Let us away," the man encouraged, wiping the flaky pastry crumbs from his kidskin hose.

Aurelia stared at Battista with tempered delight and an incongruent shake of her head. "You have done so much for me already. I did not intend my attendance to cost you."

"I owe you my life, my lady," Battista said, leaving a jumble of coins upon the table and once more pulling out her chair.

"Besides"—he bumped her shoulder with his as they strolled off—"they are for us as well. This one is a bit . . . ripe." He said it merrily, no harm intended, and the splotches of her embarrassment faded as quickly as they came.

It took but a few moments to order two simple gowns much like the one she wore, from the nearest tailor, and to order them sent to Battista's home. She could not don anything but a common woman's outfit, for to hint at nobility would restrict her movement; privileged women were not permitted to go about alone or with only men as companions.

"And you could endeavor to walk differently," Battista suggested as they turned right onto the Piazza della Signoria, the vast courtyard hosting the city's governmental buildings.

"Walk differently?" Aurelia pursed her lips at him, one dark brow raised high.

"*Sì*. You bring undue attention to yourself with the way you move. You should walk less . . . less . . . ," but he floundered to find the words to finish, instead he tried to mimic a woman's straight-backed but sinewy stride, making Aurelia laugh at the attempts.

"Regal," Frado ended the thought, perfectly and without pause.

With a moment's thought, Aurelia stopped and started, hunching her shoulders, then straightening them, taking bigger steps, then smaller, in a feeble effort to move with less grace.

"Never mind." Battista laughed at her, leading her past the Giant and through the enormous black doors with the brown wood grids just beyond.

Once inside they blinked away the blindness of the bright outdoors, nodding with no more than unfamiliar politeness to Ascanio, Barnabeo, and Ercole, whom they passed on their way out.

"Did you find it?" Battista whispered as they neared, and only Barnabeo gave a curt nod, his beaklike nose pointed away.

"Penelope," the man grunted, and Battista blinked, his only response.

He took Aurelia's hand and looped it over his arm. "This way," he told them, and crossed straight through the foyer and into the small, perfectly square courtyard just beyond.

Though much of the town hall was dedicated to the Medici family and those who ruled in their name, many rooms were opened to the city's populace during most hours of the day, and Battista walked them with the knowledge of a frequent visitor.

He hurried his companions past the tall, narrow porphyry fountain with Putto and the Dolphin on top, resting on the center of four perfectly white, perfectly circular marble stairs in the center of the small enclosure. Four stories above the opened courtyard, the Arnolfo tower stood guard, but they crossed safely beneath its shadow.

Once more within the interior of the palace, Frado led now, up two flights of stairs and along the left corridor, no pause along the way to peruse the gold-edged architecture of the frescoes dominating most walls and many of the ceilings.

They entered the last room on the left—the corner room—and stopped. Four other people toured the small room, one devoted to a marriage of conjoined desks at the center and *Penelope at the Loom* frescoed upon the ceiling and an encompassing frieze depicting episodes from the *Odyssey*. Only four paintings decorated the walls, three of them devoted to the subject of the Madonna and Child; only one included St. John.

They ignored the two familiar men as inconspicuously as they did the elderly couple, who shuffled along arm in arm, whispering together as only lifelong companions can. Lucagnolo looked up from the small square of parchment in his hand and the chunk of charcoal blackening his fingertips, but made no outward sign of acknowledgment. After a few more scratches, he and Giovanni quit the room, though with a feigned casualness worthy of any actor upon the stage. The couple soon followed and the trio left behind jumped to the painting upon the left-side wall with a fervent anticipation they had denied since arriving.

The rendering and its subject matter were even more eerie when seen in person; the red of the Virgin's gown beneath her cloak and the robe encircling St. John leaped out like splashes of blood and the faint halo about Mary's head seemed to point directly to the strange shiplike shape hovering in the sky. There all eyes were drawn, but now they could see the yellow glow encircling it.

As if it were an arrow, their eyes followed its direction outward, beyond the curved edge of the painting, the round gilt frame, and along the wall. The ship's bowsprit did indeed point to another painting, one hanging to the right and just above the Mainardi . . . the only one in the room not depicting the Madonna and Child. A woman dominated the rectangular canvas pitched horizontally, only one and seen from the back, her blond, almost-white hair hidden by a golden veil that matched her gown. She stood upon a path, one step ahead of the spot where it split into three. Upon three stones of each trail, symbols were etched on the markers, symbols repeated and hanging in the sky, prominently placed over three of the many points of interest dotting the panoramic landscape of a canvas far wider than it was long. Pagan symbols all.

"Threes," Aurelia whispered.

Memorizing as many of the details as possible, they slipped from the room, turning away from the confounding painting, scurrying away before more curious visitors entered, before any strangers could look upon the unsettled expressions most surely blatant upon their faces.

Aurelia stared vacantly at Lucagnolo's rendering; images of Florence crowded her vision, images of a day well spent in the embrace of the glorious city. With silent chivying, she berated herself for her silliness, at her juvenile delight over things seen and done. She struggled to center herself, to find the balance within to serve that which she craved and the purpose she could not forget.

"I think you need to add a few more buildings, between the large one on the left and the mountain in the middle." Battista's suggestion broke her reverie.

They huddled over Lucagnolo's sketch, placed in the middle of the table, witches watching over their bubbling cauldron. Each one proposed details Lucagnolo had missed or forgotten to include, and though they came fast and furious, the young artist did his best to infuse his rendering with the proffered elements without a smidgen of impatience or irritation.

Lucagnolo added the structures as Battista suggested: small and simple buildings, no doubt a row of basic housing for a merchant's family or an artist's studio.

"The symbols are definitely pagan," Aurelia mused aloud as she studied the hieroglyphs, each repeated three times, on the three paths and in the sky. "The first is fire, I am certain of it." She tapped one tapered finger upon the elemental triangle shape.

"*Sì*, fire," Battista mumbled his agreement. "And the last is for God or higher being. But the one is the middle is a mystery."

"Climbing?" Ascanio offered, but with little certainty in the soft suggestion.

"Could it be rebirth?" Lucagnolo offered, his charcoal never relenting from the parchment, unable to desist the fine-tuning with the addition of shadows and layering. He took the tip of the dark tool back to the rune in the center of the sky, the swirl of lines ending with the tip pointing upward.

"Rebirth it might be," Aurelia agreed. She scoured her memory of the years and years of tutoring and lectures, though clearly much had been left out of her education, purposefully so.

"There were waves crashing against the castle." Ercole jutted his chin toward the fortress standing to the far right of the sketch. A correct observation. Lucagnolo added a froth of lines upon the base of the structure, though the detail only confirmed that the castle stood on a coastline, not informed of it.

The touch added, the study fell silent and intent, so engrossed not a one looked up as Pompeo entered the house and joined the group hovering around the drawing, wedging himself between Aurelia and Battista.

"We are discussing Dante?"

Aurelia grabbed him by the arm, fingers digging into his muscular forearm.

"Dante!" Battista and Ascanio barked in harsh unison.

The youngster flinched back, soft brown eyes bulging.

"Have I offended?"

"No, no, of course not, Pompeo." Battista reached over to give the young man a consoling squeeze of the shoulder. "We were just taken aback, no more. The name of the great poet has come up before in this quandary, but we did not think to put it in connection with this painting." He calmed as he questioned, pulling the recently arrived youngster back into the group. "Why do you?"

Pompeo stepped close to the table once more, visibly relieved. "Is this the painting from the palace?" He leaned over to get a closer look as they confirmed his query. "I know this work; it is by Duccio, *sì?*"

Lucagnolo nodded; though he had not copied the artist's signature upon his simple copy, it had been on the painting. Duccio di Buoninsegna had been one of the most influential Italian artists of Dante's era. That Pompeo knew the work, and the artist, gave credence to his mastery of the topic.

"The three paths are said to symbolize the three phases in the *Commedia*." Pompeo took up his lesson with more confidence. "Here the first leads to a great palazzo, but beneath its beauty lie all the ravages of Hell. In the center is the mountain, the hurdle of Purgatory to lead to Heaven if one can survive. And the last, the castle, it is the heights of Heaven . . . of Paradise . . . itself."

His tutorial brought the rendering to life, a simple statement of a complex subject and yet it gave the work all its meaning.

"But where are we to go?" Battista voiced the question all pondered. "I do not recognize any of these places, though we cannot doubt—by their construction, by the landscape and the architecture—that they are all somewhere in the vast Republic of Italy."

"Of this we can be sure," Ascanio offered. "The first stop is a palazzo, a very large and opulent palazzo, the next a mountain, and the last a castle."

"It is so very literal." Giovanni looked unconvinced, smooth forehead crinkled with doubt. "The *Commedia* was a masterful allegory, a scathing statement against all the evil in the human spirit. Dante strove to reveal the nightmare of consequencces caused by avarice and pride and greed. It was a condemnation."

"Allegory, yes." Barnabeo sat, pulling a basket-encased bottle toward him, filling the closest cup with the white, lemony-scented liquid. "But of a soul's journey to God. We are all born with sin staining our souls. It is how we live that we wash ourselves of it."

Aurelia stared down at the man; she never imagined such depth lay beneath the gruff exterior.

Ascanio shook his head. "Dante offered us a lesson, one of the world's order and man's place in it."

Aurelia tipped her head in agreement; she had always seen the work in such a light herself. But being among these men, she realized she had learned little of humankind at the Mantua court. A statement on world order could never have explained how such men as these—thieves, hedonists, and artists among them—could possess such complexities that most hid beneath her sight.

"I think Dante intended all this and more." Battista took the chair beside Barnabeo. "He represents the epitome of all that is knowledgeable and superb of Florence."

Dante was indeed a son of Florence. Many considered the poet, born the son of a lawyer, one of the greatest philosophers of his age, a master of the literary as had rarely been found on the peninsula. The language he had used to create the *Commedia*, a marriage of Latin and the Tuscan dialect, had quickly become the unofficial official language of the Republic.

"I can tell you what it is not." Ercole's ever-pessimistic demeanor entered the debate. "It is not a map. It is symbolic, not literal."

"Yes, yes, I agree," Battista countered. "But perhaps if we take it in conjunction with this painting, the symbols with his text, we could see it as a set of instructions. Hand me my copy, would you, Pompeo?" Battista held out his hand toward the cluster of wing chairs, couches, and tables. "It should be just there, on the small table behind you."

"I shall get mine as well," Frado said, setting off to his room.

"I have mine here." Giovanni pulled a small, leather-bound volume from the inside of his doublet, a tassel-ended ribbon marking his spot somewhere in the middle, somewhere in *Purgatory*.

"You carry it with you?" Aurelia asked him. She sat then herself, drank as well as she appraised the company in which she found herself.

He smiled down at her almost bashfully. "Always." He sat beside her and opened the thin-leafed volume. "I will gladly share with you."

These men had welcomed her into their coven without question, with a kindness and a chivalry reaching far beyond honor among thieves. Their intelligence and breadth of knowledge astounded her as much as their methods alarmed, and yet she felt an alliance with them, one she had never experienced before. She tucked her face into her cup, hiding her smile behind its rim.

Hours passed as pages turned in silence, a crinkle here and there to mark one or another's progress through the piece. Written in the first person, it told of Dante's journey through the three realms of the dead.

"Ah, to have loved with such all-consuming passion," Pompeo sighed, looking at the very round form of the day maid's backside as she helped Nuntio to place a late supper upon their table. The plain though pretty girl giggled at his words and probing gaze, smiling back at Pompeo.

Throughout the epic poem, Dante's love of Beatrice rose thick and sweet. Legend held that he had met the love of his life at the tender age of nine and though he spoke to her but a few times his passion for her—the sweet innocence of courtly love—had never wavered. He had never stopped loving her, not when she died at the young age of twenty-four, not when he took another woman as wife. Beatrice breathed in every whisper purling amidst Dante's works; never once had he written of Gemma, his wife.

Aurelia laughed; she had seen many enactments of love at the sophisticated court of Mantua, seen them and through them. "Men speak highly of love when it causes them no trouble."

"Such skepticism. Perhaps our guest has been burnt by love," Battista scoffed, though not unkindly.

"No. I have not," Aurelia responded without guile. "But one need not taste a lemon to know it is bitter."

He laughed with her then, as did some others, and she lowered her gaze back to the poem yet did not read the words.

Had she known love in her life? She had known attraction, the kisses of flirtation, even infatuation. But love? She could not answer the question with any certainty and her ambiguity formed a sad commentary in and of itself. Would she wish to know the joys and anguish of love? That she could answer, though she cared for the response not a bit.

Battista slammed his book closed with a thwack and the gathering jumped and flinched.

"I am convinced. The painting, the poem, the triptych . . . it is all very clear. We must make to a palazzo that is a living hell, a mountain that will be as hard to overcome as Purgatory, and to a castle that reaches up to the heavens."

Aurelia had come to the same conclusion more than an hour ago, when one passage in particular—no more than a few choice words—had resounded with familiarity, words the marquess of Mantua had spoken to her when they had made a journey together. In the minutes since, her decision had been whether to tell, a puzzle for which there was perhaps more than one solution.

"Then it is to Hell, to Purgatory, and to Heaven we must go." With a heavy sigh, Battista raised his dark eyes to Aurelia, and she met his look, matched it with equal parts of determination and apprehension.

"I am not sure if you should continue, Aurelia," he muttered, anticipating the argument before she gave it her voice.

She shook her head, mouth set firm with indomitable conviction and the hint of a smile. "You have brought me for a reason. We cannot deny what the fates intend."

"You believe in the fates, do you?" He hitched himself forward in his chair, drawing closer, leering at her, so near she spied the pinpoint reflection of light in his coal-like eyes. "And what do those fates have in store for us? You believe in that as well? That we cannot fight against it?"

"I believe in predestination, yes." Aurelia's smirk did not falter beneath his scrutiny, but instead grew wider. "Not that we *cannot* fight it, but that we shouldn't."

His stare he did not surrender, but a smile touched him, crinkling the corners of his eyes. Battista shook his head in denial or bemusement, either would suffice. "There is more danger here, Aurelia. I cannot expose you to it, not as an honorable man."

His chivalry once more surprised her, as he wore it as easily as the cloak of a scallywag.

"You allowed me to bring you home, to return you safely to Florence. Why is this any different?" She admired him, true, though if he intended to leave her behind he was a fool.

Battista tossed back the waves of dark hair from his face as he laughed. "I had no choice, we both know it."

"Do not delude yourself, or me. You brought me to Florence because you were convinced I could help you. And I can." Aurelia stood, the undeniable regally straight posture now a testimony to her conviction. She leaned over the table and stabbed one finger into the pictured palazzo they agreed was Hell. "I know where this is."

Twelve

The path to Paradise begins in Hell.

—*Inferno*

He didn't move, nor speak a word. Battista's smile faded from his face, a star snuffed out by a dawn sky. If he stared at her long enough, he wondered, could he reveal the truth, if she had known all along the location of their first destination? But there was nothing of it in her face, her beauty as ever in the forefront, her determination a hard, implacable stone wall just behind.

"Where is it, Aurelia?" he asked with a ruthless whisper, and not a man in the room stirred as they awaited her answer.

"It is the Palazzo Prato. No more than a half day's journey from here."

There was not the slightest hint of hesitation in her answer, nor had he expected there to be.

"How can you be so convinced?" Battista interrogated her as the barrister, the men gathered among them her judges.

"I have been there," she stated flatly. "When put in the context of Dante's words and the setting of this painting, I recognize it easily."

Battista allowed not a quiver of expression, not the belief in her decisive statement, nor the fear that she duped them all. He sat back slowly, probing gaze riveted upon her face, his silence demanding she offer more evidence of her contention, and she complied.

Aurelia rose and pulled Lucagnolo's sketch closer. "Here? See this cliff-sided pass? I have seen it through the curtains of my carriage. And this small golden dome? It is the chapel of the compound. This palazzo was one of the few places where my guardian allowed me to travel, in his company, of course. It is more heavily guarded than the Palazzo del Te."

She sat back down, brows knit, puzzled gaze staring off into the distance of her life. "I have often wondered why the marquess brought me there. He said many times that the barone di Prato and his wife are the very worst sort of people, as if they were the devil's own children."

"Devil's children?" Ercole repeated the phrase with a sharp edge of disgust. "Why?"

Aurelia crinkled her long, slim nose. "They are hedonists, unabashed and unashamed of it as well. They live for pleasure, of every type. The marquess allowed me only to sit at table and then insisted I retire, locking myself and my ladies in when I went." Her slim shoulders shook as if she threw off a chill. "The sounds I heard continued all through the night. I often thought they were the sounds one might hear in Hell."

Not a one of them missed the portent of her words. Frado caught Battista's gaze over the woman's russet head; in his friend's countenance Battista saw the same thoughts: Aurelia's pronouncements were difficult not to believe, nor did they have anywhere else to begin, and a quest must begin somewhere.

"You say you know these people? They will recognize you?" Battista turned back to Aurelia.

"*Sì,* they know me. And I them. I know just which names to mention to gain us not only access but a warm welcome as well." Aurelia pinned him to the floor with her sharp stare. "And I will speak those names for you, at their door, if you promise to bring me. If you swear, on your honor, that you will allow me to participate in every juncture of this journey."

Battista snorted derisively; she had invoked honor to elicit his cooperation. He added cunning to his growing list of her surprising characteristics.

"It is, as you say, your fate to do with as you please. If it is your choice to risk your life, then it is mine to allow it."

Aurelia tipped her head, clearly pleased, a strange little smile playing at the corners of her lips. "I will have to disguise myself. As will you."

Battista balked. "Me? Why me?"

"My guardian is no doubt convinced you have kidnapped me. If you remember, his guards saw you pull me through the hall, from one room to another. He would never believe it was anything but abduction."

With a respectful grunt-like scoff, Battista raised his eyes heavenward, remembering clearly the moment she forced him to clasp onto her arm. This woman was indeed crafty, far too crafty.

"You must alter your appearance should any of the marquess's men be in attendance at the palazzo when we arrive. I imagine he looks for us both and has from the moment we left. Any search order would contain a description of you, the best they could compile from others who took note of your presence, as did I."

Battista stewed in sullen silence; this mission became more convoluted and perilous as it continued. Why did he feel as if Dante's own fraught-filled journey would pale in comparison before it ended?

He turned to Ascanio, a narrow-eyed stare at his snickering friend who was clearly amused at the notion of Battista in costume. "Would you make for the Teatro Comunale?"

Rubbing his sensual mouth still stuck in a grin, Ascanio jumped to the task. "Fine idea. I am sure the community theatre will have just what we need." He chafed his hands together merrily. "A mustache, and beard . . . oh, and a plumed hat. No one will know of the rascal you are beneath a nobleman's regalia."

"It should be as ostentatious as possible," Aurelia called after him with a reserved grin. She met Battista's annoyed gaze. "It is the type of people they prefer, these Barberini, those as flamboyant as they themselves."

"So then we shall have to order you some new clothes also, madonna." Battista put his elbows on the table with a thump and clapped his hands together. "One with an immodest neckline and some cosmetics for your face." He stared at her, at the unadorned beauty needing no enhancement, waiting for her determined demeanor to crumble, for her amusement to vanish, but he was soon disappointed.

"If it is what we must do, then we must." She tipped her head to the side with an easy shrug. "A noblewoman's heavy veil will allow me anonymity."

Battista pushed out of his chair, pacing away from her insufferable acquiescence. "Barnabeo, Pompeo, I want you with us," he announced, choosing one for his brawn and the other for his youth. The group would encompass Frado as well, as always.

Battista stalked about the house, thoughts flung in every direction. They had to follow Aurelia's clue, for they had nothing else to go by. He believed her, believed her assumption that the temple of profligacy that was the palazzo in Prato was their destination. Her motives troubled him, though, for he could not gauge them.

Battista possessed clarity of vision, the ability to see the truth in others, and his refined intuition had enabled him to surround himself with those dedicated and loyal to him his whole life. But Aurelia remained a mystery, though he had spent more than a few days in her company. There were mysteries beneath her depths, and though he found enigmas intriguing in other women, he found them disturbing in her. Beneath all these thoughts lay one . . . did she lead them into some sort of trap?

Such musings went round, as he himself did, but there was naught for it.

"Pompeo, you and Barnabeo will set up a camp as close to the palazzo as is safe," he continued his instructions.

"It will not be close, I assure you," Aurelia piped in, but he gave her words no pause.

"Frado, you will be the humble servant of the conte and contessa di Panzutti and will accompany us into this den of vipers."

"Humble servant, forever the humble servant." Frado closed his book with a snap and shuffled away, whether to return it to its place or rid himself of the company no one could be sure.

"It is only because you are so very humble," Battista tossed at his friend's back, but Frado would not be pacified, waving the consoling words off with the flap of a hand.

"Conte and contessa?" The squeak in Aurelia's voice rivaled that of any fleeing mouse.

Battista stopped his pacing, turned with a barely suppressed sneer, and smugly crossed his arms upon his chest; ah, at last he had wrought a reaction.

"Well, yes, of course." He sauntered toward her, narrow hips below broad chest swaying with masculine grace. "I imagine to present ourselves as anything but married would put you in a very precarious position, would it not?"

No simpering smile spread upon her lips now, he saw with a snide sort of pleasure.

"Uh . . . I s-s-suppose . . . uh . . . y-y-yes . . . ," she stammered.

"An unmarried woman, of your beauty?" Delighted to have finally flummoxed her, he leaned down over her, one hand on each arm of her chair, pinning her into it. Though she tried to hide it, he saw her push back into the cushion, as if to escape him. He allowed a rakish gaze to scour her, from bottom to top, and he saw the heat of it rise up her neck and onto her face. He lowered his voice to a sultry growl. "You would be the toast of the evening, *sì?*"

Her jaw jumped; she understood exactly what he meant, and for a moment he thought—hoped—she would bow to the threat. But she denied it, the fear he taunted her with, and the steely narrow gaze of her eyes turned thunderously dark; she refused to be cowed, not even by this.

She raised her chin at him in unquestionable defiance. "Then when do we leave . . . Husband?"

It had been four days since they had finalized their plans, four days to give Battista's wound time to finish healing, four days in which the tingle of excitement, the anticipation of the journey awaiting them, riled her with unrelenting restlessness.

The light patter of spring rain upon the shutters sang to her, keeping the day huddled in the darkness all the longer, as if to further tease her with the possibility of leave-taking. She knew not what transformed her; she had become an addict, the adventure she had lived the last fortnight was no longer enough, she yearned for more—it was the opium she craved.

Aurelia deluded herself with thoughts of duty and purpose, with arguments that one could serve both while enjoying oneself simultaneously, but she knew it all as sophistry, saw it for a petty pretext, one allowing her to continue without guilt. She had done her duty for so long, she deserved these moments of pleasure at last, she had earned them.

Battista had not permitted her another excursion into the city on her own and the long, monotonous days had found the walls of his home growing thicker with every passing moment; she began to wonder if she had exchanged one prison for another. Only the certainty of the coming expedition smoothed the hard edge of her wanderlust.

For the third time, she arranged the new gown and all its frilly undergarments and accessories in the satchel that would hang across her horse's back, but she saw it for the busywork it was, activity to pacify hands refusing to remain idle. Aurelia pulled down on the doubletlike bodice of her honey-colored travel costume, pleased with its fineness and finesse, its almost-masculine lines.

Battista had surprised her with the clothing he purchased on her behalf; his knowledge of women's fashion far exceeded her own and she wondered who had offered him such tutelage. Too much about this man she could not reconcile, a dimension of this adventure that sat awkwardly upon her shoulders.

Quiet caught her attention, and she turned to it, returning to the shuttered window. Aurelia heard no more than discordant dripping, the last remnants of the gentle storm slipping off the roof. She pushed open the carved wood, breath catching on the greeting vision; there, in the distance to the east, the pale glow of dawn beckoned with a smile, the coming sunlight pushing through a crack in the cloud cover. She backed away from it, stepping back to the lone chair in her small chamber on the third floor. Aurelia sat and stared out across the rooftops of Florence, her eyes following the road to the north, past the ancient Porta alla Croce marking the edge of the city, and the unknown land beyond.

The glory of departure was imminent, and she longed for it with unfeigned delight; she conceded to the truth of it. Aurelia gave the hands clasped tightly together in her lap a squeeze, as if to remind herself of the greater purpose she served; she must never forget it. Though niggling self-doubt pestered her, poking a finger at the question of whether her purpose might be more forthrightly served had she stayed in Mantua, she refused to allow it to gain hold. She could serve both masters—those of the universe and those in her heart—and she would.

Beneath her, wood creaked as a man's weight shifted upon it and just outside the window, on the abandoned street below, she heard the whinny of horses and the jangling of tack. With a smile that would not loosen itself from her lips, she snatched up her satchel, raced down the stairs and out through the door.

As Pompeo and Barnabeo tied the horses to the post, as they removed her sailcloth bag and hitched it to her horse, Aurelia stood grateful beneath the fading stars that had come out to bid farewell to the receding night. She did nothing to stop herself; she threw back her head and laughed softly into the twilight depths. Now, as the moment was upon her, Aurelia would be worthy of the challenge of her life.

Thirteen

Pride, Envy and Avarice,
The three sparks which have set the hearts of all on fire.

—*Inferno*

Many a lord held residence in the hills and mountains of the Italian peninsula; many the castle had been built on these cliffs as a stronghold against the violence of a less civilized era. In the wake of those turbulent days, these same castles had become palaces of luxury. To the fortress-type structures, large windows and columned porches had been added, nexus points for an unfettered view of the rolling hills and meadows at the feet of the privileged. These pleasure domes had neither political nor economic purpose, but existed solely for the intellectual and aesthetic gratification of their masters.

The cliff passage appeared unnatural: straight and precise, as if the incision into the mountain had been carved out with a mighty chisel. No fewer than ten guards armed the imposing black steel gate at the end of the dusty stone corridor. The troupe observed the soldiers huddled at the foot of the scrolled metal, scuttling about like ants at the foot of a giant. From the crest of an opposing hill they studied the obstacle before them.

"We dare not go further." Battista held them with a hand in the air. "To step one pace upon that path would be to reveal ourselves."

Not a one offered an argument, for there wasn't one. Aurelia had warned them how well-protected the palazzo would be; if all her information was as accurate as this, they had indeed followed her rightly.

"Your verdict appears justified, Aurelia. Well done." Battista gave grudging credit where it was due.

She accepted the praise with a silent nod, yet not even her thickly thatched black veil could completely guise the sliver of her smile.

Barnabeo lifted himself off his saddle, straightening legs anchored in stirrups.

"Then it is up we must go." He jutted his square chin toward the forest-covered slope to their left. "Those trees provide both perfect camouflage and aspect. We will be hidden yet able to watch for you."

In silent acquiescence, the group followed his lead, the only sounds the snapping of twigs and crunching of bracken beneath horses' hooves. In the dappled shade, Aurelia folded up her veil and lifted off the velvet riding hat, revealing the pile of pinned plaits, and the line of moist sweat gathered beneath its brim. How strange she looked with the heavy kohl lines around her eyes, their blackness intensifying the green flecks by contrast. Battista cared little for the cosmetics she wore, the thick powder, the berry stain on her lips. What may enhance a plain face only obfuscated her beauty, disrespected it with but mocking refinement.

With an equal relief, he pulled the fuzzy *beretto* from his head, feeling the cooling breeze rake its fingers through his ponytailed hair. He had refused to wear a wig, allowing only for his long tresses to be bound and tucked under. He couldn't recall a spring so hot, especially this far north on the peninsula, or was it simply that they drew ever closer toward the fires of Hell?

From their vantage point on the northern edge of the foothill, they discovered that the swath cut through the stone curved itself round each side of the mountain, a castle's empty moat. From that lowest point the mountain and the palazzo rose up like a hovering leviathan, splendor its weapon.

Pompeo jumped from his horse, tied the reins to a nearby pine tree, and retrieved a hatchet and a small, thin saw from his saddlebag. As if he studied a painting, he surveyed the sparse forest with a purpose.

The group dismounted, more than a few stretching away the kinks of the five-hour journey. Aurelia reached down, plucking one five-pointed flower from the hundreds covering the forest floor, raising it to her face.

"A gentian," Battista told her. "Have you never seen one?"

"I do not think so." She shook her head, gaze flitting about, too much beauty to see at once. Like a magnificent carpet, the blue, almost-violet flowers rose but a few inches off the ground, covering their feet. "Certainly not like this."

"This one, I think," Pompeo announced, slapping the thin trunk of a scraggly pine.

Battista looked up. "It is already half-dead, that is for certain," he said, spying the brown needles protruding from the top of the partially denuded tree. "It will go down easily."

"And see there?" Pompeo pointed to a fluffy, healthy olive tree beside it. "It will catch there. It will be easy to see against the pale green."

Battista nodded, pleased with the marking Pompeo would put in place once darkness descended. He turned his gaze back to the palazzo; the felled and angled trunk would create a clear demarcation from any escape point south or west of the mountainside palace. Pompeo and Barnabeo could not risk lighting a fire, exposing their presence; the fallen tree would be the only sight to mark their location. If necessary, Battista would launch a burning rag from one of the windows visible from this hilltop, a signal for help.

A shaft of sunlight found them as it lowered into the descending posture of late afternoon, and they stepped back from it.

"We should present ourselves," Aurelia said, climbing into her saddle once more. "It would not do to arrive after dark. They will look more kindly upon guests who call before the meal is prepared."

Battista conceded easily to her superior knowledge of court life. He bobbed his head, scratching hard at the fake black beard gummed to his face, and stepped to his horse.

"Are we ready then?" Aurelia did little to hold back on the reins, as eager to be off as her black stallion, bucking and pawing the air with his front legs.

"You smile, my lady, as if we were off to a party." Battista scowled at her.

Aurelia bit at her top lip, sucking one corner of the pink flesh into her mouth, but it did little to stem her smirking. "Are we not? Every night is a party in this household."

Battista was not amused. "One does not make merry with the devil. One pretends to, in order to avoid his scorching touch."

"*Sì*, it is like a performance." Aurelia's horse spun round, and she with him, as if in a dance. "It is all very . . . stimulating?"

"Stimulating?" Battista scoffed as if he spat on the ground. "You had better return that hat and veil to your head, before you are recognized and stimulated all the way back to your ward's keeping."

Sufficiently chastised, Aurelia did as instructed, Battista mimicking the act with his own uncomfortable hat.

Once more disguised, Aurelia urged her horse forward, her two companions following, though not nearly as enthused.

"God keep you," Pompeo called to them.

Battista turned back to the man he thought of as a younger brother, raising a hand, hoping it would not be the last he would see of him.

"Tell your mistress the cousin of her cousin, Catarina Colonna, comes requesting shelter for the evening." Aurelia spoke to the man standing by her horse without looking down at him. Her gaze roamed over the palazzo autocratically, as if she judged whether it met her lofty standards.

The guard reached out a hand to gather the stallion's reins, holding him still while studying Aurelia through the slits of his visor. "Your name, signora?"

"I am Livia and this is my husband, Gaetano, the conte di Panzutti. She will remember me, I am sure. We spent a summer together once, as children."

The guard had not yet moved and Aurelia kicked her foot out at him, though she pulled it up just short of his body. "Go. Now."

With a shallow bow, the soldier retreated, moving quickly.

Aurelia turned to Battista with a roll of her eyes, a condemnation at such ineptitude. Battista longed to applaud; she played her part well, as she had pledged, far better than he would have guessed. Were he the guard, he would believe every word she said; most nobility had more distant cousins than they could keep track of. It would be no surprise should one make a random visit.

As quickly as he bolted, the guard returned.

"The baroness bids you welcome, *sua signori.*" He bowed respectfully, their patent of nobility somehow confirmed, leading their horses through the gate and into the courtyard.

Battista dropped from his mount, swallowing away his admiration at the beauty of the palace. Perfect in its symmetry of rounded arches and sculpted plinthlike columns of finished ashlar, so polished as to look almost white. Windows stood out from their moldings guarded on each side by statue-festooned niches. This courtyard boasted every architectural elegance and extravagance, and they had yet to enter the palazzo itself.

The smaller door within the massive double gray portal opened as they approached. Once inside, they squinted at the change of light as Frado followed behind, one small satchel in each hand. Aurelia strode on determinedly, shoulders back, chin high, but Battista read the trepidation in her fingers as they fiddled with the edge of her bodice, tugging on it again and again as if it threatened to rise up and reveal her truth beneath.

Their boots clomped stridently on the foyer's green striated marble floor, the clatter not loud enough, however, to drown out the raucous laughter reaching out from the long corridor just beyond. Four doors stood open on each side of the passageway, bronze statues posted between them, gilded forms of naked women and men, the light of the curly-armed brass candelabrum sparking off every curve of the vulgarly posed bodies. Groups of men and women passed between these doors, refreshments in hand, almost all tottering with some level of intoxication.

Battista turned from the tableau, catching Aurelia's gaze, seeing his own troubled thoughts in it. If this was the household's demeanor so early in the evening, how would these people behave as night's concealment gave license?

"If you will wait here, the mistress of the house will be with you shortly." The guard held them with a hand, tipping a curt bow and making for the door and his post once more.

The aperture thumped to a close behind him; a shattering of glass burst in the hall, followed closely by a small cry and a spate of laughter.

"Is this how you found this place before?" Battista leaned toward her, putting the proprietary hand of a husband on the small of her back.

"Never this bad," she responded with a barely perceptible shake of her head, her face implacable should any look upon it. "Perhaps they behaved themselves when the marquess paid a visit."

"Then we have only each other for protection." His hushed caveat took in Frado as well, though it was only a matter of time before the servant was separated from the masters.

Of a sudden the music began, a spirited *gagliarda* that sent up a rousing cheer. More revelers spilled out into the hallway—overly jeweled women, overly laced men—streaming from one room into another, the location of the musicians, no doubt.

Only one woman noticed them, and she threw up her hands and eyes heavenward, approaching them at a rush.

"*Per favore, miei cari.*" The woman's round cheeks dimpled as she smiled at them, her voice high and breathy like a child's, though powder clogged thickly in the lines of her face. "I truly am so very sorry, my dears. They told me you were here, and I completely forgot."

She giggled at them, and from behind her laughter rang out as if in answer.

"Have no fear, Baroness di Prato." Battista quickly took up her hand and bowed over it. "Yours is a beauty worth waiting for."

The woman looked to swoon, but there seemed little that was genuine in the act. She returned his playful glance with a hard edge. "Please, call me Ringarda, all my guests do. And you are so very welcome here, Gaetano, is it, and Livia? It is our pleasure to open our home to . . . my . . . cousins?"

"Well, your cousin's cousin, actually," Aurelia corrected with a graceful courtesy, hearing the question for the snare it might be. "I am so very sorry to impose upon your hospitality. But we were delayed in our journey with no chance to make for the inn."

"My skittish wife had no desire to spend the night out in the wild." Battista laughed with a hard, belittling edge.

"A cousin's cousin would make us still cousins," the woman twittered. "Why, I think I can see a resemblance between us."

"*Certamente,*" Battista assured her as Frado busied himself with picking up and setting down the bags once more. The short, round woman could not look any more different from Aurelia had she tried.

A great hue and cry rose up behind them and they turned to spy a man, a woman on each arm, fall from a doorway, sprawling indecorously into the corridor, rolling together with the women as if the spill were all part of the dance.

Ringarda laughed as loud as the merrymakers, offering no comment on the degrading display she found amusing but clearly not anomalous, and set off for the staircase to the right, its mullioned banister curving up to the floor above. "We can offer you a room and some food, have no fear. Though whether you'll be out of the wild . . . it remains to be seen. You have come on a night when my husband entertains, as he so often does. There is no hope for it, or for anyone who comes here."

The three guests followed, Aurelia almost tripping on the first step, no chance to reply, no chance to run from the warning their hostess offered in jest, one so similar to that prognosticated by Dante. If astonishment and trepidation could stop time, the world would freeze in that moment.

"Giuseppe!" the baroness cried out, and within seconds a sloppily dressed majordomo appeared behind them.

"*Sì*, madonna?"

"We will put the *conte* and *contessa* in the blue room for the night." She gave her instructions over her shoulder, leaning toward Battista, who had taken her arm. "It is just down the hall from my own room."

Battista smiled, as he ought, but said nothing.

"Help their man with the bags and then take him to the kitchen," Ringarda ordered curtly.

Without further word, Giuseppe took one of the satchels from Frado's hand and stepped quickly around and beyond the group of nobles.

Frado scissored his short legs to keep up, a narrow-eyed glance backward. "To the kitchen," he said pointedly, and Battista acknowledged the message with no more than a blink of his eyes.

Far narrower than the one below, the first-floor corridor branched off in two directions. The baroness led them to the right and to the third door on the right, one left open by the already-retreated set of servants.

Battista beckoned Aurelia in, then turned at the threshold and offered a bow, holding their hostess at the door with a gallant maneuver.

"Why don't you two freshen up a bit and join us." Ringarda included them both with her words, but not with her glance; that, she reserved for Battista alone.

"What a lovely thought, Baroness, but I think we will rest a bit." He reached out and took her hand once more, this time closing it warmly in both of his. "Could you send someone to fetch us at mealtime?"

Ringarda batted her eyes at him. "If you wish, Gaetano."

"I do," he purred, and quickly shut the door behind her, as if he kept the wolves at bay.

Aurelia stood in the middle of the large room; she looked small amidst the large furniture—the canopied bed, the double-doored garderobe, and the latticed privacy screen hiding one corner from view. Upholstery of burgundy, ceiling frescoes of naked cherubs edged in gold, and thick velvet cushions everywhere, it was a most masculine, intensely sensual chamber.

Across the expanse they stared at each other; all that was real and frightening and awkward in their situation rose up between them, until Battista could bear it no longer.

With one raised eyebrow, he looked at her askance. "Gaetano? Is that how you see me, as a Gaetano?"

Aurelia laughed heartily, hand to her stomach, releasing the noose of tension pulling her straight, and with the tinkling sound the curse upon them cracked. "It was my favorite dog's name."

"Oh, now, you go too far!" Battista squawked with a laugh as he crossed the room and pushed back the heavy embroidered curtain.

They were on the east side of the building; the view took in a lovely path-strewn garden touched with the purples and yellows of spring. Peering left, he found the building stretched far back, away from the front entrance, as if it receded into the mountain itself. "We have come to the right place, Aurelia, forgive me if I ever doubted you."

She blinked at him, bottom lip dropping before she caught it. "Her words and Dante's, *sì?*"

He turned back with a nod, thoughts rushing to the undeniable, haphazard reference.

"What do we do now, Battista?"

In her voice he heard unfamiliar doubt.

"We rest," he said, gesturing for her to take the bed, dropping himself onto the leather settee along the opposite wall, and stretching out his legs. "I have a feeling we're going to need it."

She did as he suggested, all too eagerly, removing her riding boots and lying back with a soft sigh of relief. It wasn't long before her breathing settled and lengthened. In the quiet of her sleeping form, his mind whirled, not only of his quest but also of the woman with whom he shared it.

He was attracted to her, of course; she was far too beautiful a woman and he would forever be a connoisseur of beautiful women. But there was something else, something both troubling and intoxicating about her, an uncanny feeling he could not reckon or name, though he chewed hard upon it as the shadows lengthened and enshrouded the room. The time had come for them to face the creatures of the house.

Without waking her, he changed into his own dinner clothes, cursing Ascanio for the dandy he was, for the dandy he forced Battista to be. The finely wrought black velvet doublet boasted puffed upper sleeves and slashed lower, where the bright red silk shirt peeped through. The silk trunk hose hugged his thighs and the striped stockings matched the small bows on his pointed shoes. He had never worn such a fanciful costume and he growled at having to do so now. His one reprieve, the long skirt of the doublet, though open in the center, concealed—for the most part—the uncomfortable and boastful codpiece.

He would have to leave his satchel of tools, his dagger-sheathed belt, and his leather cuff behind, blatantly incongruous with this outfit, but their lack made him feel defenseless. If he and Aurelia could get through the meal unscathed, they could make their excuses with the early morning departure and return to their rooms. It was the immediate goal and he would focus on it alone.

With another heavenward glance, one offered up for strength, he stepped to the bed, gently nudging Aurelia on the shoulder until she woke.

"Ah, yes, Gaetano has arrived, I see," she snickered, peering up at him.

"*Sì*, and it is time for his wife, Livia, to arrive as well." Battista refused to be baited; he held out a hand to help her from the bed. "I have put your gown behind the screen with your shoes and jewelry as well."

Battista fumed at her crooked grin, glaring at her as she made her way to the corner of the room.

"Have you always been so exceedingly . . . cheerful?" he asked a tad unkindly.

But she laughed, a cluck of surprise. "No, actually, I haven't," she answered from behind the screen. "But I am liking the change, truth be told."

Her playfulness rebuked any slight; his lips twitched with the contagion of it. Battista listened as she rustled around with the voluminous material.

"Have you ever thought to be a lady's maid?" she asked, giving him a turn to laugh.

"No, though I can think of some benefits to the position."

"Well, prepare yourself," she called. "Here comes your chance."

She stepped out from the screen then, and his breath caught. He coughed away his reaction, not wanting her to hear of it, not wanting her to know how the vision she offered affected him.

Aurelia shrugged her now-silk-covered shoulders. "Would you tie my laces, Battista?"

She showed him her back, revealing the golden ties falling along her skirt, the empty eyelets she could not reach, and the gossamer linen below. The tight bodice of the jewel-encrusted emerald gown displayed the curves of her narrow waist and full hips. A thin line of jewels trimmed the high-necked, transparent chemise and the square neckline of the bodice sat low upon her full, rounded breasts.

He thought of all the traps he had escaped from, all the guards he had outrun; surely he could meet this challenge as well. As if he had done so for years, he laced her gown, pulling it to just the right fit.

"The poor are lucky, I think," Aurelia remarked.

"Indeed?" He finished his work and stepped back, appraising the finished product, allowing a glimmer of his pleasure to show on his face. With almost every wisp of her hair hidden beneath the matching emerald snood with its heavy lace veil, her face was barely discernible, but he would know those green eyes no matter how camouflaged. He only hoped no one else would.

"They need no one to help them don their simple dress."

Battista nodded his agreement just as the knock and the call of "dinner" came from the other side of the door.

He held out his hand to her and she took it.

"Stay close to me," he whispered as they stepped out into the hall behind the servant leading them to the dining room. "Looking that beautiful, here, you are in far more danger than you have ever been."

Among the forty or so people sitting at the mammoth table, there were any number of dukes and knights, barons and counts. And amidst these nobles there sat even a so-called prince. There was no greater evidence of the changing face of Italian hierarchy than at this table; these egotistic Italians revered their labels, but in these bombastic days they most often denoted rank, not reputation. Aurelia cared not one whit what they called themselves, as long as they did not call her Aurelia.

More than a few of the faces looked familiar, and she did her best to avoid them without appearing rude. More than one man vied for her attention, and her every move asserted that she belonged to Battista, or "Gaetano" as it were, taking his arm whenever possible, allowing his hand to rest upon her in the most intimate of postures. She would prefer that she not like the feel of it as much.

Battista did his part admirably, chiming in to denounce the despots ruling their lands cruelly, belittling whatever religious leader's name the others tossed up for ridicule.

Aurelia had never taken part in a tournament, not a joust nor a duel, though she imagined this was what it felt like, this sparring and jockeying. She ate little, laughed much, and lied a great deal. Through it all, not a single person she knew—and she did indeed know a few—recognized her for who she was. She had long acknowledged the truth: People saw only what they wanted, rarely seeing others for who they really were.

The long banquet table was awash with engraved pewter plates and sparkling Venetian crystal; the meal continued for hours and offered the land's greatest delights . . . salted trout from the coast, pheasant roasted to perfection, sweet rice simmered in almond milk.

Try though they might, Aurelia and Battista could not detach themselves from the ever more inebriated and ebullient party until the small orchestra performed a second round of musical entertainments and a few ponderous yet lascivious attendants offered readings of some vulgar poetry, intended, no doubt, to encourage sexual stimulation.

"I am ever so fatigued, my husband." Aurelia leaned over the lap of a pudgy prince and complained loudly to Battista on the other side as the third such recital came to a close.

Jumping to his feet, Battista pried the snaking arms of the prince from around Aurelia's shoulder.

"*Grazie mille!*" Battista fairly yelled at his host at the end of the table, and still his words were barely audible above the clangorous revelry in the dining room and spreading out into other parts of the palace.

The pointy-faced baron raised one long, thin hand, a barely bothered-with dismissal, far too preoccupied with the two women beside him to care who came and who went. Both leaned forward, their breasts revealed beyond the curved tips of their nipples; one woman stroked his almost-hairless pate as if he were an obedient dog.

Aurelia silently thanked the women for their perfect diversion and, latching onto Battista's arm, set off for the door.

"You cannot leave now." Ringarda pulled them back, throwing her arms around Battista's waist as if she lassoed a pig. "The real festivities have yet to begin."

With a forced laugh, he detached himself from the lewd groping, hands inching intrepidly down his hips. "The delights of your home are indeed tempting, *cara mia*, but we must away very early in the morning."

Ringarda thrust herself between them, one arm circling each, stroking their backs with the same feathery, inviting touch. "Nonsense. What better way to spend the next few hours than in the company of admiring friends."

Aurelia tried to step away, but the woman's flabby arm was surprisingly strong. Instead, Aurelia stepped closer, thrusting her body against Battista's, hands caressing his chest, running upward until they gathered about his neck.

"We have not been married long," she explained with a low voice, licking her full lips, looking up at Battista as if he were the next course. "I'm sure you understand, signora."

Battista's surprised gaze clamped down upon the now-moist mouth so close to his, arms rising to encircle Aurelia's waist with an instinctive response.

With a salacious though crestfallen grimace, Ringarda released the hold she had on them. "I can see he will have no one but you, my dear. I will delay you no longer then." She stepped away only to spin back. "But call, should you desire more company . . . either of you."

"You shall be the first to hear of it," Battista assured her with a crooked smile and a crack in his low voice.

Aurelia led him away, keeping one step in front of him, unable to look him in the eye after her lewd portrayal. She mimicked what she had seen so many other female courtiers do, and she must have done it well, if the astounded look on Battista's face presented any evidence.

Stepping into their room, she heaved a sigh of relief at the sound of the metal rasping slide of the bolt as Battista threw it into place.

"I long to bathe," she said without turning, pleased to hear Battista bark an uncomfortable laugh.

"I know exactly what you mean."

Aurelia crossed to the window and threw open the sash, closing her eyes in gratitude as a crisp breeze washed over her, as if it cleansed her of a clinging filth. Battista grabbed the pile of his discarded clothing, his well-worn leather breeches and jerkin, and jumped behind the screen.

"You should change as well," he called out.

"I will be most happy to," Aurelia replied.

The notion stood between them then, unspoken but understood . . . neither knew for sure where next they would go, only that they would be better served to go in comfortable, sturdier clothing.

Their changing completed, an awkward silence came to sit with them, accented by the dissonance of the debauchery rising up from below; as the night progressed, the clatter changed without remittance. Unmistakable were the moans of passion; frightening were the groans of pain punctuated by cries of pleasure.

"I hope you know . . . what I did . . . how I acted . . ." Aurelia stumbled on her embarrassment, unable to forget her actions as the haunted night stretched out. "I do not—"

"Your performance was masterful," he told her quickly, "have no fear."

Aurelia exhaled audibly, tossing aside her worry, turning to the only notion worthy of attention.

"How do we know where to go?" She reached into her satchel, scurried her hand beneath the folded and packed gown, and pulled out a well-worn copy of the *Commedia.*

"We don't," Battista answered. "We can only hope to find a clue."

He pointed at the book in her hands, reached into the satchel now back in position where it belonged on his back, and retrieved his own copy of Dante's epic poem.

"You have the way of it there. The answer lies in these words. I'm sure of it."

Beside each other on the warm leather sofa, they reread the lyrical words of the *Commedia's* first canticle. Aurelia kept her focus on the first passage, on Dante's journey through Hell, as she had for many a day, ever since discerning the first clues, since knowing the location of their first destination. But it was much harder to concentrate on the poem thick and rich with allegory and symbolism in a palace filled with practicing hedonists, sitting beside a man who grew more familiar with each passing day.

For all her years, she had rarely been in the company of a man on such an intimate level. Her glance slipped sideways; Battista's dark, thick lashes almost rested on the high bones of his cheeks, gaze riveted on the book in his hands. He pulled on the tuft of hair growing beneath his curved bottom lip as he so often did when deep in thought.

What a curious species men were, she mused, feeling both drawn to and repulsed by the man beside her. His allure drew her and yet frightened her; would it cause her to reveal too much of herself, would she make herself vulnerable where she had no business to be?

The feisty spirit within her longing for adventure argued back, *Are not men part of the human experience?* . . . And if what she overheard beyond their door offered any substantiation, did not men tender a great deal of life's "amusements"?. . . Was not frivolity a master she hoped to serve herself? She had lived every day of her life as a devout woman, as faithful to her purpose as any who took a vow. But these moments existed to offer her more; she believed it.

With a sudden surge of audacity, Aurelia shimmied closer to Battista, offering him what she hoped was a flirtatious smile.

"Dante believed Hell was found below." She could have bit her tongue. Having no clue how to start an intimate conversation—ignorant of what a vamp might choose to say—she had latched onto the only topic they had in common, but there was nothing beguiling about it.

Battista quirked his brows quizzically. "Hell *is* below," he stated matter-of-factly, turning back to his book, jerking back up at her skeptical expression. "You don't believe in Hell?"

"I don't believe it is below." She laughed lightly, though with stoic assurance. "But Dante did, and therefore, I suppose, below we should go."

He looked relieved and there she found hope. Gathering herself, she put her hand on the small space between them, leaned ever so slightly, and—

Battista stood, crossed to the door, and put his ear to the crack. Aurelia sagged back in her seat; she was the most feeble seductress who ever lived.

He tossed her the most devilish smile over his shoulder. "It's time."

Fourteen

Abandon hope, all ye who enter here.

—*Inferno*

They sidled down the empty corridor, mindful of every creaking board beneath their feet, chary to the stillness now enveloping the palazzo in its embrace. At any moment, Battista expected a door to fly open, then another, releasing the slumbering sybarites caged within. Or worse, to turn a corner and encounter an armed, questioning guard. Battista knew what he would do—what he must do—but he had no wish to abuse Aurelia to nurture their charade.

Once more on the ground floor, having safely descended the stairs without incident, they turned to each other with the same indecision.

"Did you notice any other stairs?" Battista asked with an urgent whisper.

Aurelia shrugged, tiptoeing toward the wide, resplendent hall leading to the dining chamber.

"The food came to the table from a back door. We can suppose it would lead to the kitchen on a lower level. It is the same in Mantua. It is a place to start, *sì?*"

Battista stepped to her with a nod, pleased by her analytical thinking.

The pendant lamps above their heads had gone dark and nothing more than nebulous, shifting light found its way into the corridor, slithering out of the rooms along its breadth. The moonlight cast a gray glow through the windows to their right, while the pale orange of fires dying in their marble hearths slipped out of the rooms on the left.

Battista shifted in front of Aurelia, taking the lead, stepping behind each bronze statue to hide beneath their legs, peering round their curvaceous bodies to see what awaited them in the next section of passageway. With each jerky progression, they made their way to the last chamber, and slipped in, closing the beveled and gilded double doors behind them.

"What in God's name . . . ," Battista hissed, stricken by the sight before them.

The signs of carnage lay everywhere . . . broken dishes still moist with uneaten food, overturned bottles, and broken crystal strewn across the floor. Upturned chairs dotted the landscape, scree at the base of a mountain. Shreds of clothing, ripped and tattered, draped the ruins—the top layer of riotous devastation. The revelers had taken their mania to the point of destruction, sparing nothing in their degenerate quest for satisfaction.

Aurelia shivered and he put an arm around her, pulling her close.

"I have never seen such a human wasteland." Anger darkened her voice far more than fear, and he was pleased to hear it.

"This is the work of evil, nothing less."

They shared a glance, one of sureness in the face of depravity.

"Look there." Aurelia pointed to the far northeast corner of the room, the narrow aperture almost unnoticeable in the once magnificent hall.

Picking their way carefully among the wreckage, they rushed to it and any semblance of normality that may exist on the other side.

Battista pushed at the door and faltered, finding it locked from the other side; it was a galvanizing statement, one revealing the servants' fear of their own masters. Pulling a long dagger from the three holstered along the back of his leather belt, Battista slipped the blade into the crack between door and frame, raising it slowly upward until he heard the click of metal. With one last flick of his wrist, he forced the blade higher, lifting the latch and releasing the door.

A dark, narrow hallway awaited them on the other side, warmth and the remnants of epicurean aromas wafting through it.

Latching the door behind them, they rushed through the darkness and into the cavernous kitchen of the wealthy palazzo. Heavy copper pots hung from ceiling hooks like huddles of sleeping cave bats, racks and racks of wooden shelves held jar upon jar of ingredients, and inverted bunches of drying herbs hung upon the walls. Just beyond the archway, they held. Battista pointed to a scullion asleep by the house fire, no more than a boy, no one to fear even if he awoke.

"What do we look for now?" Aurelia asked; she had led them here without thought to the next step.

"I know not." He pulled his mouth into a grim line. "But I think we shall know it when we see it."

Together they stepped farther into the stone chamber, as quiet as the rats scurrying across the floor in search of crumbs and scraps of food. They stepped lightly, unsure of what—or who—might lie just beyond the next set of shelves, in the density of the next pocket of shadows.

"Battista!" the rasping whisper screeched out at them.

Battista gasped, squeezing the dagger hilt. Aurelia jumped behind the protection of the blade. Both almost fell in relief at the sight of Frado sitting on the other side of the mammoth center grate.

Battista rushed to his friend, enfolding him in a chest-thumping embrace, in shared relief at their survival.

"Where have you been?" Frado pushed him roughly away, affection forgotten as impatience returned. "I have been waiting for hours."

"As have we," Battista assured him. "These . . . people . . . continued all night. There was no other opportunity to pass through them undetected."

Frado put a hand on his friend's shoulder, halting his contrition. "Yes, yes, never mind. If half of what these petrified servants have told me is true . . ." Words failed him; he shuddered with revulsion at the demented rituals taking place within these unhallowed halls.

Dipping his head to Aurelia, equally pleased and relieved to see her, he crooked a finger at her with what appeared as a content, if tentative, grin. "Come this way."

Without disturbing the slumbering boy, now almost completely forgotten beside the distant recessed hearth, Battista and Aurelia followed Frado to a small, doorless pantry carved out of the interior wall. As they passed a butcher's bloodstained counter, Battista grabbed a crude lantern and lit it from a nearby candle before entering the cubby. More cluttered shelving covered the walls; only a small portion of the back rough-hewn gray stone remained visible.

Frado inched closer to this very space, and though his feet moved forward, his upper body arched back, as if he feared whatever lay in front of him. "Here. Listen here."

They scuttled to him. An odor reached Battista before any sound, a noxious fume of decay dripping down the back of his throat. As Aurelia did, he tipped his head to the side and leaned his ear forward.

Faint but unmistakable, what could be human groans slithered out of the cracks in the stone. No moans of pleasure these; heartbreak and gut-wrenching pain vibrated in every disquieting resonance.

"There is some . . . thing behind there, I am sure of it." Frado had backed up to the pantry's edge. "I have listened to it all night.

I could not sleep for the fright of what lay behind there. It is the sounds of—"

"Hell." Aurelia finished his thought.

Handing the lantern to Aurelia, Battista shimmied into the slim space, as much as his bulk allowed. Gripping the back edge of the wooden shelving, he planted his feet and pulled.

Wood screeched across stone in protest and the case moved away from the wall. Battista snuck in behind it as soon as the opening allowed, and pushed, pressing the set of shelves to the right and against the opposite wall.

Aurelia pressed up against him, peering round him to see what lay behind.

The stone wall gaped open with the shape of a jagged arch, but one no taller than waist high. A gust of air, fetid with humid rot, rose up and Battista slapped his hand to his face to staunch the foul air from entering his body. Louder than ever, the groaning from below seared the brain with dreadful anguish.

"It leads downward," Aurelia mumbled from behind her own hand.

Battista laughed, a nasty twitter. "Of course it does."

He turned to Frado. "You must wait for us once more, my friend."

If he expected Frado to argue, he was wrong.

"Are you sure of this, Battista? Are you sure you must go . . . in there?" Taking the satchels holding their finer clothes, he backed farther away from the pantry and its ravenous hole.

Battista lowered his hand, growing accustomed to the smell, if not at peace with it.

"Believe it or not, I am curious now," he snorted, half-amused by his illogical notion, feeling less unhinged when Aurelia waggled her head in agreement.

"I have always thought you deranged." Frado shook his head with a grin fading as quickly as it came. "Be safe, *amico mio*."

Battista smiled and held out his hand to Aurelia. The feel of her warm skin against his bolstered his wavering fortitude.

Ducking down, they passed through the low opening and found not stairs, but a smooth stone ramp leading downward. Taking the lantern, Battista held the light out, a faint circle of illumination spreading no more than a few feet in front of them. The unknown of the darkness slowed their pace, but they did not stop, even as the walls began to seep with a thick, yellow liquid.

Their breathing entered the song of the groaning, growing heavier as they descended into the dank air, as the keening grew louder, and they reached a doorless archway. There was nowhere else to go but into it.

Battista stopped and, with an ungentle yank, ripped the fake beard from his chin.

"Whatever we face, I must face it as myself," he said with watering eyes.

Aurelia nodded, plying tender fingers to remove a thatch of gummy residue from his smooth jaw.

Battista took Aurelia's hand, gave it a squeeze, and stepped forward.

Beyond the egress, the groans became screams as air rushed at them, hitting them square in the face, pulling the snood from Aurelia's head, lifting her skirts and Battista's hair. Aurelia raised her arms as if to block out the sound . . . defend against the onslaught of wind. Battista squinted to see what lay before them. The walls of the chamber opened up, becoming a long rectangular room with what appeared to be no more than a black abyss awaiting them at the end.

Taking a few more tentative steps forward, Battista raised the lantern.

That's when they saw them.

On each side of the room, statues stood guard alongside the walls, tall, pitiable giants. Of dark gray stone stained blacker with mold, their gnarled, open mouths cried out their pain. Whether men or women it was hard to tell beneath the hooded robes shrouding their faces . . . in the hopeless, helpless expressions they all wore. As the air pummeling them rushed through the statues' mouths, it scraped against their jagged teeth, the contorted lips, filling the space with the sound of anguish itself.

Battista turned his face away, desolated by the statues' song, the misery invading him body and soul. Upon Aurelia's face, now wet with tears, he saw his own heartbreak.

"The sorrow of it." She hung her head, now curtained by hair unbridled with the force of the wind.

"Don't weep," Battista begged of her, for he could not manage her sorrow as well. "It is not—"

She grabbed his hand, eyes bulging out at him.

"Weep. Weep," she repeated with bizarre elation. "The *Commedia*. Your copy. Give it to me," she demanded. Her own leather-bound volume, that given to her by Giovanni, she had left in her large bag with Frado.

Battista pulled the book from his pouch and gave it to her, watching her as she urgently turned pages, bracing her back to the rushing air, preventing it from sweeping the light tome out of her hands.

Her page flapping held; her intense gaze rose to his face. "We are in Hell."

Battista longed to laugh at the irony of it.

" 'Here sighs, complaints, and deep groans sounded through the starless air, so that it made me weep at first. I will be your guide and lead you through an eternal space where you will hear the desperate shouts, will see the ancient spirits in pain, so that each one cries out for a second death . . .' "

She read to him, though there was no need; they had come to the right place, as much as he might wish to deny it. But the first piece of the triptych would not be in this room; it would be folly indeed to think they could overcome this challenge easily.

He took her free hand as she tucked the book to her chest with the other, and led them forward once more.

The contingent of screaming statues led them onward, the expanding sound gaining momentum, an audible, devouring torture. Battista hunched his shoulders against the onslaught of sound and air, scrunching his face and eyes.

"Close your mind!" Aurelia yelled over the cacophony, repeating herself at his puzzled glance. "Close your mind to it. Put yourself . . . your being . . . in another, better place. You can do it, I know you can."

She waggled the hand he held in his in encouragement and pulled him to a stop. In their stillness, he contemplated her words. Such a strange suggestion and yet he found his spirit taking flight, returning to his mother's home, at the table with her and his sister, laughing so riotously as to bring tears to the eyes. He opened his eyes, thanking Aurelia with a smile, wondering yet again of her truth—and stepped forward.

Passing three screaming specters on each side, they came at last to another archway and quickly—gratefully—moved through it. In the next chamber, the sound did not disappear completely, but diminished enough to release them from its wretched grip.

Beyond the pillar, they found another room, smaller, still of stone, but circular. Here flaming torches hung upon the walls, three of them, enough to show them all they needed to see, and Battista set his lantern upon the floor. Once again, a statue stood within the room's confines, but only one.

The effigy rose up from a small circular dais at the back of the room, a semi-circle etched into the floor around it. A man, not a woman, and though he appeared to be smiling, on closer inspection it was most certainly a grimace. He stood very straight, legs together, one arm stiffly by his side. Bent at the elbow, the other arm stuck outward, parallel to the floor, a cupped, empty palm reaching into space.

"He wants something," Aurelia said, no longer needing to scream to be heard.

"Agreed," Battista replied. "But what?"

They separated, as if in a dance, circling the room in opposite directions, scanning the walls and floors for something to give to the sculpture to elicit his secret. They met in the middle of the slim alley behind the statue. But they found nothing; not a pebble disturbed the smoothness of the floor, not a scratch marred the walls.

"There is no door," Battista said flatly.

Aurelia turned back to the man in the middle of the room. "He is our way out. I feel it."

She hovered around the base of the behemoth, face scrunched tight in perplexity. With a sly move, Battista slipped the book out of her clutching fingers, eyes roving over the pages.

He laughed silently when he found it. Stepping to the front of the statue, stepping up on the small platform, he gave her back the book with one hand as he reached out with the other, aiming for the man's waiting limb.

"Wait—" she started, but Battista held back her protest, pointing to a particular passage upon the page.

And when, with gladness in his face, he placed his hand upon my own, to comfort me, he drew me in among the hidden things.

At the last minute, Battista's hand faltered; he urged it on with a grit of his teeth.

The stone felt cold and hard in his grasp, but with one squeeze of the granite hand the arm fell away to the statue's side, and, with a grating of stone upon stone, the wall behind him slipped away and the dais began to spin, aimed for the cavern opening in the wall.

"Aurelia!" Battista cried her name as he lunged for her, yanking her onto the platform just as it disappeared completely into the next room.

In each other's embrace they held, knowing they had avoided

separation by only a second's worth of time. Battista looked down at her, her fair skin wan yet endearingly familiar in the shared air of survival. With palpable vacillation, they stepped apart.

They found themselves in another circular room, but in its center a spiral staircase awaited to take them yet farther downward; there was nowhere else to go but down.

"The circles of Hell," Aurelia whispered as she followed his lead once more.

Though he was taller than she by a good head, the steep decline allowed her to rest a hand upon his shoulder without bending over, allowing her to descend with stability on her low-heeled riding boots and to gather the full skirts in her other hand.

After the second time round, a clanking reached their ears; after the third it became a crashing, rhythmic smash of something hard against something equally solid, but still there was nowhere to go but down. Sweat slithered along the edges of Battista's face, dripping from his nose, and he wiped it with the back of his arm, loosening the ties of his jerkin, grateful for the slight coolness the act afforded.

Finally, at the end of the fourth circle of stairs, they reached a floor and, to the left, a low archway.

Another rectangular room awaited them just beyond, another two rows of statues along each wall, six on each side. But this time they were reliefs, not freestanding statues, built into the wall. These sentries did not scream out their pain, instead they released it from their bodies.

At varying instants, huge, perfectly round boulders hurtled out from the folds of six of the sculptures' robes, three on each side. As those boulders crashed, bounced, and returned, the remaining six launched their projectiles, creating a hectic but somehow symbiotic pattern as they went. Just beyond the lines worn into the floor, crevices indicative of years of wear, lay another archway, Battista and Aurelia's next goal.

"I believe there is just enough time between them to pass through," Battista raised his voice above the crashing.

Aurelia shook her head. "I can't see it. Can you?"

Battista longed to tell her—to assure her—that he could, but it would have been a lie and he had not the stomach for deceit in this place. He shook his head in truthful denial.

She sucked in a deep breath, he heard it whistle through her nose, and he watched as she closed her eyes, as repose smoothed the creases of worry on her face. He lost her then, somehow, though she stood beside him still, and he turned back his gaze to the barrier before them. He would guess for them both.

Grabbing her arm, he leaned forward. "Now!" he cried, but she yanked him back.

"No, wait! Do not let your fear bother you." She held him with Dante's own words.

Aurelia closed her eyes once more. As fragments of seconds ticked by, her grip upon his arm tightened.

Without a word, she dug her clipped nails into his arm, urging them into frantic flight.

The boulders rolled. They ran forward, the first set of boulders crashing in front of them. They dashed quicker. The boulders began to retreat as they headed straight for them.

Aurelia slipped through just ahead of Battista.

He grimaced in pain as the last boulder clipped his heel, barely making it past the crashing. He stumbled but stayed on his feet, stayed no more than a half step behind her. The second set of boulders aimed for them, moving faster than the first, Battista would swear to it.

They ran as if the devil himself gave chase, lunging out of the way, to the other side of the room, just as the next riotous smash rumbled behind them.

As they stepped through the archway, the stone portal gave way—triggered somehow by their passage—closing with a scream of dropping stone and billowing dust. The time to turn back had long since passed.

Heaving for air, they found themselves in yet another circular room, but above another center spiral staircase, an overhead oculus cut through the layers and layers of earth above them.

Battista rushed to it, turning his face upward to the sky, breathing deep the fresh air. Moving beyond the pleasure of it, he took in the vista; the stars began to fade in the first glimpses of dawn.

"We haven't much time." Aurelia stood beside him, drinking in the snippets of healthy air trading places with the heat and smoke.

"Then we'd best continue," Battista grunted, taking her hand and placing it on his shoulder as they entered the next stairwell.

Like the first, this one circled round and round, but here the torch-lit walls boasted pictures, crude black line drawings depicting the worst of human sins . . . murder, theft, orgies of gluttony and sexual perversion.

"Look no more," he whispered as the glyphs continued after their third go-round, but he need not have bothered; she had already turned away from the bleakness.

From the depths below the mephitis rose up to greet them. Descending the last few steps, they entered a long, cavernous space, moist with a trickle of liquid running through the center, the small dribble barely visible in the reflection of distant torch flame.

"A sewer?" Aurelia asked, face scrunched in disgust.

Battista shook his head. "I don't think so, though I do believe I hear the scurry of rats."

Most women would raise their skirts and squeal in fright, but he dismissed the thought quickly; he knew her far better by now.

They set off along the path cut by the stream, keeping tight to the wall on the right, keeping their feet as far from the repugnant liquid as possible. The trail ran straight and offered no impediments; Battista breathed a sigh of relief at the ease of the passage . . . until they came to the end.

The floor beneath their feet plunged straight down; nothing but a jagged cliff connected their spot with the next. Hands clasped once more, this time for stability, they leaned together to peer over the edge and down.

"You'll never make it in those skirts," he remarked.

Aurelia's mouth stretched across her dirt-streaked face in a grim line. "Cut them."

"*Scusi?*" His head snapped up.

"With a dagger. Cut them high enough to allow my legs better movement."

Battista slipped a short, serrated blade from its holster and bent before her, muttering, "As you wish, my lady."

He made quick work of the cambric overskirt and the first layer of chemise beneath. Only when he reached the last, thinnest sheaf did his hands hesitate; this cut would reveal her legs.

"I wish it," was all she said, but it was enough.

The last layer slashed away and discarded, Aurelia reached down to the material remaining, gathering a bunch around each thigh and tying each side, reincarnating her skirts into a makeshift pair of pumpkin breeches.

Try though he might, Battista could not keep his gaze from the sculpted form of her legs.

"I walk and ride a great deal." She gave the explanation though he had not asked for one, as if she glimpsed the thoughts behind his impolite leer. "It is all I am allowed."

He heard her dissatisfaction at life in every word's intonation. Pulling away his gaze, he offered an encouraging smirk. "You will have no trouble."

Stepping back to the edge, he sat and dangled his legs over, one foot reaching out to find a hold. His search successful, he stepped out and turned round, fingers clasping the ground now in front of him, fingers stinging with the heat of the stone. A perfect round lip seemed to wait for his hand a few feet below, but as he reached for it, as he brought the force of his weight upon it, it fell away with an almost clicklike sound, the piece vertically hanging loose and useless. Battista reached out for another jutting edge; this one held.

"Follow close," he said before disappearing completely over the lip.

It was a slow, arduous descent, but short. In minutes, they found themselves once more following a thin stream of liquid, the dark red of it clear in the bright glow reaching out from a distant source.

They rushed forward, neither speaking of the liquid at their feet, refusing to acknowledge the slop and squelch of it echoing against the hard stone with every step, neither daring to touch the fluid and confirm it as blood, both preferring to deny it as a mirage.

"Quickly, Battista," Aurelia urged him.

"I know," he grunted. "We must be running out of time. Frado mig—"

"No!" she denied him, voice harsh and guttural, hair dark with dampness and sticking to her sweat-covered face. "It knows we're here. We've angered it."

He wanted to stop and ask her to explain; he wanted to cover his ears and beg her never to speak of it again. Battista grabbed her hand and ran.

As in the stairwell, pictures covered the walls of this passage, more scathing commentaries on the depth of man's depravity. Try though Battista might to keep his gaze focused forward, the glimpse of familiar faces demanded his attention. Many a great citizen of Florence, many a noble patriarch, lived in these etchings, held forever in the eternal damnation of Hell, their rank testified to by the scepters in their hands, but their sins had scarred them, and their heads sat backward upon their stooped shoulders.

"What is that noise?" Aurelia's hissed query snatched him from his study.

From somewhere behind them, where quiet had been, came sounds of movement . . . a liquid moil, a slapping, and a creaking. Battista turned but saw nothing, and told her so with a silent shrug.

They ran ever faster, rounding a bend, and the sounds clamored louder. He turned back once more.

The frozen gape upon his face said more than any words, and she grabbed his hand as she turned. Yanking on her arm, he jerked her head round.

"Don't look," he begged her between gasping breaths.

But his directive only made her greed to see stronger, and she swiveled round, running backward. She saw, then, what he had.

The trickle of blood had become a river, a rapid sloshing upon the pictures on the wall, tainting the fiends depicted with red ooze. As it hurtled toward them, its volume rose, a bloody hand growing larger as it reached out to capture them. But that was not the worst of it.

Now great blazing torches stood in recessed alcoves, their light directed in odd angles by their position, the anomalous light cast peculiar shadows upon the etched walls. In the eerie illumination, the specters drawn upon the stone seemed to move; evil men, now monsters . . . chased after them . . . and yet never reached them. It was an illusion, it had to be, one of such genius it created guards that would never die, but of such real horror it hoped to drive the intruder mad . . . and away.

Aurelia whirled back, threw off his hand, and pumped her arms; they ran for their lives.

His barely healed calf wound began to throb and his running grew labored with a limp; he kept up with her, though just.

The orange glow ahead became brighter and they squinted in the profound glare, the heat quavering the air before them.

"They're stopping!" Battista yelled, sparing a quick glance behind them, and the notion sent them running toward the light all the faster, ducking at the last moment to pass through a low arch.

Bounding through, Battista jumped to the side, pulling Aurelia with him, throwing their backs to the wall as their chests heaved, gasping for air.

"*O Dio mio!*" He could say naught else as he took in the room.

Bent at the waist, hands upon her knees as she struggled to breathe, Aurelia looked up.

"From out of the flames and into the fire itself."

The room with no exit had six sides; the one at their back held the entrance. From four of the walls—two on each side—streams of flames burst out at them in discordant intervals, creating a barrier of fire in the middle of the room. Where the flames receded, men stood, or rather detailed portrayals of men. And each time the flames withdrew, they pummeled the man trapped forever in its path.

The last section, the one directly opposite, receded into an alcove. Upon the alcove's back wall, a picture hung.

"We found it, Battista. We actually found it." Aurelia laughed, a deep, throaty guffaw of triumph and delight.

Battista shared her sense of victory as he stared at the suffering apparitions set about the room. With each glimpse, their features, their actions, and the settings became clearer, and he could not stop himself from looking upon their pain with a pleased regard.

Judas held the first place on the left, with Brutus just beside him. On the other side of the room, on the panel closest to them, stood Cassius. And the last man—

"No!" Battista screamed, lunging forward, pulled out of the grasp of flame as Aurelia yanked on the edge of his doublet, the material ripping with the force she used to keep him out of the fire.

Roughly he tugged free, but gave off his charge, dropping to his knees as near to the fourth specter as possible, yet remaining just beyond the grasp of the flame. As he squeezed his eyes closed to the sight, a great sob convulsed through him.

She knelt down beside him; he sensed the quiet of her presence, felt her hand as it rubbed across his heaving shoulders. "Who is it?" she hissed.

Battista shook his head, as if he would not—could not—answer. "My . . . my uncle," the confession rushed from his lips, but did little to appease. "His was the sin of greed and it destroyed his love for my father . . . destroyed them both in the end."

A tempered answer, but all he could bear. He saw her look of sympathy, as one would look at Goliath once David had finished with him, and he could not tolerate it. He hung his head into his hand, his face to the floor, and allowed his tears to flow unfettered, those dammed up over the years since his father's passing.

"He passed, my uncle died . . . ," Battista muttered to the hard stones below as if they were priests to hear his confession, ". . . before we . . . before I could tell him of my forgiveness, of my love."

Aurelia took his face in her hands, one on each tear-sodden cheek, and moved to tilt his head up.

"You've do—"

He lost her words in the loud hissing suddenly filling the room. Aurelia shook him, almost knocking him over, leaning toward him until her soft breath nibbled on his ear.

"You have done it, Battista. Look."

He opened his swollen eyes, swallowing hard. Tears fell still, dripping onto the floor, falling through the flame no more than inches away. It hissed in fury at him. One more tear and the flame shuddered, receded, never to come at them again.

"Your love for him has doused his flame. You were the only one who could."

He looked up and at her in disbelief, blessed by the radiance of her smile.

"And his pain, I have no doubt."

It was a thought too beautiful to bear and he shook his head, afraid of it and its promise of hope.

"There is space, Battista." She shook him again, hard, his teeth clattering in his mouth. "We can make it through now. There's enough room. Hurry."

Aurelia's fingers dug into his arm as she pulled him up and yanked him across the room.

As the flames from the men who suffered still snatched at them, they zigzagged across the chamber, into the alcove, to stop just inches from the painting, from their prize.

It was the hand of Giotto, irrefutably. His technique was apparent in the brightness of the colors and lightness of the strokes. From the right-hand edge and into the center of the painting, the partial forms of two women possessed the canvas, standing one behind the other, placed before a welcoming village, a pellucid and brilliant blue sky above. Each woman wore the same deep forest green gown, and though more showed of the woman in the back, the dark, reddish-brown hair of the one in the foreground hid her face, and her image was faintly translucent, as if she faded away.

Battista shook himself and reached out for the painting.

"We have no more time for this."

He grabbed the frame from the wall and tipped it over.

"Look!" Aurelia cried.

The hook, now bereft of its burden, shimmied upward and pulled itself into the wall, drawn away by an unseen hand. As Battista's knowing touch pried the frame off the canvas and the canvas from its wooden slats, the hook disappeared completely into the wall with a metallic click.

They held their breath in that moment of nothing. Battista saw her fear, knew it for his own; would another monster leap out to devour them, must they surmount yet another challenge neither had any strength remaining to endure?

The wall trembled, tossing stone dust into the air, and, with one last grating scream, sunk into a crevice in the floor.

"Oh!" Aurelia cried, and her squawk turned to laughter, Battista's joining in at the sight of stairs before them . . . one long, narrow set of steps . . . leading up.

"Frado," Battista called as loud as he dared. "Wake up, Frado."

"Huh? What?" Frado jumped up from his tipped-back chair, befuddled gaze flicking from the alcove where he had last seen them to his right, to the small, opened door tucked into a corner all the way to his left.

Battista held the rolled painting in the air, shook it with loud silent triumph, and beckoned Frado to them.

In the last vestiges of night, the three escaped together from the clutches of Hell.

Fifteen

If the present world go astray,
The cause is in you,
In you it is to be sought.

—*Purgatorio*

The flames licked at her back as she ran from it, the heat scorching her, the fear rising in her gullet like acidic bile. The golden light just ahead brightened, his face barely discernible in its brilliance. If she could only reach it, if she could . . . just . . .

Aurelia woke with a gasp, flinging herself up upon the sweat-soaked sheets. Knuckling her forehead with fisted hands, she brought herself back to reality, out of the nightmare reliving the last day . . . back to the bed in the small gabled room of Battista's home.

She rose on unsteady legs and stepped to the window; a flush pink dusk spread across the sky, bathing the intimate and lush garden with its rosy glow. She had slept the day away, not surprisingly. Aurelia shimmied onto the wide sill and pushed aside the shutters, the air cool and soothing on her moist skin. She felt very grateful to be here, and safe, and though she chided herself for her foolhardiness, the intoxication of this adventure gave her all she longed for, and more.

Cupping her face in her hands, shoulders high at her ears, Aurelia relived the challenges of Hell with a child's wonder and delight, a wide smile growing apples on her cheeks, the surge of excitement rushing through her veins once more. So much she didn't understand. She had done things she never thought herself capable of—and done them well. She had seen things, evil things, things she had always known existed, but their substantive reality had left its indelible mark upon her.

The voices of duty and conscience berated her; Aurelia flung back her head at them as she pushed the damp curls off her skin. She refused to listen; for once she would hear her own voice and no other.

Other voices came to her, from the floor below, from out of the kitchen windows, and up to her perch. One Battista's, another Frado's, and suddenly the voices condemned her with guilt. Did she risk their lives to satisfy her own pursuits? True, if pressed, she could justify her acts, wave off any doubt with the flag of ultimate service. But did she put these men where they had no place to be? Could she stop them?

Aurelia heard the name of Giotto; the men below discussed the painting. Jumping up, she grabbed one of the two simple gowns from the wardrobe and threw the butternut dress on over her chemise. She had to get down there, had to see the painting. Perhaps if she deciphered its message first, all her problems would be solved.

"There you are, Aurelia." Battista's cheerful call announced her arrival. He stood to greet her, reaching out with an intimacy born of shared survival, a bond knit by the extreme circumstances they'd endured together, blind to the appraising, curious stares of the men around them. He put his arms tenderly around her for a moment, only to pull away, hands rubbing the tops of her arms as the dark warmth of his eyes studied her. "We thought you would sleep forever. Are you well?"

"Well enough, if a bit sore," she replied honestly with a sniff of laughter, pleased to see him recovering, pleased to be again in his company. What they had experienced had changed their relationship irrevocably, and care must be taken; she could not allow such affinity to make her vulnerable. "I feel as if I could have slept for days and days, but my gurgling stomach said otherwise."

The congregation laughed, men who knew the impetus of hunger. The entire cortege had gathered, Lucagnolo included, though his sallow skin and sunken eyes bespoke of worry unabated. As always, the men huddled around the mammoth table, but no cards or dice or silver coin did it hold, only the painting.

Barnabeo pulled Battista back down into the seat beside him, their chairs turned to face each other as Barnabeo attended to Battista's hands.

"What about you, missy?" The gruff bald man half-turned as he smeared a malodorous salve onto one of Battista's palms with a gentle touch, its sharp, bitter scent filling the room, having already bandaged the other appendage. "Are your hands as bad as these?"

Aurelia held up her hands, turning them over as if she revealed a hidden treasure, surprised to see small blisters bubbled here and there on the pads of her palms. But they were small and pained her not at all. Looking down at Battista's inflamed hand—blisters broken, the skin beneath flaming and raw—she saw he had not fared as well as she, and the taunting voice of guilt nipped at her once more.

"Keep to Battista," she told Barnabeo. "I need no treatment."

Turning to the other men, accepting their greetings and offers of respectful welcome, she looked to the painting unfurled before them.

Small weights held down each end, an empty tankard at one, a thick book at another. These men, these art thieves, knew of the damage human hands, and their dirt, could do to oil paintings, and they took great care to avoid it.

"We cannot decide if it is two different women or the same," Lucagnolo disclosed their debate. "If they are not the same, they could be related, such is their similarity."

Aurelia understood; the curve of the women's cheeks, the color of their hair, it was identical. But without seeing the face, no one could be sure. She reached up unconsciously, tucking loose strands of her own hair back into the plaits wrapped round her head.

"Nor can we comprehend if it is the women of greatest magnitude, or where they are," Ascanio told her, rising to give her his chair. "If this is indeed intended as some sort of map, I believe the location is the true import."

"I do not find it hard to reconcile di Bone's involvement in this," Battista, Barnabeo's ministrations complete, joined the deliberations. "Here is a man who lived three hundred years ago, a poor shepherd boy, until his talents were discovered by Cimabue, and yet his work was so far ahead of his time. There were messages in his work, there can be no doubt. But this one eludes me."

"His pieces reeked with humanity. It is what drew Dante to him. It made the poet include the painter in the *Commedia*," Lucagnolo explained. "It makes me think the women are the key."

"May I have some of the *trebbiano?*" Aurelia leaned across the table, but the bottle of white wine sat just out of her reach.

Pompeo filled a small tankard and brought it round to her with a basket of bread. "I do not think she is real."

Aurelia looked up at him, brows high in question, taking the fruity beverage with a nod of thanks.

"What do you mean, she's not real?" Battista asked.

The young man raised his shoulders in a confounded shrug. "Look how pale . . . how translucent she is. It is as if she is an intangible being, not of flesh and blood and bone."

Aurelia coughed, almost swallowed whole the *pasmata* in her mouth, tossing back a large draught of wine to soften the chunk of baked roll in her throat.

Ascanio thumped her on the back. "Perhaps she is caught between worlds, as if in the act of disappearing."

"The images work in concert. It cannot be just one or the other," Battista mumbled, head oscillating slowly. "More than ever

I wonder on this relic we must find. What about it has brought Giotto, Dante, and Mainardi into collusion?"

"It is not just them. I have found some vague references to a society of men." Lucagnolo sat, bony slim hands clasped upon the tabletop, sad eyes rising to the faces around him. "They were called La Confraternita dei Guardiani."

"The Brotherhood of the Guardians," Frado repeated the moniker with a befuddled mumble. "I have never heard of them."

Lucagnolo shook his head. "Nor have I, but it included some astounding members, Dante and Giotto, *sì,* but Mainardi, Duccio di Buoninsegna, Baldo d'Aguglione, Can Francesco della Scalla, and others. More than I can remember."

Ercole whistled through his teeth. "Poets, artists, lawyers, soldiers . . . it is a ménage of power."

Aurelia found Battista's startled gaze locked upon her face from across the room.

"What would bring such men together?" He shook his head. "I confess to you all that though I would do as the king bid me, I did so with the indulgence of a parent to a child, with no belief in his claims. But now . . . with all I have seen, all we hear of these men and this society of theirs. What else but a powerful object would require such protection?"

Not a one of them could or would answer him. Aurelia searched the somber faces, seeing nothing but more confusion. As Nuntio and a helpful maid served their supper—the painting set aside upon the desk in the book-lined cubby—their debate became inconsequential, for there simply wasn't enough knowledge to do more than conjecture.

"When you are finished, Pompeo, will you fetch Maso Guffati?"

Pompeo bobbed his head, left cheek bulging with a mouthful of veal and *piselli.* "You want him to make a copy?" He chucked his chin toward the Giotto as he filled his plate with another serving of the meat and peas simmering in red gravy from the pot in the center of the table.

"*Sì.*" Battista dropped his spoon and knife and leaned back in his chair, worry creasing his smooth brow. "And then I will ask some of you to put the forgery in the original's place."

"*Sei pazzo.*" Frado's scathing denunciation shattered the stunned silence.

Battista gave a raucous snort and turned to his lifelong friend. "You know, Frado, in the last few days you have called me first a degenerate and now a crazy man. I am neither . . . and both."

"Why?" Frado asked, slapping his palms upon the table, ignoring Battista's frolicsome banter. "Why would we do such a thing?"

Pushing his tin plate away, Battista leaned his elbows on the wood, head forward, gaze touching them all as it circled around. "This antiquity, this relic, it is more than any of us can comprehend. Why else would these great men use such drastic measures to keep its location so well hidden?"

It was a declaration to which there was no debate.

"If, for whatever reason, someone found the painting gone, it would be more devastating than any challenges we have overcome to retrieve it. Clearly, there are mechanisms in place for someone to verify its safety or to retrieve it. It may mean La Confraternita dei Guardiani exists still, protects it still." Battista's ruddy face darkened. "If somehow its disappearance is traced to us, it might well mean our lives."

This man seldom spoke of fear, or bowed to it, and this rarity made his warning all the more potent.

"Do you think a group of . . . common men . . . could gain entry to the palazzo?" Aurelia broached the question, making no effort to hide her misgivings. In all her wildest imaginings, she never thought or intended for others to be put in such jeopardy.

"If they arrive bearing a delivery of food and wine and dressed as merchants, they will," Battista answered with a well-pleased smirk. It drooped then, as he raked back his black hair from his face. "But I cannot ask any of you to take this task on. Those people, those heathens, are evil's guardians. They are in that position for a reason, and what I propose is an arduous chore, to be sure. It is an undertaking that must be accepted, not given."

His weary gaze turned to Aurelia, and once more the cloak of survival wrapped them together. "We have not told you all we encountered . . . all we have seen."

Aurelia watched as the bulging cords of his throat throbbed with a tight swallow. *Will we ever be able to speak of it?* she wondered. Were there words to convey it into reality?

"It is not a mission to be undertaken lightly." Battista grappled for words that fell short.

"I will go," Ercole blustered, folding his thick arms across his chest. "If Aurelia can survive, I am certain I can."

"Be certain of nothing!" Battista commanded, voice aquiver with naked consternation. "What this woman endured—"

"We endured." Aurelia reached out, taking one linen-wrapped hand in hers, all caution cast aside in the poignancy of recollection.

One corner of Battista's mouth curled. "What we endured few could survive. It is a test both physical and mental."

Ercole's arms flopped to his lap. "I will do my best," he said, humbled.

"As will I," Pompeo chimed in with a clasp upon Ercole's shoulder and an almost-convincing smile for the group.

"*Sì,* the youngest and the oldest. You will make a good combination," Battista pronounced with assurance, though his quick sidelong glance told Aurelia something else entirely, something she heard in her own troublesome thoughts.

The forgery took Guffati but a few days to complete as they prepared Pompeo and Ercole for the journey through Hell. More than once during the telling, one or the other had balked, refusing to believe the tale. Only with repetition did they come to accept it as truth, only with a realization that turned their knuckles white.

The men had left that morning, and in a rare occurrence the *casa* that rang always with the voices and laughter of men simmered in somber quiet, empty save for Battista, Frado, and Aurelia. The others had taken to their own homes, unease over their friends' safety magnifying the innate need for the warmth of the family hearth.

"What bothers me most"—Battista rested his head onto the hand propped up on the arm of his chair—"is that we have no clue where to find the next piece of the triptych."

"Purgatory," Aurelia offered uselessly from the couch. An unhelpful answer, though answer it may be. Clearly, they were to endure all three of the *Commedia*'s levels. Where Purgatory lay, none could surmise.

"We know from the Mainardi and from Dante's words that it is to be found in or near a mountain." Battista tapped his copy of the book upon his head as he spoke of the first maplike painting, as if the repetitive motion could batter an idea into his mind.

"Agreed." Aurelia held Giovanni's copy in her lap. She had tried to return it, but he had insisted she keep it, insisting with a laugh that she needed it far more than he did.

Slapping the book closed, she jumped up. "I am for my bed," she told them, stepping around the jumble of furniture and heading for the stairs.

Battista raised his brows at her. "Already?" He glanced out the back doors, open in the warmth of the night, the sky still peachy with the glow of a setting sun.

"My head pains me," Aurelia answered over her shoulder.

He stood and stepped toward her, reaching her with his long strides just as she took one step up. "Are you all right?"

She turned back, and he found consternation in the furrow between her brows, in the darkness of her changeable eyes. "*Sì*, I just need some sleep, Battista. No need for worry."

He smiled, relieved, if not completely. "Then I will keep this loudmouth quiet and allow you some rest." He dipped his head in Frado's direction as Aurelia continued her climb.

"I am for the tavern." Frado rose, and, with a flapping, dismissive wave, took himself up and out.

"All the better," Battista called to Aurelia's retreating form. "I will make for the garden. The weeds have been calling my name for days."

His companions gone, now alone in the large room, his tumble of thoughts crept back in the unguarded silence. As promised, Battista took himself out the open double doors and stood with hands on hips as he surveyed the chaos of his small garden. His men often laughed at him, teasing him that the growing of herbs and flowers was a pastime for women, but he had helped his mother tend the family garden since he was a small boy; returning to the work brought him back to those untroubled times.

Tossing aside his doublet, lighting two pedestal torches on each side of the cozy, flora-filled niche, he rolled up the sleeves of his simple linen shirt and knelt in the dirt. Carefully he moved about the tender *imperati*, the early flowers already in full bloom—their short purple-striped petals bright even in the diffusing light—and the white clusters of *marginata* opening atop the black stems. He snapped the offensive scraggly weeds from between these beauties, as if each one represented the puzzles in his head. If not for the jangle of the front door latch, he would have stayed there till full dark drove him from his work.

"Who is there?" he called, calm though curious. His companions came and went without notice or pause, but he did not expect any of them on this night.

No answering reply came and he looked up, eyes squinting into the shadow-infested interior. The open room was empty, not even the specters of concern remained as the evening breeze wafted through, but he had not imagined the sound. A knot of fear bit into his head; he and Aurelia were alone in the house.

Pushing against his knees, he rose to his feet and crossed back into the house, heedless of the dirt prints his boots left on the polished cherrywood.

Aiming for the stairs, fearful for his guest, he changed course with a huff of air. The shadow passed by the smoky-glassed window, but he knew it as certainly as he would know his own face in the mirror. Running back to the garden, he grabbed his doublet, throwing it on as he made for the front door, opening it a crack, and peering out.

The fleeting impression confirmed his conjecture. There, just turning the corner, he spied Aurelia, her lace net and veil firmly in place.

Why he followed, why he did not make his presence known, he could not say for certain. Perhaps the nasty voice of suspicion—one he had heard speak her name in the past—kept him to the shadows behind her as she followed the ever-narrowing backstreets to a modest but simple area on the west side of the vast city.

Her unhesitant stride added to the insidious thoughts, for she had often said that she had never been to Florence. And yet she trod about with assurance and determination in her quick step.

Following her around the corner of a yellow stone house with green shutters—children playing in front of the door as two elderly men, their straw chairs tipped back to lean against the front of the building, looked on—Battista jumped back again.

Leaning no more than inches around the rough corner, he watched as Aurelia approached the third house on the left and the woman who sat at a table, a small tin cup in her hand. In the light of the street torches, he watched as the woman offered Aurelia a warm smile, gesturing to the chair on the other side of the round wood bench and the half-full carafe upon it. But Aurelia would have none of it; she shook her head and gestured, almost impatiently, to the door and the house beyond.

The woman must have been far more elderly than Battista first thought, for Aurelia helped her to her feet, the woman leaning on Aurelia's arm as she hobbled into the house.

Quick as able, Battista turned the corner, ran to the house, and flung himself into the chair just emptied. It sat below and to the right of the front, double-shuttered window. He sucked in his breath, shoving his body back against the bricks as an arm reached out to clasp the shutters, closing them with a waggle of a fleshy wing.

But the aperture boasted no glass, and the shutters did little to suppress the voices.

"I am surprised to see you again so soon, *donna mia*," the aged voice warbled with respect.

"*My lady*," Battista ruminated, *she called Aurelia my lady; she must know the truth of Aurelia's identity, at the least that she is a noblewoman.* In this notion he found yet another unpleasant surprise.

But he allowed none of his misgivings to show on his face or in his posture. As if he belonged to the house, he availed himself of the wine left behind, raising his cup with a smile to any who passed him by, to the revelers beginning to fill the street in the summerlike heat of this night. The passage would fill soon, leading as it did to more than one of the large piazzas that would host a myriad of entertainments on an evening such as this.

His smiles disguised a gruesome grimace as the merrymaking plugged the air, and he struggled to hear the conversation within.

"I could not wait . . . needed . . . ," Aurelia said, impatience clear in her clipped diction.

The woman responded, but only a smattering of words reached his ears. ". . . I am doing my best, I promise you. But the painting you . . ."

Battista longed to scream with frustration as he lost the older woman's voice behind a bout of boisterous laughter, the hilarity of a group of young men passing along the street, full of themselves and their amusement. But what he had heard . . . His jaw hurt as he bit down upon his anger. Aurelia spoke to this woman about a painting, but which—the Duccio or the Giotto—he could not tell, but it did not matter. Her complicity with this woman could only be a disloyalty to him, and it stabbed him with its vile purpose.

The women's voices reached him again, words of thanks from Aurelia, imbued now with gratitude replacing irritation.

"I understand, Signora Alberini, really I do, but . . ." Aurelia breathed deep on the proclamation and he heard a tone of deference, and yet she clearly urged the woman to give her more . . . but more what he didn't hear.

Battista threw back a full mouth swallow of wine, poured another dose, and tossed that down his gullet as well. He supposed she could be trying to help their cause, one respecting his goal. But if that were the case, why would she not have shared her efforts with him?

From the very start, Battista had often wondered if Aurelia's actions were in the service of her guardian; the marquess of Mantua was a well-known art collector. Her devotion to him, her gratitude for her care and sustenance, might easily induce her to such a challenge, to obtain not only the triptych but also the antiquity, for the Mantuan collection. Battista's first fear returned to haunt him once more, laying waste to all the trust his and Aurelia's collective experience had built between them.

"Then if I am still here, Signora Alberini, I will return in a week."

He heard Aurelia's words clearly, realizing with a start that she stood at the door, that the portal inched open.

Clasping onto the name she tossed out so casually, a revelation that would allow him further inquiry into this incident, Battista jumped to his feet, almost crashing the chair to the street, dashing off in the opposite direction than that from which they had arrived.

Hidden well within a gaggle of people—a family of both young and old—Battista dared to look back at her. As he surmised, Aurelia lowered her veil before her face, dipped a shallow curtsy in parting, and headed back toward his house. He glared at her back, at the retreating figure of a woman who had become, once more, a stranger.

The dead of night stretched out long and hollow; in its dimness he found no ease, thoughts tangled on Aurelia and her nocturnal encounter. Like specters—one by the name of anxiety, the other agitation—two women, though they were one and the same, stood in his mind. The stranger thrust into his life by necessity, the friend who helped him survive and triumph. What he felt for each was equally as powerful, two encompassing emotions that tipped each end of a broad spectrum.

More than once, he had made for the steps, lifting one leg to make the climb, to barge into her room and demand an explanation. But each time, the face of the woman who had pulled him from the grip of fire rose up before him, holding him in place, preventing him from destroying what lay between them.

And yet if allegiance was their truth, why did she not come to him of her own accord?

"Damn it," he swore under his breath, the same thought pelting him like hard nuggets of hail. He had to end the torment, had to ask her. He jumped up again, jumped to the stairs, and—

The front door banged open, the blood-covered face in its threshold the countenance of the devil himself.

"Battista!" the apparition cried out, one trembling hand raised, reaching out.

The specter knew his name. Battista drew his daggers, held them before him in defense. Until he rushed forward, until he saw the black hair and round dark eyes beneath the dirt, the blood, and the tears.

"Pompeo!" Battista yelled, shoving the blades back into their scabbards, thundering across the room, jumping the furniture to get to the man before he fell to the floor.

Just as he dropped, Battista reached him, catching him in his embrace, controlling the descent as they both lowered to the polished wooden planks.

Battista pushed the sweat- and dirt-crusted hair from the young man's face. "Are you injured? Is this your blood?"

He searched Pompeo's skin, his hands, his doublet, but found no wound, nothing to cause such a stain.

Pompeo opened his mouth to answer, but naught more than a

sob came from his throat. As the tears dribbled off his chin, he shook his head.

Footfalls thundered on the stairs, first one and then another, lighter.

"Ercole? Where is Ercole?" The words scratched Battista's throat as they squelched out, for he needed nothing more than this solitary ravaged form to answer the question.

Battista panted, he couldn't find enough air; his heart pumped, though he would stop it, unable to believe his life continued if one of his men's had ended.

Pompeo squeezed his eyes shut tight, great dollops of tears forced through the crinkled lids, as he whispered the harsh declarative, "Dead."

Frado wailed as if struck, staggering away from the men on the floor.

Battista kissed the boy's head, holding the young man close, rocking Pompeo as he offered up a silent prayer for this boy's safekeeping and the care for the immortal soul of his lost comrade.

Over the top of Pompeo's head, Battista's gaze found Aurelia, stabbing her, as if she alone had killed Ercole.

Sixteen

To doubt is not less grateful than to know.

—*Inferno*

The darkest days of death do not occur as the loved one is laid in the ground, but rise up as life continues, their absence keen amidst the forever-changed normality.

Aurelia saw the descending of such grief upon Battista in the days following Ercole's funeral; she saw the dashing of his hopes each time the door opened and the roly-poly man did not stand in the threshold, imparting good news in the dour manner so particular to his contrary demeanor.

Aurelia did her best to distract him, to keep his thoughts on the next piece of triptych, to the puzzle of where their Purgatory awaited them. But the days of frustrated study—hours spent over the paintings and the poem—only served to exacerbate his misery. He had found Purgatory in the passing of his dear friend.

Withdrawn and sullen, Battista barely spoke, and if he did he offered naught but clipped and choppy words filled with frustration. His irritation seemed most often directed toward her, and his petulance wounded her, though she pushed the nonsensical injury away as best she could. He blamed himself for Ercole's death, she was sure of it, and wondered if perhaps he blamed her as well. He worried that the forgery had not been put in place—destroyed in the same fiery end as Ercole—worried more that the missing piece would bring attention and more danger to their quest.

Aurelia studied the book in her hands, gaze flitting from the words devoid of meaning for all the many times she read them, to the face of the man impenetrable no matter how often scrutinized.

With a knock needing no answer, Barnabeo pushed through the door; even this barreling man shuffled beneath the weight of loss.

Tossing a velvet pouch upon Battista's lap, Barnabeo plopped himself onto the settee beside him. "The duke was very happy to pay top dollar," Barnabeo declared with little pleasure. "He did not even bother to haggle."

Battista pulled at the tasseled drawstring and peeked into the purse, a wan, if satisfied, smile appearing on his gloomy face.

With little enthusiasm, Battista handed out the coins, dispersing the bounty earned, in some way, by them all.

Frado eagerly skipped forward, palming his coins, and, with a curt nod, quit the room with the same expeditious efficiency.

Aurelia followed him, holding the door open as he rushed from it, squinting into the sunny day as the small man trundled quickly away, lost in the swirling activity on the busy street.

"Again?" she asked of his retreating form, turning to Battista as Frado strode out of sight. "You pay him and he cannot wait to leave you. Where does he rush to with such urgency?"

She flounced back down in the wing chair she favored, the soft maroon velvet cushions squishing beneath her in a comforting manner. Elbows on knees, she perched on its edge, her query held in the air as she stared pointedly at the men. She did not miss the glance they shared, a masculine intimacy glinting with amusement.

She tilted her head to the side, the snippet of lightness most welcome in a house bereft of it for many a day, the pale cheer infecting her own lips. "What?" she asked them, expecting some bizarre tale of heavy drinking and carousing.

Ascanio pushed his chair from the table, fussing at his lace-edged cuffs. "Frado gives most of his earnings to the orphanage."

"Or the Church," Giovanni offered from the chair beside him.

Aurelia's mouth gaped, floundering like a fish abandoned on dry land, but she could not contain her astonishment, and her fluster pleased the men to no end.

Battista chuckled, and it was the sound of a man longing to come back to life. "He lives here and I feed him, without charge for either. He believes his is a blessed life and that he should bless others in return."

Aurelia spun back to the portal in wonder, eyes squinting as if the shadow of the surprising Samaritan stood in the threshold still.

She closed her flapping lips, unable to respond. There was so much to this world she would never understand, and yet so much to be held in glory.

Of a sudden Battista pulled up from his slouch, rubbing his face with both hands as if washing it, growling a bit as he did. "I have had enough of this."

Yanking his hands from his face, he looked at the company of mournful men.

"Ercole would hate this," Battista told them contritely. "It is the feast day of San Giuseppe, his favorite of all the holy days. . . ."

"Because of the *zeppole,*" Barnabeo mumbled, but not without the rumble of laughter.

Battista smiled, looking almost relieved to do so. "*Sì*, the *zeppole*. How he loved them. He would rail against us all for sitting here, moping, when such a party was to be enjoyed."

He stood up, pulling Barnabeo up with him, pushing the rock of a man toward the door.

"Go, all of you. Exchange these dark, dreary clothes for your brightest red. Meet back here as quick as you can. In the name of Ercole will we eat and drink, and drink some more."

The men responded, Ascanio the first, all too willing to become resplendent once more. In the wake of their departure, Aurelia held her breath. Battista had not seemed to include her, but then it might only be her own apprehension.

He faced her then, unable to hide the shadow in his eyes from her knowing glance. "Come, Aurelia, don your prettiest dress. On my arm you will enjoy this day."

Aurelia released the breath she had held for what seemed like days and stepped to him, hand brushing his arm lightly. "You have given them what they need . . . what we all need . . . as you so often do," she told him, soft voice loud with admiration; this man was a leader and a friend, he nurtured and protected them.

He mumbled something, but she paid it little heed as she rushed away, lifting her skirts to run up the stairs, eager to be out of the house, to enjoy a festival in public rather than behind the walls of a well-guarded palazzo, her craving for fun and adventure making her deaf to his response.

"The whole town is about," Battista said as he licked the yellow custard from his fingers.

They ate the *zeppole* purchased from a street vendor's cart, the sweet goo oozing from the light and flaky pastry with every bite, as they stood at the side of the crowded street, wedged between the pastry vendor and another offering aromatic portions of *stufator*, serving the stew in hollowed-out, crusty bread.

Aurelia closed her eyes to the delight, allowing herself to feel nothing but the flavors and textures assaulting her mouth.

The procession of children had just passed—little boys in their first pair of fancy hose, little girls with garlands of flowers in their hair—each carrying a gift to lay at the feet of St. Joseph in the Duomo, the great cathedral in the center of the city, where the saint's statue stood. Their little arms overflowed with flowers, limes, candles, wine, and more, carrying on the tradition begun in Sicily in the Middle Ages, thanking San Giuseppe for ending a devastating drought.

On every corner of the city, bedecked in flags of red, its people offered a different delight, every piazza a joust or a pageant, even the churches—restrained in the late days of Lent—held Scripture readings, lighthearted words to celebrate the saint's day. And everywhere floated the strains of music.

Aurelia lunged forward, bumped into from behind by a laughing, handsome young man, but smiled as the offending gallant kissed her hand in apology.

"You speak the truth," she chuckled to Battista. "I have never seen so many people in one place before."

Ascanio laughed as Frado took a stand at her back, a protective guard dog at his post. She rubbed her hand on his arm, acknowledging his care, and he winked over his shoulder at her. They had lost Giovanni and Pompeo somewhere along the path, the younger men called away by the rattle of the dice or the giggle of a woman.

"Perhaps you will see someone you know." Battista leaned down, lips close to her ear.

She tilted away with a frown, not recognizing him behind the intense expression. "I know no one in Florence save you and your men," she told him with a shake of her head.

Battista's brows bolted up his smooth forehead. "Really? No one?" His voice bit her with scathing sarcasm.

Her breath escaped her, as if he squeezed her with his large, powerful hands rather than a withered glare.

"N . . . no, not a one," she replied, taking yet another step away, her voice sounding tentative, even to her own ears.

Battista sneered at her with the disguise of a smile, and the band around her chest drew a notch tighter. Something disturbed him—some knowledge—she was certain of it, and his knowledge frightened her as nothing thus far had.

"Come." He took her almost roughly by the arm and led them west, along the crowded Via Largo. "We do not want to miss the ceremony."

As the red-tiled dome of the Duomo rose up in front of them, Aurelia lost all taste for the celebration. Should she speak to him, should she tell him more, enough, at least, to end the jabbing questions?

Her jaw ached as her teeth ground together; if only he asked her a direct question instead of this spiteful meandering, this intellectual sparring. She could better handle pointed confrontation than speculation at what boiled in his head.

Aurelia rankled at the itch of vulnerability, a frightening state, especially after so many years in the protection of the marquess.

"Battista," Ascanio hissed. "Look!"

Turning back with Battista, Aurelia followed Ascanio's narrowed glare.

On the other side of the widening avenue, a group of men stood stiff and motionless, a mammoth boulder in the stream of frolicking humanity. Though dressed in a similar fashion to Battista and the other men in their group, this posse wore their swords and daggers with greater number, wore their aggressive attitude upon their slashed and colorful sleeves, the chips on their shoulders, and the sneers on their lips. They gave no way as the crowds tried to pass. One stocky man stood at the front of the group, a pale-skinned black-haired man, his coarse beard covering most of his face, a snarling thin lip visible behind the untrimmed mustache, a bone white scar running from the edge of his mouth toward his jaw.

As Battista turned, they found each other. With slow deliberation, the man raised his hand to his mouth, put the tip of his thumb to his teeth, and, with a hateful glare, flicked it out at Battista.

Aurelia sucked in her breath. Ascanio bounced on his toes, launching himself toward the brigade of men.

"No, Ascanio, do not bother." Battista pulled him back, grabbing both of Ascanio's arms to contain the man's anger. "*Sfacciato*. They are not worthy of our consideration."

Aurelia watched as the gang of brigands ambled away, studied the miscreants Battista had labeled as lacking face, one of the greatest condemnations an Italian dared bestow upon another.

The depth of a person's honor they held in the face, or so people believed.

"Who was that man, Battista?" She had seen much in their time together, but never had she seen someone act so purposefully and publicly *sense vegogna*, without shame.

Battista looked at her oddly, as if suddenly remembering her presence. "That, dear Aurelia, is Baldassare del Milanese. As I do, he calls himself an art dealer, but everything he does, he does for his own profit."

"He is nothing like you," Frado growled from beside them. "He takes with no compunction, hurting whoever may stand in his way."

"I did not know he was back in Florence." Ascanio calmed, voice thick and clogged with distaste, as the dangerous *bravi* strode away. "I thought they were staying in Rome these days?"

"Apparently not," Battista mumbled, none too pleased at the turn of events. "Find Giovanni and Pompeo, would you? We need to tell them of Milanese."

"We will meet you at the Duomo," Ascanio called, stepping away to his errand.

Battista nodded, putting one arm around Aurelia, the other around Frado. "Come, *mei amici*, to the ceremony."

Aurelia puffed with relief. The amiable Battista had returned, forgetting—or so it seemed—the prying questions he had put to her, and the appearance of his enemy.

"I am not sure if that hat matches your lovely gown." Battista's hand hovered with amiable propriety at the small of her back as he led Aurelia through the now-dark streets. "But it becomes you."

She had had no red to don, had chosen a simple pink dress and matching snood, but as the day progressed, as Battista pulled out whatever pebble niggled in his shoe—the fugue of irritability that had plagued the start of their outing—he had bought her a bright red broad, circular hat to perch upon her head.

Aurelia raised her eyes to see the brim. "*Grazie mille,* Battista. I will have a gown made to match, for this has become my most favored headpiece."

He beamed at her as Pompeo fell upon them, arms thrown upon their shoulders, fumes of alcohol—of wine and ale—coming off him in waves.

"I will buy you that dress, *donna mia,* for I am a verra rich man." The slight youth laughed as he leaned heavily upon them. He may have drowned his sorrow in whatever libations he found, but he had won at every game of chance he entered. The purse at his belt jangled with coins of all shapes and sizes.

Battista jerked his head back, eyes fluttering beneath the barrage of Pompeo's breath. "I think you need to find a bed before you fall." He chuckled. "Stay with us tonight. I do not think you will make it home."

"No, no, I mus return to the pary." Pompeo pulled away, spinning ungainly in the opposite direction.

Battista grabbed his arm, wrapping it back around his shoulders as Frado took the other.

"Nonsense, silly boy," Battista chided Pompeo lightly. "We are no more than steps from home. You will pass out in a few minutes anyway."

Pompeo blinked with surprise. "I will?"

Ascanio and Giovanni, bringing up the rear with equal inebriation, laughed at his gibberish.

At Battista's blue door, the group bade their good nights, Barnabeo promising to see the other two drunkards safely to their beds.

"Nuntio must still be at the festival," Battista remarked, waving to the others as they strode away, heading into the house shrouded in darkness. Not a candle had been lit; only the low-burning fire in the kitchen grate shed any light in the house.

Dropping Pompeo upon a couch, the youth more unconscious by the minute, Battista stumbled about, cursing softly as he lurched upon things unseen, hands out waving about, feeling his way, finding what he needed. Aurelia watched the shadow of him stagger like a blind ghost as she kept by the door and the safety of street torchlight. Finally, Battista lit first one candle, then another.

"What the—," Frado barked.

With a thud and curse, he hit the ground.

"Are you drunk, too?" Battista laughed, the merriment dying upon his tongue as he turned, illuminations in hand.

Even in the meager light, the destruction was clear. Furniture lay overturned, cushions shredded, their feather guts strewn about. The crates in the corner had been ripped open, their contents tossed helter-skelter with no care for their value.

Aurelia slapped her hands over her mouth, as if they could stifle the scream barely caught in her throat. She had never seen such purposeful devastation. Statues lay in pieces, paintings ripped from their frames, furniture broken, thrown to the ground for no good reason save the goal of demolition.

"Frado!" Battista cried, recovering from his stifling shock, rushing to his fallen friend's side, and pulling him up. "Are you hurt?"

Frado shook his round face, the bulbous cheeks turning bright red as he surveyed the wreckage. "Why would a thief do such a thing?" he hissed.

Battista's nose crinkled in distaste. "They were looking for something specific. And when they did not find it, they took their frustration out on my possessions."

"The triptych!" Aurelia cried, rushing through the debris, tripping in her hurry to the painting and the last place she had seen it, resting on the small desk in the study. But in the dark recess of the corner cubby she found only more wreckage, the desk overturned, the painting nowhere to be seen.

Her fisted hands shook, nails digging crescents into the flesh of her palms. All their work had been for nothing; this one fiendish act had erased all her good intentions. She should have destroyed the painting when she had the chance; she had rationalized her behavior for that purpose and she had failed, hesitating for the sake of Battista, for the longing for yet more adventure.

He came up behind her, pieces of a Greek figurine in his hands. "My father gave me this." Though he stood beside her, his voice came from far away, back at the time his deceased parent had presented him with the gift.

The crash echoed through the chamber, the piece of the small woman shattering against the wall. Aurelia yelped in fear, jumping back. Battista threw another piece, his scream of anger louder still.

"How dare they!" he thundered, his beautiful face mangled with his wrath, all anger and frustration boiling deep within—whether at the wreckage, Ercole's death, or something more—bubbling to the surface.

"Storm's comin'," Pompeo mumbled from his perch upon the settee, head hanging off the edge of the hard furniture now without cushions, falling quiet once more, falling into unconscious oblivion.

Ignoring the drunken man, as they all did, Aurelia stared at Battista, frightened, though more for him than herself; to be consumed by anger was to be eaten alive.

Yet her own anger refused to yield; it festered as Battista failed to see what was missing. She grabbed him by the shoulders and shook him. "The painting, Battista. The Giotto is gone."

He eyed her darkly, but said not a word. She watched as he closed his eyes and breathed deep, pushing the sweaty hair off his face with both hands, resting them on the top of his head as he gathered himself visibly.

"Did you hear what I said?" she railed at him in frustration. "The painting has been stolen."

Battista shook his head, dropping his hands to his sides as if in relief. "It is perfectly safe."

Aurelia knuckled her eyes in confusion. "What? What do you say?" She flung an accusatory finger at the overturned desk. "Look, it's—"

"It's locked away." Battista righted a chair, wiping debris from its navy and gold upholstery. "Whenever I leave the house, I secure the most valuable of my possessions in the safe room."

"In the . . . safe room?" Aurelia whispered, confounded. "I . . . I did not know you had such a room."

"Few do." He turned, surveying the totality of the damage with a sweep of his gaze.

Aurelia seesawed on her relief and her concern, pondering once more this man and his secrets . . . displeased to find he claimed as many as she.

"It is hard to know for certain, but it appears nothing was taken," Frado called out from the far corner, plunging through the debris, finding pieces left undamaged and placing them back into the crates.

"I am not surprised," Battista hissed. "No one in all of Florence, in Rome and beyond, would have the audacity to purchase a piece owned by della Palla."

From another man it would be a boast; from Battista it was a hard-edged truth.

Aurelia rifled among the rubble. "I don't think many pieces are damaged, either." She placed some cushions back where they belonged. "It seems to look much worse than it is, as if whoever did this created disarray with a purpose."

"Baldassare." Battista spat the name as a curse.

Frado groaned and slumped into a chair, hands full of broken marble shards. "*Dio mio*. Of course. He has been back, what, two days?"

"But why?" Aurelia asked either of them. "I understand the rivalry between you, the ill will, but why would he cause such chaos? Why not just take what he came for?"

Battista crossed to the kitchen, kicking debris out of the way of his stampede. Grabbing the squat, round bottle of russet-colored brandy, he did not bother with a cup but put the rim to his lips and tossed the liquid down his throat. "Because he did not find what he came for."

"The painting," Frado hissed.

"The painting," Battista growled, throat rough from the harsh alcohol.

"Baldassare is on the same trail. May the devil take him," Frado cursed.

Battista laughed without amusement. "It had better be soon, or else there are only worse days ahead."

Seventeen

He listens well who takes notes.

—*Inferno*

"Wait . . . what?" Aurelia pestered with a squelch, a hand to her forehead as if it pained her. "What are you saying? Do you mean to imply someone *else* knows of the antiquity and . . . and the triptych?"

Battista refused to answer her, out of spite to be sure; she had not answered him, had not been truthful with him. Why must he be so with her?

He steeped in the juvenile emotion; he distinguished it clearly with faultless internal vision, but he would not deny it regardless.

The door squeaked open; his hand rushed to his daggers, only to hold at the sight of Nuntio, at the alarm blanching the old man's face.

"*Madre mia,* what goes here?" Nuntio staggered into the room.

Battista threw back one more mouthful of brandy, plunked the bottle on the table, and stepped to him. "I am sorry for this." He placed a hand on Nuntio's shoulder. "Hire however many people you need to clean this up. Cost is no matter, do you hear? I will not have you exhaust yourself over this."

Nuntio looked up, face slack with shock, mouth an open silent maw.

"Do you understand?" Battista goaded him for an answer.

"*Sì, sì,*" Nuntio assured him, though he did not sound certain.

"*Bene.*" Battista nodded, pleased with that at least, and made for the door, wrenching it open.

"Where are you going?" Aurelia called after him, but he gave her no answer, showed no pause.

"Let me go with you." She scuttled after him.

The alarm in her voice held him then, the shudder of concern. It brought him up sharply, a bitter tug-of-war between sincerity and hypocrisy. He wanted neither just now.

"Where I am for, no lady should follow."

Aurelia took another step toward him, opened her mouth, and he closed the door in her face.

"*Basta,*" he said to the night. He did not intend such rudeness, but his head could stand no more. "Enough," he said again, and turned left, heading for the Via de' Martelli.

A gathering would certainly take place tonight, he mused. Though not a member of the group whose company he sought, his friend offered the invitation in perpetuity, and Battista would avail himself of it for the first time, its diversion the craved tonic.

In the streets, the merriment prevailed . . . with rousing voices and laughter of the celebratory, with the music, and the indulgences. He stopped at a wine vendor and purchased two large bottles of sweet, white Greco wine, the perfect beverage for gentlemen. He had no time to fulfill the custom of the get-together—a potluck of sorts—but Battista hoped his circumstances would find him forgiven, that and the wine.

The home and studio of Florence's most flamboyant sculptor, Giovanni Francesco Rustici, lay just beyond the Duomo, near the site of the old university. Battista found the column-flanked door thrown wide, the opulent interior aglow with candlelight and laughter, replete with the presence of La Società del Pauiolo.

"*Buonanotte!*" Battista gave herald as he entered the foyer of the mansion, heading to the left and the sound of male voices boisterous in spirited conversation.

"Who calls?" The cry found him, and though it attempted severity, the undertone of laughter dispelled it as feeble. From the left corridor Rustici rushed out, a red cape unfurling out behind him, glittering chains jangling upon his broad chest.

"Well, if it isn't Battista della Palla, as I live and breathe." The dimples in the man's round cheeks came out to play at the sight of his new guest. Though Rustici had left youth behind long ago, youthfulness belonged to him, reddish frizzy hair not yet grayed, stocky figure not yet turning to fat. It seemed his childlike attitude kept him forever young.

Battista bowed, relieved he still wore his fine festival costume. Though Rustici forsook his noble lineage at such gatherings, accepting guests in bohemian garb or even craftsmen in worn work gear, Battista thought himself better prepared in his finery, especially on this day of celebration.

"Good evening, Messere Rustici." Battista straightened. "I hope you do not mind my last-minute appearance. I have need of your hospitality and the company of amiable fellows."

The sculptor waved a chubby hand dismissively; word of Ercole's demise had swept through the city, if not that of all of Battista's tribulations. Sympathy combined with the knowledge of Battista's sponsor, and Rustici welcomed him willingly.

"The wine stays, but you must go." The feisty artist cracked with laughter at his own quip, grabbed the bottles from Battista's hands, and set off like a general at the head of a charge. "This way, young man, we have just the distractions for one in need."

Battista followed with a sigh of relief, leaving the heavy burdens of grief and worry at the open door.

At the end of a long, well-lit corridor, double doors stood open, welcoming him into the remarkable room Battista had only heard of, never seen.

In honor of the group who gathered at his home, Rustici had converted a mammoth wine vat to resemble a cooking cauldron, wherein his guests—the Company of the Cauldron—sat around a circular table amidst the unique, august environment.

"Michelangelo? You have a guest!" Rustici cried as he pushed the astonished Battista farther into the room.

"*Meraviglioso!*" a hoarse voice responded above the patter of running feet. On his short legs came the scruffy artist, arms held out and open in a fond, delighted greeting. "How wonderful!" he cried as he wrapped Battista in a warm embrace.

"I thought we would never see you here." Michelangelo released his grip, holding the younger man at arm's length, peering intently at the youth he had once called an apprentice.

Battista shrugged, a shy child's gesture, the same as when they'd first met, humbled, as always, when in the presence of this most gifted and kind man.

"*Grazie,* Michelangelo, it does me well to see you."

"Why did it take you so long to come?" The artist shook a finger at him. "You have been on my invitation list for years."

The Company of the Cauldron, an artist-based society, allowed but twelve members at any one time; only one member's death could bring the initiation of another. But each member was allowed to invite four guests, though they must be of similar artistic occupation as the members—sculptors, painters, architects, or musicians.

"I never felt . . . ," Battista struggled for an explanation, abandoning it and any need for artifice with this man. "I have never thought myself worthy of such company."

Michelangelo cuffed him, though lightly and with one of his rare smiles, the artist's amber eyes sparkling with flecks of blue and yellow. "You could have been great, had you the patience. And what you do for Firenze . . ."—the man's gruff voice hushed to a whisper—". . . well, it makes you far more worthy than half these rascals. Come, you've arrived just in time."

Michelangelo pulled him to the large, round table and pulled an empty chair beside his own place, leaning over to whisper in his ear, "You remember the one rule, *sì?*"

Battista nodded vigorously; the eccentric, ebullient Rustici had but one rule for the society he hosted, one developed after two of its most distinguished members had fallen into a nasty squabble. The question, which was the preeminent art form, painting or sculpture, the very same discussion that had sent two masters into a vicious argument, a quarrel that had forever darkened the relationship between Michelangelo and Leonardo da Vinci.

Battista gave greeting to the other men, trying his best to appear nonchalant in the company of such talent as Andrea del Sarto, Antonio da Sangallo, Lorenzo di Credi, Baccio d'Agnolo, Michelangelo's close friend Francesco Granacci, and many others, the house full on this festival night.

A wide, polished beam, the "cauldron's" handle, arched over their heads, holding a series of lanterns casting a suffused, comforting glow over the room. Servants prowled the circumference of the vat, filling the expensive Venetian crystals with costly Tuscan vintages and Battista's pale yellow wine. From below their feet, through slates of polished mahogany, the cadence of festive music wafted up, tossed about on the bang and sizzle of a busy kitchen.

Battista lost himself in the splendor of the moment, of the company by his side, by the beauty all around him, by the never-ending flow of wine.

Taken unaware, he jumped at the shrill blast of a fife. Michelangelo laughed, calming him with a hand upon his shoulder.

"Time to eat." The artist grinned with a waggle of busy salt-and-pepper brows.

Battista relaxed, but only for a moment. Yelping like a little girl, he grabbed at the table as it fell away from them, as servants manning ingeniously devised winches lowered the trencher, only to reel it back up once the scullions below had covered it with the most creative food Battista had ever seen.

The gathering cried out with delight and rousing applause at the sight of the first course, one concocted by their host. Depicting a scene from the Roman poet Ovid, the two broiled roosters were dressed up as Ulysses and his father. With the aid of iron needles strategically inserted to hold their poses, the Ulysses lowered his father into a pie, the edible representation of the Fountain of Youth.

"Are we to eat it or put it on display?" Battista laughed to Michelangelo, hands stinging, unable to cease his clapping.

Michelangelo nodded merrily, seeing it all through Battista's uninitiated eyes. "It only just begins." He chuckled with a threat proved easily fulfilled.

As the night progressed, the creations kept coming, bedazzling the eye and the imagination, as well as the palate. A cathedral made of pasta followed next, along with a pig dressed as a serving girl, and a set of blacksmith's tools, including an anvil composed entirely of pressed calf's head. The crowning glory of the meal came from del Sarto himself, a miniature temple in the classical design, its floor a shiny montage of colored jellies, columns of red sausages veined to resemble marble, the capitals of sculpted Parmesan cheese, and the roof of marzipan. The oversize altar—the pièce de résistance—was sheet music crafted of elongated pasta with peppercorns for notes.

Battista tried it all, how could he not, and sat back with a belch, rubbing his protruding tummy as the conversation turned, as it so often did with artists, to the muse.

". . . I crave something simple but about which I can feel deeply."

He had heard Michelangelo explain this before, knowing it spoke of the man's love for his mother, the loss of her as a child, his loneliness, and his hunger for love. Though he cared deeply for the man, the familiar talk lulled Battista—full of food and wine—into a half doze, until he heard the name.

". . . like Giotto."

Battista sat up, head snapping to the side. "*Scusi?*"

"I said I take much inspiration from nature, from places that capture my imagination," del Sarto repeated, "as did Giotto."

Battista waggled his head, knowing only too well of Giotto's proclivities. Suddenly sober, intensely alert, Battista took in every word, though nothing proved helpful, until the talk turned to mysticism and the unexplainable subjects artists included in their work and, again, the mention of Giotto.

"We are more highly attuned to the supernatural," Rustici gave words to the wildly held notion of those born with a creative soul. "The three stars of Pyxis. Remember his rendering above the mountains to the south? His painting came decades before their discovery. How do you explain that, I ask you?"

"The Pyxis above the mountains!" Battista slapped the table, a clap of thunder crashing above the lively conversation, deafening and muting all and at once.

Michelangelo leaned toward him, brow furrowed over his crooked nose. "Are you all right, my friend?"

Battista came back to the room, his stunning inspiration tucked safely away.

"*Sì, sì*, pray forgive me," he bade the whole group. "I had forgotten how beautiful that particular piece was. Perhaps I have had a bit more wine than is wise."

"Nonsense!" Rustici yelled from the opposite side of the table, grabbing a bottle and leaning over to fill Battista's goblet once more. Battista threw back his head and laughed, grabbing the beverage eagerly in celebration.

He gulped from his cup as he stewed in his thoughts, hand trembling with the triumph of finally having some clue where next to look, where the next piece of the triptych may be. Granted, there were many mountains to the south of Florence, but few had been the subject of Giotto's painting. They had only to study his work, and perhaps the Duccio again, to discover it. Aurelia would be so thrilled, so incensed, to have some concept more precise upon which to set her great mind. She—

Battista shook his head, euphoria at his discovery diminished. His second thought had been of Aurelia, of sharing it with her, and he pulled himself apart on thoughts of her. Was she the most intriguing woman he had ever—would ever—meet, or was she his enemy, sent by other enemies to obstruct him?

He stood on shaky legs, grabbing at the table to steady himself.

Michelangelo raised bloodshot eyes at him. "You are leaving us so soon?"

Battista bowed, if awkwardly so. "I must, I'm afraid. The arms of a woman await."

Other men heard his proclamation and the lively heckles followed him as he bid his deep gratitude to his host, as he walked a crooked line out of the room, away from the men who would continue the festivities straight on until dawn.

"Battista!"

The chorus of greetings found him as soon as he threw open the tavern door; here, as among the Cauldron, many knew his name and reputation. But here the starving artists of the city celebrated, those too young, too unknown, or too untalented to gain entry to the private club. The floors were filthy, the furniture cheap and tattered, but the drinks were powerful and the company equally amiable. He would find as much ease with these rapscallions as he had with those geniuses, perhaps more, for there were women here, and many an agreeable wench among them.

Battista grabbed but one slug of brandy from a dear friend, whose name eluded him, before searching among the women for the perfect one.

"Well, how fine it is to see you, Battista," she purred at him from behind, running her fingertips up his back from waist to shoulder, sending him shivering with delight.

He reeled round, recognizing the voice. "There you are, Nerina. I was looking for you."

"You were?" The woman slipped languidly into his arms, the small puffed sleeves of her low-cut gown slipping from her shoulders, revealing smooth, creamy skin from her neck to the low, round curves of her breasts, the flesh nuzzling against him.

Battista studied the woman pressed against him, the chestnut hair, the large green eyes—yes, this was the woman he came to find. Wasn't she? He shook his head, shaking loose his already-muddled thoughts.

"Is this the woman I saw you with at the festival, della Palla?" The greasy voice cleaved through his head.

Battista pulled Nerina to his right as he jerked to his left and the repugnant visage of Baldassare del Milanese.

"You dare speak to me, you son of a dog." Battista shook with fury. "How dare you look at me after what you have done?"

Baldassare smiled, black gums and yellow teeth revealed with an ugly fleer. "What have I done, you fool? I am an innocent man."

"You lie through your throat!" Battista screamed, flinging the most condemning insult at the man, lunging at him, their confrontation taking center stage amidst the tavern rabble.

"Bastard!" Baldassare countered, any feigned amusement lost at the slap of the slur, shoving Battista with his dirty hands.

"Liar!" Battista shoved back.

The fist connected with his face before he could move, reactions slowed by the glut of alcohol in his blood. Battista plummeted to the floor, the bitter taste of blood filling his mouth.

But Baldassare failed to grasp how many men Battista called friend, how many rushed to his defense, throwing Baldassare and his men to the street, a few following to ensure their retreat with a well-pitched and colorful slur.

Nerina fell to the floor beside Battista, gathering the grimy hem of her gown and holding it to his bleeding lip.

"Are you all right?"

Battista nodded, rising up unsteadily, pulling her with him.

"Many thanks, *mei amici*," he called to the room and the men who had defended him so swiftly. "A round for them all, on me!" he cried to the tavern-keep, and the room thundered with cheers of approval.

She led him away then, without argument or resistance, to her room at the top of the rickety stairs, where he pounded away his confusion in her arms, his fears and trepidations forgotten in the release.

He gasped and flung himself up, chest heaving with labored breath, head soaked with sweat. In his alcohol-induced sleep, in his sexually sated repose, the dream had come upon him . . . Aurelia's words congealing with those of Rustici . . . and he knew. He knew where to find Purgatory.

Jumping up, he jostled the sleeping woman beside him, having forgotten her presence, if truth be told.

"Battista," she complained without opening her eyes, naked back revealed to the upper curve of her buttocks, chaotic tangle of hair fluttered across the coarse bed linens. "What are you doing? Come back to bed. I am not done with you yet."

He laughed, but with no intention of conceding to the lewd invitation. He threw his wrinkled linen shirt over his head, threw his arms into his jerkin, and grabbed his breeches, stockings, and boots. Bending over the bed, uncovered derriere sticking out from beneath the hem of his shirt, he bussed her smartly upon the head. "Many, many thanks, *cara mia*."

Her muttered protests left behind, Battista ran from the room and down the stairs, heedless to the stares and laughter greeting him from those breaking their fast in the tavern.

He waved happily at them, skipping out of the building, hopping on one foot as he shoved the other in a leg of his breeches, tumbling out into the street where the morning coolness cleansed his skin and swept away any jumble remaining in his head. He had a mind to keep his hose off—to feel the invigorating air on his genitals all the way home—if only it would not have landed him in jail. Such was his happiness, such was his eagerness to tell them of his discovery.

Battista ran so fast, though he wangled his behind into his drawers, he cared not a whit about his stockings and boots, throwing them upon the floor the instant he threw open his blue door.

Her first thoughts, when Battista burst in the door, were prayers of thanks, gratitude to the forces of the universe that had brought him back safely. Aurelia's second thought was of the blood staining the front of his shirt, visible through the untoggled jerkin.

"Are you all right?" She rushed to his side, forgetting all else, in her fear for his well-being.

Battista grabbed her at the waist and twirled her around, and she yipped with surprise.

Frado came running, as did Nuntio, alerted by her cry, though neither seemed surprised to find Battista just now returning.

"My friends, my friends, we must celebrate," Battista sang.

"I think you have been celebrating for a very long time," Frado sniggered, and Nuntio nodded with amused agreement.

"*Sì, sì.*" Battista laughed, pulling Frado into his embrace.

"Your lip, Battista." Aurelia pulled away long enough to dunk a cloth into the pail of water by the fire, dabbing his split lip gently.

"It's nothing." He allowed her ministrations. "Baldassare's fist."

"Baldassare? What?" Frado thundered.

"He fared far worse, I assure you," Battista said. "But forget it, forget him. I know! I know!" he sang once more, this time dancing, forming a circle to include Nuntio in his silly jig.

"You know what, *messere?*" The older man laughed, struggling to keep up.

"I know where Purgatory lies."

They froze, all three of them, staring at Battista with mouths agape and eyes gone round.

"You do?" Aurelia gasped, hand to her heart.

Battista danced without them, swirling through the room to the back doors, throwing them open to the sun and air. "The mountains of Ciociaria, in the grottos."

Aurelia knew nothing of the place, but she saw the light bursting in Battista's eyes, the brilliance of his conviction. Relief made her bold and she launched herself back into Battista's embrace, prancing about with him. This time her hand pulled at Frado. She laughed at Battista's unvarnished joy and the true abandon of it, so relieved to see it after his days of dark moods, so thrilled to know where to find the next piece of the triptych. She had never behaved with such elated unrestraint; she became addicted to the freedom of it in that instant, the child who was never allowed to play had learned how.

Frado laughed despite his best efforts. "And how did you make this discovery?"

Battista finally slowed then, telling them some of his night, the time spent with the Cauldron, the words of Rustici.

"You were with Michelangelo?" Aurelia blurted out, unable to help herself. She heard little after the mention of the artist's name. But Battista ignored her interruption to finish his story.

Frado nodded, grin stretching wider. "It makes a great deal of sense."

"Doesn't it?" Battista trilled, wrapping one arm around his friend, the other around Aurelia.

Frado scrunched his nose and pushed Battista away. "You need a bath, you buffoon." He laughed. "Hot water, Nuntio, and lots of it. He reeks of wine and women."

Aurelia's feet faltered, her smile fading. She had smelled the strangeness, but attributed it to too much drink, blood, and a night without sleep.

Of course he had been with a woman. He was a beautiful,

young, healthy man. Where else would he have spent the night? Disappointment keen for all the logic of the thought, but she had no right to it.

She thrust it aside, as much as she could, smiling again with the joy of Battista's return and his breakthrough, if perhaps not as brightly as before.

❧ Eighteen ❧

The wisest are the most annoyed at the loss of time.

—Purgatorio

The maps covered the small table before him, the star charts as well, but the images swam beneath his dry-eyed gaze, the roads snaking across the parchment, the stars no more than blurred blotches. Battista rubbed his stubble-covered face as if to chafe clarity into his befuddled mind; his tongue felt covered with dirt and the ache in his head swelled with each passing moment.

He had bathed, slept, eaten, and slept some more, but still had not recovered from the residual effects of so many libations, too much rich food, a fist to the face, and a nightlong ride on a willing and energetic partner. Battista leaned his heavy head upon the tall back of his favorite chair, allowing the study's afternoon shadows to wrap him in their comfort, and smiled. How long the pangs of his debauchery would plague him he didn't know, but it had all been worth it; from the dregs of his cups had come the answer.

The more he studied the *Commedia,* the Duccio, and the chart depicting the three-starred Pyxis, the more logical his discovery became. Pyxis, Latin for "compass," its name, by definition, delineated it as a guidepost. He charted the route upon a map; it would be an arduous journey to the grottos, requiring a minimum of two days and many long hours in the saddle. He could not be sure of the availability of inns along the path or if they would need to bed down upon the ground.

Battista didn't doubt for a moment that Aurelia was up to the task; nothing she did or accomplished would surprise him. Of all he felt for her, grudging respect ranked high upon the list. If only he could cleanse himself of his suspicions, if only he could surrender unconditionally to the bond they had formed when in the grip of Hell. The connection was unlike any other he had ever experienced, not even with his own dear mother, or the men he called family.

His eyes drooped, each blink lengthening, the lids moving slower and slower. Her enigmatic eyes rose up before him, the genteel face disguising the cunning and capable paradox of her, his recollections so clear it was as if she stood before him.

When the light stirred behind the spotty glow of his lids, when he opened them against his own soundless protests, it was not her image, but Aurelia herself, veil in place, dressed in her simplest gown, heading for the door and quickly out of it.

"Oh no," Battista grumbled, rushing to his feet as fast as his pounding head allowed. "Not again."

"Aurelia, wait!" he cried as he flung himself from the door, groaning as the bright sunlight stabbed his eyes, closing one, then the other against the agony. "Aurelia!"

She turned round quickly, but he could not tell if fear darkened her pale features or alarm.

"Are you all right?" Aurelia rushed back, reaching out to take his hands.

Battista swallowed hard against her sympathetic supplication. He wished he could lock up his meddlesome thoughts with one of his fancy locks and make no attempt to pick it.

"Where are you off to?" He raked his straight black hair off his face, only to have it fall again as he lowered his gaze; he could open both eyes, but only if he shielded them with a bowed brow.

"I . . . I-I-I am . . . ," she stammered, pursing her lips. "Is that why you stopped me? There is nothing amiss?"

"No, nothing." He straightened his shoulders in a gruff gesture of righteousness. "I was concerned for you to be out and about by yourself."

Her mouth formed a thin white line across her face. "I am to the *sartoria* if you must know. If we are to go about searching through caves, I must attire myself appropriately."

"I see. And how are you to pay for such clothes?"

Her face burned with anger; it festered clearly through her heavy veil.

In silent thunder, she opened the small drawstring purse hanging about her wrist and joggled it over her other palm. As the small incandescent pearls tumbled into her hand, Aurelia bit at him with a snapping glare.

"They did me little good upon my veil." She tipped her head sideways so he could see her headdress; the thick strands of her hairnet, the color of summer's oak leaves, no longer bore the pearl punctuations at each intersection.

"Ah, of course. You make the most—"

"May I be on my way?"

Battista cleared his throat against her antagonism. He forced a smile and responded with cheer, raising a crooked arm. "It will be my pleasure to escort you."

She looked at his appendage dubiously, but took it nonetheless. He had peeved her with his suspicions, it pained him in the stiff grip she had on his arm. Would a guilty person feel such anger? He didn't think so, but for a man who stooped to thievery with great frequency, he knew little of dishonesty.

"I do not think our next task will be as . . . as warm as our last." He offered what he hoped would be an amusing reflection.

Aurelia bit her top lip, constraining the smile elicited by the sardonic suggestion. "Agreed. But it may present other challenges. The souls of Dante's Purgatory struggle for salvation. It is the greatest torment of human existence . . . that most like the state of life, always struggling for something better."

"But it is a struggle for peace, and goodness," Battista argued. "Don't you think?"

Aurelia dipped her head with a quick nod. "*Sì,* but it is an unnecessary one if they had lived within goodness to begin with."

Battista frowned. "Such a condemnation, Aurelia. You do not think much of your fellow man."

"If it is a condemnation, I do not spare myself with its sharpness."

She looked away and he lost what her eyes might tell him, the sadness in her voice undeniable. He covered her hand with his free one and gave it a squeeze, touched by her melancholy.

"We will have many a decision to make, I believe," she continued, turning back, her hand relaxing in his embrace. "It is what sends a soul to Purgatory in the first place, the decisions they make along the journey of their life."

He jostled her shoulder with his in an amiable gesture. "You have been studying Dante well."

Her gaze pierced him. "I promised you I would have insight to this journey, and I meant it."

Battista wondered how he could doubt her with such a proclamation.

"Ah, here we are." He turned from his confusion, pointing to the large wooden scissors hanging above an opened door. "This clothier is trustworthy and reasonable. I'm sure we will find you what you need here."

They stepped together into the busy shop, deluged by the earthy scent of raw fabrics and the visual brilliance of an array of colors. A chattering group of women bustled over bolts of material, the pale pinks and yellows of spring, light silks and cottons for the warm months to come.

"Mario!" Battista called a fond greeting to the merchant hurrying toward them with a callused hand outstretched, a wide smile beneath the thick and bushy gray mustache. "*Come stai?*"

"Battista della Palla. I am well, my friend, and you? It has been far too long since I have seen you in my shop. It's about time you purchased new hose. That leather must chafe you terribly in this heat. Come, come this way, I have a fine pair of thin suede that will fit—"

"Hold, my dear fellow." Battista laughed, barely halting the excited man and his effusive greeting. "I have not come for myself, but for the lady. Pray you make your greeting to Madonna Aurelia."

The man's mouth formed an almost perfect O as his gaze fell upon Aurelia.

Folding her veil back, she bobbed the proprietor a most graceful curtsy.

"I beg your pardon, my lady." With a flourishing hand, Mario gave her a fine leg. "I am at your service, of course. What may I get for you this fair day?"

Aurelia smiled at the elegance of this simple merchant. "I need a pair of sturdy boots, signore, if you please. Ready-made, if available."

"Of course, of course. Right this way."

He led them past the group of women, each one offering Battista a flirtatious smile, even those old enough to be his mother, along the shelves on the right-hand wall, until he reached a small cubby. With a flourishing hand, he invited them into a U-shaped grouping of shelves covered with shoes and boots of all shapes and sizes, pungent with the strong aroma of leather.

"Ah, here we are, just what I had in mind." Reaching out, Mario picked up a pair of ankle boots, the smooth, light footwear a dainty confection of kid leather and lace, slim heels and large bows. "These will look lovely on a beauty such as you."

Aurelia shared a look with Battista; in her face he saw his own silly grin, the same twinkle at the absurd in her eyes.

"They are beautiful indeed, signore," she told the man with gracious respect. "But I really did hope for something much sturdier. Something not unlike Battista's, in fact."

The two fuzzy gray caterpillars above the merchant's honey brown eyes merged together and his round head fell to one side.

"Like those?" He pointed at Battista's worn and manly footwear, voice rising to a squeak.

Aurelia nodded, a smile spreading across her flushed face.

Mario shook his head. "I am sorry, my lady. I have nothing such as those, made for a woman."

"Perhaps a pair of men's boots small enough to fit?" Battista suggested. Aurelia was not the daintiest woman he had ever met, as feminine as she may be. There were men with feet of a similar size, Michelangelo for one.

The merchant's eyes bulged, then sparked with ingenuity. "I believe I have just the thing." With a snap of his fingers, he took himself off, returning in seconds with a pair of supple black boots, laced to midcalf with rawhide, almost flat with but a sliver of a heel. "They are not the fanciest, I grant you. They were ordered by a foreigner passing through, a small man who never came to pick them up."

Aurelia reached for them eagerly, turning her back, discreetly removing one day slipper beneath the folds of her skirts, replacing the dainty shoe with the clunky boot. Jumping up, she stomped about with an off-kilter gait.

"They are perfect," she crowed brightly.

Mario shook his head, though not unpleased. "Then they are yours, *donna mia*. But you will need better stockings to wear beneath, something stronger." With an emphatic finger poking the air, the merchant set off on his search.

Aurelia walked a circle, lifting her skirts just an inch, so the boot showed on one foot while her slashed and bowed slipper showed on the other; in their dichotomy Battista thought he glimpsed her truth.

"I have always wondered what it felt like to walk in men's shoes." She laughed as she sat back down. "I wonder if I will belch more and think less."

She intended her words purely to tease, but Battista did not find it funny, perhaps because he saw some legitimacy in the jest.

Reaching down to unlace the boot, she raised her merry gaze. "What if I begin to lus—"

Her stare stuck, frozen on the open door and the street behind him. Her mouth fell open, her face blanched. Battista's hand jumped to the small scabbard at his back.

"What is it?" he hissed, turning slowly, not knowing what threat might lie behind him.

Aurelia swiveled in her chair, face to the back of the store. "Gonzaga's soldiers . . . t . . . two of them."

Many a man passed the open portal, but Battista saw two—two opulently dressed with a hint of the military about the black leather jerkins and swords dangling from their sides—men who scoured the streets and the buildings, decidedly looking for something, or someone.

Battista needed to see no more. Yanking Aurelia's arm, he pulled her up, just as she grabbed the one slipper and one boot not on her feet, crushing them to her chest with one hand as she lifted her skirts with the other.

They hurried through the store, hastening toward the curtain separating the main salon from the private back rooms. With a flick of a raised hand, Battista lowered Aurelia's veil back in place. Rushing past a startled Mario, Battista ripped a small drawstring pouch from his belt and tossed it to him, a great jangling erupting as Mario caught it.

"For the boots, *amico mio,*" Battista said, ignoring the merchant's confounded regard. "And for two pairs of those hose you spoke of. One for me and another, much smaller, for her." He jerked his head toward Aurelia as he snuck a look out the door in the distance, just in time to see the two men pass beyond it.

"For . . . what?!" Mario yawped, holding the purse before his confused gaze.

"But we must have them by the end of tomorrow, *sì?*"

Mario's head swiveled as his gaze followed them to the curtain. "I . . . uh . . ."

"Can you do it?" Battista hesitated for the quickest of moments, Aurelia already beyond the camouflage of the heavy maroon screen.

"Yes. Yes, of course." Mario shrugged, almost helplessly.

Battista cast him a quick grin and nod. "Good man."

Stepping swiftly through the split in the curtain, Battista followed Aurelia as she rushed through the narrow space—part kitchen, part storage—a quick glance at the plump woman stirring a pot poised over a small center grate.

"Smells wonderful." Battista smiled at her as he and Aurelia plunged toward the back door.

The woman gawked at them in stunned silence as they pushed open the portal and rushed out.

In the narrow back alley, Aurelia stepped back, giving Battista the lead.

With the confidence of a lifelong resident, he led her through the dirt-packed side streets of the city, the narrow ribbons of pathways lined with modest two- and three-storied brick homes, no glass in the windows, lines of dripping laundry strung over their heads like colorful banners decorating a noble procession.

"No more, Aurelia. No more wandering out and about." He tossed the demand over his shoulder, no need to slow to berate her. "Are we not challenged enough? Now we must contend with the men of Mantua?"

"I know, I know," Aurelia replied breathlessly, brooking no argument. "I did tell you he would search for me."

He tossed her a scathing sidelong glare. "Which would not warrant such urgency were you to stay indoors."

Aurelia rolled her eyes, tight jaw buckling beneath flushed, moist skin. "I know, I know," she repeated impatiently. "One need not hammer a nail already buried in the wall."

Nineteen

In the middle of the journey of our life
I came to myself within a dark wood
where the straight way was lost.

—*Inferno*

Aurelia felt scandalous in her boots, hose, and stockings, though she wore all beneath her sturdy riding gown. She cared little if the wind rose up and tossed those skirts about, if the male apparel peeked out. The sun beat upon their heads with a scorching heat and she had forsaken her veil as the road led them through the forest and unpopulated fields in the journey south from Florence. Like her skirts, her hair flapped out behind her, whipping up with each bouncing gallop, the breeze cool and invigorating on her sweat-soaked neck. Her mouth grew dry, but she could not close it to the pummeling air, her smile unrelenting; here, at last, she basked in the unrestrained freedom she craved.

Not long after they had passed beneath Florence's city gate, where the strong gray blocks of *pietra forte* gave way to hard-packed earth, Battista had led them easterly rather than true south, galloping off the wide Via Cassia and onto a narrower, less used road. As they moved closer to the curving mountain range slicing the peninsula in two, Aurelia had not asked for an explanation, for one was not necessary; who knew what manner of beasts may follow them, they could take no chance continuing on upon the main thoroughfare.

The logic of it did nothing to dampen her disappointment; their trek allowed only glimpses of the resplendent villages they passed from a distance. This urban land boasted many lovely towns; cresting any given hill, a traveler may see more than a few upon the horizon, their encircling walls marking the boundaries, their bell towers providing a compass point to guide them onward. Nor was the architecture confined to the rolling meadows and low flatlands; imposing mountains were terraced almost to their summits, the pale stone villas as natural a part of their façades as the gray-green olive trees and the umbrella-like *pineta* filling the air with their piney redolence.

As the sun hovered near the horizon, its heat casting a vivid magenta and tangerine hue over all it touched, she pulled back on the reins, lifting herself from the saddle, peering with ingenuous awe at the mammoth city rising out of the distant plane to the west. Did she spy the walls surrounding the Vatican or perhaps the Pantheon? Could those pillars thrusting up from the ground be the columns of the Forum? She hoped they were, dared to by her desire to see such sights.

"I'm sorry, Aurelia." Battista's voice came from her side; her disappointment apparent even through the dappled light filtering through the trees.

"Perhaps, if we . . ." He shook his head. "Someday, perhaps, I may show you the great city. But not now."

Aurelia lifted one corner of her seamed mouth; it was a hope she would wish for then, if he were to offer it again, pleased he spoke to her in a kindly manner. They had not exchanged many words over the last few days, over the course of the hard travel of the day, and when he did speak she heard again a hard edge, though if it was anger, mistrust, or impatience she did not know him well enough to determine. Their relationship had somehow fallen into disrepair, obstacles rose between them as surely as the mountains stood between the coasts, and she knew not how to bridge the divide. But she would not waste any moments on what was done, living only in each one offered her, immersed in the adventure and her goals.

Battista turned, looking at Frado slumped in his saddle with commiseration. They had been on the road since early morning, and the older man faltered beneath the weariness they all shared.

"I think it best we make camp for the night," Battista said, slowing to a trot, waiting for his friend to catch up.

"Are you sure?" Aurelia pulled up as well, though not eagerly. "Will we still reach the grottos by tomorrow if we do?"

He turned a flat, dark gaze upon her, the coolness of gloaming back in his demeanor. "We are more than halfway there. As long as we set off at first light, we will arrive soon after midday."

His assessment proved accurate, if conservative, and as the sun reached its apex on the following day, their horses struggled to climb the foothills of the Ausoni Mountains, hooves slipping on the loose rock of the craggy passage. They leaned as far forward in their saddles as possible, heads almost butting with those of their straining mounts.

"We'll have to walk," Battista called out as he quit his steed.

Only too keen to follow suit, Aurelia dropped from her saddle. Rubbing her fine stallion's sweat-drenched mane, she leaned her forehead against him as she would any other beloved friend. "You have worked hard, my dear," she whispered, and the horse whinnied softly with a toss of his head.

"Walk?" Frado whined. "How far must we walk?"

It was a good question, one without an answer. Battista raised his head, hand to his forehead to shield his eyes from the glaring sun, gaze following the path as it thinned and scaled the formation of rock and earth above them, where it blazed a brown swath through the low scrubby green vegetation. He insisted the cave they sought lay in this karst region with an innate certainty, but where the entrance may lie he could not say.

"We must go up just a bit further, to that plateau. See it there?"

He pointed to a ledge not far in the distance, and though a majestic mountain rose up beyond it, it was difficult to see what lay between. "I think we will be able to get a lay of the land from that vantage point."

Frado toppled from his mount with a clumsy thud, grunting and mumbling his curse-strewn dissatisfaction.

"We will take our midday repast from there as well," Battista tossed back as he crested the ridge. The mention of food and wine would lessen the pain of exertion. Predictably, Frado's grumbling subsided though he continued to move at a sluggish pace.

"Dio mio!"

Aurelia hesitated at Battista's stunned utterance, moving faster when she moved again. "What is it, Battista? What is wrong?"

It took but a short sprint up the path and she stood beside him, sucking in her breath with an audible gasp, hand to her heart.

They stood on the rim of a circular basin; below them, sheltered in the arms of the curved stone valley, lay a hidden paradise.

Curvilinear formations of rock and vegetation sat around and among shallow pools of water, the surface so still and clear, perfect images of the curvaceous arrangements were duplicated in the reflections, their beauty multiplied again and again, an unending oasis of cream rock, green growth, and azure sky.

"When I see such things, I see the hand of God," Battista murmured reverently.

Aurelia turned a tender gaze on the man beside her; she had never seen him attend church, yet he wore his faith with the same ease as his leather jerkin, and with equal relish. His was a spiritual soul, and she silently celebrated such theology.

"Life's true beauty is often concealed where the eye cannot see it. It may be found only if one is open to it," Aurelia replied, turning back to the breathtaking panorama.

Frado reached them, panting, only to drop to his knees as his sight beheld the vista. They laughed together, Aurelia and Battista, at his unadulterated joy at the place they had found.

They fell silent, allowing the stillness to envelop them, offering themselves completely to it. Minutes passed uncounted, but without a care.

Battista broke the peace, with a gesturing finger and a soft declaration. "Look."

They followed his signal to a spot on the curve diagonally across from them. Though not readily detectable, a jut of rocks formed an arch over an outcropping of boulder. On top of the striated stone, a cap of spiky green fronds stuck out, like short hair hackled in fright. A rim of darkness stood out between the boulder and the formation just beyond it, but whether space existed between the arch and the outcropping it was hard to tell from this distance.

"It could be an entrance, to be sure," Aurelia said.

"Let's find out." With a cluck of his tongue and a tug on his reins, Battista pulled his horse forward, edging down the stony embankment.

"Do we dare enter this refuge? Are we worthy?" Frado whispered.

"I think we were meant to," Aurelia assured him, reaching out to squeeze the man's clasped hands, thinking without saying that the passage and this chasm could easily be symbolic of the anti-Purgatory, that which must be traversed first in Dante's poem.

The journey downward became ever more treacherous as they fought the pull of the earth, as they struggled to control their descent. Arriving safely if sweat-soaked, they splashed onto the plateau on the bottom, their horses dipping their mouths eagerly into the fresh, clean water. Bending at the knee, Battista, too, refreshed himself, bringing the water to his mouth with a cupped hand.

Aurelia kicked at it gently, sending gemlike droplets sparkling up into the sun, splashing her face with the cooling fluid. She wished she could shed all her clothes and baptize herself with the rejuvenating liquid. She settled for cleansing her face and hands and the back of her neck, shivering as a bead of water dribbled down the hollow of her spine.

Battista reached the outcropping first, tying the reins of his horse to a smaller but similar projectile beside it. Peering around one side, and then the other, Battista turned to them in displeasure.

"There is no more than a crack between," he said dejectedly.

Aurelia secured her horse and stepped to the stone monolith. It rose over her head at least ten men high and half as many wide. She squinted to see less distinctly but far more clearly.

"It is a robed man," she said, head tipped almost straight up on her long, thin neck.

Battista came to stand on one side of her, Frado on the other, each tipping his head back in a comparable posture.

"I see him," Battista said, voice strangled by the awkward position.

The craggy lines upon the rock face drew an abstract but interpretive form of a bearded man, a long nose and deep-set eyes, his head tucked into the mantle of his robe falling in folds to the ground.

Battista lowered his head. " 'I threw myself devotedly at his holy feet, asking him to open out of mercy; but first I beat three times upon my breast.' "

Aurelia recognized the opening stanza of the *Commedia*'s second canticle, the beginning of *Purgatorio*. She held her breath as Battista knelt and, with a fisted right hand, beat upon his breast three times.

A black bird cawed overhead as a gust of wind swooshed around them, but the rock cropping did not move.

"Wait," Aurelia demanded. Lifting her skirts, she fell to her knees, and then to her stomach.

"What in Heaven are you doing?" Battista demanded.

"Dear lady, you'll hurt yourself," Frado insisted, then threw up his hands with a laugh, as if the absurdity of the situation suddenly dawned on him.

" 'From beneath the robe, he drew two keys.' " The words came out in muffled grunts, spoken into the moist stone beneath, one hand stretched out in front. With a happy yelp, her digits moved beyond the edge of the outcropping, disappearing into the tiniest crack between rock and ground. She squirmed forward, hand completely engulfed by the gap of stone.

She yanked her hand—now fisted—out and jumped to her feet with one swift, graceful move. Holding out her limb, she unfurled her fingers, quoting Dante once more, " 'The one was made of gold, the other of silver.' "

The men bombarded her, jostling her as they squeezed closer. On her scratched, gritty skin lay two strange pieces, one whitish and one yellow. Though clearly keys, they were more akin to dowels of metal, not carved nor bright, straight cylindrical shafts with unique indentations, the metal tarnished and worn.

"Do you think they are truly made of silver and gold?" Frado's hushed murmur spoke of value, not discovery, and Battista bumped the man's shoulder with his own, knocking Frado's attention back to the matter at hand.

"Well done, Aurelia," Battista praised, though grudgingly. "But where are the keyholes?"

They separated, each heading for a different part of the mammoth boulder, each searching—with eyes and hands—for indentations to accommodate the unique keys.

"Here, here. I've found it!" Frado cried, his thrill to be an active part of the quest ringing in his high-pitched squeal. With a squelch of shallow water beneath his boots, he ran to Aurelia, swiped the keys from her hands, and returned to the left side of the boulder. Patting the stone surface, finding the two small barrel holes, one sitting atop the other, he pinched the small yellow dowel between thumb and forefinger and raised it up.

"Stop!" Aurelia and Battista cried together, rushing toward him, Battista passing her with his long-legged stride.

Frado froze, hand poised in the air, face awash with fright.

"You must put the other in first." Battista reached him, placing a calming hand on his startled friend's shoulder.

" 'First with the white, then with the yellow, he plied the gate so as to satisfy me,' " Aurelia quoted the instructions.

Frado heaved a cleansing breath, switched the devices in his hand, and raised them once more. He gently pushed one in and then the other, turning first to the right without yield and then to the left, where the small pins slipped and then receded, as if pulled by someone, or something, on the opposite side.

"They c—"

With a thunderlike boom and a grinding of stone, the monstrous boulder shuddered and fell to the right, creating a gap no more than a foot wide, broad enough for Battista to slip through sideways.

The stone dust fell upon them, fluffy as snow, the motes dancing in the sun's bright glare.

With wide-eyed eagerness and the hint of a grin, Battista leaned toward the opening, slipping one foot and one shoulder into the space.

"No, not yet!" Frado pulled him back, grabbing and tugging his friend's arm. "You have not eaten a thing since early morning and only God knows how long you may be in . . . there. I insist you eat, rest, and drink before embarking on this journey." He stood with arms akimbo, mouth set tight and firm.

Aurelia lowered her head, hiding the smile born of the endearing man's attempt at fierceness.

"You make fine sense," Battista replied, and slithered back out of the crevice.

As they each took a place atop some flat, moss-covered rocks, passing the wine-filled goatskins and strips of dried meat, Aurelia leaned her back against the chasm wall, eyes raised heavenward as if in prayer, feeling at the same time small in the face of such splendor and large as a part of such a creation.

"I think you may safely give us more than the usual two hours." Battista chuckled around a cheekful of food. "But I would give it no more than a rise and a set of the sun."

"Oh no." Frado shook his head, bald pate uncovered and shiny in the sun. "No, no, no. I will not leave you. This is not the same. This is not someone's home. I wi—"

"Frado, you—," Battista tried to argue, to no avail.

Frado sliced at Battista's words with a pointed finger and a narrow-eyed glare. "I will come looking for you, should you not return."

Battista sighed, tipped his head to the side, and smiled. "You are correct, *amico mio,* this is not a palazzo I am set to plunder. . . ."

Aurelia lifted her head, raising a cynical brow.

"Poor choice of words." Battista shrugged, having the grace to look sheepish. "This is not a guarded palace that may find me captured, but a cavern of unknown depths. Nor am I alone. Surely you have a care for Aurelia's well-being?"

Frado curled a lip at him, at the unfairness of using a woman—one for whom he felt a fondness—as a bargaining chip.

"If we do not return by this time tomorrow," Battista continued unashamed, "you must make your way to Rome. Find Vispasiano di Polisena. He will have the tools and the men . . . should you need them."

Battista's gaze found hers and all manner of animosity seemed set aside. They had seen Hell together, true, but as too much knowledge did at times, it brought only more fear. She watched as his dark gaze rose from the narrow opening in the cliff side to the mountain of rock towering above it; no one could survive the weight of it, no matter how many men and how many tools tried to lift it away.

She lifted a shoulder a smidgen, one side of her mouth curling, a gesture of cautionary acceptance. He cast her doubts aside with his smile, slapped his hands upon his thighs, pushing himself up, and offered her a hand.

"Are you ready, Aurelia?"

She gave no answer—who could be ready for such an expedition?—but took his hand and stood. Packing a few extra pieces of food in his pack and slinging a skin of watered wine around his shoulders, Battista led her away.

With Frado hard on their heels, they approached the portal. Turning sideways, pulling in his breath, Battista slipped through. With her small frame, Aurelia turned only slightly askew to fit through the space.

They stopped but a few feet into the cave, each taking a bearing on the mammoth structure in which they found themselves.

The late day's light streaming through the crevice shifted and Aurelia turned back, almost laughing as Frado stuck only his head in to see them away. Any hint of laughter died in her throat at the man's confused gaze; something bothered him, but his befuddled expression put no name to it. She looked down at herself, where his gaze led hers, finding a blaze of light suffusing her whole body with its brilliance.

Aurelia sprinted forward, jumping into Battista's shadow.

"This way, Battista." Tugging on the sleeve of his jerkin, she led his gaze in the opposite direction.

The entrance hall of the cave was as large and vast as a great cathedral, one filled with boulders and fist-sized stones gathered in haphazard piles, their composition of mostly pale gray and watered red. A large and fast-flowing stream rushed through the center, its trickle echoing in the emptiness. More like a chamber than a cave, there was a complete absence of any of the concretions normally found in a grotto.

No more than a few steps inward and the path diverged, trails formed by nature itself. One branch followed the rushing water, veered to the left and down into darkness. The other headed up, toward a golden glow.

"*Sì*, upward to the light, as all those passing through Purgatory desire," Battista agreed.

The path rose round the circumference of the cave at a constant angle, the gradient never increasing or decreasing. And yet its tedium—igniting fear of endemic infinity—fatigued them. Here and there a recessed opening revealed a graying sky; on the opposite side the golden light of dusk set the cave aglow, so close to the outside of the mountain did they travel.

As they passed one such opening, high upon the wall, Battista stopped beneath it.

"Look, Aurelia, the Pyxis." Battista pointed at the cluster of stars hovering over the mountain, just as the painting had shown. "It hangs in the northeast sky. If we see it again, we may keep our bearings."

Aurelia agreed with a halfhearted nod, turning back to the path before them. The pale drawings upon the walls had started just a few paces back, and she ran her hand along the bumpy stone surface, gently rubbing off dirt to see them better. Seeing her motion and the glyphs uncovered, Battista pulled a small handled brush from the pouch at his back, sweeping the dirt of untold years away from the crude sketches.

If they feared that—as in Hell—the tortured souls depicted would appear to spring to life and give chase with the illusion, the fear subsided as their stories became clear. Death came calling in each of the three scenes, the harbinger of the hereafter brought forth by a different means. In one a soldier died upon the battlefield, in another an old man died upon his bed, and in the last a young man fell to a scarring illness. In every instance, the recently deceased reached upward, for the Paradise awaiting him, if he was worthy, in the heavens above.

"Will death come for us now?"

Aurelia spun round; Battista's angular face, ever more beautiful in the shadows cast by the eerie light, creased with worry.

"We can never know when our ultimate moment may come. We can only hope to be worthy of it," she replied.

Battista frowned at her as if her words meant to insult, not encourage as intended, but an explanation faltered on her tongue.

Just ahead of them, the passage narrowed, not only in width but also in height. From a wide barrel-vaulted passage, it shrunk to a single-file lane and finally to an almost-complete blockade. Her reflection at the ease of the ascension had come too soon, as she had known it would the moment the idea slipped through her mind. Aurelia regarded Battista's tall, lean physique with a sidelong study; neither of them would make it through the small opening, not even if she scurried on her belly.

"Ah, our first challenge," Battista said as if reading her thoughts.

"Not a challenge," Aurelia grumbled. "An impasse."

They reached the barricade just as the path tried to turn once more to the left. It was not a pile of stone, but a wall; the opening was not a hole, but a fissure, no more than a missing tooth in the mouth of the wall.

Aurelia stepped to it, hands running along the sharp, hard surface, fingers searching for some sort of latch or perhaps another keyhole. Finding nothing, she banged on the stone, a desultory attempt; her physical strength could not overcome such a surface.

"Are we stymied?" She turned to Battista, surprised to find him standing quite still, face contorted in deep thought.

"No." His head waggled slowly, changing direction, becoming an enthusiastic nod. "No, we are not done yet, *donna mia,* not at all. We must bow."

"Bow?"

"Yes, bow. Did you not see the rendering of Satan falling from Heaven?" he asked, referring to the last drawing they had passed. "What brought his fall?"

Aurelia tilted her head. "Pride?"

He gave her that smile then, the one so striking, so intimate, and she lost thought for a moment, swimming in the sight of him.

"Our humility must bend us to the sin of pride." He stepped forward, voice full of more than just explanation, but of genuine repentance. Looking down and around, he pointed to the floor.

Aurelia saw it, too, an outline of a basic rectangular shape, carved shallowly into the stone floor directly in front of the fissure.

Stepping to the rim of the stone square, they clasped hands, kneeling upon the slab as they bowed.

The instant their weight shifted from their feet to their knees—shifting to the carved-out shape—it lurched beneath them.

Aurelia yelped in surprise; Battista reached out, hand flapping in the air, finding nothing to grab onto to keep them from plummeting downward.

With a rasp upon their knees, the slab struck bottom, having fallen no more than a few feet. No longer did an impassable wall tower in front of them; what had been little more than a fissure had become a triangular crawl space, its existence revealed by their plunge upon the stone.

Battista bent low, staring through the opening. "There is another chamber but a few paces away," he told her, inching forward. "Our next stop, though it seems far too easy."

"We are only just beginning," she reminded him as she watched him fall to his hands and knees and inch forward, as she did, following his waggling posterior.

It took a few short minutes to traverse the crawl space; Battista stood on the other side, reaching out a hand to help her to her feet.

Brushing off the dirt from her skirts, she raised her gaze, breath snatched from her lungs. Sparing a furtive look at Battista, she found him in an equal state of awe.

The enormous cavern opening out from the point of entry defied imagination.

"It is a sculpture," Battista breathed. "As fine as any by the hand of Michelangelo or Rustici."

With the wonder of an ant looking up to a flower, Aurelia stared enthralled at the formation above their heads. "It looks like a willow tree."

Battista laughed with unabashed delight. "It does, doesn't it?"

Long, lean projectiles of a pale clay-colored stone hung from the unbearably high ceiling, as if the protrusions were fluid and swayed from the stone overhead, some of the trickles so thin as to look feathery, fuzzy, like the fronds of a weeping willow.

"As if you could picnic beneath its branches," Aurelia envisaged fancifully.

"Where is that light coming from?" Battista pointed to the far left corner of the chamber and the circle of golden light illuminating it to near brilliance.

Aurelia followed the crepuscular stream of light upward, but that portion of the ceiling lay hidden behind the largest froth of protrusions. "There must be an ocular above."

Battista shook his head. "But it is dark out. The sun set some time ago."

With a shared grimace, they set out across the hall, the tinkling of tiny streams following along, the air whistling and moaning through the projectiles. They followed the course of the streams as they would the narrow streets of Florence, the light at least three lanes away. As they drew closer to its brilliance, they spied a huge form rising out of the ground, the rounded top no more than inches from the roof.

There was nothing illusory about the shape. The mammoth wings, the heavy robes, the halo carved above its head. The gigantic statue was an angel; in its two crossed hands, it held two swords, both aflame.

They circled around the base of the angel, the faithful at the feet of the deity. Just beyond the sphere of light, the ceiling lowered and curved, forming a plainly discernible but closed archway. In silent negation they agreed, neither perceived how to open it.

"Is that a lever?" Aurelia stepped behind the giant seraph, pointing straight up.

Battista came beside her; the stone pin sticking out from the angel's back looked like nothing if not a lever, for the trough it sat in ran down the figure for several feet, the opening and the dowel at a height just above Battista's reach, the bottom end of the furrow level with his knees.

"Let's give it a try, shall we?" With a gentle tug on her arm, he pulled her back, out of harm's way. Eyeing the lever, he spat on his hands, rubbed them together, bent his knees, and jumped.

He grabbed onto the stone bar, hung, all his weight upon it, and for a moment it moved not an inch. With a sudden grinding of stone, it plunged, taking Battista with it. At the same time, the angel's mammoth wings flapped, the breeze a brutal gust, buffeting and pushing Aurelia backward with its force.

The light grew dim, the whoosh of air threatening to douse the swords' flames.

Battista's feet touched ground once more, the lever not reaching the bottom of its gully. The wings stilled, and the flames grew full and bold again, the stench of burning oil thick in the air.

"To your knees, Battista." Aurelia braced herself against the wall. "Pull on it until you drop to your knees, pray for those in Purgatory."

"*Sì, sì*, yes, yes," Battista mumbled, nodding with understanding. With a flex of his arms and a stretch of his neck to either side, he sucked in his breath and launched his body once more. This time, as he gripped the lever, he lifted his calves, legs forming an L, allowing his weight to carry him, and the lever, all the way down, until his knees skimmed the hard floor.

The angel's wings flapped harder, the air a gale force. It hit the flaming swords, extinguishing the fire, setting the room into virtual darkness. Behind them, the stone door shuddered and fell away.

"Run!" Battista cried, jumping to his feet, reaching out behind him.

Aurelia pushed herself off the wall, barely regaining the breath knocked out by the driving thrust of the wind. She took his hand, a natural instinct, and they rushed together through the portal, both expecting it to close behind them at any instant.

Panting and wheezing in the next chamber, they stared—almost disappointed—as the egress remained clear. They laughed together at their unnecessary urgency.

She felt it then, as she thought he must, the reweaving of the bond they had formed in Hell; Aurelia saw it on his lovely face and she reached out. "I—"

Battista turned, stepping away and up the gradient path before them. She could see nothing but his back, nothing of the reason for his denial. With a pang of disappointment wedged in her heart, she followed.

It was a short climb to a perfectly square terrace, the most room-like chamber encountered since they had entered the grotto. Man, not nature, had formed this space, its walls distinct—smooth and straight—with two squares carved into the floor, a matching design chiseled upon them, the straight, even lines of a cross atop the curled pagan coil.

"We have no need to search for a door." Battista crossed the floor and stood before the clearly demarcated portal, one without latch or keyhole. "But how do we open it? You would think a painting would hang in a room such as this. It would look at home upon these walls."

Impatience sharpened his voice as his fingers traced the crack of a door.

"These two squares," Aurelia mused aloud. "Perhaps they are the key."

With a scowl, Battista joined her in the middle of the room between the carved tiles. He stepped on one, the resulting click loud in the tranquil chamber. Excited, Aurelia stepped on the other, and with a matching clack the door slid sideways, disappearing into the wall, revealing another climbing pathway on the other side.

Without discussion, they stepped off the tiles, heading for the door. The instant their weight lifted from the squares, the door shuddered to a close, Aurelia and Battista still many paces from the closed portal.

"We have to run for it," Aurelia said, heading back for the tile.

"We'll never make it," Battista groused.

Aurelia rolled her eyes and shoved her hands onto her hips. "What is yo—"

"Did you see these pots?" Battista ignored her, giving her no ground to continue.

There were indeed two terra-cotta pots, one in each corner flanking the door. A ribbon of design encircled each at its fattest point, a chain of the same motif found on each tile.

"I think if we place a pot on each spot, we will keep the door open."

Battista grabbed one as Aurelia did the other, placing them on the tiles simultaneously. But no click did they hear; the door budged not an inch.

"They're not heavy enough." Now it was her turn to sound petulant, but she no longer cared, and turned to the puzzle before them.

"Humph," she muttered from the back of her throat. Stepping to one pot, she removed the doubletlike jacket of her travel costume and the small chain she wore around her neck, and stuffed them in the pot's bottleneck. She added the small band of fine leather around her waist and . . . *click.*

Battista stepped to the other pot, pulling out a fine dagger from his pouch and an odd lock, a silver tool, and a small coin purse, and plunked them all in. The tile lowered but with no answering sound.

"Too much, you have given too much . . . you must take some back, for only with equal giving can another rejoice in the gift," Aurelia said, leaning over to peer into the containers. "Dante tells us, through Virgil, that the value of material possessions decreases with sharing while the value of spiritual possessions increases, but only if of a balanced nature, so that one does not feel beholden to the other."

She offered a profound commentary for their situation, its every ordonnance. Aurelia looked at him pointedly, surprised to find him staring back.

Without a word, he reached into the pot and drew out the dagger and the purse and returned them to his satchel. As the pot inched up, the click resonated and the door shimmied open.

Battista bowed with little gallantry in the gesture, and she stepped across the room and through the opening.

In this tight silence, they climbed once more, the path winding up and up, around and around. Dust, settled for years, kicked up in the air, covering them with a light coating of fine clay-colored particles. Infesting their throat and their nostrils, the smell and taste of dirt clogged their senses.

As they trudged onward, the path became muddled, infused with smoke as the passageway widened. Through the thickening haze, it appeared as if the trail split into three paths, but the air became too murky to see clearly. The higher they climbed the smokier it became, the vapors turning from white to gray to black. The miasma burned their throat and their eyes, tears poured down their faces.

"We must cover our eyes," Aurelia croaked. Reaching beneath her skirt, she pulled on the thin linen of her underchemise. With a grunt and a great tug, the entire skirt portion ripped from the seam at her waist. Grabbing each side of a seam, she pulled and tore it into strips, handing one to Battista, bunching the other over her own bloodshot eyes, and tying it behind her head, sighing with the relief.

"And how are we to see?" Battista asked with no mention of thanks as he blindfolded himself.

Grateful he couldn't see her, knowing the tale of her irritation was written plainly on her features, she told him, "It is not a time to see, but to know."

Reaching out blindly, she found his hand and pulled it to her.

"Put your hand on my shoulder. I will lead you."

"I see no—"

"Just do it, Battista! Trust me!"

Aurelia made the desperate plea in this moment and in the entirety of their shared experience.

He said naught; his large hand covered her shoulder, fingers closing firmly on her small bones.

Aurelia breathed deep, freed by his faith. In the infinity of sightlessness, she inhaled again, listening as the air entered her body, feeling her lungs expand with it. In the sound—in the sensations—she found the stillness she needed, and started forward.

She sensed his hesitation, reached up, and placed her free hand calmly upon his. His movement gained sureness and they advanced together. For a truly blind moment, her instinct faltered. Aurelia veered to the left.

Instantly a terrible anxiety possessed her; her stomach churned into knots, her head ached, and she shivered in a cold sweat. She turned away, straightening her course, and all fretfulness flittered away.

"We must keep going," she said, as much to herself as to Battista, and her throat burned as smoke entered her mouth and lungs. They had not passed the vapors and she walked on.

Without visual stimulation, the sounds of the cave grew ever more distinct. Amidst the trickles and dripping of water, within the swooshing of air through stone concretions, moans—like those of voices, both low and high—chanted rhythmically. Had these sounds been here all along? Had she and Battista refused to hear them in the name of self-preservation?

The mantra led them onward; Aurelia's instincts clung tenaciously to the keening. Time slowed in the darkness and yet her confidence grew. As the voices became louder, another sound joined in.

The whoosh of rushing water floated toward them on a fresh mineral scent. Aurelia and Battista drank it in in large draughts, cleansing the filth of the smoke from their bodies.

"Can we—"

"Just a short bit more," Aurelia answered, knowing what Battista longed for.

She directed them to the right, answering the insistence to put them snug against the rock wall they bumped into, and took several more paces forward. The dogged assertion that they stop and remove their eye coverings tore into her.

"Now, Battista," Aurelia told him, and pulled the strips of cloth from her eyes.

"Merda!"

Vista revealed, Battista cursed, splattering his body against the cold rock at his back.

The small tunnel had poured them out into an enormous cavern like the flow of wine through the long neck of a wide-bottomed bottle. They found themselves perched upon a slim path traversing the circumference of the chamber, hundreds of feet above the lake bottom. Across from them, a frothing waterfall fed the lake, the water so pure—moving so fast—it churned blue-white, a chill breeze drifting from the cool liquid.

As Aurelia surveyed the room, she put her hand upon her heart, closing her eyes once more in silent thanks. To their left, the two other paths ended abruptly, no path beyond the egress, nothing but a sheer drop to the bottom.

"I cannot believe we have climbed so high. The mountain did not look this large from the outside."

"Perhaps we have passed beyond any physical confines," Battista replied calmly.

Stepping around her, he took the lead once more. "I can see a hollow on the other side. It must be the way forward."

The path before them expanded wide enough to be easily negotiated, and the wall it hugged curved outward, allowing more sureness of step. They moved quickly in the absence of impediments.

Battista took the first step away from the tunnel and onto the suspended path and the entire mountain began to shake, as if the earth itself quaked.

"What now?" cried Battista.

"Hang on!" screamed Aurelia, pushing her body against the wall to their right for stability.

The simple path became a fatal obstacle course. They hurled themselves forward as the chamber shuddered around them, the tremors dislodging huge boulders from the cliffs above, sending the projectiles crashing down on the path around them.

Moving in fitful starts and stops, they jumped ahead of one rock, screeched to a halt before another. The propelling boulders pounded downward—crashes ringing in their ears—to splash into the lake below with a smash and a starburst of water.

"Back, Aurelia!" Battista screamed as another massive stone pelted down over the path before them, his body thrusting in reverse, one booted heel grinding into hers.

Aurelia jerked back in pain.

Battista rushed forward in the boulder's wake.

Four, maybe five feet separated them.

Aurelia, recovered, rushed to catch up.

The boulder passed her, just inches away, smashing onto the path, breaking off a chunk just as Aurelia made to step upon it.

She screamed as she fell, falling so quickly, she couldn't comprehend what happened to her body. As inertia pulled her downward, her hands flew up, and the grasp, when it came, jerked her to a stop, halting her descent and swinging her against the hard wall, knees scraping painfully upon the jagged stone.

"Your other hand, Aurelia!" Battista cried, teeth bared with exertion, broad shoulders leaning back to offset her weight at the end of his arm. He reached out his other arm. "Give me your other hand!"

With a push off the wall, she swung her dangling limb with all her might, and found him, hands clasping forearms.

With a growl of straining effort, Battista pulled as Aurelia found toe-sized footings, pushing upward with her legs and feet.

The edge scraped her face as it rushed by, dug into her gut, and tore against her legs. With a last yell, Battista pulled her over the edge, the impelling force carrying her forward against him, and they tumbled to the ledge, air whooshing from Battista's lungs as his back hit hard stone.

Aurelia held on to him—in the safety of his embrace—but they could not linger. The chamber continued to quake, the boulders continued to fall.

Jumping up, he pulled her to him like a sack of feathers. "Stay with me!" he cried.

She had no time to answer. He latched onto her hand and yanked. They ran again with erratic progress, heads bent, hurtling toward the dark orifice and the safety it teased them with.

Wheezing with exertion, they flung themselves into the dimly lit tunnel and stopped, breathless and safe . . . for the moment.

"You . . . saved . . . me," Aurelia puffed, doubled over, only her hands upon her knees keeping her from falling. "*Mille grazie, uomo buono.* You are indeed a good man."

Swigging deeply from the goatskin, he handed her the soft-sided flask, drawing closer as she drank. "I have never been so frightened as when I saw you falling."

The naked honesty in his voice pulled her up. Aurelia found the emotional truth in his eyes, but unlike the chasm, she knew not how to cross the space between them.

"Come." He slung the strap once more about a shoulder and began climbing yet another incline, another swirling path upward, Aurelia close on his heels.

"Hell may have been more dangerous, but this seems to be taking forever," Battista grumbled as they trudged along, impatient with the unbroken ascent. "It feels as if it will never end."

"No doubt the lost souls stranded in Purgatory feel the same," Aurelia replied, hoping to ease the burden with the contrast of a harsher reality.

His voice took on a hard edge. "I am sure your own soul will not be so tortured. You, by your own words, are free from sin."

Aurelia cut a look at his back, as if to see the puzzle of his words deciphered upon it. "I have never been free *to* sin." She laughed softly with a shrug. "If given the luxury of choice, would I have still chosen the righteous path? I don't know. The first real decision I have made on my own has been to come with you. My first taste of temptation and I have been lured away."

She stopped; her own thoughts created the hurdle she must overcome.

"What makes you think you made the wrong choice?" He held, heel grinding in the dust and dirt.

"I do not know if it is the *right* thing. I know only that it is what I wanted . . . to have an adventure, to be actively purposeful." Aurelia chuckled. "I suppose only time will tell if I have sinned in doing so."

"Perhaps the old woman you snuck away to visit in Florence warned you against me, against this quest."

His words hit Aurelia with the full force of his fury, knocking her into silence. She stared at him, at the truth of his ire finally revealed.

"You followed me?" she croaked, choking on anger.

"You kept secrets from me?" He jumped forward. Toe-to-toe they stood, his released anger splotching his ruddy skin.

"I . . . y-y-you . . ." Aurelia stammered.

Battista laughed a nasty guffaw, spinning back round and trouncing upward once more.

Aurelia followed, feet stomping like a child having a tantrum, hands fisted by her sides. She fought against the red-hot fury, willing herself to see the situation as he did. Why wouldn't he follow her? She had snuck from the house without telling anyone and had said nothing about her visit. She chewed on her top lip as she remembered the occasions she had denied knowing anyone in the city. He had a right to his anger, and an explanation.

"Battista, I . . . I . . . needed to ask after my guardian," she sputtered a confession of sorts, one given uneasily but with true remorse. "He had been unwell for some days before I left and . . . and I have a care for him. I owe him much."

Battista pivoted round, jaw flinching; he gave her a cold eye and pursed mouth.

"Do you love him?"

Her brows flew up her forehead; of all the responses she had imagined, she never expected this.

"No . . . I mean, yes. But it is the love of a brother, of a caregiver."

Battista's shoulders drooped, but he did not let it rest. "Why did you not tell me?"

She raised her face skyward, wagging it at her own foolishness. "I did not think you would approve. I feared you would think it too dangerous. I—"

He grabbed her by the shoulders and shook. "I trusted you with my life. I took you into my home, and you betrayed me with your secrets."

Aurelia pushed a hand against his chest, his condemnation only too real to be debated, though he did not know the depth of it. "I would do nothing to hurt you, Battista, ever." She gave him that truth willingly.

"I want to believe you." He lowered his puckered brow, his face stripped of anger, wreathed with vulnerability. But as she reached out, he drew away. "I long to believe you."

He resumed the climb, Aurelia quick on his heels.

"We are united by the desire to help our fellow man. You can be—"

But the words died on her tongue, dried up by a blast of scorching air that battered them as they reached another plateau.

Pushing against it, they turned right, following the path as it narrowed and flattened, as it opened into yet another cavernous room. But this one held them as none before had.

The room burned as if alive with flame; waves and waves of it burst up from the floor and out from the walls, a maze of fire. But at its end, perched somehow safely, a painting, though one too distant for them to tell for certain if it was a part of the triptych, yet how could it be anything else?

Their anger put aside, they stared at the blasts of flame, perspiration bursting on their skin, soaking their clothing. The explosions burst with jarring arrhythmia, only the most meager hint of a path carving its way through the fire.

Battista looked down at her with naught but concern. He held out his hand and she took it gladly.

With the same jerky motion that had brought them along the ledge, they leaped and bounded, held and reversed their way through the flames. Reaching the center of the room, they found a space devoid of all fire, so small an area, they could but stand with their backs pressed against each other, a hair's breadth from the snatching flames.

In the distant left, they had left the entrance behind; toward the right, the painting waited beyond the remainder of the maze. From this perspective, there was no denying it as part of the triptych. A quick glance revealed it as almost identical to the first, a mirror image of the two women, though the landscape behind them appeared different.

"It must be the left piece!" Battista shouted over the whoosh of the fires.

The truth of it washed over her with a wave of gratitude, and upon the emotion came a painful pinch of guilt.

"I'm sorry, Battista." She swung round.

"I think I see a pattern," he said at the same time, turning as well, their bodies pressed against each other once more, their faces no more than inches apart.

But instead of gracious forgiveness, Aurelia found his face contorted with alarm.

He plummeted to his knees, hands beating against her legs, at the flames feeding voraciously upon her skirts. Sparks flew in the air as his hands pummeled the disintegrating material. But the flames ate away the fabric like a ravenous beast, the heat reaching through to her skin, and she groaned in discomfort.

Battista reached back, drew out a dagger—the same dagger she had insisted he pull from the pot—and with savage but precise slashes cut the layers of her skirts away, thrusting the tattered, burning silk from them and into the path of flame. It caught completely, disappearing in seconds in a burst of spark and ash.

As he crouched at her feet, his stroking gaze climbed her lower body, all her curves revealed through the tight-fitting stockings and hose. He straightened slowly, intrusive stare rising with him.

Aurelia could not move, afraid of the penetrating glare and yet enthralled by it.

He met her gaze and broke away from it, not with anger but respect.

Aurelia wiped the sheen of sweat from her face, only to have the hand wrenched away.

"We must away from here. I can stand it no more."

Battista pulled her along, along the path and through the pattern amidst the flames he had somehow reconnoitered.

They reached the end of the maze, no more than a few feet from the painting, and just beyond it, a closed but obvious portal. The painting seemed to hover in the air, but in truth hung from the thinnest thread hooked to the stone ceiling hundreds of feet above their heads. On the floor between them and the door, another stone slab, one with the same pattern as before. But here there were no pots, nothing to put on the slab to keep it down and the door open.

Battista stepped forward, onto the slab. As expected, the door scraped open. He stepped backward, off the sunken stone. But instead of slamming shut, the door closed slowly, the edges inching together bit by bit. At the moment it closed, a belch of flame darted up from the ground at its threshold. With an almost-comical roll of his eyes tossed to Aurelia, Battista stepped on the stone and off it again, this time counting silently.

"We can make it," Aurelia said, knowing—with irrefutable certainty—they could.

He smiled at her, nodding. "Indeed, we can. But we will not do it without the painting." He stepped beside her and pointed. "You run to the right, while I will move to the left. I'll grab it on the run."

Aurelia swallowed, throat raw and dry. If he did not snatch it perfectly from its perch, if he moved no more than a hair in the wrong direction, the full force of the bursting flames could scorch both him and the painting.

Battista pushed the strands of sweat-saturated black hair from his face, neck muscles bulging as he breathed two deep cleansing draughts, and stepped onto the square. Aurelia stepped up beside him, just to the right, at an equal launching point.

They shared a look, one potent and full, and turned back, eyes forward on their goal and their exit.

"Go!" Battista shouted.

He stepped off the stone and they took off at a sprint.

Aurelia pumped her arms, her legs.

He outdistanced her, but he needed the time.

The door slithered downward.

With a warrior's cry, Battista leaped up at the painting, long arm, large hand, reaching out for the unframed but mounted painting. His hand grabbed it, his arm yanked, and the ropelike string snapped like a whip. Battista bounded back, impelled by the opposing force.

"Watch out!" Aurelia screamed, certain he would lose his footing, land on his body now off-kilter with his legs.

Battista growled, pitching his head forward, righting his balance with sheer force of will, landing on his feet, free arm windmilling for stability.

Ten feet away and the door crept lower still, a high window now half-closed.

Aurelia curled her body in anticipation; they would not make it through without ducking.

Battista crouched as he ran, back almost horizontal, head down, face pitched up to see.

Three feet away, the door tumbled to waist level. One more

gait, one taken blindly, Aurelia's head bowed, and she hurtled through, somehow unscathed.

Battista puffed with exertion no more than a step behind.

Aurelia wheeled round, now on the other side. He was too big; even compacted, he would never make it.

"No!" With an anguished cry, she threw out her arms, as if she could pull him through.

With an answering reach, Battista stretched out not only his arms but also his body, as if diving into water, thrusting the painting ahead of him as he hurled himself through the remaining narrow gap.

His body, a projectile, propelled into the space beyond the door, hitting Aurelia as if she were the target.

With startled cries and pain-filled moans, they tumbled together through a small cubby, along a rocky path, and out into the open air.

Twenty

Thence we came forth
to see again the stars.

—*Inferno*

"Are you—?" His voice rumbled into her, through his body lying prostrate at a cross angle atop hers.

"Yes, yes. You?"

"*Sì*," he panted. His body ached in more places than he could count, his lungs burned, and he could barely breathe for the stitch in his side. "Somehow, yes, all right."

"The painting?" Aurelia grunted at him, straining to talk beneath the weight of his body.

He rolled off, coming to rest on his back beside her, face turned to the star-brilliant sky and the moon above them. In silence, he raised his right arm sluggishly, fatigue protesting against every movement, and held the wood stretched canvas in the air.

Her body heaved with the sigh of relief.

The laughter bubbled in his belly, rising upward, refusing to be denied. It squelched in his throat till he could stand it no longer.

With the braying of a donkey, he burst into laughter, loud and raucous, of relief and the ridiculous.

Aurelia lifted herself up on her elbow and stared at him. Battista laughed all the harder at her astounded gape, a guffaw now out of control.

She answered then, only a giggle at first, but as she flopped once more onto her back it grew to a chortle and then to a riotous cackle, the high-pitched harmony to his baritone buffoonery.

They laughed until they grew weak—weaker—from it, until it exorcised all the pent-up stress and fear from their bodies, releasing it into the fathomless night and the twinkling stars.

"This is complete madness," he said; a cat's purr of laughter still textured his voice.

Aurelia gave a snort, but no argument.

"Life there could not be any stranger than this." He pointed at the crescent of moon in a caliginous purple sky, no less bright for its partial form.

She giggled again. "I had thought my existence before was bizarre, but this . . ."

Battista sat up, though not without a creak of bones and groan of protest, and pulled the painting from its casing. He spread it upon his lap and bent over to squint at it.

Aurelia sat up, leaning into him to get a better look herself.

"It is the other side. There can be no doubt."

"Agreed." Aurelia rubbed her forehead. "But there is not enough light to see what it may tell us."

Battista rolled the thick canvas and tucked it upright into his satchel.

"Help me, Lord," he grunted as he rose to his feet, holding out a hand to her.

She took it with a smile, pulling as he did, till she stood beside him.

Without thought, he wrapped his arms about her, lowering his tall body to embrace her better.

Aurelia stiffened, but only for the briefest moment, relaxing into his hold, reaching up to put her arms around his neck, resting her cheek against his chest. It was a posture of succor given and received, of forgiveness and shared survival. His honor had brought her with him, a promise given and respected, but he knew he would not have survived this challenge—yet again—without her.

He had no desire to pull away, feeling as if they could fall asleep in their cozy nuzzle.

Until her stomach rumbled noisily.

Battista pulled away, holding her at arm's length, the bombastic braying threatening to topple out once more.

"I'm hungry," she said, grinning with no shame.

He laughed at her candor, at her alacritous appetite. "Then let us away, my lady. If I know Frado, he has found whatever game may live in the basin and has it roasting deliciously at this very moment."

Aurelia stepped away, her arms releasing him slowly, and turned for the narrow path hugging the side of the mountain, all gray in the dim light of the moon.

Rocky crags rose up sporadically along the rim of the trail, creating railings that came and went. Battista eyed the steep path downward with a modicum of relief; the journey to the bottom would pass much quicker than had the one to the top.

"I have a confession."

Aurelia's voice came on the wind, and he smiled, not only at the sway of her hips as she led him down the mountain, clearly visible in her tight-fitting clothing, but also at the absence, in his heart, of the anger and mistrust of the past days. It had been a bitter morsel stuck in his craw and he was well pleased to be rid of it.

"I am not sure I am strong enough for another," he told her with no true concern.

She laughed merrily, doing her best to roll her thick hair into some semblance of a bun and pin it up, revealing her long sweaty, sooty neck. "I know the last few hours have been trying, b—"

"Trying?" Battista roared. "Is that what you call it? I would call it insane, outrageous, monumentally difficu—"

"*Sì, sì,* fine. Perhaps I misspoke. Ouch." Aurelia tripped on a fist-sized stone in the path, unable to see well as they passed around the dark side of the mountain. "What we survived was extraordinarily difficult, but . . ."

"But . . ." His voice lilted up with skepticism.

Aurelia swiveled her head round to look at him over her shoulder, smile bouncing as she continued the climb downward. "But I am having the most wonderful time of my life."

Battista threw back his head and laughed; even in the dark, he could see the green glow of her eyes.

"No, it's true," she argued, her smile broad and bright as she shrugged her shoulder up to her chin like a cunning child. "Did you see how fast I ran? I have never r—"

"*Dio mio!*" Battista screamed, lunging forward, but too late.

Aurelia tumbled off the side, screeching in pain and fear as her body plummeted downward . . . head and shoulder, legs and feet, swirling round and round . . . until her anguished cries died away, until her limp body came to rest on the next twirl of the path at least thirty feet below.

"Dear God!" Battista cried again, jumping off the path through the jagged hole where Aurelia had found no footing, almost tumbling himself, controlling his mad, frantic pace so as not to lose his traction and fall himself.

"Aurelia, Aurelia!" He scrambled down to her, calling her name, praying she would raise her head and offer him her mischievous grin.

He came to her side, fear frenzied at the sight of her. Thick patches of blood covered her flawless skin, slashes cut over one eye and across one cheek. Her palms were scratched raw, one wrist crushed beneath her body at an inhuman angle, her clothes were torn and bloody in more places than he dared count.

With a strangled cry in his throat, he shoved one arm beneath her knees, the other beneath her shoulders, and growled as he gained his footing. Running now down the side of the mountain, heedless of his own blind repelling, he repeated one mantra over and over as her lifeless body flopped in his arms.

"Let her live. *Dio mio, per favore.*"

The path released him into the basin a far pace away from the low glimmer of fire pinpointing Frado's position.

Battista ran again, not knowing how his body continued to move, his arms screaming with red-hot pain, her body falling farther and farther down the front of his body, his exhaustion pulling her down.

"Frado!" he shrieked.

The slumbering man started violently, grabbing at the sword lying beside him. Jumping up, twirling round in confusion, he blanched at the apparition hurtling toward him.

"What in God's name happened in there?" Frado screamed as he ran to meet Battista, putting his hands beneath Aurelia's limp form, helping ease the burden.

"It was . . . There is too much to tell." Battista's voice cracked. "She fell, Frado. Not inside, but out, d-down the side. I c-cannot rouse her."

Frado's eyes bulged white in the darkness. He asked no more questions, pulling Aurelia's body, still partially in Battista's clutch, toward the small fire and the bedroll.

They laid her gently upon the thick wool. Battista watched helplessly as Frado lowered his ear to Aurelia's mouth, as he patted her face and jiggled her hand, and though her chest rose and fell, it was a shallow movement and none of Frado's attempts brought her round.

"We must get her to a healer." Battista sat back on his haunches, refusing to relinquish the hand of the unconscious woman.

Frado reached into a large saddlebag, pulled out a thin, if soft, blanket, and draped it over Aurelia's body, tucking it beneath her shoulders and legs. "Will she survive the journey? Two days, Battista."

Battista could have struck out with frustration; he knew full well how long it would take them to return to Florence.

"No." He shook his head, but at what he did not make clear. "We'll take her to Rome. Michelangelo may be there. He . . . he told me he meant to travel there soon. We'll take her to Michelangelo."

Twenty-one

The experience of this sweet life.

—*Paradiso*

The pain did not barrage her at first, but thirst—a consuming, maddening thirst—swelling her tongue and chafing her throat. Aurelia willed her eyes to open, pushing her brows up on her forehead, stretching her skin until the lids had no choice but to separate. She blinked against the light—a radiant magenta glow—startling to her long-closed eyes nonetheless.

The small brick-walled room had little in it, the four-poster bed upon which she lay, a scored and varnished coffer at its feet. In the corner beside the velvet-curtained window, a privacy screen of dark puce silk and a single chair of the same color, winged and claw footed. In it, a giant of a man slumbered, one who looked vaguely familiar. Aurelia turned her head to see him better, her tangled hair rasping against the linens and her dry lips cracking as they split slightly into a feeble grin.

Battista's head, face dark and shadowed with fatigue and a thick layer of stubble, hung sideways off the chair, a swath of dark hair falling across his forehead. His mouth hung open in a crooked droop of utter relaxation, a low drone of slumber and a tiny droplet of drool dripping out.

A congestion of church spires, cream stone buildings, and red tile roofs crowded the vista beyond the window, all swathed in the brilliance of a fiery sunset. A magnificent view, one she could not name. Aurelia had no idea where she was, only that Battista sat beside her and it was enough. She stared at him, taken by his beauty, even in his awkward posture. Like his spirit, his splendor was both rugged yet graceful, an intriguing dichotomy.

Aurelia could no longer deny what she felt for him, feelings transcending a bond born of shared trauma, an attraction of the physical and the kindred soul. And yet the sentiments crossed at odds with her existence. She had left the safety of her lodging for adventure, but could she stretch its boundaries to encompass the heart of another? Could she be that selfish?

Aurelia turned her gaze from him, troubled eyes staring blankly at the rough-beamed ceiling, as if the answer lay above. She breathed deep of warm, fecund air, of thick blossoming in the fullness of early growth, of dirt rising up from a busy street. She sniggered silently at the boisterous greetings, at the deep rattle of a heavy-burdened cart, at the clopping of horse hoof upon hard-packed earth. She became again part of the flurry of life, and she healed in the energy.

"Aurelia?" A frog's croak broke her reverie.

Battista blinked at her, rubbing his eyes with the heels of his palms, chanting her name once more as if to assure himself what he saw was no illusion. "Aurelia? You are awake?"

She smiled silently with a swishing nod against the pillow.

He dropped to his knees at her bedside, taking one hand in both of his, resting his forehead upon their knuckles.

"I did not think . . ." His voice trailed off and he shook his head in denial of any more words or thoughts. Looking up, his weary, pale countenance flushed with relief. "It is a blessing to see you awake."

"Drink, *per favore*," Aurelia begged of him with a thin rasp, a lump of emotion in her parched throat, thicker now for his tender attention.

He jumped to his feet. "Of course, of course."

From behind the privacy screen Aurelia heard the tinkling of glass upon thin metal, and he rushed back, with a mug of heavily watered wine. With tender ministrations, he slipped one hand below her neck, lifting her gently, as he held the rim to her parched lips.

Aurelia closed her eyes in the ecstasy of the liquid upon her tongue, its coolness as it slithered down her throat. He moved it away, but she raised a weak hand, pulling the small, stemless chalice in his hand to her lips once more, and drank deep.

"Not too much." He chuckled. "You have had little for a long time. You seemed to wake now and again, and we fed you water and broth, but not very much. You must not overdo."

Aurelia's brows knit, a stab of pain her reward. She raised a hand, feeling the linen bandage across her forehead. "How long?"

Battista's shadow-rimmed eyes evaded her as he busied himself, refilling her drink behind the safety of the screen.

"How long, Battista?" She pushed against the bed with her elbows, inching upward with a frail attempt.

Rushing back, placing the cup on the lid of the coffer, he lifted her shoulders. "Eight days," he mumbled, rearranging the pillows at her back and shifting her upward, allowing her to lie in a more bolstered position.

"Eight days!" Aurelia did not know if he lied or if some terrible dream had manifested itself. But the pains coursing through her body gave hard testimony to her consciousness. She looked down at herself; a bandage covered her left arm, something thin, straight, and hard keeping it stiff at the wrist. With her right she lifted the covers, shocked to find herself clothed in nothing but a wisp of a chemise bunched around her buttocks, her legs and arms a mass of bandages and cuts, lumpy with dark maroon scabs.

She shook her head at him, squinting. "I do not . . . We made it out of the mountain, *sì?* With . . . with the painting?"

"Yes, yes." Battista sat back down, scraping the chair closer to the side of the bed, and tucked her back beneath the covers with a motherly gesture. "You fell as we climbed down, down the side of the mountain." He pinched his eyes shut, as if to block out the memory. "But only partway. I carried you . . . we, Frado and I, brought you here. Michelangelo's physician has been caring for you. I knew he would. He wasn't sure if you, well, if—"

"We are in Florence?" Aurelia frowned, the fuzziness and weakness obfuscating any recollections, but she could not reconcile the view from the window with her knowledge of Battista's city.

Battista shook his head. "No. We are in Rome, at Michelangelo's house."

Her lips fell flaccid in a gaping maw, her head jutting forward on her slim neck, a turkey about to trot. "Rome, Michelangelo's house . . . is he . . . is he here?"

With a low-throated chuckle, Battista nodded. "*Sì,* he has been here for the whole of your convalescence. He has been quite worried about you."

Aurelia flumped her head back upon the pillows with a flush of pure joy, mitigating, if only for a moment, the marks of injury and illness. "I am to meet Michelangelo, at last," she muttered with the profundity of a prayer.

"He will delight in your beauty," Battista told her, then shrugged. "As he does mine. It is his way."

Battista's words piqued her, and she lifted her head off the pillow with a raised brow. He smiled at her almost sheepishly, but said not a word in further explanation, and yet she understood. With the curve of his lips and the veiled salacious look, she grasped, then, all the unspoken intentions of the artist's great works, of the troubled life she had heard he led. No talent so vast could overcome the misery of living a life in constant conflict with itself.

"I thought I heard voices," the slightly hoarse greeting hailed them from the doorway; in it stood the slight form of the man himself. "I am so relieved to see you awake, *cara mia.* Battista and I have worried much for you."

Aurelia's chapped lips formed a soundless O. She knew this man, recognized at once the flat forehead, the thatches of dark chestnut hair shot with grays falling forward upon it, and the heavy-lidded, amber-colored eyes.

"Signore Buonarroti," she breathed with unbounded amazement. "I . . . I know you." Aurelia blinked wide eyed, at the same man she had shared those poignant moments with at the foot of the Giant, *his* Giant.

The artist nodded, face showing no surprise and but a little dabble of amusement. "*Sì*, I recognize you as well. It is a strange world we live in, my dear, is it not?"

"Most certainly." If she possessed the strength, she would most surely have laughed. All this time, all her desire to meet this man, and it had already taken place. She may think herself wise, but knew, in that moment, she had much to learn.

Michelangelo narrowed his eyes at her with a tilt of his head; she saw a puzzling thought cross the high-boned ridges of his face, but he gave it no voice. Stepping away from the door, he gave her a shallow bow.

"I will have Agniola bring you some broth. And then you must sleep some more. I want you well so you may tell me of all your adventures."

"*Grazie mille*, Signore Buonarroti," Aurelia called as he left them.

He turned back with that ghost of a smile and shook a finger at her, one covered in paint and roughened skin. "No, *per favore*, I am Michelangelo, your most humble servant." He bowed again and disappeared, a ghost vanishing with the coming of dawn.

"He wishes to hear of our adventures?" Aurelia whispered. It was a question not of Michelangelo's desire, but of his knowledge.

Battista met her uncertainty straight on. "There are few men who walk this earth that I would trust as much as Michelangelo."

* * *

He knocked upon the threshold, tilting his head around the doorjamb before an answer came.

"May I come in?"

"*Sì,* Battista. I am ready."

Aurelia sat on the edge of the bed, the middle-aged Agniola hovering around her, tucking in a strand of hair, checking the laces upon Aurelia's back, squinting at Aurelia's just-plucked forehead for any stragglers.

It was the first time she had been dressed in a fortnight, and though she looked stronger than he had seen her since her tumble down the mountainside, the plum silk gown he'd purchased hung on her thin frame. He had loved the fullness of her, and though there remained some hints of it in the fine curve of her hips and the roundness of her breasts, they were not as voluptuous as they had been when first she and Battista had met. He promised himself he would see them fleshy and vivacious once again; if he had to hand feed her for the next month, it would happen.

"*Bellissima.*" He smiled at her, seeing the anxious question in her eyes.

She dipped her head, now free of bandages but not scars, a lovely blush spreading across her cheeks. With her own strength, she rose and approached him. "*Grazie,* Battista. Shall we go?"

Battista laughed, wrapped her good arm around his, and led her to the door and the top of the stairs. Though she had been up and around for a few days, she had not left the confines of her room, gaining her strength with short walks from one side of the chamber to the other. Tonight would be the first meal she would take at table, with Battista and Michelangelo as her companions. Excited energy radiated from her, a firefly peeping with light.

As Battista led her down the stairs, taking one slow step at a time, hesitating between each, he gave her a friendly warning. "Michelangelo is the most amiable of companions, but you must not look overlong at his nose, nor speak of it."

Aurelia quailed. "His nose?"

In the few instances she had seen and spoken to the artist, it had been impossible not to notice the crooked shape of his nose, but why Battista thought it imperative she not comment upon it puzzled her.

"It is but a symbol of his vanity, and his broken heart," Battista said with a whisper and a shrug. "Pietro Torrigiani did it to him, both in fact."

"Torrigiani, another sculptor, yes?" Aurelia felt certain she had read of the man. "He studied in Florence, did he not?"

Battista nodded, concentrating for a moment as he helped her across a small landing, turned them to the left, and onto the next section of stairs. "Yes, a fellow sculptor. Michelangelo met him at the age of fifteen, when they were both apprenticed to the great Bertoldo."

"What was it between them?" she urged Battista on his tale with an insistent whisper.

"I believe Michelangelo loved him." Battista flicked a shoulder. "Or perhaps it was just lust. Torrigiani is, or at least was, a beautiful man, tall and powerfully built, with the face of a god. Whatever they shared, for a time it was mutual, though Torrigiani was envious of Michelangelo's talent."

Aurelia slowed, rapt fascination holding her feet upon the step.

Battista held back with her and finished his tale. "Michelangelo outgrew Torrigiani, who used the slightest offense of words, one some say was no offense at all, to punch Michelangelo savagely in the face. He shattered Michelangelo's nose, desecrating it beyond the repair of even the Medici's physician, for it was in the sculpture garden of Lorenzo the Magnificent that they were both apprenticed."

"How awful!" Aurelia put a hand to her mouth.

Battista nodded. "Unfortunately, our waiting friend always thought himself ugly, long before the accident."

"Physical beauty is but a curtain to anyone's truth," Aurelia protested with almost-fanatical vigor. "It has nothing to do with who we are."

"For the most part, I agree," Battista replied, blinking at her vehemence. "But not for an artist, not for one who lives to create beauty upon the stone and the canvas."

"I suppose," Aurelia mumbled as they continued. "But he must know his name will live on, not for the shape of his nose, but for the beauty he has created."

Battista smiled down at her, at this beauty of a woman who had so little value for her own loveliness. "Perhaps you should tell him, without actually mentioning his nose, of course."

Aurelia laughed softly. "Of course."

They reached the first floor of Michelangelo's house, one given to him by his most powerful sponsor, Pope Clement, a modest house with a courtyard and another building at the back, set in the valley near the foot of Trajan's column between the Quirinal and Capitoline hills. The aroma of roasting meat and baking sweets reached for them as they crossed through a small but well-furnished sitting room and into the dining room.

Michelangelo jumped from his chair at their approach, pulling down his finely fitted tunic, a muted marigold matching his eyes, and smoothing his hair forward upon his brow with an unconscious gesture.

Aurelia released Battista's arm and rushed to the artist's side, aches denied in her zeal, a greeting hand reaching out.

Battista held back, watching joyfully as they delighted in each other's company, two souls of such significance in his life.

"Monna Aurelia, how splendid you look!"

Of almost the same height, though Aurelia stood perhaps an inch or two taller, they looked perfectly paired for their dance of greeting as one bowed with a flourish and the other curtsied deep.

"It is most splendid to see you," Aurelia replied as her host led her to a chair, one set between two others at each end of the table, and helped her into it.

"You are feeling very much better, *sì?* I can see it in the glow of your lovely face."

"Much better, *grazie.*" Aurelia turned to Battista, as if suddenly remembering his presence. "You have all taken such very good care of me. I can never thank you enough for your efforts and your hospitality."

Michelangelo waved a hand, dismissing her gratitude. "Think nothing of it, my dear. And now that you are up and about, I can truly play host. Agniola! Antonio! We are ready!"

At his command, the door at the back of the room swung open and the housekeeper rushed out, hands braced on the handles of a large silver platter, a young man behind her, each hand carrying two more heaping salvers.

"Monna Aurelia, this young fellow is Antonio Mini from Pontassieve. He once kept house for me, but now, with dear Agniola here, he assists me in my studio."

The lanky young man bobbed his dark-haired head as he placed the overflowing dishes on the table. "*Piacere,* signorina."

"Nice to meet you as well, Antonio." Aurelia smiled. "You must feel honored to work with the great master."

"Oh *sì,* of course," Antonio nudged Michelangelo as he passed him by on his way back to the kitchen, a mischievous grin to palliate his sarcasm. "Exhaustion is not so hard to take when levied by the hand of a master."

"Michelangelo is finishing work on the great Julius's tomb," Battista told Aurelia as Agniola served him first, the male guest, from the deep dish of cannelloni stuffed with chopped beef and mushrooms.

"Finishing, yes." Michelangelo laughed. "I have been finishing it for many years now. And many more will pass, no doubt, before the work will come to an end."

He smiled up at Antonio, thanking the young man for filling his goblet with thick and pungent garnet wine. "The Holy See has called me off the project, yet again, to work on his library."

A deep furrow formed between Battista's brows. "You are not well pleased. I can understand."

"Whatever you create, you must know it will be a masterpiece, now and hundreds of years from now." Aurelia leaned toward the artist, bruised face scowling with ardor, laying one hand gently upon his.

Battista lowered his head and smiled; she did as promised, assured Michelangelo of his true legacy, and did it with grace and elegance.

The blush rushed across the artist's wizened face. "*Grazie, donna mia*. You are most kind."

"I mean no kindness by it," Aurelia said with startling brusqueness. "I speak the truth. Do not doubt it."

Both men looked at her, both surprised and intrigued; what was in her to speak with such authority neither could say, but it was there and they both knew it. Battista caught Michelangelo's gaze, saw the question in the dark amber eyes, and turned from it, unable to answer.

"You liked my *David,* did you not, Aurelia?" Michelangelo asked her as Agniola filled her plate with *pappardelle alla lepre,* the aromatic hare sauce drenching the thick, wide noodles.

Aurelia smiled, peering at him mischievously from under her lashes. "You know very well how beautiful I think him to be." She laughed. "You really should have made yourself known."

"I feared it would have changed the way you looked upon him," Michelangelo replied candidly.

"Will you tell me about him?" Aurelia put her fork down, clearly having little appetite for anything save this man and his words.

Michelangelo shrugged modestly, yet still the pride showed through upon his lined face. "I often wonder if I managed to convey all I wanted to say with him. I wanted him to be a real man, not some boy with a man's face. It is the curse of so many sculptures. I wanted him to be fully realized, fully functional in a rational world. He is a man who triumphed over evil, one much larger than himself, but I wanted you to look at him and believe it, not as a miracle, but as truth."

Battista smiled at Aurelia as she flicked him a besotted gaze, one of wonder and gratitude.

"I believed it the moment I saw him." Aurelia turned again to the artist. "In fact I wondered, as I stood at his feet, just how you came to render him so realistically."

Michelangelo glanced at Battista with a jaunty, if barely perceptible, waggle of his bushy brows. "Shall I tell her my secret?"

"I think you must," Battista said, smiling into his cup.

Michelangelo leaned toward her, one conspirator to another. "I dissected them, bodies I mean."

Aurelia's face shifted with emotions, crumpled confusion opened to startling awareness. "You did not?"

"I most certainly did, *donna mia*," Michelangelo preened. "I would creep down to the hospital morgue in the wee hours of the night. The Prior Bichiellini believed in me, you see. His belief allowed him to turn his eyes." Michelangelo almost smiled. "I almost died of exhaustion, working night after night, after long days at the studio. But there, beneath my knife, the spirits of the bodies told me their secrets."

Aurelia sat back with astonished surrender. "It explains much of your Giant. Though"—she cupped her chin in her hand and tapped her lips with thought, regarding the artist narrowly—"I see some of you in him, the forehead and the brow, the scornful manner of your lips."

It was Michelangelo's turn to sit back in his chair, for a fleeting moment held captive, his secrets exposed. "You are frighteningly perceptive, Aurelia. I did indeed pour all of my disdain and melancholy into him as I worked. But the Giant's proud nobility, his almost-barbarous vulgarity, that is the *David*'s alone. And I did make a few mistakes with him."

Aurelia shook her head. "I do not believe it."

"No, 'tis true. His great face is set in a small head and his thin arms are at odds with his enormous hands and heavy fingers."

"It only makes him more human, for are not all humans unique and flawed?"

Michelangelo accepted her grace and looked to Battista, a light in his eyes Battista had not seen in a long while.

"You have brought me a great gift, *amico karissimo,*" Michelangelo said humbly.

Battista raised his goblet in reply. "To you, my friend, may you return to your chisel very soon."

"I will drink to that." Michelangelo tossed back a gulp. "True painting never will make anyone shed a tear. Good painting is religious and devout in itself. Among the wise nothing more elevates the soul or raises it to adoration than the difficulty of attaining the perfection—with sculpture—which approaches God and unites itself to Him."

"B-b-ut . . . b-b-ut . . . ," Aurelia stammered, stunned by his critical assessment. "The Sistine Chapel . . . oh!"

Her bottom lip sagged; her hands slapped the table.

The men eyed her, waiting.

She gaped at one, then the other, then back to Battista again. "May we see it? While we are here? *Per favore?*"

Michelangelo answered her, "If it is your wish, *donna mia,* I will take you myself."

"Tell me ho—"

"We will talk of it then, yes?" He reached out to pat her hand, not to dampen, but to postpone her enthusiasm. "We have other things to interest us this night." He turned his heavy-lidded eyes to Battista. "You will tell me of your adventures now, *sì?* Now that we know the lady is recovered?"

Battista could avoid the insistent look, or the question, no longer, having put off his friend with the excuse of Aurelia's ill health.

With a modicum of words, Battista told the artist of his assignment from the king of France, of the strange piece François craved, of the intricate challenges required and what they had completed thus far. Battista mentioned the Confraternita dei Guardiani and he told Michelangelo of their precarious dealings with Baldassare del Milanese, the ransacking of his home in Florence, and his certainty that del Milanese was on the search for the same powerful relic.

"*Dio mio,*" Michelangelo breathed. "I have never heard the like. Will you show me the painting?"

"Frado did not take it with him, did he?" Aurelia asked of Battista.

The dedicated man had just taken his leave of them that morning, returning to Florence to tell the others of the events and the reason for their delay. He would return to Rome, after filling a purse or two from their coffers, and then make the final return to Florence once more in their company.

Battista pushed away from the table. "Of course. I have only the portion we have just retrieved. We thought it imprudent to bring the other with us."

Battista heard the rumble of their voices as he climbed the stairs, as Agniola brought out fruit and cheese to end their meal, and some waferlike *pizzelle,* always remembering Battista's favorite cookie whenever he came to stay.

Retrieving the rolled canvas from beneath his bed, he thought of the long hours bent over it as he sat by Aurelia's bed, as he waited with prayers upon his lips for her to awaken. Without the other, there was little to glean from this piece, except for the background.

At his approach, Michelangelo stood and cleared any plates or platters from the table before him. Battista rolled out the thick canvas, and Michelangelo's eyes flamed with keen interest.

"This was the beginning, you know," Michelangelo murmured. "It changed technique and approach to its very core."

"What do you see?" Battista stood behind the artist, towering over him like his Giant, more than a passing resemblance to the sculpture's warrior bearing.

Michelangelo rubbed his weak chin, rough skin rasping against the wiry beard. "There is little to gain from the woman. She is the main subject of the triptych as a whole, but in this piece her secret is still hidden. But here, this background, it is but a simple landscape, a pastoral meadow, a well-rowed farmland, and yet it looks distinctly of the peninsula."

"I thought the same," Battista agreed, turning to Aurelia for corroboration, but she stared blankly at the painting, seemingly devoid of any impressions; perhaps fatigue got the better of her.

"And you say the other side showed a village?" Michelangelo asked.

"*Sì.*" Battista waved his hands as if to conjure the image. "A well-cared-for village rendered with warm, welcoming colors. We thought it meant to tell us where the other piece could be found, but that is the sole function of the Duccio. We believe the triptych—all of its clues—are meant to bring us to the relic."

"A piece by Praxiteles that will ensure the king's victory." Michelangelo sat down and flopped back, both hands to his face, searching gaze flung upward into his mind or the heavens. "Such a perilous, divine mystery. You are right, Battista, where these two backgrounds meet, a place that lies between a village and vast farmland, will be your ultimate destination. But whether you find the woman, the piece, or both is yet another unknown."

"Only the last piece of the triptych will tell us where to go."

"And what of the Brotherhood of the Guardian?" The older man closed his eyes, rubbing hard at the space between them. "The words tickle my memory, as if I knew them before, heard them before, but have forgotten."

Battista filled his tankard and drank deep. "After what we have seen, in both Hell and Purgatory, they were near fanatical in their duties. These challenges are masterful, meant to kill those too feeble or too impetuous to hurdle them. Yet clearly constructed to enable those with knowledge to pass unscathed to the paintings if need be."

"Such devotion and ingenuity is to be admired," Michelangelo said.

"Indeed," Aurelia breathed with almost-grudging respect.

"They were clever to leave the center for the last," Battista echoed her esteem. "For the other two are useless without it."

Michelangelo raised his eyes. "And do you know where to find it?"

"No, not really," Battista said with disappointment. "The Duccio showed us a castle upon the shore."

The artist snorted gruffly. "Well, that narrows it down to a few hundred."

"Exactly." Battista collapsed into his chair, threw back another long swallow of wine, and plopped the empty goblet back upon the table with a thud.

"But it is not just the Duccio, but Dante which guides you, *sì?*" Michelangelo asked.

Battista smiled as his friend fell under the ensnaring, enticing entanglement of the quest. Battista was glad of it, for it would not only add a brilliant thinker to the puzzle, but the puzzle might, for a time, relieve Michelangelo's heavy burdens as well, the layers of concern over his work, his family duties, his loyalties, and his aloneness.

"True," Battista replied.

"I must reread the *Commedia.*" Michelangelo rubbed his hands together. "It is a most religious piece, a most Catholic piece, and yet it speaks to the true nature of humanity in a way Catholicism refuses."

Aurelia blinked at him. "Are you a pagan, Michelangelo?"

Battista put his nose back in his cup. Lifelong friends, these men knew every one of each other's intimate truths; Battista knew well of Michelangelo's spiritual struggles. He held his breath as he waited to hear if the artist would admit to them or not. Battista's friend was a private man who had learned, through scarring tribulation, to keep his deepest feelings close to his chest.

"When I was a young man, I learned much in the library of Lorenzo de' Medici, surrounded by the greatest thinkers of the age, men who found the majority of their answers in the teachings of Plato." Michelangelo's voice grew distant as he recalled days long passed. "The pagans understood, as do the Humanists, that we need not destroy a man's mind, his creativity and independence, to ensure the safety of his immortal soul."

He laughed, though with no great amusement, leaning forward, hands brushing along the sage linen atop the table. "Yet I know myself to be a son of God, a disciple of Christ. I simply choose to practice my religion in creating beautiful and harmonious human bodies."

Michelangelo turned his smile upon Aurelia, and she answered with one of her own, one of understanding and gratitude.

She sighed heavily and Battista laid a gentle hand on her forearm.

"Are you tired, *cara mia?*"

Weariness had come to dampen the spark of delight in her eyes.

"A bit," she admitted with a reluctant shrug.

Michelangelo jumped to his feet and to her side, pulling out her chair, holding out his arm gallantly to assist her. "I will keep you no longer, *donna mia*. But we thank you for your splendid companionship this evening."

He took her injured hand and brushed his lips softly across her knuckles, the only portion not covered by wrappings.

"I will remember this night for as long as I live," she assured with no coquetry, and Michelangelo could only bow humbly at such a pronouncement, handing her to Battista's waiting arms.

As he led her away, Aurelia turned back to Michelangelo, the delighted imp returning.

"You will not forget your promise, Michelangelo? You will take me to the Sistine?"

Michelangelo chuckled, raising his hand into the air with his vow. "I promise, my dear. Have no fear."

One lone candle, guttering low with flickering flames, revealed the outlines of her chamber and the few pieces of furniture in it.

She and Battista stood together in silence and stillness, an awareness of each other and their place vibrant in the air between them. Her bed had been turned down and her freshly washed, thin chemise spread out upon the linens.

"I will fetch Agniola for you." Battista stepped back from her warmth and light, so vivid in the dimly lit room, afraid, but of what he could not say.

"No, leave her be. I am certain she is fast asleep by now." Aurelia turned, showing him the curve of her back and the laces requiring attention, her dark green gaze finding him from over her shoulder. "You do it, Battista."

No coyness hid in the request; its truth hummed in every vibration of her low whisper, in the thick provocation of her glowing gaze. He stepped to her eagerly, fear denied, if not forgotten.

With a delicate touch, he untied the laces, pulling the silk ribbon through the eyelets with slow languor, reveling in each inch of flesh revealed, in the sensuous hum of the slick trimmings sliding against fabric.

Reaching the bottom of the laces and the glorious curve where her back ended and her buttocks began, he lowered his lips to the smooth creamy skin on the back of her neck, lips smiling against the flesh as bumps of delight broke out upon it. His mouth and tongue drank of her, wrapping one arm around her waist as she fell against him. Pushing her body into his, Aurelia reached up one hand to encircle the back of his head, to thrust her fingers in his hair with a tug of insistence.

Battista groaned with urgency, flung her round, and lowered his lips to hers, the full, moist flesh open and waiting. Gently at first, he rejoiced in their secret as he did in the prizes he had sought all his life. As her tongue reached out for his, he captured the mouth, taking ownership of it.

Aurelia leaned against him, bandaged hand at his waist, the other rubbing against his chest, moving downward.

He gasped and pushed her away, staring at her as she blinked owl-like at him.

"Are you sure, *cara?* Do you know what you are doing?" The strangeness of her life came to him, the consequences of their actions—if they were to go further—all the more precarious.

Aurelia sniffed softly, looking up at him with unfettered desire. "I know exactly what I am doing . . . well, not exactly. But I am fully aware, Battista, fully conscious and in *this* moment. This—you—is exactly what I want."

He hummed low and feral, her assurance tantalized him. Abandoning all rational reflection, he lowered his mouth to hers once more.

Twenty-two

Do not be afraid; our fate
cannot be taken from us; it is a gift.

—*Inferno*

"That was almost as exhausting as the mountain." She giggled in the darkness.

Against hers, Battista's cheek blossomed with a smile, but the belly she stroked beneath her fingers did not move, his chest did not rumble with any answering laughter.

Raising herself up on her elbow, she peered into the face, the masculine bone structure so precise as he lay back, yet the features so indistinct in the dearth of light.

The candle had burned to a stub and snuffed itself out with an unheard hiss; the hours spent indulged in each other's arms had passed without intrusion or notice.

Though she had never heard the cries of a man in the throes of ecstasy, she had known them from Battista's lips, known he had been as overwhelmed as she. Yet she saw nothing of delight upon his still countenance.

"Have I . . . have I offended you?" she whispered, not with the fear of being overheard, but of the answer. "I know I am not as experienced as your other—"

Battista lurched upright, swells of stomach muscle undulating, and took her by the shoulder. For all his sudden intensity, he eased her back down gently, his physical control at odds with the heat of his touch, the passion in his eyes.

"Speak not another word, Aurelia." He leaned over her, silky black hair falling over a flushing face. His gaze narrowed and flitted, not—she saw clearly—with disappointment, as she had feared, but with shame. "I did not expect . . . I was surprised to find you a . . . a maid. You're so . . ."

Aurelia waited, feeling as if she were perched on yet another cliff. But she did not rush him; she saw the conflict in the puckers upon his brow. With a tender touch, she pushed the silky floss from his face and tucked it behind one ear. "I am . . . what?"

And then it came to her.

The chortle rose from deep in her throat, quivering with cynically tainted amusement. "Old?"

Battista flung himself back on the bed, ruddy face now scarlet with embarrassment.

"No, well, yes, but . . ." He rose back up and faced her, an honorable, courageous man who would not retreat in the face of adversity. "Not *old,* but not a child, either. I would have . . . I could have done things . . . differently . . . better, perhaps."

She could not allow him to suffer anymore.

She hushed him with a brush of three fingertips upon his swollen, well-used lips. "I would not have wanted it differently. You could not know I am . . . was . . ."—she giggled again, rich and deep with lascivious satisfaction—"the world's oldest virgin."

Aurelia saw the smile tugging at his mouth, try though he might to disguise it, and sighed with relief. She would not want a shred of regret to taint what they'd shared.

"But what of conception? At your age, it could be dangerous."

Her harsh laughter silenced him this time.

"Do not fear on that score," she assured him. "It is not possible."

"How can you be so sure?" His voice rose in the quiet of the house, in the stillness that lived as one day traded places with another.

"I know." Aurelia put her hand forthrightly upon his chest as if to stifle further questions before they formed. But it was a futile attempt.

Battista sat up, thin linen falling to the crook of his hips. Aurelia's eyes followed the thin line of dark hair as it dipped below the sheet, longing—with an innocent, awakened curiosity—for the sheet to fall away completely.

"You are not old enough for your courses to have stopped," he said with more conviction than she expected. "It is a possibility. We must—"

"I tell you it is not possible." Her clipped, harsh invective squelched his insistence like an ax bent on beheading. "I cannot conceive, Battista. I am infertile, as are all of my kind."

Aurelia bit hard on her upper lip; he had pushed her one step too far, pushed her to loosen the guard standing sentinel over her words. She cursed silently, turning her head from his poignant stare.

With an insistent finger upon her chin, he brought her back. "Your kind?"

"My . . . m-m-y family, many of those in my f-f-amily," Aurelia sputtered, hoping her stammer appeared as embarrassment rather than deceit. "It is an inherited disorder of sorts."

She watched as his befuddled gaze softened with sympathy, as he lowered his lips, kissing her gently, sucking playfully on her heavy top lip. "I am sorry, Aurelia, and for your kin," he said, and she believed him, making her feel all the worse.

"Tell me of Michelangelo." She rushed to other thoughts, other words.

He smiled. "I have a feeling you know a great deal about him."

"Of his work, and his adult years, *sì,* I have read much of it," Aurelia replied. "But I know little of his childhood."

"It was not a happy youth." Battista's face crumpled at the recollections. "His mother died when he was but six, and his father was useless with his grief. His aunt Cassandra ran the household, but she was cold and efficient. I fear he endured much loneliness, unwanted, too, by any save his Nona, and the Topolinos."

Aurelia shook her head. "I do not know the name."

"It was the stonecutter's wife who suckled him when his own mother became too ill. As a child, Michelangelo fled there at every opportunity, an urchin running wild on the streets of Florence." He laughed brightly. "Some say he ingested stone dust with Signora Topolino's milk, and that is how he came by his talent."

She smiled at the thought. "Do you believe it?"

"I believe he found the stone and the stone found him, for they were fated to be together," Battista decreed, laying bare his belief in divine providence with the pronouncement.

"And what of you and Michelangelo?"

"There is not much to tell." He bent at the waist and lowered his head to rest it upon her stomach, his voice vibrating through her body as he spoke. "I was, for a short time, apprenticed to him, but it was clear I had no talent with a brush or a chisel. But we were such kindred spirits, as lovers of art, as loyal Florentine Republicans, a bond quickly formed. He never asked . . . it never . . . it is and always has been a very pure friendship."

He smiled at her, a soft grin full of love, and she laughed at the odd picture created with his head turned sideways upon her belly.

"My father died, Michelangelo never had children . . . our relationship gave us each what we needed. We have always been there for the other no matter the delicacy of our tribulations."

His revelation intrigued her; Aurelia waggled her brows at him. "Tribulations?"

He sat up and lowered his voice, as if, even in the dead of night, those who opposed him lurked just beyond the door, as if the crickets chirping beyond the window could fathom his confession and carry it away to those who would do him harm. "Those loyal to Florence are not always loyal to the Medici, whether they rule or not. We have each struggled with them. We have called upon the other first at times of such struggles."

She turned on her side and curled into a ball, her knees snuggled into the angle of his crossed legs, pulling the linens closer about her shoulders. "You are very blessed, both of you."

Battista nodded. "Are you cold, *cara?*"

"I am. And quite thirsty," she hinted.

"I shall get you wine and a blanket. I will return in an instant, have no fear."

He stood with a smirk but no modesty, the pale flesh of his hard, rounded buttocks aglow in the dark room. A surge of desire roiled through her. She had never seen a man such as he completely naked; she had prepared men for burial, old men whose physical beauty had long since passed. But what she saw . . . the powerful build, hard muscles, and sharp angles of a man in his prime . . . it was a sight not soon forgotten. She understood why an artist longs to capture such beauty in the immortal form of a sculpture.

With another giggle, she nestled into the bed, stopping herself from reaching out, grabbing his arm, and pulling him back to her bed as he slipped wraithlike from the room. She felt wanton and languished in it. Aurelia understood, for the first time, why her guardians shielded her from the pleasures of the flesh. How would she return to a life without it? She did not know, had no care to think of it at all.

Her drowsy stare made its way out the window, finding the stars blazing in a moonless, inky sky. She had come so far in this adventure, and she looked back upon it with more than a modicum of guilt; she had gone places and done things severely prohibited.

As if her guardian stood before her, Aurelia shook her head and laughed low in her throat; she would keep doing them, there was simply no question about it. Oh, the time of reckoning drew closer, but she wrinkled her nose at it, dispersing it like water under the heavy weight of a falling rock. She would see Rome, see Battista naked before her again . . . see this quest to its conclusion. Consequences be damned.

He eyed her from the doorway, unseen in the gloom, watched her delicate features as they changed from delight to concern and back again. From here, he glimpsed the smattering of freckles beginning to blossom over the bridge of her fine nose, and they taunted him, as if each one were evidence of the ways he had led her astray.

Battista knew every inch of her, going where no man had ever gone. But who was she? The enigma of her nibbled away at him, stopped him from stepping over the threshold, though a blanket to warm her fell over his shoulder and a small carafe of wine to refresh her he held in his hand.

Aurelia stretched then, her soft skin shushing against the sheets, arching her back, her curves abounding beneath the thin fabric. The linen clung to her sweat-moist skin like fog upon a rolling meadow, the translucent beauty just beyond sight yet not beyond imagination. His passion devoured him, erasing all thoughts to the contrary, and he fairly ran into the room.

She smiled up at him in the darkness as he laid the blanket across her body.

Without a word, he filled a small tumbler and held it as she drank. Assured of her satisfaction, he pulled back the coverings and laughed as her flesh broke out in chilly bumps. As Aurelia stared at him in astonishment, Battista tipped the bottle slowly over her body, dribbling the wine into the hollow of her belly.

He trembled with control as she shivered at the sensation. His dark gaze never leaving her eyes, he lowered his head, and drank of her, her moans of pleasure wafting into the peace of the night.

Aurelia's slumbering breath crooned in his ear, but he attained no equal peace.

With as little movement as possible, he slipped his arm from beneath her head, slithered from beneath the covers, and stood for an expectant moment by the bedside. Looking down at her—at the slumberous serenity upon her exquisite, almost-exotic features, the russet curls tossed and feathered about her head—he stood rooted to the floor, wanting only to submerge in the vision, to fill himself with the masterpiece before him.

It was a beauty in its prime, not one just beginning. But how could such beauty have gone untouched for so long? No one would call him unworldly or naïve; it was only the common and the poor who valued virginity, not those of Aurelia's class. Courts were replete with sexual entanglements. So how could she have preserved her innocence for so long? The better questions were why, and how dare he be the one to deny such perpetuation.

Slipping into his breeches, picking up his undershirt, Battista could bear her beauty and the questions it created no more.

The wooden steps creaked as he descended, the groan of a nightly specter, and he tiptoed into the dining room, pushing at the swinging door leading to the kitchen.

In search of food, more of Agniola's delicious *pizzelle,* he pulled up quick at the sight of his friend perched by the low-burning embers of the house fire, rocking in a straw and wood chair, a parchment on his lap and a piece of charcoal in his hand.

Michelangelo's face brightened in the dimness. "You could not sleep, *amico karissimo?*"

Battista grinned at the silly endearment, one the artist had used since his childhood. "I am exhausted and yet slumber eludes me."

He searched the cupboards until he found the cookies and brought the platter, a pitcher of spiced cider, and a tin cup to the table. Michelangelo lit a slim taper from the embers by his side and placed it in a stick upon the table as Battista filled his mouth with the sweet, flaky pastry.

"Aurelia," Michelangelo breathed her name with a sigh. "She is . . . is . . ."

Battista sniffed. "I have no sufficient words for her, either."

"Do you love her?" Michelangelo asked with little need of words, seeing the answer in his friend's gaze.

"As much as any man such as I can love another."

"Bah!" Michelangelo scoffed, slapping the air between them with an impatient hand. "You have used your own legendary reputation to avoid love. You are more capable of it than most."

Battista released his head into the hand propped on the small kitchen table and rubbed his forehead. "But I can't think of it now. I must see to my mission. Things grow more perilous by the moment, do they not? What have you heard of the emperor and the pope?"

Michelangelo placed the chunk of charcoal down upon the parchment and let the thick paper roll up of its own volition.

"No more than a week or so hence, King François renounced all intention to abide by the Treaty of Madrid. He will not be bound by it, as he swears he signed it under duress."

"He was Charles's prisoner for nearly two years as his country faltered, as did his health. I imagine his days involved a great deal of duress."

Michelangelo agreed with a curt nod and continued. "The pope has given François his blessing."

"That is good." Battista bit off another mouthful of a cookie.

"But many are angry with the pope. They consider him the dregs of the Medici and call him the Mule. He antagonizes those of the Republic by bringing his family into Vatican Palace, obviously grooming them."

"He ca—"

"And yet the emperor not only refuses to release François's children, he continues to move south from Piacenza."

Battista dropped his cookie to his plate, his hands to his lap, and his jaw to his chest.

"It is madness." His head shook in disbelief. He had begun this quest, this mission for François, out of a keen sense of loyalty, in the hope that it would bring the king's promises of military support for the Republic to fruition. But as Battista's exhausted, unfocused gaze reached out to the future, he knew that finding this relic, that which would bring the king of France the power he claimed it to possess, was more vital than ever.

"Go to bed, Battista." Michelangelo rocked back, the well-worn chair creaking rhythmically. "Go back to the woman who warms it, and find your comfort there, for there is little to be had elsewhere in this world."

Twenty-three

Art, as far as it is able, follows nature,
as a pupil imitates his master;
thus your art must be, as it were, God's grandchild.

—*Inferno*

She had waited three more days, but she would wait no longer. She had been resting for almost a fortnight; she could bear to rest no longer.

Aurelia needed no one to help her stand or walk or move about, required but a little help in getting dressed, the fingers of her left hand still too swollen and achy to do her much good. The cuts and abrasions had healed, leaving little mark upon her flesh, and what she yearned for most of all was to be free from these walls.

"Battista?" she called out from the bottom of the stairs, as she had for the third time in as many minutes. "Are you not ready yet?"

Pacing between the foot of the stairs and the threshold she so longed to cross, she wondered what took a man so long to prepare. He wore no gown, nor did he have need to worry much over what clothing to choose or how to pin up his hair. Battista favored the same type of breeches, jerkin, and silk shirt as always. Not that she would be so foolish as to complain about his attire; the form-fitting fashion displayed his build to its utmost, and she had grown quite fond of simply watching him, clothed or not. There was something so very enticing about a muscular, masculine man who moved with almost-feminine grace.

Light footfalls creaked upon the stairs, and Battista floated down with the lightness of a dancer and the sureness of a soldier. Even on this outing, daggers hung from the sheaths hung from a thick brown belt slung low about his hips. His leather jerkin, tailored to mold his form like skin, was slashed at the top shoulder points and lashed with trim, long laces.

Aurelia smiled up at him. "Do you think Michelangelo will join us soon?"

She had no wish to be rude or abrupt, especially with their generous host, but she could contain her eagerness no longer, it twitched her knees beneath her skirt and chewed upon her lips.

"I am here, *cara mia*." Michelangelo poked his head out from behind Battista, so small as to creep unseen in his friend's shadow.

"You look very fine," Aurelia said as they reached the bottom of the stairs.

"*Grazie.*" Battista preened, pulling his jerkin down by the hem to better shape it about his strapping form.

"I was talking to Michelangelo," Aurelia quipped, laughing at Battista's crestfallen expression. The artist chuckled low, but Aurelia held him. "Truly, *messere*, I was. The lovely color of your tunic brings out your eyes."

Michelangelo looked down at his light cotton shirt of fallow brown with pleased, if humble, delight. She had not seen him in it and thought it new, as well as the long hose and sandals he wore. The abnormal warmth of spring continued, and though this day began cloudy, it promised every intention of providing the same heat as the last ten. Michelangelo had long since taken to donning the cooler footwear Roman men preferred during warm summers.

"You do look rather fine," Battista agreed with good nature, any perceived slight forgotten in the spirit of the day's outing. "And you, Aurelia, look mag—where is your sling?"

Aurelia's shoulders drooped like a denied child's and she inched her bandaged, splinted hand behind her back as if he would forget her injury were he not to see it.

She pointed toward the door with her good hand. "This is Rome, Battista . . . Rome. I will look an elderly frump in such a contraption."

Battista shook his head with a lick of his lips as his eyes fell upon the creamy skin beneath the high, thin fabric of her chemise, above the low, straight neckline of her gown. "There is nothing in this world that could diminish your beauty."

He came toward her with a sway of his hips, and she thought he meant to kiss her there, in front of Michelangelo. They kept their intimacy secret to no one in the house, most especially Michelangelo. His room sat between theirs and each had tiptoed past his door in the middle of the night, their muffled moans of passion cresting as the moon rose and fell.

But Battista veered past her and into the dining room, swiping the rough calico sling from the table where she had abandoned it.

"And there is nothing in me that will allow you to risk further harm to your hand."

Her lips compressed upon her somber countenance; she did nothing to help, nor hinder, as he cradled her arm in the strip of fraying fabric and brought it over her head to rest on her shoulder and neck.

Michelangelo frowned with sympathy at her crestfallen visage; gone was the vibrant beauty ready to take on the grandest city in all of Europe.

"Wait, my dear. Wait just a moment."

He rushed away with the insistent command, hastening up the stairs and just as quickly back down. He brought with him the loveliest shawl she had ever seen, a shimmering silk triangle, the tassel beads sparkling as they tinkled together, the green vines and yellow flowers vibrant against the purple background. It matched, to perfection, the pale lavender of her new spring gown.

With tender attention to her hand, he wrapped it round her, positioning it with an artful eye and a motherly cluck of his tongue, perfectly camouflaging her sling, tying the ends upon her opposite hip. It made her look ever more festive despite the lump of her cradled arm beneath.

"It was my mother's," he told her softly, stepping back to survey his handiwork.

Aurelia's heart trembled; she could but imagine what it must mean to him.

Michelangelo reached forward, one last adjustment made with thumb and index finger, as if he took his chisel to stone for one last perfect strike. Aurelia took his hand before he drew it away. "I will cherish the moments within its care."

His lips twitched beneath the wiry black hair and he closed his eyes in silent acknowledgment.

"Then let us be off, shall we?" He held out one crooked elbow and led her to the door. "There is so very much to show you."

Aurelia smiled at Battista from over her shoulder as they stepped out into the overcast day.

"Rome needs no sun to sparkle with brilliance," Michelangelo chirped, waving at the low clouds, denying them any power.

From his doorstep, he led them to the left, along the rising Via della Bottegha Oscure, toward the hill in the near distance.

"Oh, what a disappointment." Michelangelo pouted as he watched Aurelia drop the veil over her eyes. "I had hoped to squire about a beautiful woman through the streets of Rome. All my friends would be so very jealous."

Aurelia tossed her head and laughed. "I am sure there are many beautiful women in Rome, far more beautiful than I. It is only proper for me to don my veil."

Michelangelo peered at her through the tops of his eyes, a dark skeptical glint in the bright amber, and she squirmed beneath the scrutiny; the artist saw far more than was good for either of them.

"Even through your lace, *donna mia*, your particular shine blazes through."

She dipped her head at him as he called to Battista over his shoulder.

"Come, *amico karissimo*, I would have both my beautiful guests beside me."

Battista caught up to them with a few large strides and smiled at her over Michelangelo's head. The artist began his tour as he used their strength and youth to assist him up the rise.

"This is one of the seven great hills of Rome. From here, we may see much of the city spread out before us, a banquet at our feet, to be devoured, each delicious bite." As they leaned into their climb, he gestured his bearded chin at the great palazzos flanking the broad lane. "If you look closely at some of the surrounding grounds, you may see the protrusion of ancient ruins, those built by the Sabines."

They came to the summit and he led them into a small circular cobbled piazza, open on both the north and south sides, a petite fountain at its center, the small cherub dribbling water stingily from its overturned vessel. As a haze of sunshine struggled through thinning cloud cover, the splendor of Rome created a sparkling vista.

Aurelia could not breathe for the beauty of it; everywhere she sent her gaze it landed upon triumphs of architecture and antiquity, grandeur enticing visitors to this city from the world over: temples, chapels, arches, and palaces. Masterpieces both ancient and modern, designed and constructed by artists far ahead of their time, like Hadrian, and those of recent years, such as Bramante, who did their utmost to be as worthy as their predecessors.

"The city is so very different than the first time I saw it," Michelangelo said pensively.

Aurelia tugged her gaze from the landscape to the small man beside her. "Were you not happy to be here?"

He dismissed his past with a twitch of his shoulder. "I had left Florence an unhappy young man . . . frustrated and confused . . . and came upon this metropolis that was, then, no more than a waste heap."

"*Certamente, no!*" Aurelia protested with a breathy objection, throwing back the veil as if it distorted the truth.

"It is true, my dear. I thought the Vandals had sacked it once more. More than half the buildings were gutted or abandoned, goats and pigs grazed as if they owned the land, garbage was piled everywhere. And the stench?" His wrinkled face scrunched at the memory of it. "Between the refuse, the dead animals left to rot in the streets, and the open dung holes, it was hard to walk about without becoming nauseated. Only the assurance of my friend Leo Baglioni convinced me it was the truth of the city. At the time."

He took a step away, holding out his arms as if to embrace the city. "But even then the work had begun, and now . . . look. It is magnificent, no?"

Without waiting for their agreement, for they must agree, he reached out a hand, guiding her eye to the treasures surrounding the hill with a heavy-knuckled finger. In the distance to the east, the half-tumbled, dark stones of the Coliseum stood amidst the glimmering bright stone of the resplendent palazzos edging it; the imposing ruins of the Forum poked at the sky in the foreground, almost at their feet.

"In Greek, the word *Pantheon* means 'to every God.' Did you know that, Aurelia?" Michelangelo pointed north, directing her appraisal to the sharp roof and columns of the temple.

"I did," she answered without hesitation. She thought more lay in the depths of his query and she knew subterfuge to be a futile exercise with this man and no longer bothered with it. "Rome was a great pagan Mecca. A shining example of acceptance for any faith and spirituality, such as it was, before Constantine and the Vatican."

Michelangelo sniffed. "*Sì*, before the Vatican."

As if called forth at the mention, the artist swept his hand toward the west. Clearly visible across the sparkling Tiber River snaked the outlines of the Leonine Wall surrounding Vatican City, distinct against the clearing sky, the pointed obelisk rising up into the air. Just to the east of it, they could see the daunting silhouette of the fortress of Sant'Angelo.

"Shall we make our way there?" Michelangelo suggested, his young company agreeing heartily.

As they trudged down the hill and through the narrow, winding streets, Michelangelo continued his monologue, detailing the history of every church and palace, temple and ruin they passed, rising to the role of guide with palpable relish.

The city roiled with a bevy of activity, humming with noise and dynamic energy. Though its population had declined greatly in the scourge of plague that passed but five years ago, still a bit more than half a million people called Rome their home. There could be no avoiding the odors of life with such a populace, though the municipal improvements had done much to keep it but a thin tang lost almost in the redolence of cuisine and cultivation.

He brought them through the Campo Fiori and its vast marketplace scented by the fecundity of fresh vegetables, cheese, fruits, and flowers. They scuttled through rows of colorful stalls and the crowds, the conflux of languages spoken creating a pastiche of sound.

"Rome is not a city unto itself, but many within the one." Michelangelo raised his gravelly voice over the din. "There are Germans, Arabs, French, and more, each with their own quarter, even the Jews. It is a celebration of mankind, but one that could easily become a riot with the utterance of a single wrong word."

He preened as he guided them, like a cock of the walk, and though he did not stop to speak to anyone—avoiding the need for introductions—he displayed them by his side with a protective pride bordering on the possessive. Many recognized Battista and called him greetings and good cheer, but he dallied no more than demanded by good manners, guarding Aurelia's anonymity as stridently as Michelangelo.

"What draws those people?" she asked of her guide as they meandered through a small intersection, a crowd of people gathered before a curved wall.

Michelangelo clapped his hands together. "Wonderful. There must be a new posting. You will find this most interesting."

The triumvirate approached the gathering, peering over and around the dozen or so people. One fresh piece of vellum, its ink clear and its edges untattered, stood out upon the layers of others much less intact, and gummed to the stone base of the oddest-looking sculpture Aurelia had ever seen. Missing both its arms—a rusted metal rod protruded from one shoulder—and both its legs—one cut off at the knee, the other at the hip—the face of the figure had all but vanished as time and weather had worn it down.

"What manner of lunacy is this?" she whispered, incredulous.

Michelangelo smiled. "It is, or was, a bust of Menelaus," he explained. "The creator has never been definitively attributed. However, common thought places its genesis in the Hellenistic period, a few centuries before the birth of Christ, or thereabouts. But only recently did the gentleman obtain his current moniker. They call him Pasquino."

Aurelia raised a brow at him. "Pasquino?"

"Indeed." Battista smiled, taking up the story, clearly one he warmed to, though he lowered his mouth closer to Aurelia and his voice dropped in his throat. "Censorship is strong in Rome, perhaps more so than elsewhere on the peninsula. It has become the custom for those who wish to speak against the popes and the Vatican to post their criticisms on such effigies scattered throughout the city."

"Talking statues," Michelangelo interjected.

Battista nodded. "Just so. This one in particular has become quite famous. For many years, it was the site of the most erudite and scathing slander made against the pope. It became clear to the locals that the broadsheets were the work of the tailor, one who served the papal court, whose shop lay very near to this spot. Just around the corner, there." He pointed to the narrow road running off to the east. "He was as widely known for his intellect and wit as for his skill with needle and thread. Not long after the neighborhood folk surmised that the tailor, Pasquino by name, was the author did he go missing. Never to be seen or heard from again."

"Never?" Aurelia's voice squeaked.

"Never," Michelangelo and Battista chorused.

As the word died upon his tongue, the slim and slight Michelangelo turned, slipping sideways into the crowd, leaning close to the parchment with squinting eyes.

"What is it?" Battista asked as his friend rejoined them.

Michelangelo shook his head. "Nothing. It is . . . no, nothing."

"Are you sure?" Battista put a hand upon the artist's shoulder. "You seemed troubled."

"Not troubled. Thoughtful, no more. Come, there is much left to see."

The sun, now fully revealed, beat down upon their heads from its early afternoon perch and the stream of people in the streets thinned as the residents made for their repasts and their rests.

"I shall take you to the Hostaria dell'Orso. It is not only the cleanest inn in the city, it is my favorite," Michelangelo chirped as he led them through the Piazza Fiammetta, so named for the mistress of Cesare Borgia, the son of the pope, and on, to the shade of the Palazzo di Riario. Diagonally across from the square angles of the cream stone building stood the Inn of the Bear. The tables, set out on a flagstone terrace, were tucked into the coolness of a vine-covered arbor edged with classical columns.

Both staff and owner of the *hostaria* greeted Michelangelo with the acquaintance of family, seating them at the best table, in the far corner snuggled deep in the shadows, only pinpoints of dappling sun dusting the cubby with its light. They sat at the round cherrywood table—their backs to the vines with the little yellow flowers—one on each side of Michelangelo, as instructed. From here, they could see the comings and goings on the crisscrossing streets and the other tables on the terrace.

"Just beyond that turn, on the Via Sistina, is my old house, my first home here in Rome." Michelangelo pointed the way with a small snigger. "It was very small and very cold, and yet some fond memories linger."

"People have a wonderful capacity to forget the pain and remember only the pleasure," Aurelia said.

"You speak the truth, my dear, for the preservation of our hearts and our souls. And yet we must learn from our pain, while we forget it." He raised a tankard in salute. "To the human conundrum."

Michelangelo ordered them all a serving of the soup of the country, crusty loaves of bread scooped out and filled with fish and tomato gravy. Aurelia ate greedily, soon finishing the broth, spicy with oregano and garlic, and the chunks of tender fish, and began tearing off pieces of the edible bowl, now soaked and flavorful, and munched on them slowly, enjoying every morsel. The activity of the morning had done much to restore her spiritless appetite, and the fresh air—the tang of the river just to their north—did much to reinvigorate her thirst. Once more, she found herself swelling with joy at forbidden adventure.

Her hearty feasting continued unabated, the indulgent smiles of her companions as they watched her unnoticed.

"It is not often I find myself in the company of such beautiful people," Michelangelo mused, sitting back, taking his tankard with him. "I am a lucky man to have such companions."

"We are equally as grateful for your company, *amico mio,*" Battista assured him, taking a last bite of his bread and a hand-covered belch, having eaten every bite put before him.

Michelangelo grinned. "I agree. We three make a fine group. But I regard your physical beauty." The artist's critical appraisal brushed along the curves of their faces and the dichotomous yet equally pleasing shapes of their bodies.

"What there is between you enhances each other's beauty," he continued, ignoring the shared tender gaze between them and the slight bloom warming Aurelia's cheeks. Michelangelo threw back a gulp of wine and leaned forward, elbows on the table as he looked keenly at her.

She smiled back at him curiously, as if she could see all the thoughts working behind his amber eyes.

"You know, I rarely paint women; I find more that is interesting and worthy in the structural power of the male form, as I was taught."

He did not say it as an insult, though it would be easy to perceive the words as such, and Aurelia did not take it so.

"But when I look at you, Monna Aurelia." His gaze, burning now with creative passion, flitted between them. "When I look at you two together, I cannot help but wish for a brush and some canvas. Perhaps I shall put you both in a painting."

She sputtered out the wine like water from a busted well, spattering the table and her face with red splotches.

Battista jumped to her side and dabbed her chin, blotting the drips of wine clinging there as he slapped her gently on the back.

"Are you all right?" he asked, hovering with concern.

Aurelia could only nod as the coughing spasm subsided.

"Does the thought not please you, Aurelia?" Michelangelo chortled as a serving maid rushed over and cleaned the table with a stained, damp rag.

"No . . . I mean, yes . . . but no." Aurelia's tongue tangled in her mouth, bereft of any coherent word to ply upon it. There was so very much of the absurd in the turns of her life—especially those encountered on this adventure—but that would be one far too bizarre to abide. She turned her acuity from Battista's frowning inquisition and settled herself with a deep breath.

"Of course, *messere*, to be rendered by the master Michelangelo would be the greatest compliment of a lifetime." She smiled with only the slightest quaver of deceit upon her lips. "However, I fear there is no time. As I am so much healed, I believe Battista and I will soon be continuing our quest."

"Ah, *sì*, your quest." Michelangelo seemed satisfied by her reply, if not pleased. He stood, the legs of his chair scraping against the stone terrace. "Then let us continue our tour. There are things you must see before you leave Rome."

He brought them across the bridge at Sant'Angelo and slowly passed the towering cylindrical edifice, guarded and topped by stone angels.

"It was a mausoleum, first and foremost," Michelangelo told them, "built by the Emperor Hadrian in the first century."

"Second," Battista corrected, but without a peep of superiority.

"Ah *sì, sì*. The second," Michelangelo nodded his thanks. "It did not become a fortress until the late thirteenth, under Nicholas the Third. See that passageway?"

Aurelia followed the artist's gesturing finger, her gaze finding and trailing the path of an elevated walkway, the Castel Sant'Angelo anchoring one end, the Vatican the other. Continuous parapets crowned the covered corridor of pale russet stone as the arches held it up from below.

"It provides safe passage for the pope, should a quick guarded retreat be needed."

Battista glared with ill-disguised disdain at the fortress.

"You care not for this place, do you?" Aurelia asked him.

He looked down at her, crinkles of contempt smoothing away, though not completely. "No, I do not. Many a good citizen has been imprisoned in those walls."

"Yes, it serves as a prison, and a place of execution," Michelangelo said. "And in its center, it is rumored, there lies a treasury, a safe room for all the riches obtained by the popes, the art and the relics of both ancient and current civilizations."

"Relics?" Battista stopped, staring at the castle, curiosity replacing his disdain.

Michelangelo pursed his lips with a vague shake of his head. "If the relic you seek was in the possession of the Vatican, I can assure you, any evidence of its existence . . . and any who know of it . . . would have disappeared long ago. Never underestimate the power within those walls, a force that has nothing to do with God."

It was a respectful condemnation, if such a one existed, but a truth. She had heard the same from her guardians as they warned her never to come to this place.

Michelangelo led them west, to the right, and along the curving Borgo Santo Spirito. The crowds around them grew, cramming the lane with many a bowed and hooded head, many a rattling prayer bead. A tranquil hum filled the air, the sound of voices low with mumbled prayers. Soon, the looming wall surrounding the Vatican rose up before them.

As they turned into a vast courtyard, as soon as Aurelia placed one foot onto the pale, uneven flagstones—worn rounded and smooth by hundreds of years and thousands of pilgrims—she stopped, clutching her good arm over the injured.

"What is amiss?" Battista grumbled, throwing one arm protectively about her shoulders as his gaze flitted warily about the crowded courtyard. He pulled her close to the massive walls—at least seven stories high and fortified with circular towers—surrounding the grounds, the cool stone creating a shaded oasis.

"No, I am fine. Truly, Battista," Aurelia assured him, touched by the fierce gentleness of his concern. "I just felt . . ." Her voice trailed away and she turned to Michelangelo. "This is the place of St. Peter, isn't it?"

"It is." Michelangelo stretched out his arms. "All of this land, stretching to the castle, was part of what the ancients called the Ager Vaticanus, the Vatican Field. And it is just there where Peter was martyred, there he was crucified upon an inverted cross." He pointed to a pink stone obelisk rising into the air, just to the south of the Basilica.

Aurelia shivered and Battista pulled her closer. She smiled up at him. "I can feel his spirit embrace me."

"Many visitors say the same," Michelangelo said. "Though it is only those who possess great spirit themselves."

Stepping out of the walls' shadow, he took them into the sunlight. As the crowd milled around them, Michelangelo pointed out the other highlights of the compound, the churches and palazzos, monuments and chapels, an ever-expanding hodgepodge of buildings, with each pope contributing his own touch to the structural composition.

"In the Basilica, you will find Giotto's mosaic." Michelangelo faced due west and the old building surrounded with scaffolds and men. "It has been under construction for years now. I sometimes think it will be lifetimes before it is complete."

He moved toward it, as if impelled by his own eagerness to see it finished. "I have seen Bramante's plans. It will be one of the greatest buildings known to man, if they can construct it."

Aurelia stepped up beside him. "I have no wish to see any but your masterpiece."

The artist ducked his head humbly. "Then far be it from me to deprive you."

With Battista, he led her east, to an enclosed marble staircase and two large bronze doors at the top, two halberd-armed guards stationed to each side. With a barely perceptible tic of their heads, the guards parted for Michelangelo, who murmured a soft, "*Grazie.*"

"What do you think of their uniforms?" Michelangelo waggled his brows and flicked his head at the guards left behind, his low voice echoing in the empty passageway.

Amused, Aurelia turned back. Brilliant and distinct with bold stripes of yellow and blue, the soldiers' puffed pantaloons matched their stockings and their doublets, the latter accented with edges of bright red beneath crested breastplates. The skullcaps beneath their pointed, shiny helmets bore the same stripes.

"Quite debonair," she proclaimed.

To which Michelangelo smiled broadly and, with a finger over his lips, declared, "I designed them as well."

Aurelia's face burst with stunned delight, turning to Battista and finding confirmation in his prideful grin.

Inside the portal, a barrel-vaulted hallway bright with white-washed walls and multibranched chandeliers split in two directions.

Aurelia followed Michelangelo, staring curiously about, unable to contain the puzzled expression from creeping onto her face.

"I am sorry to disappoint you, my dear," he said. "But we must traverse a part of the Apostolic Palace in order to reach the chapel."

"What of its own entrance?"

"There isn't one, really," he told her. "Nothing large or ornate at any rate. It can only be reached through the palace. But none of its grandeur is lost for it. On the outside, it is but a plain rectangular building, as Pope Sixtus wished. There is no external decoration or architecture of any note. There is nothing to miss."

"How extraordinary," Aurelia breathed.

"It should not be overly crowded," Michelangelo said as he led them through a series of small though resplendent rooms and passageways. "It is not open to the public at this hour and only a few are permitted access at this time of day."

The hallway let out into a courtyard, which led to a small door in the side of a nondescript brick building. But just beyond lay Heaven itself.

A few steps in and Aurelia's gaze, her whole head, lifted, and lifted still more, her whole body almost toppling backward at the exquisite vision opening above her. If not for Battista, and a steadying hand at her back, she would have fallen to the floor.

They were alone in the chapel, as Michelangelo had predicted, and she almost wished she could—dared—abandon all propriety and lie upon the cold stone at her feet, all the better to see the splendor overhead.

"T . . . tell me," she eked out the words, voice strangled through her bent throat, nostrils full of thick incense and burning wax.

Michelangelo snorted but with little glint of humor in it.

"It was nothing but blue paint and gold stars. The commission offered was enormous, or so I thought at the time. But the pope paid far more to others for far less work." Michelangelo rubbed the space between his eyes, hand held almost protectively over his distinctive nose, the lines of struggle etched tellingly across his face. "It must have been Raphael's charm, my own could never compare to it, which brought him such treasures."

Battista stepped behind the artist, wrapping his strong, protective arms over the man's chest, leaning down to whisper in his ear, "Raphael will be remembered. You, *caro mio,* will be glorified. True compensation is far more satisfying."

Michelangelo rested his head onto the arms creating a shield about him, taking in all the succor offered. Aurelia stared at these men, their tenderness heartbreaking, their beauty a creation of God as surely as the masterpiece above them. How many people had the tools to create such masterpieces and simply refused them for their own misguided fears.

"When Julius set me to the task, I knew it had been at the urging of others, those who would keep me from my chisel, those who would see me fail."

Aurelia wrenched her gaze from the ceiling to look at Michelangelo, needing to look him in the eye. "You triumphed, over them, over all. You created this, but this made you the grand master."

The hollows beneath the elder man's eyes grew darker, a brush of fatigue painting his wrinkled face, and he stared at the nave before them, unwilling or unable to turn his gaze upward. "It was an ascension that felled me, I assure you."

They stood side by side in the narrow center aisle of the chapel, his voice a low guttural rumble echoing through the cavelike chamber. He told them of the long years of anguish and turmoil as he set about his task, beginning with the design of an appropriate scaffold, one that put no holes in the ceiling, as that proposed by Bramante would have done. Michelangelo spoke of his struggle with vertigo, the dizzying, nauseating condition that had assailed him since he was thirteen and working on the Santa Maria Novella.

"How many times I vomited into a bucket through . . . all this." He waved his hand at the ceiling twenty meters over their heads. "It is a wonder I had any meat left on my bones."

"I have heard," Aurelia whispered, bending now sideways from the waist as her neck grew fatigued, "that you were obliged to convince Pope Julius of your design."

Michelangelo laughed at her polite choice of words. "We argued like Crusader and infidel, I being the Crusader, of course. But to answer, yes, what I wanted went far beyond his original vision and I had to convince him to love it, though love it in the end he did. He interrupted me constantly, and constantly I had need to assure him."

The artist walked farther up the aisle, Battista passing him and continuing on, as Michelangelo gestured to the three horizontal tiers of the side walls. On his right, the muted tones of golds and blues detailed the stories of Christ as rendered by Pietro Perugino, Sandro Botticelli, Cosimo Rosselli, and Domenico Ghirlandaio. To the left, the south wall depicted the Story of Moses with the same diffused shades by the same artists, the paintings frescoed upon the middle tiers.

"Julius wanted the Apostles to be adorned over these stories, simple renderings, one for each of the pendentives."

Aurelia stretched her neck once more to the triangular segments supporting the vaulted ceiling.

"But there was far too much more of man's spiritual journey to be said. There was too much space available in which to say it." Michelangelo sat on the edge of a pew, elbows upon his knees, head in his hands. He recalled painful memories; they were there in every curve and bow of his slight body, the pleasure of the achievement muddied by the struggle of its creation.

Aurelia moved not an inch, eyes locked upon the vision above as if locked upon Heaven itself. She could only imagine how such an achievement had drained so much of his energy—every creation kept a piece of its creator—and why he had failed to be productive for so many years afterward, his creative juices dried, the blood of it painted on this ceiling.

"Is that—" The words tripped over her lips as she pointed to a particularly intriguing scene within a lunette, but Michelangelo stopped her.

"There are more than three hundred figures above us, my dear. I would need many days to tell you of them all." He reached for her hand, his affection tempering his glibness. "I am not sure it is meant to be taken as individual pieces, but as a whole. Yes, I could tell you that there are nine scenes from the book of Genesis. There are the Apostles and prophets, and the ancestors of Christ. But there have been so many who have analyzed the work." He shook his head. "They try to wrench the spirit of it away with their academia."

Aurelia stepped closer, keeping his hand in hers as she stood beside him. "And tell me of the spirit, Michelangelo, of your spirit and your message."

He looked up at her and she almost staggered back at the wave of gratitude in his powerful gaze. It was as if no one had ever asked it of him, though he longed to tell.

"Need," he answered simply, a powerful, potent whisper. "Man's need, of God, of salvation. It terrifies us and yet we pray for it with every morsel of our being. There is . . ."

He faltered, voice catching with emotion. "There is more, much more than I could ever, should ever, tell."

Wiping his face brusquely with the back of his hand, he looked back up at her, and held. He turned to the stone he loved so very much.

All sadness and heartbreak, need and despair, disappeared, swept away as if wiped with a harsh cloth. His amber eyes bulged from sunken sockets, his throat bobbled up and down, swallow after dry swallow. Michelangelo stared at her . . . at one of the renderings just beyond her face . . . and back, again and again. His skin burst with red splotches. His hand trembled in hers.

Aurelia dared not turn, dared not look at what he had seen; she had no need. She saw it in his face; he had seen something, something he had created with his own hand, but only just now—in that very instant as he looked upon her face—did he discover its meaning.

She leaned down toward him, moving her head closer and into the fore of his vision.

"You . . . ," he mumbled.

Aurelia squeezed his hand tighter, a quick glance at Battista, who ambled near the altar a distance from them, a silent plea for Michelangelo, holding him with screaming silence. Slowly, Michelangelo closed his mouth, moving his other hand to cover hers with a rasp of his rough skin.

Aurelia begged him softly, "You were speaking of things better left unsaid, secrets needing to be, that must always be, buried."

Battista turned round and headed back toward them from the east, just as a Swiss Guard creaked open the door in the west wall.

The time for any more words ended. As he turned to the guard, Michelangelo twitched one eye at her. It was the vaguest sign of collusion but one she must hang on to, at least for now.

A pall fell upon Battista at the sight of the soldier. Their day had been so filled with enchantment, but their truths lay just below the sound of gentle laughter, ever ready to end the pleasure of each moment. Was the guard there for him or Aurelia? Either possibility put him on the defense, and he checked his hip for his daggers with a slow nonchalant motion as he hurried back up the aisle.

"Signore Buonarroti." The guard offered a straight-backed, sharp nod as he approached.

"Yes, young man?"

"The pope graciously offers his hospitality to you and your guests."

"He does, does he?" Michelangelo looked to his companions with a half smirk hidden beneath his bushy facial hair. "Then we'd best not keep His Holiness waiting."

He held out his arm to Aurelia as they stepped away.

Battista followed, fisted hands by his sides, his unspoken fears yet to be realized. He had thought it imprudent to visit the Vatican, held in the sway of a Medici, but had not been able to deny Aurelia a sight of the chapel or Michelangelo's delight in showing it to her. That the pope knew of their presence after such a short length of time came as no surprise, though Battista had hoped—prayed—they would come and go long before his all-seeing eye fell upon them.

Battista was no friend to the Medici, nor was the fact a secret; it had not been for quite some time, and as Aurelia tugged on her veil, pulling it down, covering as much of her face as possible, he wondered on her relationship with them as well. Or perhaps it was the pope, as the master of the Church, whom she had no wish to encounter. It mattered naught, served only to exacerbate Battista's apprehension.

With another precise bow, the guard led them forward, halberd held tight by his side.

"No, not that way." Michelangelo stepped forward with his protest as the soldier took them through a smaller chapel, heading left. With a flapping, insistent hand, Michelangelo directed him to the right.

Behind them, Aurelia raised her brows and her shoulders to Battista. Leaning down sideways, his hand on the small of her back, he whispered in her ear, "Raphael's rooms."

Aurelia opened her mouth in a silent *oh* of acknowledgment, smiling at Michelangelo as he turned back, as they turned right and descended a series of stairs.

Out into the bright sunlight, they passed a tall, square building on their left.

"This is the Torre Borgia," Michelangelo said. "The infamous pope used it as a refectory, is that not right?"

"*Sì.*" The wide, protruding bones of the soldier's hard face barely moved as he spoke, his dark eyes fixed firmly forward.

They entered a large rectangular courtyard, one filled with people, terraces, fountains, and statues as well as plots of formal, sculptured gardens and angled stairs. A festive atmosphere lived in the air, one dictated by the beauty and sophistication of the setting.

"Ah, so he is in the library," Michelangelo murmured, not expecting, nor receiving, a reply.

"You are in for a treat, my dear." The artist offered again his arm to Aurelia. "You have mentioned your dedication to study. You will think you are in Heaven when you see this library. I hear at last count there are more than three thousand books, codices, and incunabula within these walls."

"Cannot be!" Aurelia cried, thunderstruck.

"*Sì*, 'tis true," Michelangelo assured her. "His Holiness, like so many before him, is a devoted scholar, and not just to works of the faith. You will see."

The guard held open one door of the large two-sided entrance and they stepped into a massive hallway, checkered marble tile upon the floor, delicate paintings of cream and blue, and soft umber upon the vaulted ceiling, the rows of columns, and their thick box-shaped bases.

Within the column-formed arches stood rows and rows of shelves filled to capacity with books of every shape and size. Battista found occasion to smile as Aurelia breathed deep, closing her eyes in pleasure at the pungent scent of leather, parchment, and ink as if she were in a resplendent and redolent garden.

Their heels clattered upon the tile, echoing in the quiet chamber. Here and there scapular-hooded novitiates and long-robed priests crossed their path, hovering silently through the hall, books in hand, academic specters intent on naught but gaining knowledge, vexed that any disturb their study.

Stopping with a squeak of a leather-heeled boot on the slick floor, the guard turned, directing them to his right and into a small cubby of two-sided mahogany writing desks and thickly populated bookshelves.

"His Holiness will be with you shortly."

The soldier tromped off, weapons jangling in the stillness.

"I am not sure this is a good idea, Michelangelo," Battista whispered brusquely. He paced the narrow length of the space, hands clasped behind his back, clenched tightly together. Peering out of the cubby to the long corridor trailing away in two directions, he watched for more soldiers as well as the presence of the pope himself, listening for the jangling of more weapons.

"Nonsense," Michelangelo waved off his friend's caution, taking a turn about the room with far more relaxed leisure, studying the half-dozen paintings hanging in a tight pattern along the outside, windowless room. "If the pope were calling you forth to question your . . . your activities, it would not take place in the library."

Battista scoffed at himself with critical amusement. "Quite right."

"Don't forget, *caro*, you and the pope now have a mutual friend, *sì?* No, I'm sure this is no more than—"

The artist's words broke off like a dead branch in a vicious windstorm.

"What is it?" Battista rushed to his friend's side, Aurelia but a step behind.

Michelangelo stood before a painting, a long vertical rectangle of dark grays and whites and blues. Upon the canvas, a walled castle stood on the edge of the ocean, gray stone harsh against brilliant white waves crashing upon it, spraying up to the third- and fourth-story loopholes. Circling the exterior of the fortress, a constricting snake winding about the main keep, a staircase spiraled upward. From the artist's viewpoint, it appeared as if one could climb the staircase up to and into the twilight sky, one speckled with night's first stars.

Michelangelo's slight, stiff body hummed with energy; it buffeted against Battista and he feared for his friend's health, paying little regard to the painting. Until Michelangelo raised his hands to it, gnarled and shaking limbs hovering over the rendering.

"Michelangelo?" Battista reached out and took the slim shoulders in his grasp, ready to shake them if he must.

" 'I was pure and prepared to climb into the stars.' "

"What?" Battista scolded with his apprehension, unable to hear the meaning of the artist's words through his fear. "What are you saying?"

" 'I was pure and prepared to climb into the stars,' " Michelangelo repeated, but with the same singsong voice that alarmed Battista for its peculiar articulation.

"Dante," Aurelia breathed.

Battista cut his eyes at her; her dumbfounded stare now joined with Michelangelo's upon the painting.

He looked at it then, really looked, and in a rush the words made sense as Dante had spoken them, as he passed from Purgatory to Paradise in the *Commedia*. With one true glance, Battista noted the similarity to the castle in the Duccio, the last location on the map, the location of the last piece of the triptych.

"Where is it?" Battista hissed, leaning between them, brusquely nudging them aside with his large form. "I can't make out the signature."

Michelangelo shook his head. "Nor can I. But I know where this is."

"You do?" Battista heard Aurelia chorus the question.

Michelangelo slapped his hands upon his forehead, head falling backward as he left them upon it. "Now I understand. The words stuck in my head, but I had no idea what they meant, only that I *should* know it."

Battista took a deep breath, summoning all the patience he could muster. Placing his hand once more upon his friend's shoulder, he turned Michelangelo around with gentle insistence.

"Slow down, Michelagnolo," he hummed, plying the endearment given to the artist long ago by his father, one spoken only by the artist's closest compatriots, hoping it would calm Michelangelo and allow him to focus. "Tell us from the beginning. Of what words do you speak?"

Michelangelo's vague stare focused sharply upon the face of his dear friend. "Earlier today, when I read the notice posted to the Pasquino. I found a sentence that had no place."

Battista skimmed a look to Aurelia and saw his own consternation; so many of the clues they had needed existed where none belonged.

"It was yet another derisive commentary against the pope and his allying with the French king and yet, in the middle passage . . ." Michelangelo brought his fingertips to his brow and rubbed, as if calling forth the words as one would tempt a genie from a bottle. "It spoke of calling the dragon to his home. I thought it complete nonsense, the ravings of a lunatic. And yet I could not forget it. The words have been in my head for the whole of the day. Someone intended for you to find the words, you or someone else." He poked his temple as if it offended.

"And those words." Aurelia stepped into the crook of their entanglement, her body forming a triangle with theirs. "What do the words tell you of this picture?"

Michelangelo turned with the most reverent of slight smiles. "I know where it is, *donna mia*. I know this castle. It is not far from Florence, just to the north." He looked back to Battista. "It is the Castello della Dragonara."

"The Cast—"

"Ah, my dear Michelangelo, how dare you come to the Vatican and not say hello to me?"

The pope barged toward them like a ship pulling into port, one with no anchor, his tall, wide body larger than life in the pure white *sottana* and *mozetta* covering every inch of his body. He tipped his head and the slim line of jewels trimming the white zucchetto upon his almost-bald head sparkled, as did his dark gaze. He held out his hand and the Anello Piscatorio to the artist.

With a barely contained sigh, Michelangelo stepped up and, with a slight bow, brushed his lips across the Fisherman's Ring, the same worn by every pope. The relief of pure yellow gold depicted St. Peter fishing from a boat, a reminder that all Apostles were "fishers of men."

"I meant no slight, Holy Father, I swear to you. I know how busy you are and had no wish to disturb you." Michelangelo swept his gaze and his hand to his young companions. "We are here as tourists, no more."

Pope Clement laughed heartily. "You can never be a tourist here, Michelangelo, not anymore." He turned to the others, keeping a smile upon his bearded face. "Ah, and this sturdy young man must be Battista della Palla, if I guess correctly."

"You do, Holy Father." Battista dropped like a stone into a bow, reaching upward to kiss the offered ring, thoughts gnawing on how the pope came to know his name though they had never met. He straightened, catching the peculiar sight of Michelangelo squeezing Aurelia's hand behind her back, a covert gesture. "Your palace is a testament to God Himself."

"As it is meant to be, my son. You and I have mutual friends, or so I am told, important friends."

There could be no doubt he referred to King François, and Battista relaxed a bit at the mention of the ruler. "It is true, Holiness. I have called him friend for many years."

"I would ask you of him," the pope replied, turning his gaze upon Aurelia. "But first you must introduce me to this beautiful woman by your side. She is a mystery to me."

An irksome note sounded in the last words, and Battista thought to dispel the pope's ignorance quickly.

"This is the Lady Aurelia, she is . . ." Battista gave a shallow bow as he made the introductions, tongue sticking on a credible concept with which to clarify her, having never envisioned the need to do so, especially to a man such as this.

"My cousin," Michelangelo interjected with a bark. "From the north, on my mother's side."

It was true his late mother came from a noble lineage, unlike his father, and Michelangelo did indeed call more than one noblewoman cousin. But it was rare to find any member of the family in the company of the artist; they had all but abandoned Lodivico di Buonarroti and his motherless brood at the moment of Francesca's passing.

Aurelia bent over the pope's ring in silent obeisance, as expected from any woman, keeping her head bent low and her gaze humble through her veil.

"Are you enjoying your visit to the Vatican, my child?" the pope asked, his long face crinkled and quizzical as he looked upon Aurelia, and Battista recognized it with empathy; he had felt the same thing many times when looking at her himself, a strange mixture of fascination and suspicion.

"Very much, Holy Father," Aurelia replied softly.

"And what have you enjoyed the most?" Clement took a step back, penetrating gaze slipping slowly up and down the length of her, not with lascivious intent, but in study, as if she were one of the precious works of art held in the Holy City.

Her lips inched up at the corners. "The ceiling of the Sistine, Your Holiness. I have never seen the like, not even in my imagination."

Clement nodded sagaciously. "It is the same answer these days, though I myself agree. Why do you think that is? It is, after all, just a painting."

He plied the statement with outlandish intention, particularly with the creator standing beside him. Purposefully instigating, Battista thought, a question posed more for the nature of Aurelia's answer than the answer itself.

With her gaze upon Michelangelo, she answered forthrightly, "It is the physical realization of his spiritual gift. Few are able, in this life, to find it. We all know it, recognize it when we see it, and we envy and worship it at the same time."

The flood of words flew off her tongue, and Aurelia sucked the corner of her top lip into her mouth, as if to stem the tide.

"You have an astounding clarity of vision from those startling eyes of yours, my lady." Clement held up a hand, two fingers straight, two tucked down, and made a small sign of the cross before her. "And what were you to see next?"

"Actually, Holy Father, we were about to head for home," Michelangelo replied before the others could say different. "You know how easily fatigued I am. I fear I have no more strength left, for today at any rate."

"Then I shall see you out myself, shall I?" The pronouncement disguised itself as a question, and the corpulent pope took his place beside Battista as he led them out in the same direction they had come, Aurelia and Michelangelo behind, two Swiss Guards bringing up the rear.

"You feel François can be trusted, do you, della Palla?"

Battista found no words, taken aback by Clement's blunt approach to the matter. The irony of the discussion was not lost on him. "Indeed, Holy Father."

The pope scratched at the white skullcap upon his head. "I hope you are right, young man. I hope *I* am right. And what of Henry, the English king? What do you know of him?"

"Very little," Battista answered honestly. He knew the sovereign to be but another player in the juggling for power that had gone on between France, Spain, and England for time untold. He knew what François thought of his English counterpart, for the king and his mother and sister had railed on against the aggressive sovereign many a time when in Battista's company.

"I think he may be a bit mad." Clement chuckled with dark amusement. "He has taken one agreement to think he can secure another." The pope's voice plunged to a barely coherent mumble. "Divorce. Utter madness, I tell you."

Battista said nothing, for surely nothing could he be expected to say to such a proclamation. The pope shook his head and turned back to Michelangelo.

"And what of my library, my friend? How does it progress?"

Michelangelo nodded with his specter of a smile. "Quite well, Holy Father. Better than I anticipated. In fact, I shall be returning to Florence within the next few days, in the company of these two delightful young people."

"Well, aren't you the lucky man?" the pope said.

"Oh yes," Michelangelo replied, avoiding Battista's pointed stare. "Very lucky indeed."

Twenty-four

Less than a drop of blood remains in me
that does not tremble; I recognize the signals of the ancient flame.

—*Purgatorio*

A rooster crowed in the distance, a raucous laugh at those who thought to stay abed, and the soft bells of morning called the faithful to mass. Aurelia snuggled into the stillness of daybreak, one unlike any found at other times. Dawn built a bridge for her, one out of her body, one allowing the stillness to enter her, to cleanse her thoughts of clutter.

Gliding down the stairs, slipping silently into the dark kitchen, she took a long draught of mulled cider and threw open the shutters, breathing in the unsullied lush air of a new day. Mourning doves cooed in the trees between the house and the studio, and Aurelia closed her eyes, letting the soothing sound fill her. Curling up in the well-worn stuffed chair before the window, she tucked the layers of her homespun gown beneath her legs. As the sun crept over the horizon, the enveloping blanket of light and warmth tucked her in.

The strange sound pulled at her, a low but insistent scratching. Aurelia struggled to open her eyes, so deeply had she fallen into meditation, the surface of consciousness lay far above.

Aurelia peered across the room through the hazy slits of her eyes and glimpsed Michelangelo, perched on a corner stool, almost hidden in the opaque shadows the room accommodated, hand flying furiously across the paper he hunched over, eyes jumping from her to the creation of her he conceived and back. She should stop him, but each stroke felt like a caress, as if he brushed her jawline with his fingers instead of rendering it with his charcoal. It was a wondrously soothing feeling, and she luxuriated in it, banishing all thought of consequence, allowing him—and the birth of the day—to continue without disruption.

Too soon the floor above them creaked as others in the household awoke; groggy, companionable voices passed outside the window as men made their way to the studio. The day had commenced against both their desires.

"No one will ever see it, *donna mia*," he spoke without lifting his eyes, using the finest point of the charcoal now, making only the minutest movements with his hand.

She chuckled softly, but didn't move. "Ah, so you know it is forbidden."

Michelangelo shrugged one shoulder, but continued his work. "I knew when the vision came to me all those years ago in the chapel. And I know it now. But my adoration will not allow me to stop." He shrugged again. "Of course it is forbidden, or else you would not be on this quest, *sì?*"

He looked at her then, head cocked to the side, brow furrowing as his hand stilled.

"Why *did* you come? Surely there are others who would be, should be, charged with this task?"

Aurelia opened her eyes, calamitous thoughts barging their way into her mind; there would be no turning back, not for this day.

"You will think me frivolous and selfish." She hung her head, unable to look him in the eye.

She heard his scuffling steps approach, found his kind face appear in her downcast gaze. Michelangelo knelt at the side of her chair, one hand taking hers, the other holding his parchment.

"I should not have a bad thought of you, Aurelia." He breathed a laugh. "Who am I to judge one such as you? Or anyone, for that matter."

"I came," Aurelia found the words in his unconditional empathy, "for me."

He tilted his head yet again. "*Scusi?*"

Aurelia patted his hand with a smile. "I had, of late, found the burden of my position difficult to bear, the isolation of it most especially, the terrible sameness of it." Her smile fled. "I wanted to experience this life, not just be a witness to it, but the lighter side of life, not that of duty and responsibility."

"The lighter side of life?" Michelangelo's raspy voice fairly squeaked with incredulity. "And you have chosen this . . . this quest . . . to find the *lighter* aspect of life?"

Aurelia threw back her head and laughed with unadulterated delight. Michelangelo, jaw dropping for half an instant, joined her, dancing with her in the irony.

Their laughter flittered away, the lark on a soft spring breeze, and he placed her drawing in her lap and released his charcoal to the floor. Taking both her hands with his, he kissed them.

"You and those who will follow you have my heart, my fealty, and my silence, Madonna Aurelia." He whispered his pledge with formality. "Now and forever."

Tears came to her eyes; she found the feel of them strange. In all her years, she could not remember a moment so breathtaking, so heartbreaking, as to bring her to tears. Whatever the consequences of her impetuous actions might be, to know this man, to experience him and Rome and all he had shown her, was a joy worthy of it all.

"I ask but one thing." Michelangelo lowered his forehead to the knuckles of her hand, voice muffled into the puffed and worn fabric of the chair arm. "That you bring no harm to Battista, to *amore mio*. That I could not bear."

Aurelia sniffed a sigh, it was a difficult request, but one she had already pledged herself to. How much easier things would have been were Battista not the man he was, possessing such beauty, of every incarnation.

She picked up the parchment in her lap, studied the face so skillfully etched upon it, one so familiar and yet alien. "I must do whatever I must, but I can promise you no hurt shall befall him, least not while our lives intersect, for he is m . . . my love as well."

She gave him a conditional answer, and she saw the edge of dissatisfaction in his honey-colored eyes. His throat throttled a swallow and his ethereal smile peeped out at her once more.

"I shall come with you, then, if I may," he requested with a giddiness more suited to a child. "I would see the end of this, at least from Firenze."

"A wonderful idea," she assured him. "You shall be marvelous company on the journey. It will be well that you are near, once—"

"*Buongiorno.*" Battista popped his head into the kitchen, face bright with glee. "Frado has returned. We make for Florence."

Just as quickly, he darted out, leaving Aurelia and Michelangelo warm in the wake of him.

Michelangelo stood and took the parchment, gaze roving over it with a critical though pleased eye. As she stood and joined him, as they headed for the door, he stepped to the low house fire, no more than burning cinders not yet stoked for the day, and placed the thin drawing material upon the glowing embers.

They left the kitchen, Aurelia's likeness turning to fluttering ash behind them.

❧ Twenty-five ❧

Beauty awakens the soul to act.

—*Purgatorio*

They passed the Porta Flaminia as the midday sun arched overhead, their horses tossing their heads as they crammed through the northernmost gate leading out of the city with hundreds of others, on foot and on horse, who came and went on any given day. Just beyond the gate, just past the dirt-stained brick face of the Aurelian Wall constructed more than a century and a half ago, the hard-packed, well-traveled road split into two. Battista led his small group to the left and onto the Via Cassia, the major thoroughfare leading all the way to Florence.

He was not well pleased to have left so late in the day; he had all intentions of setting off at day's first light. But Michelangelo did not travel as quickly or as well as the others, and Battista made concessions to his elder friend with but a little annoyance.

"I will enjoy this journey so very much more than the one which brought me here," Michelangelo grumbled to Frado, who rode beside him. "Granacci and Gianotti were very cranky for the entire two days."

Battista shared a sidelong glance with Aurelia, seeing the same amusement in her light-dappled eyes, never so brilliant, even through her veil, never so green, as when the sunlight gleamed through them. Michelangelo complained halfheartedly; his two friends were invaluable to him, as loved as he was loved in return. No doubt they were as miffed as he by the artist's sedate pace.

"We will spend the night in Poggibonsi." Michelangelo raised his voice to reach the two young people ahead of him. "At my favorite inn. I stop there whenever I pass from Rome to Florence or back. They know me well."

"I can well imagine." Battista rolled his eyes at Aurelia, and she stifled a twitter in the thickness of a forced cough.

It had rained the night before, a hard, drenching rain, and the dirt of the road had yet to dry, had yet to turn to dust and be kicked up to clog their throats and their eyes. As the crowds of travelers thinned, as the other wayfarers made their stops or their turns along the way, Aurelia pushed back her veil. As the horses trotted along—for Michelangelo was inclined to move no faster—her body bounced gently in the saddle and she raised her closed eyes to the sun.

Battista laughed at the sight of her.

Aurelia opened her left eye at him. "What is so amusing?"

"You." He laughed again fondly. "You are quite the sight."

The soft breeze in the hot, dry air picked up the long strands of curls streaming down her back, a chestnut profusion of shimmering floss. No longer did she feel the need to pin and tuck it beneath her veil, but she allowed it to fall free like water from a cliff.

"You are hardly recognizable as the same woman I met not so very long ago."

Even as he said the words, his mind chewed upon their time together. He had known her a lifetime but knew her not at all. Thrust together more than a month ago, they had found pleasure and succor in each other's arms for more than a fortnight. And yet the air of mystery still hung about her, one he could not unravel, no matter how hard he tried.

"I hope the woman I have become is a better one," Aurelia said with as much of a question.

He smiled, and with it he revealed all. "Better. More. You are more alive than you were."

Aurelia's smile stretched across her face, she closed her eyes again, tossed back her head, and threw open her arms, as if she embraced the world. "Alive. I am so very alive."

Battista shook his head kindly at her silliness, how very beautifully it became her.

"You will have much explaining to do when your guardian sees those freckles."

Pallor of face lent a woman nobility and prestige, the fairer of her sex charming men, while tanned skin betrayed those of low birth who labored out of doors.

The shadow of what awaited Aurelia crossed her face; his stomach lurched at the thought of it. It quivered his intestines, as did the prospect of a dishonorable death.

Aurelia shook her head at her future. "Pale skin is but a badge we are forced to wear, one proclaiming us to be controlled, kept safely locked away in our cages."

He reached out and captured her horse's bridle, pulling her closer, their horses rubbing flanks as they traipsed along.

"You are a spirit that can never be contained." His gaze caressed her face, his vision touching what his lips longed for. "You are free here." He touched her then, unable not to, cupping the back of her head in one large palm, caressing her cheek with the pad of his thumb.

"You could be free forever, if you choose. I would always protect you. I know—"

"Don't," she begged him even as she leaned into his touch, closing her eyes as she nuzzled her head into his hand.

"Look!" Michelangelo called from behind them, a finger outstretched. "The turn to Poggibonsi. It is just ahead."

Battista took back his hand, but with a look assuring her it was only for the moment, and sniffed a laugh. "We have been on the road but for a few hours and already he wants to stop for the day."

Aurelia grinned. "We will make an early start. We will give him no choice. Even at this pace we will see the gates of Florence by tomorrow's end, *sì*."

"We had better," Battista grumbled, lighter, though, for her encouragement. He turned his horse onto the craggy stone road, leaning forward as the path steepened.

"This is a very important road, Aurelia. Did you know that?" Michelangelo asked, still playing the part of her guide with relish.

"I did not," Aurelia replied with equal zeal.

"Some say it was first blazed in the ninth century. Sigeric the Serious, the Archbishop of Canterbury, most assuredly used it at the end of the tenth. Upon this road he traveled to and from Rome to be consecrated." Michelangelo raised his eye to the tips of the tall trees lining the upward-inclined trail, evening's breeze pitching them gently to and fro, the soughing of the leaves full and rich. "Since then thousands of pilgrims have passed upon it to make for the Holy City."

"Our faith knows no boundaries," Aurelia mused, casting a fey smile over her shoulder at the artist.

Battista had seen the same smile on her face that morning, as he came upon Aurelia and Michelangelo together in the kitchen. Something had grown between them, and though it bore no similarity to what Battista shared with her, he could not help but feel a nasty pinch of jealousy. He wanted her to stay with him, but she had brushed away the first and only mention of it. He had no wish to share what little time he did have with her, as selfish as he knew that to be.

They crested the long gradient, and a rolling landscape spread out before them, one rich with towering dark green cypress trees and thick with rows of grape- and olive vines. Atop the next hill, the next *poggi*, the village of Poggibonsi sat like a crown. Once a fortress owned by Bonizzo Segni, the remnants of the multitowered ramparts were still visible at the top, spaced teeth in a smiling mouth.

With a click of his tongue, Michelangelo bounced in his saddle as he urged his horse into a plopping canter and surged forward.

"I will lead now," he called. "I know just which gate to use to bring us straight to the inn."

Battista scoffed kindly and shook his head. "I have never seen him this . . . this cheerful," he told Aurelia, surprising himself with the use of the word in context with his moody friend. "This is your influence, *donna mia*. I have no doubt."

Aurelia did nothing to deny it. "Sometimes it takes others to bring out our best." She smiled at him shyly, but with an edge of potent sensuality, one that found him urging his horse on a bit faster, to the inn and the beds within it.

As they loped up to the charming building of pale ochre stone, no one came out of the dark wood doors of the same polished and carved walnut as the shutters and window frames. Pots of lush, newly budding flowers overflowed from the flat roof with the promise of a splendid terrace just beyond, but it appeared deserted.

"How very strange," Michelangelo said as he allowed Battista to help him from his horse. "The hospitality here is always exemplary. I have never *not* been greeted within an instant of my arrival."

Frado tied the horses to the weather-hewn posts as Michelangelo, with Battista by his side and Aurelia just a step behind, entered the coolness of the common room.

The room was invitingly outfitted with round wooden tables and wide-based chairs. Wine bottles—those full of a variety of vintages and those covered with doused candles bumpy with dried drippings—circled round it, perched on the surrounding shelf and sharing the space with pots of redolent herbs and bunches of dried flowers. The smell of the morning's bread and the sweetness of fruit clung to the air, and yet not a patron filled a seat, not a voice could be heard from beyond the other side of the two-sided fireplace.

"Stranger still," Michelangelo hissed.

"There is something amiss here." Battista reached behind him and drew a dagger from his sheath. He thrust out his other hand as a shield, stepping in front of Michelangelo and Aurelia protectively.

Booming footfalls thundered down the steps set back in the far right corner of the room. Battista swiveled on his heels, falling into a slight and ready crouch.

"Is that you, Conchetta?" The urgent call cracked with concern as a young man plunged down the stairs, pinwheeling to a stop at the sight of the four strangers.

Battista held up his free hand, tucking his dagger-wielding fist behind him. "Have no fear, *messere*, we are but travelers come for food and lodging."

The man shook his head of shaggy golden hair. "I am very sorry, signore, but I am afraid we are closed today." Though he spoke politely, his soft brown eyes rose up, back up the stairs to whatever concerned him on the upper floors.

"Jacopo?" Michelangelo stepped around Battista. "Where are your parents?"

The man, if he was indeed Jacopo, squinted at the newcomers, their faces shadowy with the light of the windows at their backs.

"It is me, Jacopo, Michelangelo."

"Oh, *Dio mio*, Signore Buonarotti." The gangly youth rushed forward, taking Michelangelo's hand, the clinging odor of tension thick on his simple tunic and hose. "I am so sorry. I did not see you."

"What is happening, dear boy?" Michelangelo reached up and placed a soothing hand on the bony shoulder. "Are your parents not here?"

"No, signore, they are traveling. My . . . my wife and I have come in from the farm for a few days to watch over the inn. But . . .

but she is . . ." Jacopo inched backward to the foot of the stairs, shoulders turning away. "Ornella labors, badly I fear. I have called for the midwife, but she does not come."

Battista's mouth went dry; so many women were lost in the throes of childbirth, he had heard of it all too often. "Where is this woman, the midwife?" he asked.

"On the next lane to the right. In the third house on the left."

Battista turned to Frado, and without a word the pudgy man set off at a run.

Battista looked to Aurelia. "Do you know of such things?" he asked softly.

"Only a little," she replied with a slight but fearful quaver. "You?"

"A little." Battista shrugged. "We will do what we can, *sì?*"

"Yes, of course." Aurelia stepped forward, holding out her hand to the frightened man. "Take us to your wife, Jacopo."

The youth's eyes grew wide with alarm as Battista came up behind her.

She grabbed onto the man's forearm, insistent but gentle. "In times of great need, we must accept any and all assistance offered. We cannot be burdened by propriety when lives are at stake."

Jacopo looked down at her and Battista watched, fascinated, as the worry lines between the young man's eyes smoothed away. With a quick nod, Jacopo led them up the stairs that turned right and then right again, stepping out onto a short hallway with two rooms on each side and one at the end.

As soon as they reached the second floor, low moans thick with pain and anguish reached out to them with unrelenting torment. In the far corner room, dark with closed shutters, fetid with human sweat, the woman lay on her back on the bed, her huge belly protruding from a slight frame, the sheets atangle about legs clenching and flexing as the pain ebbed and flowed through her body. Thick red hair bulged in a snarl from the back of her head, half-drenched with sweat, and her thin hands fisted in the linens.

They stepped forward just as another pain gripped her. The woman, who looked no more than a child to Battista, curled upward, head rising, eyes pinched, teeth grinding as the pain took hold.

Aurelia rushed forward, coming round the far side of the bed, laying one hand upon the woman's arm, the other on the swelled stomach.

"Easy, *cara mia*, do not fight it. Allow it with strength." It was a whisper and yet an assured mandate.

Ornella's eyes flashed open, crystal blue eyes, almost white against her face blotched red with effort. They narrowed in fear at the strange faces hovering over her, and she yelped at the sight of the tall Battista in her bedchamber.

"Have no fear, *piccolina*." Jacopo fell to his knees beside his wife's bed. "You must let them help us. Conchetta does not come."

The fear wrenched at the girl, as did the pain, and she growled into it.

"They are friends of Signore Buonarroti," Jacopo insisted. "Friends of Maestro Michelangelo."

The name worked its magic and the pallor of dread fled features still twisted in pain.

"How long has she toiled like this?" Battista whispered, as if to speak louder would disturb her.

Jacopo looked up at him. "Since early this morning, as I was making the bread."

Battista caught the flicker of concern in Aurelia's eye.

"Open the shutters, Jacopo," Aurelia told him, doggedly jutting her chin at him. "Yes, do it. The clean air will do her mind good, and the mind must be a partner in this chore."

Jacopo did as instructed, allowing Battista to take his place at the bedside, and they all breathed deeply as a waft of fresh twilight air swept through the room.

"Some cool water and some watered wine," Battista added. "She will feel so much better for a drink and a wash."

"I'll get it!" The hoarse cry came from the hall, followed by a scurry of feet as Michelangelo set himself to the task gratefully.

Ornella flung back onto the pillow, panting as the pain subsided.

"A drink." She smacked her parched lips at the thought of it, her voice sweet and melodic, if ragged with exhaustion.

Battista lowered to his knees near the bottom corner post of the bed, hands clasped on the edge as if in prayer.

"*Buonanotte,* signora," he said softly, keeping his distance, cooing as if to a frightened animal. "My name is Battista, Battista della Palla. And this is the Lady Aurelia."

Ornella's pale eyes switched from one to the other. "*B . . . buonanotte,*" she said finally.

"I know you suffer, my dear," he coaxed. "But do you think you might allow Aurelia to look beneath you, to make sure there is no blood," he rushed on at her uncertain look.

With cautious agreement, she nodded. Battista whirled away, before she could deny them, and listened to the shuffle of fabric as Aurelia lifted the sheets.

"That is well, Ornella, very well indeed."

Battista heard the smile in Aurelia's voice and turned back in time to see her lowering the sheets upon Ornella's thin legs. She looked so fragile, and it frightened him, but he knew the strength of women, one indeterminate by any physical appraisal; theirs came of the spirit and far outshone that of most men. He had learned it from his mother and his sister, watched them recover and soldier on as both lost their husbands. He had seen it by Aurelia's side, learned of her strength as she glimpsed and survived things he still could not reconcile.

Jacopo stepped to the threshold at Michelangelo's call, returning with a small pitcher set in an empty basin and a simple sterling chalice slopping with pale pink liquid. Aurelia took them and set them on the table at the bedside, first giving the woman a few sips, then immersing a cloth in the water to ply it soothingly upon the young woman's furrowed brow and gritty neck.

Ornella heaved a sigh as the coolness touched her skin, as the beverage dripped down her throat. Battista inched closer, watching as her face began to harden with another pain.

"We are going to look at your belly, Ornella." With methodical slowness, he moved one hand closer to the edge of the sheet as he signalled to Aurelia, instructing her with a pointed glance.

"What?" Jacopo yelped. "You cann—"

"We need to." Battista kept his smiling eyes upon Ornella. "It may tell us why you suffer so."

The young girl looked to her husband standing impaled with fear at the end of her bed. With a hard swallow, jaw clenching, head lifting as the pain thrust its way upon her, she gave a curt nod.

Battista lifted the edge. "I will turn it back no more than I have to, I promise. And Aurelia will lift your gown, *sì?*"

They did not wait for an answer; the pain possessed the girl wholly as they revealed the pale protrusion of her belly, her navel completely distended and flat, no more than a dimple on her smooth stretched skin.

Ornella grunted, gritting and grinding her teeth. It took all the control Battista had not to allow his jaw to drop and the dread to slip from his tongue. He dared a glance at Aurelia; she saw what he did. As the woman's body clenched with labor, tightened to the hardness of steel, the baby beneath the skin gyrated, one lump undulating out on Aurelia's side, the other toward Battista.

The baby lay crosswise in the mother's womb.

The girl's cries rose.

Do you know what to do? Aurelia mouthed the words at him.

Battista licked his lips, wiping his mouth and pulling on the tuft of hair below his lip.

"Maybe," he said, scuttling a bit closer to Ornella again. He took her hand as the pain crested, as Aurelia rubbed her shoulders, lifted all the way off the bed. He leaned toward her as she collapsed. "We need to rock you, Ornella, from side to side. Your baby may not be in the right position. We need to give it but a little help."

Ornella shook her head, tangled hair scratching on the linens. "No. No, I cannot . . . the pain . . . I am too . . . tired."

Aurelia went to her knees, leaned on the bed with her elbows, her face no more than inches from Ornella's. "You can and you must. This child longs to meet its mother."

Ornella quivered with refusal, eyes squeezed shut, but Aurelia would not be denied. She stroked Ornella's forehead, pushing back the burgundy strands stuck to the skin. "Listen to me. Ornella, listen."

Her petition verged on the severe and the tired woman opened her eyes at it.

Aurelia's face softened with a smile, as did her voice. "Do you see that corner of your room, just there?" She looked over her shoulder at the corner above the two windows where wall and ceiling met, her shadow long upon it in the glow of the single candle burning by the bedside. "We shall go there, you and me, and watch."

Every gaze in the room fell upon Aurelia, each person dumbstruck at the sound of such strangeness.

Aurelia placed one hand on Ornella's chest. "The you in there, and in here." She moved her hand to the woman's head. "That part of you. Send it out of your body and you won't feel as much pain. I promise you."

"How . . . how do I do it?" Ornella's eyes narrowed to a dubious stare, but in the very question, she revealed her hope.

Aurelia smiled. "We will close our eyes, breathe very slowly and very deeply, and we will picture ourselves there. *Imagine* yourself up there looking down."

Ornella said not a word, but with no more than a smidgen of

hesitance closed her eyes, forcing her breath to slow, chest rising with expansion. Aurelia looked to Battista.

"Wait only a few minutes," she said, and closed her eyes, too, breath humming to match Ornella's.

The men became captives to the moment, Jacopo and Battista from the bedside, Michelangelo from the door. A lively wind wafted in the portal, as if tossed in by the burgeoning stars, and a serenity settled upon them. Battista had never known the like and he shivered at it. He remembered then, remembered his own mind's journey—at Aurelia's insistence—when the fear of Hell threatened to overcome him.

The two women now bore the same expression, almost vacant, yet purposefully so and with a beauty that snatched his breath away. He jarred himself to action; the moment arrived.

"Jacopo, help me," he hissed.

The young husband stepped to his wife, putting his hands on the side of her belly, opposite Battista's. Gently they began to rock her, rolling her slowly from side to side, the arch of her body growing.

The baby twitched beneath his hands and Battista almost crowed with the delight of it; he had never felt a life before it was born. Ornella's brow furrowed and he feared her pain would dislodge her concentration. The baby kicked again, a hard thrust against his hands, and he pushed timidly back. With a jerk and a roll of flesh, it slipped away, the large belly buckling with the movement, and suddenly the entire protrusion flopped beneath the skin, expanding along the length of Ornella's body as if the baby lay with her, rather than against her.

Ornella's eyes popped open, a glimmer of a stunned delight in their paleness.

"The baby . . ." She slapped Aurelia's arm, bringing her back from the perch they had shared. "The baby comes."

Aurelia dipped her head, eyes slowly opening, her smile wide upon her face. "Then let us greet him, shall we?

"Leave us." Aurelia stood up and hefted Ornella into a sitting position. Moving to the foot of the bed, she pushed gently at Jacopo. "Have no fear. All will be well, Jacopo. Battista?"

Battista pulled his astounded gape from the bed to Aurelia, allowing his feet to move. He took Jacopo's arm, partners in disbelief, and headed for the door. At the threshold, Battista stopped and turned back. With unearthly calm, Aurelia helped Ornella to bend her knees and brace her feet upon the bed.

Aurelia's eyes, vivid green and bright, found his, and she tossed him a smile to send him on his way.

Her hushed voice reached him as he stood just beyond the door, in a language he did not know, had never heard, but a prayer it was, there could be no denying it. One of such intimacy, it sounded as if she conversed with her deity. He knew not what god or gods she prayed to, knew only that he would say a prayer of his own, a prayer of thanks.

Twenty-six

Oh human race,
born to fly upward,
wherefore at a little wind dost thou so fall?

—Purgatorio

The rumble of voices, pleasant and deep, reached up through the floor, penetrating her slumber and scattering it away. Aurelia lifted her head off the edge of the bed, back popping as she straightened, one hand rubbing the tight, sore muscles of her neck, stiff from a few hours of sleep curled in half.

Her heart thumped at the first sight of this new day, at the baby curled in the crux of his mother's arms—cheeks rosy, eyes little slits with a feather of golden-red lashes. He possessed his mother's coloring, this special child, Battista Michelangelo di Petra by name. Aurelia laid a gentle hand upon Ornella's brow, sighing with relief at the coolness of the skin.

Falling back in her chair, Aurelia turned her gaze to the windows and the pale yellow glow of dawn just beyond, her thoughts bursting with the memories of the deepest hours of the night.

The birth had been so easy once the baby moved into position, once he had seen the light awaiting him and rushed for it eagerly. When he slithered into her hands, covered with the blood and the fluid of his mother's care, Aurelia trembled with the wonder of it.

Praying then, as she did now, not only for his safe delivery but also at the blessing of her own part in his birth, minor though it may be. She had longed for adventure and amusement, to feel an active participant in the condition called life, but she never imagined what awaited her when she had left her home with the dark, mysterious stranger. What she and Battista had encountered in the caves and beneath the palace paled in comparison to the ecstasy of helping a life enter the world, to be present when a soul and a physical form united.

Aurelia shivered, not with a chill, for already the cicadas buzzed at the warmth, but with the thrill, one that would live in her blood until it ceased to pump through her veins.

The male voices percolated once more beneath the floorboards; she recognized Battista's as well as the young father's. Other voices joined theirs, a man's and a woman's, and Aurelia heard enough to fathom the polite refusal of service from Jacopo and the trill of congratulations from the would-be patrons.

"Good morning, *donna mia*."

Michelangelo peeped hesitantly around the threshold, respect holding him unhappily at the door, longing inching him forward.

"*Buongiorno*, Michelangelo," Aurelia whispered.

"May I come in?"

Aurelia nodded with a cautioning finger pressed against pursed lips.

Michelangelo tiptoed in, shoulders crunching up as wood creaked beneath his weight. Ornella moved not an inch, her slumber deep and all encompassing. The baby Battista twitched, but only slightly, a tight-fisted hand—one no larger than a grape—escaped from his bundling, flapping haphazardly in the air, rubbing against his face with no more control than an instinctual one. The child's bud mouth opened, stretching in a perfect circle, nose crinkling as he yawned.

Aurelia put a hand to her mouth, stifling the delighted giggle. Michelangelo heaved a quivering breath, surprising Aurelia with the bright tears shimmering in his eyes.

"This is the true masterpiece. God's greatest creation. I am nothing but a rank imitator."

Aurelia stood and crossed to his side, taking his hand as they stood over mother and child.

"Perhaps." She surprised him. "But his life, all human life, is made rich by art, and yours is the greatest of our age. Civilizations are remembered not for the mundane, but for the breathtaking."

Michelangelo breathed deep, a sigh of acceptance, and squeezed her hand.

From beyond the windows Battista's voice came in on the breeze, teasing Jacopo affectionately, as men were wont to do, his deep baritone at odds with the chirping starlings.

Aurelia stepped to the window. On the cobbles below, the men walked together, each with a bucket in his hands, heading for the cistern in the middle of the courtyard. The inn shared the cozy space with three other buildings of a similar construction of wood-trimmed brick. Chairs dotted the circumference, snug groupings tucked into arbors and vine-heavy lattices, cool cubbies where neighbors socialized and guests took the air.

From below came the sound of the front door creaking open, heavy footfalls, and a rumble of deep voices.

"It must be others looking to break their fast," Aurelia remarked.

"There is no one below," Michelangelo whispered. "Frado has gone to fetch us some pastries and cider."

"I will go tell them the inn is closed." Aurelia headed for the door.

"B-but . . . b-but . . . ," Michelangelo stammered, hands gesturing to mother and child, shoulders creeping up to his ears.

Aurelia laughed, took him by the arms, and sat him in the bedside chair. "You need only stay by their side. I will be back in a moment."

Michelangelo perched himself on the edge of the seat, back straight, hands held tight in his lap. His gaze locked upon the woman and the baby, an expression of attentive joy upon his craggy face.

"You know you long to be here and nowhere else," Aurelia teased him as she slipped from the room, pleased to see a twitch of a smile play at the corner of his lips.

The bliss of these moments wrapped her in a tight embrace, cheeks swollen with smile-born apples, bouncing as she skipped down the stairs.

Two men stood just inside the door, turning away from the emptiness of the inn, to make their way back out to the street.

"I am sorry, signori, I am afraid—"

Aurelia's heart slammed against her chest, blood boomed in her ears.

Like terrifying specters come to life, Baldassare del Milanese and a savage, brutal-looking man stood in the common room of the inn.

For a suspended moment, Battista's nemesis blanched in shock—in that instant, Aurelia ran.

Croaking with fear and exertion, she bunched her skirts in her fists, groaning in pain as her slippered toes skimmed off a step, calf bone crashing against a hard wood edge. She whimpered as she found her feet and hurried upward, words and warnings screaming in her head, berating herself for bounding up, where no escape lay ahead, rather than out the back door, where Battista, Jacopo, and their safety awaited.

But her thoughts were of the mother and child and aught else.

"Stop there, missy." It was a growl of anger, a threatening command.

The thudding of Baldassare's footsteps rang in her ears, as loud as her heartbeat. She longed to turn, to see how close he came, but she dared not spare a second.

Dropping her skirts, she used her hands to propel herself onto the second-story ledge, rushing into the first doorway toward the back of the house. Dashing to the window, she crashed the shutters open against the outer wall with a shove.

"Battista!" she cried, the fear-saturated scream caroming off the walls of the courtyard.

Battista spun, as did Jacopo, finding her face in the upper window. Dropping his full bucket, water splashing on the cobbles, Battista ran.

"Milanese!" The word flew out of her mouth as she turned round.

Booted feet trampled heavily on the floor just beyond the door.

Aurelia jumped to the wall beside it.

Baldassare passed the room by, blind to her flattened form against the wall.

Aurelia pushed off and away, searching the confines of the room for anything she could use as weapon. She stood amidst a simple guest room . . . a bed, a chest, a table with ewer and basin, and nothing more. She jumped to the table, grabbing the pitcher. But it was no more than a lightweight, cheap ceramic piece; she didn't believe for a second it could cause much harm, even if smashed upon someone's head.

"What have we here?" Baldassare's coarse voice snickered.

He had come upon Michelangelo . . . Ornella and the baby.

The growl rumbled deep in Aurelia's throat and chest; she heard it as if it came from someone or something else. She looked at the pitcher in her hand. Without thought, she turned her face and smashed the pitcher against the wall, a sneer spreading upon her lips at the pointed, jagged piece remaining in her fisted hand.

With it held before her like a talisman, she ran from the room.

One step into the hall and a black-gloved hand reached out at her, grabbing her skirts around her ankles. Baldassare's companion—poised still a few steps down on the stairs—tore the fabric of her gown as Aurelia leaped away. She kicked out, struggling to get free.

"Leave her alone!" Battista bellowed from the foot of the stairs.

Aurelia shot away, freed as her attacker turned to his.

A hard male caterwaul burst out behind her, with it a slamming of bone against flesh, a thudding of body upon floor. She flashed a look back as her feet continued forward, catching a bone-chilling glimpse of Battista and the man launched in combat.

Aurelia plunged forward, into the corner room.

"Take thee away, Milanese."

Michelangelo stood between the intruder and the bed, small hands fisted and raised before him.

Behind him Ornella—now fully awake—curled her body away from the fracas and around her child, head turned over her shoulder, face stricken with fright at the sight of the strange, evil-looking man in her bedchamber.

"You have no business with these good people." Michelangelo remained undaunted in the face of portentous villainy.

The baby whimpered and mewed, too new to comprehend the evil in his midst. Ornella hushed and soothed him without taking her gaze from the threatening scene beside her bed.

"Signore Buonarotti, I have no fight with you." Baldassare stood a foot from the artist, towering over the small man, a dagger spinning in his right hand. "But you conspire with the wrong sorts of people. A dangerous practice, I can assure you."

"You are the wrong sort, Milanese. Do not delude yourself into thinking otherwise. You are no better than a sewer rat."

The man's fisted hand flashed up and the heel of his palm crashed into Michelangelo's head; the frail body dropped to the ground like a stone.

"Watch your tongue, old man." Battista sneered at the semiconscious form at his feet.

Blood thundered in Aurelia's ears, fervor thudded through her veins.

"Leave him alone!" she cried.

Launching her body forward, she shoved the jagged piece of porcelain into Baldassare's back.

With a howl of pain, Milanese arched against the attack.

Aurelia pulled away, drawing her weapon with her, devastated to see no more than the tip of the makeshift dagger red with blood, frustrated to find no more of it had penetrated the thick leather of his jerkin or his skin.

"*Schifosa!*" Baldassare pounced with frenetic rage, left hand swinging out and colliding with her cheek. "You bitch!"

Pain burst on her face, and Aurelia staggered from the blow, dropping her makeshift dagger, throwing her hands out to catch herself as she careened off the wall.

Aurelia yelped as two clenching hands dug into her shoulders, her feet flying out beneath her as they jerked her backward. Her shoulders thumped against a hard body, her senses assaulted by a reek of body odor and foul breath.

"How lovely you feel, signorina," Baldassare whispered in her ear, the rank pant defiling her skin. "I feel for myself why della Palla takes you wherever he goes."

The bolus of her last meal rose with burning acid in her throat as Baldassare's left hand stroked the curve of one hip and the other circled her neck in a threatening, ever-tightening, caress.

"Perhaps if you cooperate, if you show me some of the kindness you have bestowed upon Battista, I will spare you any further discomfort."

Aurelia turned, forehead rasping against the wiry black stubble upon his chin.

"I would rather rot and give my body to the worms than give it to you."

"*Vaffanculo!*" Baldassare shouted, shoving her roughly.

Aurelia hit the wall, too quickly propelled to catch herself, slumping to the floor as black spots danced in her eyes.

"Bat—," she began, losing the word as Baldassare grabbed her once more, two hands clenching the collar of her gown. Her head snapped back as he picked her up and off her feet with one powerful move. He shook her like a rag doll, their faces but a hair's breadth apart.

"Where is the painting?" Spittle flew off his yellow teeth, spraying her face. "Tell me where it is or I will kill you."

Aurelia squeezed her eyes shut, clearing her head. Hysterical laughter clogged her throat, bitter with the irony of his threat, a self-sabotaging act, though he knew it not.

"God cursed you as a fool," she hissed, meeting his narrowed gaze. "You will see every drop of my blood spilled before I tell you a thing."

Baldassare's upper lip curled; his chin jutted out with hate and anger.

His bloodshot gaze darted left; from the hall, the sounds of fists crashing against skin and bone beat like a battle drum. From their right, the baby's whimpers turned to cries, high pitched and needy.

Thin white lips spread between black stubble. Baldassare pushed her away again. She stumbled but did not fall, and he jumped to the bed.

Drawing again a dagger with one hand, he reached for the baby.

"No!" Ornella screeched, weak hands flailing against Baldassare as he palmed the newborn in his broad hand, the baby's head flopping dangerously in the space between thumb and forefinger.

"Then perhaps you will be willing to spare the life of this child." Baldassare glared at Aurelia, taunted her with the newborn he held in his hand.

The baby's cries became a wail; it filled the house, filled Aurelia with a bloodlust that quaked through her body.

"No, stop." She tiptoed forward, hands out before her as if in surrender. "I will tell you anything. But please, put the baby down."

Baldassare laughed low and fiendish, pulling the baby closer to his chest, placing the dagger point but an inch away from the infant's heart. "I will put the baby down, when you bring me the painting."

"My baby!" Ornella screamed, kicking out, a hard heel connecting with the back of Baldassare's knee.

"Oomph!" Baldassare grunted as his leg buckled, his hold on the baby collapsing. The infant plunged from his hand.

Ornella screamed incoherently, lifting up from the bed, hands reaching out.

Aurelia lunged forward, one hand grabbing Baldassare's dagger-wielding wrist, the other grabbing the second dagger at his waist.

Ornella caught the baby, the force of his weight against her weakness bearing him, and her hands, down toward the floor, her knuckles brushing the cold wood. With a gnashed groan, she pulled him to her.

"Damn you!" Baldassare cried, struggling against Aurelia, tossing her off him, and turning his fury upon Ornella.

Ornella curled her body away, spine nubs clear through the whisper-thin chemise, cupping herself about her baby.

Baldassare wrenched his hand and his dagger, lifting it over his head.

"No!" Aurelia screamed as he plunged the dagger downward, as the dagger disappeared . . . into Ornella's back.

The woman's body stiffened, blood spurting from the gash as Baldassare withdrew the blade, spreading like the plague against the white linen. Ornella shuddered, and collapsed.

With the screech of a rabid animal, Aurelia leaped upon Baldassare.

The baby wailed as his mother's weight fell upon him.

Battista staggered through the door, blood running from his nose and lips.

With a moan, Michelangelo awoke, sitting up with a yap of terror.

But Aurelia saw none of it, heard none of it.

With her legs wrapped around Baldassare's body, she grabbed the side of his head with her left hand, fingers snarling and pulling in his greasy hair as she shoved her thumb into his eye. Pliable flesh giving way with nauseating fluidity.

He screamed with the pain of it.

Aurelia's body jerked around as he tried to shrug her off, but she clung on with the tenacity of a barely sated leech, one thirsty for fullness. Baldassare roared with frustration and pain.

But Aurelia heard nothing.

She tossed the dagger in her right hand upward, switching her hold upon it, the steel shank protruding now from the heel of her palm.

She raised it up, her bloodcurdling cry calling the devil into the room, into her heart. She screamed again as she plunged it into Baldassare's neck and yanked it across.

Hot, red sticky blood spurted out, a wellhead uncapped, the fetid odor infesting her nostrils, gagging in her throat. Baldassare's eyes bulged out, gaze locked with hers in astonishment, but only for a moment.

As the blood ran from his throat, as the light was doused in his eyes, all life slumped from his body, and he tumbled to the floor, Aurelia with him.

Twenty-seven

No one thinks of how much blood it costs.

—Inferno

The pain quivered upward as the tip of her spine slammed against the floor, her head bounced against the hard wood planks. But Aurelia gave not a pause to the pain. The dead man's blood dripped down her face, but she thought only of Ornella.

Crawling upon her hands and knees, Aurelia heard her own whimper as if it came from afar, a wounded soul lost forever in Purgatory. Aurelia threw herself against the edge of the bed, pulled Ornella toward her and off the baby.

In the young woman's dead eyes Aurelia saw the price of her folly. Even as Ornella's blood spread across the bed, Aurelia shook her.

"Please, Ornella, do not die. You cannot be dead," Aurelia pleaded, weeping. "I never meant—"

"Ornella!" The anguished howl came through the door as Jacopo reached the threshold. Rushing forward, he pulled his dead wife from Aurelia's hands. Wrapping his arms around Ornella, rocking her as he sobbed her name.

Michelangelo scurried to the bed, lifting the wailing baby, wrapping the infant in his arms and a blanket as he ran from the room and the sight of the carnage.

Battista staggered to Aurelia, pulling her up as he called the artist back. "Michelangelo! Take her!"

With a face the color of a rain-drenched sky, Michelangelo turned round, cupping the baby against his chest with one arm.

"Come, Aurelia," he beckoned, stepping back to grab her hand, to pull her forward, as her feet seemed unable to move themselves. "Come."

As Michelangelo led her, Aurelia watched over a shoulder as Battista dragged Baldassare's bloody body away from a keening Jacopo, the red fluid flowing from the dead man's neck leaving a staining line upon the floor as Battista pulled the corpse from the room and kicked it into another, slamming the door closed.

She turned away as Michelangelo led her down the stairs, as Battista caught up to them and came to her side, wrapping his arm around the small of her back.

They reached the ground floor in time to see Baldassare's companion, loyalty abandoned, hobbling from the inn, door banging against the wall in his urgency to be gone.

Battista led her to a chair as Michelangelo cooed and walked the infant in circles around her; she heard little but the loud humming in her ears. She held her hand up before her face, certain it was no longer there, the numbness so pervasive, it seemed impossible to believe her form still existed. But there it was, trembling in front of her eyes, still wet with the stain of blood.

Jacopo stumbled down the stairs, a wraith heavy with the shroud of death, sobbing as Battista reached out and placed him in a chair beside Aurelia. Running to the kitchen and back again, Battista placed two tumblers full of dark amber liquid in their hands.

"Drink, both of you."

Aurelia stared at him and the cup in her hand with little cognition. Battista led the cup to her lips and tipped it back. The liquid burned her throat, and she turned from it. But he grabbed the back of her neck and forced the remaining liquid upon her until it was all gone, until her eyes watered with the strength of the brew. She coughed and sputtered, pushing him away.

Jacopo needed no such ministrations. He tossed it back, gulping it down, wiping the remnants of it from his mouth with the back of his hand.

"I cannot live without her!" He threw the tin cup across the room. With a fracturing crash, it collided with two wine bottles, shattering them into pieces matching those of his heart.

"Oh, but you can." The force of Michelangelo's decree startled them. "You can and you must. You may no longer have Ornella, but you have the greatest gift she could give."

The artist stepped to the grief-stricken man, squatting beside him with the baby still in his arms. The child sucked upon his own fist, the slurping a precursor to his need for nourishment that must come soon. Jacopo looked upon his child and through his grief his smile was born, marking the moment the rest of his life began.

"He needs milk," Jacopo muttered.

Michelangelo closed his eyes for a brief moment, a quick sigh of relief. "He does indeed. We will find him a wet nurse, yes. But for now we can make do with some goat's milk and cheesecloth if you have it?"

Jacopo raised his brows and swayed to his feet. Taking the baby in his arms, he made for the kitchen. "Come, my son, your father will feed you."

Michelangelo jumped to Jacopo's side, turning back with a smile, one fading at a glimpse at Aurelia.

No longer passive in her chair, she'd jumped up and paced a tight circle in the far corner of the room, detaching herself from Jacopo and his grief, having no right to disrespect it with her presence.

"Come sit, Aurelia." Battista beckoned, pouring her another cupful of the powerful brandy.

But she would not be coaxed. She walked about the chamber, head shaking, mumbling incoherently, thoughts and emotions tangling within her, clogging on her tongue. As she came to his side, she thrust her hands out at Battista. Dark and dirty with dried blood, the red now ugly brown.

"I have . . . I have killed a man."

Before Battista's grasp reached her, she set foot upon stone once more, circling again and again, motion perpetual in the madness.

He was ready when next she passed; his hands flicked out and captured hers, his strength overpowering her mania. She allowed him to pull her down, capitulating with fatigue, slumping in the chair as he ran once more to the kitchen, returning with a bucket of water, a clump of hard soap, and a cloth.

She stared at his face as he knelt before her. Would she return all she had found by his side and his arms if it gave Ornella back her life? Aurelia thought she would, she believed she could, and prayed for it.

Aurelia closed her eyes to the succor of his ministrations and the warm slippery feeling of soapy cloth and hands upon her own.

"I can't believe you killed him. . . ."

She stiffened as the words slipped from Battista's tongue. Aurelia pulled on her limbs, trying to wrench them from his grasp. "But he—"

Battista held her, dropping the cloth to caress her wet skin with his own. "No, you misunderstand. He deserved death, and more." Battista leaned toward her as he took her shoulders in his hands. "May he burn in the fires of Hell for eternity, for he has earned that as well. It's just . . . it's only that you . . . you're so . . . untrained, so completely female. I could not believe the mastery with which you plied the dagger."

Aurelia scoffed at him with a curled lip. "Why? Because I have no member twixt my legs? I cannot long for vengeance, cannot be consumed by bloodlust? You believe one not taught to fight cannot brandish a blade and kill?"

She rose, looking down at him with frightening magnificence. "A woman can kill as well as a man, or better. What we feel, we feel through every fiber of our being. Bloodthirsty anger does not belong to the male species alone."

"I . . . I'm sorry, Aurelia, I did not mean . . . ," Battista sputtered, reaching to capture her hands with his once more, but she pushed him away. "Believe me, I know how strong—"

"And because my breasts are meant to feed a babe, I suppose I cannot lust like a man?"

Reaching down, she grabbed him by the sides of his head, pulling on his silken black hair, pulling his face up as she leaned down.

Her lips were hard and cruel on his, as if she discharged the emotion ripping her in half by tearing at him. Her tongue assaulted his mouth, her teeth nipping at his lips, the madness on fire within her combusting.

"Aurelia!" Battista wrenched his mouth from hers, pushing at her shoulders with all the force of his arms.

With the craze burning bright in her eyes, her gaze froze upon the small drop of blood trickling from his lip . . . another's blood she had drawn . . . and she could bear it no more.

Collapsing in a ball, knees buckling as she folded at the waist, she crashed to the floor, sobs of guilt and fear and revulsion convulsing her body.

As Jacopo rocked his motherless son in the next room, Battista pulled Aurelia onto his lap, rocking her as if she were a child in her father's arms, until—like the babe—Aurelia's sobs subsided to hitching breaths, to the deep draughts of exhausted slumber.

Twenty-eight

For he who sees a need
but waits to be asked
is already set on cruel refusal.

—*Purgatorio*

Like two flowers in a row, they sat side by side in the garden. Their bodies drooped, petals hanging low, burdened by their wounds, a pain that bound them.

From the moment they had returned to Florence, as soon as Battista entered his home and found Lucagnolo asleep on his couch, he knew. Battista had no need to ask if or when the man's wife had died, the truth of it lay in the hollows of his face and the emptiness in his eye. Battista said not a word, wrapping the young man in his arms, begging God to relieve Lucagnolo's burden and lay it upon his own strong arms as the bereft man sobbed in them.

Aurelia found a kindred spirit in the young widower, a spirit smothered—at least for the moment—by the darkness of grief. It drew them together, cocooning them in the healing powers of passing time.

Battista stepped out into the tiny courtyard and the heat of the day, a heat of high summer though it was only the first days of May. The plates and bottles upon the metal salver bounced as he walked, though he trod slow and cautiously, yet the pair remained ignorant to his presence, unmindful of the tinkling and clicking, their hushed conversation unheeded in the shelter of the solitude.

"Do you believe it, Monna Aurelia?" Lucagnolo turned sunken eyes to the woman sitting beside him, their chairs facing the large cherry tree—fluffy and pink in full blossom—prominent at the apex of the garden's back stone wall.

"I do, Luca, most assuredly."

She turned, and in her profile Battista thought he saw a smidgen of healing; in giving of herself as a healer of another's grief, she'd found the path to overcome her own. No longer did her freckles stand out in stark relief against white skin; no longer did sooty circles rim her changeable eyes. She was not the vivacious woman who had saved his life or led him through the darkness of Purgatory, but she was there, waiting to return.

"Death is hardest on those left behind." Aurelia took Lucagnolo's hand, the breeze tossing their hair, sprinkling them with wispy and pale cherry blossom petals. "Those who do not realize their loved ones are still with them."

Battista stopped a few steps behind them, unwilling to break the bond, unwilling to dispel the healing hovering betwixt them.

Lucagnolo closed his eyes, a low hum of a sigh settling in his chest. "I feel her beside me," he whispered, as if to speak too loudly might dispel his wife's presence. "It is the loveliest of feelings. I sense her often."

Aurelia tipped her head upward, face offered to the sky above. "And you always shall. Those who touch our soul in this life will be with us forever. The soul lives on. The spirit—the essence of being—is never ending."

As if she felt him—spoke of him—Aurelia sat up, turned, and smiled at Battista; he could not breathe for the beauty of her.

Needing no further encouragement, Battista stepped to them, placing the small bowl of fresh grapes and figs on the table between them, handing both a cup of clear *vernaccia*. Taking his own serving of the pale Tuscan wine, he sat in a chair across from them, long legs sticking out, spanning the distance with large, booted feet.

"You look lovely today, *cara mia*." He raised his cup in salute.

"*Grazie,* Battista," Lucagnolo said, humor crisply dry.

Battista laughed, merry that his grieving friend attempted humor, let alone succeeded at it. "You are as ugly as ever, *amico,* yet I love you more."

The small mouth on the narrow face twitched; Lucagnolo sniffed a wee laugh.

"Have you seen them together?"

The question would be nonsensical, were it not for all these three had experienced over the past weeks, if it were not for the two canvases lying upon the large table just inside the door.

Lucagnolo nodded. "I have. They are truly remarkable, as if Giotto copied the women with incredible precision, or the other half of the women." He hitched in his chair, sitting forward with enthusiasm. "And yet the background is so conspicuously dissimilar. I am anxious to see how he ties it together in the center piece. It will be masterful, I have no doubt."

"No doubt," Battista mumbled into his cup. The cost of this mission had been far greater than any other he had undertaken in his entire life. In his darkest thoughts, he railed against François for forcing this path upon him. In his strength, he prayed for success, for a prize worthy of the price. "Have you heard of the Castello della Dragonara?"

"Most certainly," Lucagnolo replied, popping a fig into his mouth, tucking it into one cheek like a squirrel with a nut.

"What do you know of it?"

"I know it was built of a mammoth rock bulging out of the earth on the shoreline of Camogli," Lucagnolo said with a shrug, looking off as he gathered his thoughts. "Legend claims God carved the castle from the rock, for no one knows exactly when it was built."

Battista heaved a sigh through a crinkling nose; he had lost all taste for the mysterious.

"The myths allege it is haunted as well, for it has served not only as a defensive fortress, but as a prison." Lucagnolo turned to Aurelia. "Souls that live forever."

Aurelia answered with a fey grin, sipping from the cup she held with both hands, the left once more bandaged, her injury revisited after the struggle at the inn.

Battista laid his attention upon her. "You should go no further on this . . . this mystical journey. It is a journey into madness." He drank deep of his wine, ready for the debate to begin. "I would be the worst sort of cad were I to allow you to continue."

Aurelia's gaze pierced him from the tops of her eyes. "Allow me? You think you—"

Lucagnolo jumped to his feet. "I should go."

"No, stay, Luca." Battista held up a hand. "There are no secrets here."

He spoke the truth; all his men had gleaned the change in his relationship with Aurelia, all claimed to have known it would happen long before Battista himself.

"Have no fear, Battista." Lucagnolo tipped his head in leave-taking. "I really should visit Bettaccia's family. It has been a few days and it does them much good to see me."

The loss of their only child had left Bettaccia's parents floundering, no other offspring to fill the hole in their hearts. Lucagnolo had promised his dying wife he would remain their family; it was a promise he would forever keep.

He waved to them as he passed into the dim recess of the house, as Aurelia hissed at Battista, "You would deny me Paradise after climbing out of Hell and Purgatory?"

Her words caught him up quick. Battista had not thought of her plight in such terms; he felt a twinge of shame for his selfishness. Until his gaze fell upon her bandaged limb, rising to the fading marks upon her fair face. He knew of the concealed wounds, perhaps better than she did herself, the scars left by the death of Ornella and the killing of Baldassare. The constable of Poggibonsi had cleared Aurelia of any wrongdoing, Jacopo's parents had returned to care for him and the baby, and yet she would carry those dark moments forever, for they had changed the very essence of her.

"But this is my challenge, my commission, not yours," Battista argued. Dark gaze wandered away with worrisome contemplation as he fiddled with the tuft of hair beneath his lip and shook with a contrary jog of his head. "I have received an urgent message from the king of France. The pope plies great pressure upon him and yet François will not commit his troops until he possesses the relic."

Aurelia gave a cold eye and pursed her lips at Battista. "Any who need rely on another's strength have no belief in their own."

Battista raised his brows at her. "I cannot argue, but I cannot wonder if it is not true, the myth of this piece. I have never known such challenges in a search, never encountered the like. Surely the struggle is equal to its power." He sat back, hands racking through his dark hair. "It is my chore for a reason."

She waggled her head, lips moving as if she could not find the correct words. "It . . . it has become my task. I assure you."

Pushing against the arms of her wooden chair with both hands, showing no sign of the pain it must have caused, she stood and towered over him, an eagle perched on a cliff side.

"You cannot, you must not, complete this alone." Terse and tense, jaw flinching with a hard edge, she would brook no argument. "I must finish this."

The fervent Aurelia returned, she so full of life it buzzed from her like the drone of an angry bee. He longed to take her then, or be taken by her, warmed by her concern, set afire by her passion.

He rose slowly, body inches from hers, her musky sweet scent filling his head. "Then we will finish it." With gentle fingers, Battista lifted a strand of her chestnut hair and tucked it behind her ear, blowing gently to loosen the blossoms frosting her hair. "We will finish it together."

Battista saw the relief in her gaze gone soft and golden and he could bear it no longer. Taking her by the hand, he led her into the house, safe and secure in her care.

The rattle of the soldier's armor clanged discordantly in the quiet of the marble halls, his heavy hobnailed *calige* clanking on the stone floor as he marched toward the chamber.

Without a word, the Swiss Guard parted from the opened doorway and the warrior bounded in with the force of a plundering army.

Pope Clement raised sunken eyes as the man approached, saying not a word as the warrior strode through the rows of cardinals, toward the pope's raised dais between. The soldier's presence stilled every tongue, captured every gaze as he removed the steel-etched *galea* with gold gilt highlights from his head, revealing the tight black curls beneath and the black gaze filled with angry concern.

"Di Ceri," the pope acknowledged with nothing resembling politeness. He had no quarrel with the man charged with leadership of the papal militia, but he had had enough bad news already this day.

"Holy Father." Renzo di Ceri bowed his large form over the pope's proffered hand and brushed his lips across the ring. Straightening, he tucked his helmet beneath his arm, wide shoulders thrown back, spine stiff and straight like the trunk of a massive tree, one that had withstood thousands of years of nature's brutality.

One of Italy's most decorated *condottieri*, a professional soldier who had fought against the Borgias, fought for Venice, for Spain, and now for the Medici, di Ceri had not always reigned triumphant, but he had always survived.

"What brings you here, di Ceri?" Clement rested against the high back of the red and gold chair of St. Peter. His pointed glare ignored the rows of cardinals flanking the room, perched in the square, high-backed chairs of carved wood, bright yet somber in their bloodred cassocks and mitres, birds in rows upon the rooftops, looking down at him as if he were the day's first worm. In his pure white vestments, the pope stood out, the white-hot center of flame amidst the red cardinals surrounding him. A few young, most old, there were few he called friends in these dark days.

"My scouts have just returned," di Ceri said flatly; he would yield his report though the Council of Cardinals clearly needed no more kindling heaped on their fire. "The emperor has taken Arezzo, and the duke of Bourbon marches on Acquapendente."

The gasps of horror and anger circled the room like a cyclone.

"The wolves are at the door."

The pope sneered at the quivering pudgy coward sitting in the front row. Cristoforo Numai played with the guise of power and might, his red tent a curtain over his yellow skin.

Clement turned from the sickening sight. One elbow perched on the arm of his chair, the pope braced his bearded chin in his hand, speaking through his white-knuckled fingers.

"How many swords at the ready, di Ceri?"

Renzo's expression was as implacable as if he wore his helmet still. "There are no more than five thousand militia, and the almost two hundred Swiss Guards."

"And what of Bourbon's forces, the imperial forces he commands?"

For the first time in their long acquaintance, Clement saw the shadow of concern cross the mighty warrior's coarse features.

"The word is they have not been paid for a fortnight and are ill fed."

The pope's eyes narrowed. There was nothing more dangerous than an unhappy soldier, except perhaps thousands of them.

"How many?" The demand slipped from between Clement's clenched teeth.

Di Ceri flinched on a telltale blink and turned his soldier's gaze forward with a clip of his head. "Close to thirty thousand, Holy Father. Maybe more."

The stench of abject fear burst in the room in a timeless moment of silence. As if in the wake of a rushing tide, cries filled it, four of the many in the chamber took to their feet and, without pause for dismissal, quit the room.

Clement saw the truth in the faces remaining, which others would be gone before nightfall, which ones would leave him and the Holy City in order to save their own skins.

"What of your François? What of his forces?" The impertinence in Cardinal Colonna's voice was undeniable; the man who would be pope if not for the Medici took malicious delight in Clement's impending doom.

Clement slammed his open palms on the arms of his chair as he flung himself upward, the sound like a clap of condemning thunder echoing up into the painted sky.

"He makes excuses, but they make no sense," Clement railed. He paced about, stopping before the window, leaning against it as if he longed to jump from it. A harsh breath rattled through his nose, but it stilled his tremble of fury, tempered the rage in his voice. "In one sentence he whines that he has no funds to raise a sufficient force, while at the same time he pleads for my prayers to save his sons."

"It is not surprising," Cardinal Ridolfi quipped, a young man with high aspirations and little patience. "Any man in his position might long for the same."

"*Sì*, of course." Clement turned with an impatient cluck of his tongue. "But then he prattles on of a power, a specific power, as if it were a tangible thing. That he waits for this power to come to him, and then he will set his course. He makes little sense."

"Blasphemy," Ridolfi berated.

"He was the choice you made," Colonna needled him. "Now what will you do?"

Clement stopped midpace, motionless before them, the deer caught in the hunter's target. He opened his mouth, but found no answer to suffice; no action could set them from this course. He had longed to wear the pope's mitre not to lead armies, but to spread the faith and the word of God. Yet in a moment of preternatural prescience, he knew he would be inexorably lost. For the sake of the Vatican and his faith, he could but make an attempt at salvation.

"Send your swiftest soldier to Passarini and Ippolito in Florence," he commanded of the soldier awaiting an order. "Have them send as many troops as they can, as quick as they can."

"Holy Father." Di Ceri bowed and spun on his heels, heading out of the room with the same determination with which he had entered.

Amidst the clatter of his boots, Clement listened to the silent rebukes, perspiring beneath the heat of the denouncing glares. The men remaining at the table had as little faith in him as he did in himself.

Twenty-nine

But then my mind was struck by light that flashed and,
with this light,
received what it had asked.

—*Paradiso*

Seagulls screeched with riotous laughter above their heads. Morning fog scudded across the ground, wraithlike souls tentacled to the mortal earth.

They had traveled through the night, just they two, leaving Frado and his rousing chorus of protests behind. Aurelia thought to question Battista's decision, but in truth had no need to hear the answer; he trusted her without reservation. He required no one else with her by his side. The certainty of it brought a tender pain to her heart.

If they had questioned their fate—entertained even the smallest possibility that they were not meant for this destiny—it had withered as surely as a tender shoot in the grip of scalding heat. As they turned north onto the main road leading along the coast, they shared an ironic laugh, for they had set their horses upon none other than the Via Aurelia, the main thoroughfare winding northward up the coast.

The small fishing village of Camogli remained blanketed in slumber. A few men walked the streets, eyes swollen with sleepiness, heading for the boats bobbing upon the gentle waves, the rows of white sails waving to the shore with each undulation of the sea beneath them. The sun rising behind them peeked over the horizon, reflecting off the water, sending sparks of light back into their faces.

Aurelia breathed deep the salty air, briny with the coming tide, eyes wide toward the shoreline curving in a crescent away from the center of the village.

"We should eat before we continue on," Battista said. "I am sure the sweet rolls Nuntio packed are still fresh."

Aurelia led her horse onward, approaching the low stone wall separating the edge of town from the beach. She closed her eyes, slowing her breath to match the soft *shush* of the waves as they crept up the gray pebbles of the shore.

"Aurelia?"

Battista's call niggled in her ear, but she paid it no heed.

"Aurelia? Are you all right?" He bumped his horse into hers, joggling her into awareness.

"*Sì*, Battista, I am fine," she assured him, lips curling softly upward. "It is so very beautiful. I lose myself to it."

"Have you not seen the ocean before?" he asked with an incredulous whisper.

She shook her head, grin growing wide. "Never. It is magnificent."

"Indeed it is." He laughed.

"Its beauty is but the tip of its splendor." She could not tear her gaze from the frothing waves and the turquoise sea. "It pulls at me, a power I cannot name."

"You are not alone, *cara*." Battista reached for her hand and she gave it gladly. "Many feel as you do. The grandeur of the sea, the earth, is one of God's divine gifts."

Aurelia turned, dreamy eyed, her soft expression fading at the sight beyond his shoulder.

Battista twisted in his saddle, following her stare with sudden caution.

The wall before them trailed off to the right, heading up the coast and hugging the curve of the shoreline. Not far in the distance, beyond the row of brightly painted houses and shops, the wall ended at a jutting promontory. Thrusting upward from the outcropping—tall, powerful, and imposing—the castle rose into the sky, a finger pointing to the heavens, a clear arrow directing those worthy to the path to God.

Without a word, they turned their horses upon the packed dirt road, thankful for the anonymity of dawn. Reining their horses in, they quit their saddles at the end of the wall, humans and horses dwarfed by the fortress towering above them.

White droppings of seabirds—scavenging seagulls and profusions of pelicans—speckled the dark gray stone, dotting the monolith like spots on a robin's egg. As the wall ended, a staircase began, a curving external flight of steps leading around the outside of the castle, its outer rail forming the outer wall of the structure.

A burst of tide rushed in with a crash of waves, the white foam colliding against the castle, spraying up the tall side of the citadel to the rounded tower at the top of the stairs and splashing over them as they stood at its base, a brief flash of a rainbow forming in the scattered droplets.

Aurelia laughed, at the cooling sensation upon her skin, at the sight of Battista covered in dots of sea spray, glittering as if plastered with small jewels. The beads of liquid traced the fine lines of his face and she quivered at the loveliness of him. She saw the emotion in his eyes, beyond the spark of delight, all the thick and rich emotion she had no right to feel reflected back at her in the soft brown depths.

"Shall we sit upon the wall and break our fast?" Aurelia led her horse to the posts along the side of the castle, tied the reins securely, and returned to Battista's side. He stared upward, gaze locked upon the narrow, dome-topped tower at the peak of the stairs, a deep furrow creasing between his brows.

"I am not sure if I can wait," he rumbled, voice thick with apprehensive zeal. "I fear what we will find, yet I cannot bear another moment without finding it."

Aurelia neared him, laying a soft hand upon his arm, rubbing it soothingly, yet the hard power of it served as a succor to her own hesitation. "You must wait, I fear."

He looked down at her, furrow of incomprehension rutting between his dark brows.

"Dante and Beatrice ascended at noon," she told him. "We must do the same."

"They arrived at noon, *sì*, on the vernal equinox," Battista countered. "I will not wait another month."

Aurelia shook off the ludicrous notion. "Of course not. But I think it imperative to wait for midday at the least."

Battista tossed a wary look about the cobbled square in front of the castle, hand moving protectively to his satchel and the two pieces of the triptych within. He had insisted on bringing them, expressing the hope—success assumed—that putting the three together would immediately reveal the location of the artifact and set him and Aurelia on the final leg of this maddening quest.

"By then the city will be awake. What of those who attend the fortress? Will they not obstruct our entrance?"

"I do not believe so." She led him to the bottom of the stairs and pointed to each in turn. "Look. See there? Those layers of dirt and sand have not been disturbed for many a day. I venture no one uses them. It looks as if they all enter by the front."

Battista could not argue against the testimony of the thick and crusted layers of earth and grime covering the rough stone steps. Without further dispute, he tied his horse beside hers, retrieved a bundle from his bag, and brought it, and her, to the wall.

They turned their backs to the square, feet dangling over the wall, lifting their legs and laughing each time the splash of a wave threatened, munching their sweet rolls in companionable silence. Aurelia licked her fingers, wiping her sticky hands with unladylike coarseness upon the lap of her plain muslin gown. She wore her breeches beneath her gown, and though she gathered her hair in one long bunch upon her back, she wore neither jeweled net nor beribboned veil; she marinated in the freedom of the simple attire.

Battista barked a laugh. "What has become of you, Lady Aurelia? I fear I am a bad influence upon you."

Aurelia smiled, shimmying closer to him upon the rocks, and laid her head upon his shoulder without rebuke. She had no desire to speak, or to think—to chew anymore on what could be or what must be—wanting only to be in that moment, in this place, with him.

She opened her eyes, head flopping against his arm as he raised his hand and dabbed at the beads of sweat upon his brow.

Aurelia straightened up and squinted into the sky. The fog had evaporated, the translucent curtains drawn back to reveal a pure blue firmament—a deep azure to rival the aqua sea below—and the sun had inched its way toward them, the heat of inevitability thumping upon their heads.

She turned to the man beside her, gaze locking in the potent cusp of what lay before them. Battista swung his legs back over the wall, stood, and held out his hand. For a fleeting moment Aurelia thought to deny it, to jump off the wall and run up the shore, away from the destiny awaiting them.

Taking his hand, Aurelia followed him to the shadows now inching away from the base of the castle, and together they stepped upon the first stair.

As the steps led them around the building, it seemed as if they walked on the water. Their direction changed with each step, the path of stairs, uneven hot stones beneath their feet, winding them over the ocean and toward the sunlit tower above.

Beside her Battista grunted from deep in his gut. Aurelia raised her gaze and flinched back; the piercing sun stabbed her eyes. She squeezed them shut, vision a blur of brilliant red, the blood in her lids emblazoned by the light. Their feet faltered on the steps, for they could see nothing, became fearful to move in the sightlessness.

"Aurelia . . . *cara* . . ." His whisper beckoned and caressed her, urging her to open her eyes.

Her lids fluttered open. All around her the world quivered with pure white light, only the faintest image of the stone castle, the steps beneath her feet, and the outline of the arched tower entrance, no more than a few steps away, discernible. So blinded, Aurelia could not tell if the angle of the sun was so perfectly aimed as to cause their loss of sight or if they had stepped into a patch of mist—one so dense the sun set it ablaze with its whiteness.

"Aurelia."

The hushed, lyrical call roused her, and she turned.

Battista's smooth, tawny skin appeared colorless, yet the glow of his eyes—drenched with adoration—she would know anywhere. The light tricked her, urging her to believe that only the translucent essence of his form subsisted beside her, a brilliant, sparkling shimmer of his being. Aurelia's breath quivered, yet it felt as if she need not breathe. They looked as if they had become, in a sense, transhumanized, their form—meaningless in the obfuscating light—traversing beyond the human and yet continuing to exist, the light surrounding and entering them.

"How strange I feel," Battista said with a low, enraptured voice. "Can this harm us, do you think?"

Aurelia smiled. "No, we have naught to fear." She would not attempt to explain what he could not begin to fathom, instead allowed space for a thought of gratitude for his presence. "It is the trap of Paradise. Those who protect the painting knew perfection itself could waylay any would-be thief."

Battista hovered closer, and she tingled at his nearness.

To love beyond substance . . . no emotion as powerful existed. They glimpsed what might lie in the beyond, and the power of it—of what would continue to survive between them—enveloped her. Her heart thudded as Battista leaned down, the brilliance of him drawing ever closer. It was not a kiss but a merging, a sensual overlapping of their beings, and she basked in the perfection of it.

If this were eternity, Aurelia would gladly surrender to it. And yet she could not.

She pulled away, one hand caressing the sharp planes of his face, her hand tingling with the feel of his skin.

Together they turned, feet moving upon the steps once more, aiming for the grayness of the long, narrow archway ahead.

As they passed through it, into what seemed to be a shadow, they found only more light, only the faintest silhouette of a passage visible, one stretching out to blinding infinity, or so it appeared. Aurelia thought it no more than a hallway, long and narrow with a low vaulted ceiling above her head, all of pale stone, the *pietra serena* of Michelangelo's Giant. Panels of some type of glass picketed the ceiling, intensifying the power of the light. The scent of the ocean dissipated, replaced by a clear freshness . . . cleansed perfect air. Aurelia stepped forward eagerly, progress instantly stymied by Battista's hand upon her shoulder.

"Hold," he insisted. "I am not sure this is the way."

"It is, Battista. I am certain," Aurelia argued. "It is a long passage, but I believe I can see its end."

"I see nothing, not even the floor." Battista held her, bending low, eyes squinting in the light. "It is too bright."

With a gentle but insistent flinch, she shook his hand off, moving forward.

"Aurelia, wait!" he called with irritated doggedness, but she did not yield.

She took one step and then another, slippered feet finding solid ground, smooth and cool through the thin soles of her shoes.

"See, Battista." She turned back with a grin. "This is the way."

Battista followed with nagging caution. "Slow down, Aurelia. Be sure before you step."

She moved another pace, her right foot leading her onward . . . to nowhere.

For a split second, her foot fluttered into nothingness. Her mind screamed for retreat, but her body responded too slowly. She caught a flash of black abyss, receding darkness, below; just ahead, the barest glimpse of a white square of tile floor. Aurelia toppled forward, plunging into the square chasm. She threw her arms out, thrust her body forward.

Her feet found nothing, but her ribs collided with a hard, sharp edge and she grunted in pain as her breath expunged from her lungs. Kicking her legs, pressing up on her elbows, a low guttural hum of effort rumbling in her throat, she pushed herself over the edge. Panting, she flopped onto her back, quivering with relief as all her weight rested safely on the floor once more.

Tilting her head up without rising, she looked at Battista. "I am sorry," she said penitently. "I allowed my own eminence to make me brash."

"Are you all right?" Battista rushed forward, heedless to the pitfalls they now knew hid within the light, drawing as close as he dared.

"Stay back, Battista." Aurelia's became the voice of caution. Rubbing away the ache in her midsection, heart quaking beneath her fingers and the thin layers of fabric, she eased up to her feet. "I am fine."

Concern set at ease, Battista rammed fisted hands on his hips, stabbing her across the distance with a withering look. "You cannot move headlong," he chastised. "It may be Paradise, yet it is fraught with danger still."

But already Aurelia looked ahead. "I know, I know. But . . ." She held up a hand with her plea. "But I think I have seen something meant to be seen."

His face crinkled with irritation and confusion. "What? No! Stop!" he demanded as she stepped forward.

"Wait, please. Give me but a minute."

With a wary eye to the floor, fixedly chary of its traps, Aurelia inched forward, Battista's voice no more than the sluice of fluttering wind at her back. She needed only to progress a few paces when the object became clear, its form at least, if not its purpose.

Aurelia stood before it, head tilted, hands crossing upon her chest as she studied it.

The full-length mirror was oval in shape, set on a pedestal of the same glittering gold that rimmed the glass, connected to the frame by two side axles. At its current pitch, one angled downward, she saw naught but her legs, from the knees down. Stepping forward, she reached out and pushed the top backward. It moved with far greater ease than she expected and it swung backward, out of her hand, angled upward now at the same degree it had pointed downward.

With a flash of lightning, the glass caught a beam, pummeling straight down, directly upon the mirror, in a tight, small circle. The light shot from the glass, across the room. Like a hummingbird rushing from one blossom to the next with frenetic need, the ray bounced off another glass, and then another, until a zigzag beam snaked its way through the room, defining it and laying a path from where Aurelia stood to the end of the corridor and an arched threshold.

"I'll be damned." Battista's grudgingly mystified snip made her smile.

Aurelia tried to erase the grin from her lips as he made his way cautiously to her, but she failed miserably. Battista possessed the good grace to snicker as he arrived at her side, though not without a small, petulant shake of his head. He reached out, wiping the sweat off her forehead, wiping his hand on his own soaked-through jerkin.

"You are a lucky lady." He bussed her clean skin as he removed the thick leather jacket, dropping his favorite garment to the ground with a sorrowful expression. "Lead on, *cara*."

Though the crisscrossing beam of light illumined the floor and the square holes spattered throughout, they made their way with slow caution. At the verge of the arch, Battista stepped ahead.

"Let me b—"

His words shriveled on his tongue and he stared at her bug eyed, mouth agape.

"What is it? What's wrong?" She grabbed onto his arm, fingers digging crescents in the skin so little protected through the thin, light linen of his flounced sleeve.

But he ignored her fright, covering her hand with his, face softening with lucid rapture.

"I have never seen you more beautiful," he proclaimed, though somehow sounding strangely unconvinced. "From the moment I saw you, I thought you the most beautiful woman I had ever seen, but now . . ."

He shook his head, his expression one of such worship it pained her to see it.

Aurelia smiled tenderly. "It is just the light."

"Perhaps." He took her hand in both of his. "But you are far brighter than I. It looks as if the light comes from you. From here."

He placed one hand on her stomach, and she trembled, at the touch and the intuitive notion.

She lifted his hand, urging him forward with unfeigned curiosity. "Look ahead, Battista. What lies there?"

Just beyond the portal more light glowed, but of a far more tangible form.

They stepped across the threshold and onto a square landing that creaked at the intrusion of their weight. Instantly the light—perfect globes of it—encircled them in two rows, each moving in opposite directions.

Aurelia stood with her back to Battista, their eyes swirling in their heads as they struggled to focus on the spheres hovering around them at waist height.

"I think there are twelve of them!" she cried, raising her voice over the harsh whoosh, for each sphere sizzled with vibrant energy.

"*Sì*. Torches come up from the floor. I can just barely make out the bases and their tracks." Battista twirled round, as if he danced with the lights, all focus intent on first one and then another down the rows. "But there is room for thirteen. There is an empty space in each row. Watch."

Aurelia did, turning as he did, her movement allowing her eyes to focus better. At one position, one of thirteen, as the line of lights twisted about, the two spaces created an opening, aligning to provide a gap large enough for them to pass through, were they ready. There it was and there it went, the instant of escape coming and going before their reaction.

As if to taunt them, as the space revealed itself, it quickly vanished and the movement hurried—the torches spinning more and more rapidly. Aurelia shut her eyes, rubbing against them with the heels of her hands, feeling dizzy and nauseous with the effort to focus on them.

"We have to jump through!" Battista cried.

Facing the far side of the room, no more than inches away from the radiant orbs, he pulled her before him, his hands poised at the small of her back. Hot air buffeted them, a blistering breeze forcing their eyes to close in defense, sending their hair flying back away from their faces.

"Wait for it!" Battista cried, his voice harsh in her ear, hands tensing against her. Aurelia's eyes crossed as she watched the two openings draw together.

"Almost . . . almost . . . now!"

Her body lurched; he shoved her forward from a half step behind. Aurelia's body moved faster than her feet and they tangled in her skirt, fabric tearing with a rasping rip, pulling her down, and Battista with her. She cried out in pain as he landed on top of her, her healing left arm crushed beneath.

Battista rolled off, but she could not rise, could only curl into a ball as she tucked the throbbing limb to her.

"*Dio mio,*" Battista cursed, "I am sorry, so very sorry."

Aurelia shook her head, biting back the sob of pain clamoring for release. "It is not your fault, Battista, but mine." She turned round and sat, still clutching her arm in her lap. "Or rather these damned skirts."

Battista's mouth formed a perfect O. "I have never heard you curse, Monna Aurelia," he teased her with a smirk.

She managed a pale imitation of it, no more.

"Give me those damn skirts." He reached beneath the top layer of muslin and grabbed onto her chemise, the torn opaque fabric hanging offensively. With one hard tug, he finished detaching what had already unraveled with the fall. With his teeth and his hands, he created wide strips of cloth and proceeded to wrap one piece around her wrist; tying the other into a loop, he reached out to sling it about her shoulders.

"No." She held him with her good hand. "I cannot continue so encumbered. The wrapping will have to do."

Battista eyed her skeptically. "Very well," he acquiesced, tucking the remainder of the fabric into the satchel slung upon his back.

Sitting back on his knees, he studied her. "For all your pain, my lady, you truly grow more splendid with every step we take."

Aurelia tipped her head at him. "There is no nee—"

"No." He stopped her with a raised hand and a puzzled look. "I do not mean it as cajolery. You're changing, I vow. You are becoming more ethereal with every step we take."

Aurelia bit her lip and swallowed hard, forcing a smile. "You grow more tired and fearful," she quipped with forced gaiety. "It is naught but the extreme circumstances of our situation."

"No," he said again. "I would swe—"

But Aurelia allowed him no further discourse, struggling to gain her feet, knowing he would stop to help her. Together they stood, clothing drenched, pupils reduced to pinpoints in the brightness, and surveyed their surroundings.

Beyond the swirling lights, the room opened to another flight of stairs. Aurelia rushed to and onto them, leaving behind the penetrating discussion.

With each step, the blazing light grew brighter, scorching a harsh, painful glare upon their eyes. Battista rummaged in his rucksack, pulling out more of her chemise, tearing it once more into strips. Holding her with a hand, he wrapped one thin layer around her eyes, the other about his own, creating a thin buffer between their eyes and the glare, without diminishing their vision. Sight protected, they continued on, rounding the spiral staircase, reaching another landing.

"Not again," Battista grumbled, shoulders slumping, as they examined their environment.

They stood in yet another room without an egress, a small chamber of nothing more than two short walls on the sides and one wide wall at the back, another puzzle to solve.

But even as he moaned against it, his mind chewed upon it. As they inched forward and removed the cloths from their eyes, the details upon the huge back wall revealed themselves.

Separated into four distinct panels, each panel bore the likeness of the same man, that of Jesus Christ or, at least, what the world accepted as his likeness. A penetrating blue gaze stared at them from a serene and bearded face, smooth and wavy hair curtained the almost-delicate features.

A decorated tile lay centered on the floor in front of each panel, one all too familiarly etched with the cross and the coil.

Battista turned to Aurelia, her tanned skin shimmering with the rich amber of a topaz, eyes bright as a fresh meadow, her face set in a bitterly amused mien, a mirror of his own deliberation.

"A choice must be made," he said needlessly.

"It is more than a choice," she agreed. "It is a test."

"A test?"

"*Sì.*" She inched closer to the etchings and he followed. "A test of faith."

Larger than life, the figure at the forefront of the pictures towered above them; they bent their necks to look up at the identical faces. But the setting of each differed greatly.

"It is your test," Aurelia whispered, the hushed words full of demand. "It is not for me to decide."

He scrunched his face at her. "Why not?"

She placed a hand on his shoulder and the warmth and vitality of it reached deep to his core.

"This is, ultimately, your journey. It did not begin with me as a part of it. Life puts before each human the tests belonging to each life. Here is one of yours."

He opened his mouth to argue, but not a sufficient word came forth. She spoke the truth, though how she came by it he could not surmise. Why he believed her he could not understand. It was a spiritual test, and yet he felt as if she tested him as well. Battista stared at Aurelia for a long heartrending moment, astounded and confused by the unfathomable beauty of her, turning away, for she made him long to sob.

Battista stood before the son of God, all of them, feeling as torn by the visages as by Aurelia. His life had always been a battle between his faith and his fortune, between patriotism and prize. This moment was no different.

He flitted a glance at Aurelia over his shoulder. He took a step closer to the tiles.

"Choose not in haste." Aurelia's words nipped at his back.

Battista studied each panel, an eye to every detail. In the first, Jesus wore the best of robes, the fabric thick and heavy with embroidery. Jewels glittered from his fingers and around his neck. Battista walked away from the inaccurate depiction.

In the next, Jesus was not quite so ostentatiously attired, but behind him stood a thick crowd of men and women, nobles and courtiers without a doubt, their faces hungry and greedy. Battista shook his head at them. Those who stood, literally and metaphorically, behind the prophet were as charitable as he. Never would they wear such avaricious expressions.

Battista stood before the last two, indecision plaguing both his heart and his mind. In each, Jesus wore simple attire, no jewels adorned his limbs, no finery lay upon his body, the differences arose in the background alone. In one, men draped in the robes of priests, cardinals, bishops, and popes surrounded him. In the other, Jesus stood alone.

The earthly truth—that which Battista had been taught by the nuns and his parents since he could first remember—placed Jesus as the leader of the Church, of the Catholic faith. But Dante's words echoed to Battista, those nearly memorized during the days and nights spent poring over the *Commedia*, leaving him confused and irresolute at the depth of meaning behind the words. Dante's Paradise overflowed with admonishments heaped upon the clergy, damning them for the deterioration of the Church, condemning them for their greed and avarice, a scathing commentary renouncing monasteries as "dens of thieves."

Battista looked back at Aurelia, and though he saw confidence in her soft expression, he found no help. Turning forward, giving the two last panels one more quick glance, Battista closed his eyes and listened to his heart.

It came to him, the truth of all mankind, no more readily apparent as when Jesus hung on the cross. Battista moved before the solitary image and stepped on the tile.

With a shudder and a crack, the wall fell away, behind it another staircase heading upward, leading to the heights of Paradise.

Battista heaved a thankful sigh as he reached back for Aurelia, as her slim hand slipped into his.

Aurelia pulled him back, just long enough to bend him toward her, rise up on her toes, and kiss his soft cheek. His skin felt warm beneath her lips and she carried it with her as they ascended the first step.

The stairway was narrow, squishing them together, their outer shoulders brushing the smooth stone as they passed. Their arms swept away the stone dust, sending motes swirling in the luster. The universe revealed itself, freed from its mantle of dirt, the planets etched and stained upon the smooth stone walls.

As Dante foretold, they climbed through the planets, first the pale moon, then an umber Mercury, and a sapphire Venus. The Sun stood out, bright and golden, followed by a vermillion Mars and a russet-striped Jupiter.

The stairs narrowed and Battista wiggled in front of Aurelia, stepping onto the first rung of a golden ladder scaling upward as the stairs ended. Aurelia followed, her legs quivering as she scaled each rung, moist hands slipping on the rails as she pulled herself aloft.

"Are you all right?"

Above her, Battista held upon a rung, one crooked elbow holding him on to a rail as he leaned backward, looking down at her.

Grateful for even a moment's pause, Aurelia pushed back the thick strands of russet hair plastered to her head, drenched with sweat. Her forehead crinkled in exertion. "I am doing the bes—"

Mouth agape, eyes big and white, his sudden expression of shock and wonder nipped off her words.

"Aurelia, look!" He raised a finger to the passage left behind. "It's . . ."

She turned in the silence of his unfinished articulation.

Images of the planets they'd passed now hovered in the narrow stair passage, their forms somehow projected in the air by the light. In the dimensional illusion, the images circled one another in the air, creating a universe in the space where the stairs had been, as if their own passage—the addition of human energy—had brought the images to life.

"*Benedicimi*," Aurelia breathed as she turned.

Battista could not speak, could not tell her that he, too, felt blessed. He dared not speak or move, for fear the apparition would dissipate. He unfurled his arm, leaned farther back, longing to draw as close to it as he could, to a beauty of such consequence he could hurl himself into it, live forever among it.

"We must continue, Battista," Aurelia urged.

In her voice he heard his own longing to linger, but recognized the imperative as truth.

With far more than a twinge of regret, Battista turned back to the ladder, placed his hands upon the rail, and began the climb again.

They had but a little farther to go, their panting breath loud and harsh, their movements slowing with each tread. Ahead of her, Battista hurtled over the last rung, turned, and reached out a hand to pull her up and beside him, holding her there for a moment, resting in her arms.

Aurelia fell into him—as she would plunge into warm, buoyant water—but for no more than an instant. She looked up at him with a mixture of yearning and vigilance.

"We have reached the end, Battista," she said, eyes skidded from his.

They were indeed at the top; no roof hovered above their heads, only an infinite sky ablaze with stars. No walls rose up to enclose them, only a low parapet, distant corner turrets, hemmed them in.

Unlike the floors below, evening's darkness shrouded this rooftop. Two lit torches flanked their point of egress, and Battista pulled one from its wall mount and held it before them as they looked around. A dazzling glimmer at their feet drew Battista's gaze away.

"It cannot be," he mumbled as he first bent, then squatted, closer to the floor.

It began as only a trickle, a tiny thread running from their feet and away, the squiggle of it expanding as it went. Their gaze followed it, wide eyes growing wider as the stream stretched away, as it ended in a pool. No more than three feet above the pool, a painting rested on a tall, wood easel.

"Is it . . . ?" Aurelia croaked.

"I cannot tell." Battista squinted.

It was a painting, indeed, and the rectangular shape was the same size and formation as the other two. She could make out no more than the silhouette of a lone figure upon the canvas, the shape curvaceous, with long flowing hair. Any more she could not perceive, but she did not need to.

It was the last piece of the triptych, indisputably, and yet the full force of Battista's attention lingered on the stream of light at his feet.

"Gold. It looks like a river of gold," he whispered as he bent farther still. " 'He triumphs in his victory; he who is the keeper of gold.' "

Aurelia heard Battista mumble the words of Dante—with the voice that had become their driving force—once more in the air.

Circling round, positioning himself between the inception of the stream and the painting, Battista dropped to one knee, bent at the waist, and reached out the torch closer to the glistening trickle, eyes squinting with the effort to see it better.

Aurelia's fingers dug in his shoulder. "Stop, Battista! Do not—"

Too late. His cuffed hand moved, tipping the torch over and down, the flame no more than inches from the stream . . . one lick dripping out . . . and lapping at it.

Thirty

The night that hides things from us

—*Paradiso*

The river exploded, the fire stampeding along the course of gold.

The whoosh of scalding air pummeled them, heat displacing it in crashing waves, knocking them onto their backs. Battista's skin burned with pinpricks of pain. The ferocious propulsion set him flying backward, head bouncing on the hard stone. His vision popped with black spots and, in between, Aurelia's face, two of them.

He shook his head to clear it even as the force continued to propel him backward, skittering across smooth stone. But his vision did not clear; the mirage of the two Aurelias did not dissolve.

The fire hissed as it snacked along the room, crossing the passage, careening toward the pool at the foot of the painting.

"No!" Battista shouted, wobbling to his feet, stumbling toward the flames. The fire could not reach the canvas, could not set it ablaze. He would throw himself upon it if he must. But equilibrium eluded him; he staggered about like a drunkard.

"Aurelia?" he cried out, but no more than the wisp of his name did he hear in return, the sound diluted beneath the plangent rustle of the fire, so faint it may have existed only in his mind.

The flame was no more than an inch from the puddle, and he lunged forward, reaching out, as did the fire.

The pool of gold burst, as if the heavens themselves exploded.

Battista screamed as the force hit him, as his body curled in half, as he hit the floor once again.

"Aurelia." Her name slipped from his lips as the blackness took him.

Pain. First came the pain upon his skin.

Battista lay on the floor, not trying to get up, hands reaching to his face and the skin that burned as if the fire had devoured him. His face stung at the touch, but his skin was still smooth, still intact, merely scorched raw by the explosion.

With a quavering breath, a groan of exertion, he pulled himself up to a sitting position, raising his knees and dropping his head between them as he whirled from the effort.

"Aurelia!" He called her name, her well-being the second thought to batter his already-battered mind. Receiving no answer, he called again, and yet again. But still her voice he did not hear. The vaguest recollection came to him, of her face, more than one of them, blurry in the haze and chaos of the explosions.

As soon as his body allowed, as soon as the nauseating dizziness subsided, Battista rolled up to his feet, brushing at the burn holes upon his shirt and breeches, feeling for the satchel about his shoulder, and looking about.

Smoke and sparks filled the air, but the river of gold no longer existed—no longer burned—only a small fire rustled, flames sputtering as they clung to life, where the pool of gold had been. He could barely see through the miasma filling the air.

Battista shoved his hands into his hair, eyes bulging as they racked backward.

He couldn't see the painting; the fire must have destroyed it. He walked forward, stumbling in disbelief, breath hitching with incoherent protests.

"Aurelia!" he cried once more, needing her to be there, unable to bear the loss of both, her and the painting. All he had hoped for Firenze, his homeland, would be lost. And yet it paled in comparison. He had sacrificed too much this time.

Battista moved closer to the small blaze popping and crackling as the last vestiges of liquid caught and flamed. Behind him, a ribbon of soot curled along the floor where the river of gold had been. In front of him—

"*Dio mio!*" Battista cried out, hand clenching his chest, heart bursting with equal parts revelation and rapture.

A few feet beyond the fire, the painting sat upon its tripod, still in existence, still in perfect condition. He could not make out the details through the smoke, an ever-billowing cloud rising from the small fire, thicker and thicker. He could not see it clearly, though he saw no soot stains, no black-charred splotches.

"Aurelia!" Battista stepped around the small fire, waving his hand to dissipate the blinding smoke, coughing on it nonetheless. "Aurelia! It's here."

No answer came; he turned from the silence, refusing it and what it meant.

As he neared the painting, an especially dense pocket of air nearly devoured it, the haze of smoke thicker than ever. Fearing he would lose it, that it would somehow disappear beyond the vapor, Battista rushed forward.

"Aur—"

Her name died on his tongue, for there she was in front of him . . . in the painting.

His knees broke . . . his legs wobbled . . . failing him.

Battista toppled to the floor, stricken gaze frozen on the canvas above him.

"What madness is this?" He shook his head, denying what he saw, looking away, for the vision burned his eyes, scarred his mind. "Dear Lord, what madness is this?"

He gawked at the center panel of the triptych . . . the green gown, the three women, the palazzo behind them.

Battista stared into Aurelia's face; he knew it as assuredly as he knew his own name, as he would know the face of his mother.

Upper lip curling, barely containing his cries, Battista dared to look up once more.

He gasped for breath, unable to tell if his heart crashed or stopped. Aurelia's changeable eyes looked down at him, dark and bereft of the glimmer of mischief that had come into them since she had met him. Teeth together, lips open, the full upper lip dominating the luscious mouth.

And there was the relic, the long, narrow piece of sculpted stone covered with hieroglyphics, gently pointed at one end, curved in an almost-circular curl at the other. He saw it in her hand, or did he? The object glowed from the center of the painting—as if it came away from it—at the very center of her body, but its radiance distorted the details, and he could not differentiate if her hands held it, if it hovered in the air in front of her or just behind her. With what he saw with a squinty-eyed glare, the main figure appeared slightly translucent as well, though not as lucent as the two on the sides.

Battista rubbed his eyes, achy with effort to see, and lifted on his knees, staring now at the two women beside her. Faintly though they were rendered—their translucence a statement of their transitory existence—just a portion of their faces visible behind the first, it was clearly the same face . . . the same woman. They were *all* Aurelia.

Thirty-one

Behold a God more powerful than I
who comes to rule over me

—La Vita Nuova

"What madness is this?" Battista said yet again, still upon his knees, crawling forward toward the painting. He asked himself the question, for he thought himself alone. He was not.

She stepped softly up behind him, as hesitant to disturb as to approach. Aurelia wanted no more of this. If she possessed the power to turn time in upon itself, no matter the danger, she would have done it gladly.

Battista reached up, two quivering hands reaching for each side of the painting.

"I cannot allow you to do that, Battista."

With a relieved cry, he flinched round. But she held him fast . . . with the tip of a dagger.

"Please, don't." Silent tears slipped down her face, her voice thick with emotion. If she must kill him, she could not glimpse his face again, could not bear the beauty and the pain of it.

"Aurelia, *amore mia*, thank God you are alive." The harsh prick of the dagger stabbed him in the neck and his lyrical relief turned into a grating hiss. "What is this? What are you doing?"

"I did not choose to be who I am." Her voice trembled with emotion and she released her head back on her neck, looking to the heavens for the strength to continue. "No, Battista, do not turn."

But turn he did, refusing to accept her threat, eyes bulging at the blade—one of his own—pressed to his throat. Aurelia swallowed hard as the tip of shiny steel dented the soft stubbled skin below his chin. She had never seen such anger, such disillusion, in the warm eyes turned hard, flicking from the dagger to her face and back again.

Pressing his hands against his thighs, Battista made to stand.

Aurelia thrust herself forward, pressing the blade farther, until a tiny drop of blood, brilliantly red in the surreal gray world, trickled out, running down skin she once caressed.

"No, I cannot allow you to stand." Aurelia shook her head; she pleaded, but did not care. She could not allow him the advantage of his size.

"You betray me?" he asked with a barely contained growl, inching toward her on his knees.

Aurelia shook her head again, her hair flying about in the air full of smoke and the scent of acidic flame. "Yes," she answered with fretful dichotomy. "But not for any reason you imagine."

"You make no sense," he barked at her, dark eyes black.

"I did not choose to be who I am, what I am, but to my truth I am, and will always be, faithful."

Battista's large hands fisted at his sides. He could fell her with one perfectly aimed blow, but he would not.

"Stop speaking to me in riddles." He unfurled one fist to point at the smoke-screened canvas. "Is that you?"

Aurelia held her chin high, her eyes narrowing with tenacity. "It is."

She took a step back, the dagger pointed still at his throat, needing space in which to reveal herself and her truth.

"I am a guardian, Battista."

"A guar—"

"One of a long line of guardians," she stifled him, "created to guard the artifact. As were those who came before me and those who will come after."

Battista's gaze darted to her face and the three mirror images on the canvas.

"Your French king was correct, Battista." Her words brought him back. He slithered toward her and she scuttled away. "The piece you seek does indeed hold commanding powers, a domination never meant for men of this world."

"Then why . . . what?!" he stumbled and sniped.

"It was created in an age when gods and goddesses walked the earth, those you would call by the names of Zeus, Apollo, Aphrodite, and others like them. It is to be used only should the time come to defend this world from those that would come from others. But its power was too great. It brought one man to destruction, then was buried by the same who wielded it. He destroyed himself, but only after killing he who created it."

"Praxi—"

"*Sì.*" Aurelia nodded. "Your king knew much, too much by far. Praxiteles knew of the others and their ways, knew that they could overpower those of our world. With his knowledge, that gleaned from the others themselves, he created the one weapon capable of defeating them. It was never meant for one man to wield it against another." She shook her head, wiping her moist forehead, creased with worry. "But like all things great, man found a way to abuse it. Like me, all guardians are meant to protect it, to keep it from ever falling into the hands of man again unless its true moment should ever arise. We are unaffected by the relic's power, it does not corrupt us. And therefore only we can keep it from all those who would be corrupted. "

"But Giotto . . ."

Aurelia's anger rose bitterly in her throat and she swallowed against it. "Giotto, yes. I do not know how he came to be involved. Those who help us—"

"The marquess of Mantua?"

"Yes, the marquess and those of his family line, the woman in Florence, they are all members of the Brotherhood of the Guardians. We can only surmise the artist somehow learned of the piece and its location." Aurelia pursed her lips like a mother speaking of an errant child. "What impelled him to produce these paintings I do not know. It is clear he worked in collusion with Dante and those of the Brotherhood, but, thankfully, they possessed the foresight to make the finding difficult. But I . . . we were told they had been destroyed long ago."

"Again?" Battista eyed her coldly, hands pressed to his temples. "You said, to keep it from falling into the hands of man *again*. What did you mean?"

Her head fell with the weight of man's history, with the devastation that comes from the misuse of power, and the pain it caused. Aurelia shook her head, peering at him through the top of her eyes. "I cannot bear to speak of it. You have heard the names, Attila, Caligula . . . and others yet, but only a few. My sisters died in the moments of their triumphs."

Aurelia sucked in her breath, set her shoulders back, and lifted her head, a blaze of determination in her eye. "I cannot, I *will* not, allow it to happen again. If victory is to be had, it must be obtained through one's own actions, deservedly or not at all. Your François was not meant to possess it. No man who would fight another is. What occurs between him and the king of Spain must follow the path meant for them to take. No matter the cost. No matter *our* cost."

Battista scowled at her. "And this . . . this object. It holds such powers? Gives such powers to he who wields it?"

"It is true, Battista, though I see your doubt." She leaned toward him, piercing him with her gaze. "Think of all we have seen? Think of the air ships? Would you have believed any of it until you lived it for yourself?"

Battista opened his mouth, yet remained speechless. His dark eyes, their whites shot through with threads of red, scoured about for something tangible. Waves of disbelief and acceptance crested over his red-splotched face. She would convince him; she must.

"Look at me, Battista." Aurelia stepped to him and held her other hand out, resting it upon his head as his skeptical gaze rose up. "Close your eyes and look at me."

He opened his mouth as if to refute the illogical command, the words dying in his throat. She pushed with her mind, his eyes closed with a flutter, and his body stiffened.

As if struck, his head flinched back, and he pushed her hand off.

"What . . . what was that?"

Aurelia smiled, though there was much sadness in it. "That—was me."

Battista's gaze locked upon hers; he sidled away on his knees. "I cannot bear this, Aurelia. It is too much." Bending at the waist, he plunked his head in his hands.

"You can and you must."

"Why, Aurelia?" Battista straightened of a sudden and grabbed the hand he had brushed away, squeezing it as if to break the small bones. "Why did you come on this quest? Why did you help me? Would it not have been easier to simply allow me to fail? I must have the truth."

Aurelia laughed bitterly, a scathing condemnation of her own actions. "I did not intend to help you, not at first. In fact, I meant to hinder you. That conversation you overheard . . . in Florence . . ." She hung her head in the shame of her perfidy. ". . . I plotted against you, as you surmised, working with others to find the paintings before you did."

With her free hand, she reached for him, her palm flattening against his chest where his heart thudded against his ribs. He let her, and with the capitulation a tear escaped her eye, her battle with her sorrow abandoned.

"I used you, Battista," her voice warbled, her hand fluttered. "Yes, to help me find the paintings, for there was no one better to do so. But I used you for myself as well. To show me a life I have never known . . . I have never been allowed to know."

She smiled timidly, unsuccessful at stemming the grin as she had the tears.

"And at that, you were the best as well."

His chest hitched beneath her hand, what lived between them prodigious to them both.

"And now I must use you again."

Her green gaze turned from his glower to the faint vision of the painting.

"You must help me destroy it. We must destroy all of them, once and for all."

Thirty-two

A fair request should be followed by the deed in silence

—*Inferno*

The inky world burned red, raw, and stained by the fierceness of his anger.

Her lies, her betrayal, he longed to scream against it, the spew of it rumbling in his chest. And yet Battista could not doubt all that his own eyes had seen, all he had experienced, what had overcome him as her hand rested upon his head.

"How can I trust you?" It was a scathing rejoinder more than a question, and yet he looked to her, to the face of inhuman beauty, as if for an answer.

"For the sake of—"

"All I have done has been for the sake of Florence, of others!" he shouted. "You know of my dedication, and yet you ask for more?"

Aurelia looked to the heavens as she bit her lip. "I know, Battista, I know of your selflessness. But this you must do, you must trust me, for the sake of mankind."

She lowered the dagger aimed at his throat, holding both arms out, laying herself at his mercy.

Battista moved not an inch; her plea provoked him, her openness beckoned him. But what he had seen her do—the killing committed by the same hand gripping the dagger—restrained him.

As if she read his thoughts, she released the dagger, sent it to clatter upon the stone, and reached out a hand, pulling on him, urging him to stand. For the sake of petulance alone, he could have denied her, but instead he allowed her to guide him to his feet.

Exhaustion made him heavy; he dragged against it as if it meant to keep him tethered to the ground. Battista closed his eyes, head dropping to his chest. He had the strength to overcome her easily, to take the painting—all of them—away and find the artifact with their clues, relieving her of her post and her burden. Battista stumbled away from her, from the small fire vomiting the thick smoke that enveloped the painting.

"The time must be now, Battista. There are too many others who know of the paintings' existence . . . your French king . . . whoever sent Balda—that other."

Aurelia bungled the name, tripping upon the essence of a life she herself had ended, pointing at the painting vaguely visible now through the thickening haze. They would lose it soon, in the engulfing smoke. She knew that if the vapor swallowed it completely, they would stumble off the edge of the roof before they found it again, lost in the failure of reaching Paradise.

"I don't—"

"There is no time!" she screamed at him.

Aurelia jumped forward, grabbed his hand, and shoved it onto her body, pushing it hard against the soft flesh of her stomach.

It came upon him again, the feeling of ultimate possession, of external control by another. But he saw not the ephemeral blazing white form of Aurelia, but blood . . . everywhere blood. Dismembered bodies, torn limbs, cities set afire, blood flooding and staining the streets, turning the world to a crimson calamity.

"*No!*" he screamed.

With a wrench, he pulled away, feet buckling as he staggered backward.

With one graceful move, Aurelia skipped forward, bent, scooped up the dagger, and raised it up before her face.

"You have two choices, Battista, and only two."

She stomped toward him, face set with such strength of purpose, her skin stretched taut across the sharp bones.

"You must help me destroy the paintings. Or you must plunge this dagger into my heart. For the only way to leave here, alive, with those paintings, and obtain the relic . . . is to kill me."

Battista threw his hands out before him, shaking them as if he washed the air before him clean, taking yet two more steps backward. He was done with this quest, with this mission, and wanted no part of it. Did he destroy the only love he had ever known, betray him though she had, or did he risk the fate of Florence, the constant love throughout his life?

Hands—fisted now—shook at his sides; he raised them up, saw her cringe at the threat, and lowered them. They hung there together, she and he—at the top of the castle, at the threshold to Paradise, if that was where they were—suspended in the zenith of this penultimate decision.

Battista gnashed his teeth together, turned, and ran, the painting barely visible as he entered the engulfing haze; in seconds he would lose sight of it . . . lose it altogether. Tilting on his tiptoes, reaching out, reaching into the vapor, he grabbed it.

He crumpled it with his fists, as if to release all his rage upon it, snapping the slats of wood upon which it was mounted. Marching back toward Aurelia, he inched his other hand behind his back.

Battista saw her eyes follow his hand, watched her frown, knowing her thoughts were of the remaining daggers at his back.

But she cowered not an inch as he approached her, nor did she recoil as he stepped past her. Behind his back, his hand scurried, not for a dagger but for the other paintings, pulling them roughly—

caring not a whit for their preservation any longer—out of his satchel.

Battista stopped before the smoldering splat of fire still burning upon the floor. He looked up at her, all the reward he needed in the beauty of her simple smile. With a grin, he held out the three canvases in his hand and dipped their edges in the flames, sighing as the fire first licked and then devoured them.

Thirty-three

And in His will is our peace.

—*Paradiso*

He left her, though not without great remorse.

As Battista tucked the bed linens close about Aurelia's curled form, her body hardly stirred, her exhaustion—like his—too pervasive. They had traveled through the night, traveled together on Battista's horse, Aurelia's tethered and following close behind. Battista had kept her as close as he could, insisting she ride on the saddle in front of him, his arms wrapped protectively about her.

They had arrived in Florence in the darkest hours of the morning, slumped in their saddle, dirt smudged, soot ridden, and exhausted. Rousing the household—Frado and Nuntio, and Lucagnolo, now a permanent resident of the household it seemed—they had spared no time on explanations, offering only quick assurances of well-being, and then had fallen into bed, and blissful slumber, together.

But now Battista could sleep no more, though it was still early morning. The heat clung to the earth like a greedy lover. Insects buzzed a complaint as chirping birds hunted them down for their morning feeding. He leaned over, plying a gentle touch to push back the hair sticking to her moist flesh.

Beneath the plaits of chestnut hair, Aurelia's skin bore the scars of their tribulations; on one cheek a slim white line, on the other an angry blister. Her injured hand, already purple with fresh bruising, lay tucked between her breasts, creamy skin and pale pink areola visible through her thin chemise.

His heart pained him as he looked upon her with eyes unclouded by misconception, his chest heaving with the physical realization of it. Battista could not imagine what she and those like her had endured through the centuries in the service of their duty. Battista understood devotion to duty above all else; he had lived much of his life with such a master. And yet the heavy weight of sympathy for her and those like her, and a greater desire to protect her from the torment of more danger, impelled him. If he could relieve her—them—from their duty, he would.

It was, ultimately, why he had destroyed the paintings; Battista could not bear for Aurelia to suffer for his decisions. Razor-sharp imaginings had shredded his thoughts, images of what she might endure had he discovered the location of the relic, retrieved it, and placed it in the hands of King François.

Battista's faith and his religion had been a constant in his life, but, like Michelangelo, his Catholic upbringing had been tempered with the teachings of the pagans. That an object such as a one Aurelia described existed—one others had been all too willing to kill for—he did not doubt for a moment. There were more things in and of this world that could not be logically explained; only man's fear, intolerance, and ignorance allowed them to deny it. Battista could not count the number of artifacts and relics he had unearthed that pulsated with preternatural energy.

He looked down at her face, serene in slumber, all the words left unsaid between them parching his tongue.

Battista laughed softly as he straightened; he had never cared to speak of futures with any woman, and now he had chosen the one woman for whom the future could never be spoken of.

He moved away from the bed and shimmied silently into a pair of *brache* and a thin shirt, already clothed in his certainty. He had done the right thing; only the smallest voice chivied him, one nagging about his failed duty to the king and what it might mean for Florence.

Battista slipped down the stairs on bare feet, long legs achy but cool in the short drawers, and made his way downstairs.

No one stirred in the common rooms of his home, and for a poignant moment he stood at the bottom of the steps, simply grateful for the sight of it—the crate-cluttered sitting room, the book-clogged study, the cozy kitchen. The events of the last few weeks had tempered his wanderlust. He would continue his work, for he must, but he would find far less joy in the doing.

In the smudgy light of dawn, he poured himself a full and hefty mug of mulled cider and rummaged about the cupboard until he found some biscuits, no worse for their lack of freshness. Placing them upon the table, he pulled out a chair.

The soft knock upon the door came before he could sit, and with a brow furrowed with curiosity, he stepped to the door and opened it.

The small man hurled himself across the threshold, wrapping spindly, muscular arms tightly about him.

Battista laughed as they stumbled back, answering Michelangelo's embrace as he recovered from his surprise.

"It is well to see you, too, Michelagnolo." He chuckled. The warm concern of this man, who had become like a father, was a gift untold and Battista immersed himself in it.

Pulling away, holding Battista at arm's length, Michelangelo frowned at him. Battista had not taken the time to check his reflection, but he imagined the picture he presented, eyebrows singed, skin red, almost raw, as if he had been laid out to dry too long in the sun.

"Are you all right?" Michelangelo hissed with impassioned concern.

"I am fine, dear friend," Battista assured him. "It must look much worse than it feels."

He stepped away, back toward the table.

"Some cider and biscuits?"

"Just cider, *per favore*." The older man nodded as he shuffled along behind, and they sat companionably, sipping their cider, Battista munching his biscuit.

"How did you know I had returned?"

"I just saw Nuntio in the market," Michelangelo replied. "He prepares a splendid meal to celebrate your . . . success?"

The artist's voice inched upward, the intrusive question resounded loudly in the polite inquiry.

Battista stared down into his cup as if a better answer lay in the floating pulp of the cider.

"I do not have the last canvas. In fact, I no longer have any of them. They have been destroyed."

Battista curled his shoulders in defense, as if he expected a scolding, or at the least a barrage of questions. But not a word did Michelangelo speak, and in the silence Battista found the acceptance to continue.

"Do you remember once, after you had finished the chapel"—Battista's gaze flicked up shyly—"you tried to tell me of what came upon you as you worked your brush? A possession, if you will, of something or someone not of this earth?"

Michelangelo sat back in his chair, wood creaking below him, face placid.

Battista thought the artist would deny it, for he had been a bit inebriated at the time, if Battista remembered correctly. Or perhaps Michelangelo would scoff at the notion and the discussion. Battista looked up, surprised to find his friend with a silly smirk upon his bearded face.

"Is something funny?" Battista asked with an edge of annoyance.

"Funny? No. Wonderful? *Sì*." Michelangelo leaned toward him, one hand reaching out for his. "You have learned the truth."

Battista shot him a befuddled look. "Truth?"

"*Sì*, the truth. Aurelia's truth. The truth of the relic."

Battista fell back from the table, mouth working silently on words he could not grasp.

"It is all right, *amico karissimo*," Michelangelo assured him with the same half smile. "It is a secret I already guard."

"How d-did you . . . when d-did you . . ." Battista stammered, shoulders up to his ears, hands splayed in the air.

Michelangelo tutted as he stood and refilled Battista's cup, this time with yellow wine.

"In truth? Not until I saw the lady in the Sistine." He sat back down beside his friend, amber eyes glowing with his tale. "It is not that I had forgotten what I experienced as I painted that ceiling, the moments of being out of myself over the course of those arduous years. I believe I simply had put it in a cupboard of my mind, knowing there was naught to be done about it, that naught needed to be done."

Battista nodded, gulping on the fruity beverage, gaze never leaving his friend's face.

"But when I saw her there, her own visage rendered by my hand, though I had never set eyes upon her . . . well . . . I remembered . . . I knew . . ." Michelangelo's voice faded away into wonder. "I had heard of the guardians, in those days as an apprentice, though it took me a while to remember. Word of them came along with those of Giotto, Dante, and others still. Many thought them part of a pagan society and the guardians as part of their sect. I never learned of their true purpose. But I understood when you told me of your assignment, when I saw her face upon my ceiling."

They sat in it together, their unbreakable bond ever stronger, now with a union far beyond the imaginable. Battista could have wept the gratitude of it; he would not have to live the rest of his life as the sole keeper of this secret. It was a burden he had not wished for, nor cared to carry.

"Your face, my friend." Michelangelo finally asked with a painful expression, "Was the challenge grueling?"

Battista laughed, then drank the rest of his wine. "It was a heaven filled with the pain of Hell."

"Love and hate walk a similar path," Michelangelo mused.

The slanted rays of sunlight chased away the morning gloom as Battista told his mentor all they had experienced in the castle. Though there were earthly explanations for all they had seen and done, the words—when articulated between these two—hummed with spiritual reality and otherworldly forces.

His tale complete, Battista sat back in his chair, hands rustling through his hair. "I will go to my grave not knowing the true nature of all I have seen and can only hope God will tell me the truth of it when I look upon Him."

"You mean *if* you look upon Him," Michelangelo said, one bushy brow raised impishly.

Battista cuffed him on the shoulder with a hearty laugh, his first in a very long time.

"May I know of the jest?"

The men jumped at Aurelia's voice and turned their startled gaze to the bottom stair upon which she stood.

Clothed still in her chemise, a full-skirted cream dressing gown wrapped and tied about her, she looked an angel with her russet hair atangle upon her head, her face smooth and swollen with sleep. Battista's heart swelled at the sight of her.

With a drowsy smile, Aurelia descended the last step and crossed to them.

The two men stood as she neared, as they always had, but this time they tendered a bow.

"Please don't," she asked with gentle insistence. She rushed around the table to buss Michelangelo on both his cheeks. "You are my dear friend."

She turned to Battista, rising up on tiptoes to brush his mouth with hers. "And you are my love."

It was a provocative statement, but one she seemed eager to make.

"I would have you treat me as nothing more."

"I will treat you like the lady you are." Battista pulled out a chair between them. "And nothing less."

She smiled as she sat, gaze volleying from one to the other.

"He has told you, I see," she said to Michelangelo, who had the good grace to simply shrug and nod.

"You are at peace, madonna?" he asked.

"As much as I can be," Aurelia replied. "I have served my duty, and served it well, and have not suffered too deep a wound."

She turned her gaze to Battista. "Except, perhaps, one of the heart."

Battista took up her hand and brushed the back of it with his lips.

Her eyes closed at the touch. "I do not know how I will return to the life I lived before, but return to it I must."

"Not until you are much recovered," Battista insisted with a low rumble. "You are exhausted and thin. I would see you rested and well fed before I return you. If return you I must."

Aurelia smiled but did not naysay him, be it his hope or hers.

Beside them Michelangelo's foot tapped an arrhythmic beat upon his chair rung.

"What is it, Michelangelo? I have told you all and yet I feel as if you have something to tell me."

Michelangelo nodded, bushy salt-and-pepper brows rising precipitously upon his forehead. "Indeed, I do. I fear you read my face too well."

"Do you not wish to tell me?" Aurelia asked. "I will leave if you have need of privacy."

"Oh no, my lady." Michelangelo reached out to tap her arm

with assurance. "I fear only that it is disturbing news and am not sure if this is the proper time."

Battista rose, gathering another cup, the wine, and more biscuits from the cupboard. "There's nothing for it now, *amico*. We are forewarned. You must fess up."

Michelangelo stood as Battista sat and walked to the other side of the table, better able to see them both.

"Rome has fallen."

Battista choked on the mouthful of wine, spewing and sputtering the pale brew over his chin and the table before him.

"The deuce you say!" he swore as he wiped his mouth with the back of his hand.

Beside him, Aurelia sat speechless, stiff as a board.

"When . . . how?" Battista demanded.

"But a few days ago." Michelangelo sat with a thump. "Word arrived only yesterday, while you were gone. It is all Florence can speak of."

"Tell me all you know," Battista implored. "Was it the emperor?"

"Yes and no," Michelangelo began. "It was his forces, that much is certain. But word is they acted alone, those under the command of Bourbon."

"François's betrayer," Battista hissed.

"Indeed," Michelangelo agreed. "But it was not done at the duke's command, but over him. It seems the men lost faith in their commanders. No food or pay made them angry, and angry men do barbarous things. For his own good, Bourbon took part in the invasion. Ironically, he became one of the first to fall."

"Dead?"

"Very. And any military constraint remaining evaporated with his last breath. Those few who made it out of the city say the pillaging and destruction continues. Hundreds, mayhap thousands are dead. No one knows for sure. No one can get into the city.

They've closed the gates and guard them well." The artist hung his head, heels of his hands pushing at his wrinkled forehead. "I fear greatly for my work . . . my pietà . . . the chapel."

Aurelia reached out and pulled his hands away. "You must have faith."

Battista cocked an eye at her, something in her words disturbed him, but he could not name it, too eager to learn more of Rome.

"And the pope? What has become of Clement?"

Michelangelo's golden eyes rolled heavenward. "Held captive, in the Castel Sant'Angelo. Almost all the guards, nearly two hundred, died seeing him safely there. There remain not enough alive to get him out."

Battista jumped to his feet, chair scraping against the floor with a screech of protest. He paced about, a crazed animal locked in a cage, his heart torn as assuredly as the city. He had no care for the Medici pope, but he bristled with consuming anger against foreign soldiers plundering Rome.

His hands gripped the back of his chair, his knuckles white and hard as sun-bleached stones.

"What from Ippolito and the cardinal?" Battista asked of Florence's rulers. "What is the word on the street?"

"No one knows. The speculations swing, as does the pendulum. Half fear the marauders will make for Florence next. The other half believe the time has come to take back the Republic, in the wake of the Medici fall." The sorrowful man hung his head. "But how many more must die?"

The question hung in the still air like a noxious odor.

Michelangelo looked up at his friend looming above him, great swollen tears in his eyes.

Aurelia squeezed the older man's hand in hers. "You must not—"

"You knew!" Battista raged, turning on her, all his anger, fear, and revulsion divested upon her head as the revelation came to him. "You knew, and you could have stopped it."

The accusation was harsh and loathsome. Aurelia did nothing to deny it.

Releasing her hold upon Michelangelo's hand, she reached for Battista's. With a glimmer of repulsion, he pulled away.

But she followed, jumping up, barreling toward him, meeting his gaze without shame or weakness.

"I did not stop it, for it was not meant to be stopped."

Thirty-four

There is no greater sorrow
Than to be mindful of the happy time
In misery

— *Inferno*

She closed her eyes, arms held away from her body, palms forward, posed in a posture of acceptance and abandon. Few medicinals had healed her as well as this place; in its embrace her wounds mended, her strength returned, and her body once more boasted the curves of a vigorous woman. Her paradox branded her healing as the illness that would take her away.

Aurelia surrendered to the warmth of the sun as it crested the horizon, born of another day; she capitulated her being to the chirping birds, the gurgle of the small fountain, the air replete with all that was earthy and blooming, fresh and redolent. Droning insects buzzed near and past her, caressing wind flowed over her, and she became of her surroundings, no longer merely in them.

"Why do you cry, Aurelia?"

Battista's soft hush pulled her back to the physical world.

Aurelia blinked, returning to the earth, standing in the center of the small courtyard of Battista's home.

She raised a hand to her cheek, slim brows rising upon her freckled forehead as it came away moist.

"I did not know I did," she replied.

He stepped closer and she drank of his face: the small but full curled mouth, the narrow but angled soft eyes, the sharp planes of a face both hard and tender. Would she see it again, after today? She loathed not having the answer.

Battista stepped one foot on each side of hers, lowered his long body, and slithered it against her as he wrapped his arms across the small of her back, the graceful move of a sensual lover. Her body weakened against the force of it and she dropped her forehead onto his chest, the linen soft and the flesh firm.

"Why do you cry?" he asked again.

Aurelia shook her head against him but could not speak; to say the words would make them real.

Battista heaved a sigh; his chest rose beneath her, the air, so harshly exhaled, fluttered against her head.

"The time has come for you to leave."

Half a question, half a denouncement; she denied neither.

"Yes." She lifted her gaze to his face. "In a few hours, perhaps less."

Battista frowned, puzzled, but shook it away. "You could stay here, Aurelia."

"Battista, do no—"

"You could stay here and still serve your duty." He rushed out his plea, allowing no argument, pulling her closer, crushing the air from her lungs with insistence. "You could stay, here with me. I know we may never marry. I know we could not bear children. But I would gladly sacrifice all to keep you with me."

He leaned down, tipping his head to the right, right beside hers. Another piece of Aurelia's heart cracked at the look upon features grown so dear, where despair and hope mingled tenderly. Aurelia reached out to stroke his tawny skin; she meant to placate and he continued to refute it.

"I could protect you. I could ensure your safety and help you, as surely as the Mantuan does."

There it was, the name rose up from out of the ground, a thick vine to separate them.

Aurelia closed her eyes, tenebrous brown with sadness. "The guardians must live a sequestered life. If any learned who they were, who they loved, it would be used against—"

"I would not tell a soul." Battista flapped his hand at the opened door at his back and the men who had gathered in his home, drawn there once more, as their days and their lives returned to something resembling normalcy.

The men had offered little in the way of recriminations, though she and Battista had fully expected it, fully anticipated them to grouse and question the losses, not only of any hope of finding the relic, but all three pieces of the triptych as well. Battista had blamed destruction by fire, a truth maligned by his failure to include their part in it. Only the loss of Ercole tainted the mission as a true forfeit, his life taken for the sake of an unsuccessful quest. But loss was inevitable, no matter the course of life, as the passing of Lucagnolo's wife showed them. These men had learned much through these hard days.

Aurelia smiled as the sounds of their antics flowed out into the courtyard—the shuffle of cards, the affectionate chiding between men who cared for one another.

And yet she could not accept Battista's offer. "I believe you, Battista. And I believe *in* you. But we can never know who may come into our lives. We could never know how to trust those who learn of my truth." She splayed her hands upon his chest with a slow to-and-fro of her head, heavy with the profundity of her existence. "The kind of power I guard is poisonous. It creates monsters out of the most commendable of souls. It is a virulent disease. Even your men could be weak to it."

Battista pushed her away, face cross and shadowed, as he stepped back toward the house. "No, you know not of what you speak. These men are pure of spirit. I know it. I know it as surely as I know how desperately I love you."

He turned back, his own fruitless argument slumping his shoulders, dropping his chin upon his chest.

Aurelia rushed to his side, taking his hands and holding them against her chest. She longed to fly away if she could, end this parting and spare him the pain of it. "They are all good men, Battista, I do know. As good and true as you."

As if the men heard her commendation, a great ruckus arose, voices lifted in what seemed tomfoolery, but the tattered croak of fear and alarm named its truth.

Battista's eyes narrowed, his head perking at the sound. Aurelia heard it for the warning it was.

"Battista! Make haste!" more than one man cried out.

Battista and Aurelia turned together, rushing forward and into the house.

The front door and windows stood open, shutters thrown wide. Men jostled one another to glimpse whatever took place beyond.

Frado scurried away from the door, rushing across the room at them, round cheeks splotched red, bald pate gleaming with a sheen of sweat.

"Florence is under siege!" he cried.

"No!" Ascanio and Lucagnolo refuted together.

As Ascanio stepped from the door, the parade of the armed rushed by. But not a soldier marched among them. Instead, the streets overflowed with their neighbors, Mario of the haberdashery, Lucrezia from the flower shop, and more, hundreds of them.

Like a rushing river tumultuous with fish, the crowd swept past them, anger and determination upon their brows, chants of revolt upon their tongues.

"To arms! To arms!" they cried, fisted hands pumping the air above their heads.

Men and women of all ages brandished weapons: swords, daggers, and bows, even a few of the costly *archibugi*, the deadly muzzles stabbing the sky.

"Guns! Guns to the people!" Voices rose up in adjuration. "Florence belongs to the people!"

"They're headed for the Palazzo Vecchio!" Barnabeo cried, so fierce in the throes of revolt his squeaking voice became shrill. "Get to your weapons!" He pulled his own sword, forever by his side, from its scabbard and entered the fray.

"Wait for us!" Lucagnolo cried as he and Frado flew up the stairs, returning in seconds, Frado with a crossbow, Lucagnolo with a sword.

"We will go first to your home," Lucagnolo proclaimed to Ascanio with incitement, then pointed to Pompeo. "And then to yours."

The four men rushed to the door. Last in line, foot upon the threshold, Ascanio came up short and quick, head spinning round. Handsome face aflame, his eyes jumped from Battista to Aurelia, no words upon his tongue, naught more than a fearful expression upon his noble features.

"Go along, Ascanio," Aurelia urged him on, holding on tightly to composure in the face of this moment as best she could. "Battista will find you in time."

"What?" Ascanio asked with an awkward tilt of his head, a puckered, perplexed brow.

Her self-possession broke and she rushed across the room, throwing her arms around the man's neck as he looked over her head at Battista in confusion.

"Tell the others to be safe. Tell them . . . tell them I will never forget them, not a one."

"Come on, Ascanio!"

The cry reached them from the street, and Ascanio's arms answered her embrace. She pushed him away and out the door, slamming it closed behind him.

"I need only a moment, Battista." Aurelia rushed past him and up the stairs.

In Battista's room—for she had made it her own since their return—she stood in the center, pulled in all directions. There were so many memories, so many things that held them; she knew not what to take and what to leave.

In the end, she grabbed only one gown, the same she had worn the first night they had made love, in the small room over Michelangelo's study. Rolling it into a ball, she pushed it into her small rucksack and, with it, a golden stone she had picked up in the caves, a seagull feather from the shore, and the small dagger, the one Battista had insisted she keep. They were naught but silliness, but they were her most cherished possessions.

Flinging the bag over her shoulder, she ran down the stairs, back into the room where Battista awaited.

He had armed himself in her absence; a long, fine sword now hung by his side.

"I am ready, Battista." She took his hand, rising on toes to sweep his cheek with a quick kiss, and pulled him toward the door.

But he would not be pulled; he jerked her back with his immobility alone.

"You must tell me all you know." It was a demand, and one he had every right to, but she could not appease him.

Aurelia turned, cleansing her face of all emotion, for it was no longer a time when their cares, wants, and desires had any precedence.

"You must get me back to Mantua." An emotionless, strident declaration. "Get me back to Mantua, then return here to your duties. It is time."

Battista winced, eyes rolling, hands fisting, shoulders creeping up. She pushed his patience with her baffling nature, perhaps one too many times. But it could not be otherwise.

"We must go, Battista!" she demanded of him harshly, though the taste of it was putrid upon her tongue.

He gave way then, looking none too pleased, and followed her out into the streets. The wide avenue continued to boil with those who would take it back from the Medici. It took many minutes to calm her and Battista's skittish horses, to pacify them enough to mount. Battista pulled on his reins, pointed his mount to the north.

"To Michelangelo's first," Aurelia said, heading in the opposite direction. "We must warn him."

With a hard click of his tongue and a squeeze of his heels, Battista followed.

"You must tell me, Aurelia," he called out as he pulled alongside, staring at her with feverish eyes, leaning out of his saddle toward her. "You must tell me what I am to do."

She heard his doubt then. He would answer the call to duty, as he always had, but for once fearful that he would not do the right thing.

Aurelia smiled at him, the best she could muster on the eve of their parting. "You will do what you are meant to do. Have no fear, *amore mio*."

Battista heaved a sigh of surrender, but not without his own smile. Moving in the opposite direction of the crowds, they galloped quickly to the shadow of the imposing San Lorenzo and to Michelangelo's house beside it.

"Michelangelo!"

Aurelia jumped from her horse as Battista called his friend's name and tied both horses to the bollard near the door. She entered without a knock, rushing up the stairs to the studio above.

"What madness prevails?"

The spare man looked ever more thin and fragile as he stood in the window, the sun's bright light devouring him, diminishing him still further.

"It is the madness we have hoped for, *amico mio*." Battista strode to his side, scanning the view as Michelangelo did, from the gabled windows.

They could not see the Piazza della Signoria from this vantage point, but they could see smoke, tendrils of it rising black and accusatory into the bright blue sky. They could see people rushing from the homes and shops of the neighborhood, all converging toward the same apex. Michelangelo pushed at the sash and the righteous, determined sounds of a people united rose up in a chorus, a loud prayer to the heavens, one screaming for justice and fairness, for the people and the Republic.

The clang of the bell called them out, deep and dark, *La Vacca,* the cow. It sang only in times of great trouble; it called the people to its tower in the piazza and they rushed to it.

"*La Vacca mugghia!*" they cried to each other, the warning inherent in the seemingly innocuous expression. "The cow lows!"

"You must—," Battista began.

"You must make your way to the piazza, Michelangelo," Aurelia commanded.

"What? No!" Battista turned, angry at the dangerous suggestion.

She laid a hand on his arm. "He will be all right, Battista. I swear to you." Aurelia turned back to the artist standing between them, turmoil cutting a deep swath in his wrinkled forehead. "There is much to protect in the piazza, much that you care about."

Michelangelo's eyes protruded.

"My Giant," he breathed.

The door below crashed open.

"Michelangelo!" the beckoning cry rose up.

The older man smiled through his fear. "It is Granacci. I will be safe with Granacci, *amico karissimo.*"

Battista's worried gaze lingered upon the man, but for only a moment. If Michelangelo's oldest friend did not keep him well, then no one could. Battista gave Michelangelo a nod, pulling him back, devouring him in a bear hug, before letting him go once more.

The artist rushed off, almost passed her by, almost.

Michelangelo pulled himself up short, turning with the saddest smile Aurelia had ever glimpsed. Her breath hitched in her chest.

"I will not see you again, will I?" The thought dawned fretfully upon him.

She shook her head, trying so very hard to smile, not daring to speak.

Michelangelo crushed her to him. His arms quivered as they held her. The muscles, so very sinewy from years of plying hammer and chisel, latched about her body.

Aurelia grabbed onto him as if she held on to life itself.

"You were with me on that scaffold, *donna mia,*" his harsh voice slipped in as a whisper in her ear, words spoken for her and her alone, words of adoration and devotion. "You will be with me forever."

"Of all that is wrong in what I have done"—her voice cracked upon the words, at the emotions so potently close to the surface—"I would do it all again to have met you."

They separated, not either happily, and she found her own bitter sweetness there upon his face. With a shoo of her hands, she impelled him, "Hurry now, Michelangelo."

With one last look at her, a quick smile for Battista, the artist ran from the room, down the stairs, and into the street, taking up the cry of his friends and his heart.

"*Popolo, libertà!* The people, liberty!"

The afternoon waned as they galloped through the countryside, the hard, quick thudding of the hooves like the beats of their hearts. They found but a little ease from the heat as they crossed through the forest leading to the edge of Mantua. They took not a moment's respite; too much urgency hung thick in the air.

As they crested the last rise, Aurelia pulled hard on her horse. "Stop here, Battista."

He reeled as he pulled back and around, his horse bucking at the harsh command. His dark eyes frowned at her as she leaped from her horse, ran to his, and pulled on the bridle.

"You cannot be captured, Battista. It is imperative you return to Florence." Looking up, Aurelia thought he would argue, but she saw only jaundiced acceptance.

Without a word, he jumped from his saddle, dropped the reins from his hands, and yanked her into his arms. Battista hurt her with his embrace, but only with loving intent. Aurelia wrapped her arms about his back, fingers digging into his shoulders.

Their love was a brutal thing, painful by its very nature, and yet more beautiful than anything they had ever known.

Aurelia leaned back; she would have one last look at him, one last moment to memorize his dearness.

Battista smiled at her in understanding; he lowered his mouth and for a stolen moment, as birds twittered around them, as wind soughed through the leaves above them, he paid homage to her with his lips.

With a grunt, or was it a sob, from deep in his throat, he pulled away, setting her at arm's length.

"I will be back," he said, and jumped upon his horse, setting it to motion with a harsh "heeya."

Aurelia waved, even as she lost sight of him in the sea of trees.

Thirty-five

The Love which moves the sun and the other stars.

—Paradiso

The maid hovered and twirled about her mistress, a lovely lark flitting about the resplendent flower, finishing the last touches of the intricate plaits, wrapping the copper tresses about the head and pinning them in place. The young girl, her own hair hidden beneath her starched white wimple, smiled with self-satisfied pleasure at her own artistry. As Teofila placed the jeweled net gingerly upon Aurelia's coiffure, clipping it together at the nape of her mistress's neck, she beamed.

"There." Teofila clucked, stepping back to admire her work from a distance. "You look quite lovely, Donna Aurelia. Your gown is perfect, your hair just so. Even those indecent freckles have all faded away. Your skin is as perfectly pale as when you left."

Her maid's words brought her round, brought Aurelia from passive tolerance to troubled awareness. She sat upon the embroidered cushion surrounded by all the elegance of her life, the opulence of the Mantua palazzo, feeling no less than a foreigner arrived upon a strange land.

Aurelia raised her hands to her face, fingers brushing her skin as if to see it with her touch. She was once again fair of face and the fact brought her nothing but sadness. Aurelia released her head into the basket of her hands and squeezed her eyes closed, pinching out a lone soundless tear to slip down her cheek.

"My lady, *mi dispiace molto*," Teofila gasped in horror, never having seen her mistress shed a single tear in all the years she had served her. "I am so very sorry. If I have . . . What have I . . ."

Aurelia forced a smile and quickly dashed the offending droplet from her face with the back of her hand. "Nothing, Teofila, you have done nothing to offend. Do not worry yourself. It is but my own silliness, naught more."

The young girl stared at her mistress, brows knitting with concern, clearly unconvinced.

"Would . . . would you care for a turn through the garden, madonna?" Teofila asked softly, still troubled. "There is more than enough time before the meal begins."

Aurelia shook her head. "I think not, *cara*. I think perhaps I shall read."

She rose, slipping slowly out of her private room into the sun-dappled sitting chamber just beyond. Crossing to the grouping of saffron velvet wing chairs and a round claw-footed mahogany table in front of the bright windows, Aurelia picked up the leather-bound book from the table's polished surface. She made no move to open it, merely tucked it in the crook of her arm and stood before the diamond-shaped panes of glass.

Teofila followed her mistress. "Are you sure there's—"

"I am fine, Teofila, truly. Take yourself to your meal and fetch me when it is time for mine," Aurelia implored, gaze locked upon the flourishing landscape beyond her window. The straight paths checkered through the formal garden, leading her sight away, where her heart longed to follow.

"Go," she implored her maid's hovering presence.

At last, Aurelia heard the swish of heavy skirts and the click of the latch as Teofila passed out of the room.

Aurelia's shoulders rose and fell with a sigh. As she stood in silent reflection, the sun inched itself around the pale ochre peak of the palazzo and drenched her face with its light. Aurelia closed her eyes, remembering the feel of the sun as she galloped about the country, Battista by her side.

"Stop it," she chided herself softly, opening her eyes. But as she gazed upon the garden, bright blooms of pink and yellow now rimmed with curled edges of brown, withering in the late summer heat, she could not stop her thoughts. Aurelia chewed upon all the nothingness that lay ahead of her, wondering if it was yet emptier for all her recollections. Was she better off when she didn't know what she was missing? She pushed the dour thought away, denouncing it.

Instead, she saw, on the panorama before her, the faces of those she had met, the extraordinary places she had seen, the laughter, the excitement. Aurelia's spirits lifted; her lips spread, the corners turning up, her cheeks bloomed as if she lived it again.

"You look happier than I have seen you in a very long while."

Aurelia turned to the door, having not heard it open again, finding the marquess standing in the threshold.

He offered a quick bow, she a simple curtsy, as he took a few steps into the room.

"I have made a decision," Aurelia told him with a glimmer in her eye. "Right in this very moment."

"Well, then." Federico crossed his hands smartly upon his chest. "I am doubly pleased to have arrived."

"As am I." Aurelia stepped lightly toward him. "I have decided to accept my life, and its purpose, without question, and to be glad only of what glory it holds, not remorseful for anything it may not."

The marquess snorted a pleased puff of air. "So, you have obtained your rightful wisdom?"

Aurelia smiled at the notion, head waggling a bit as she chewed upon it. "So it would seem."

"It is well indeed." He nodded. "Then you may greet this moment in the spirit in which it is given."

Federico stepped to the right of the door, but turned his head back and leaned through it.

"*Messere?*"

Before Aurelia voiced a word of question, before the crease of curiosity fully formed upon her forehead, Battista stood in her door.

"You . . . you are . . . here?" Aurelia gasped, staggered back, a hand to her chest, eyes wide at the sight of him.

With that dashing demeanor, resplendent in leather, and crowned with rakish charm, Battista gave her a half smile. "I am, *donna mia*."

"I told you I would be back." He stepped toward her, afraid of her greeting, cautious before her protector and the man's unerring attention.

"You did," she breathed away her astonishment. "You did, Battista, but I did not . . . I dared not . . . hope."

And there it was, the smile he believed he had helped her find. It was enough.

Battista abandoned all propriety at the door. He rushed ahead, her arms opening, and threw himself into them. His mouth found hers, covering her face, her head, her neck, with his kisses.

She laughed, quivering beneath him, and he held her all the tighter.

The marquess of Mantua sputtered a grumbling cough with a smidgen of embarrassment, an inchoate announcement of discreet leave-taking.

Aurelia looked up at Battista, swallowing any boisterous surprise. "What did you say to him? I cannot believe he has left us alone."

As the nobleman closed the door quietly behind him, Battista blinked, round eyed, shoulders rising to his ears. "I said nothing, I swear." He looked down at her. "Did you tell him, Aurelia? Did you tell him all of what you . . . we . . . experienced?"

She had the grace to look shyly away. "I did. I thought he deserved the truth."

Battista nuzzled her nose with his. "All the truth?"

The flush creeping across her smooth, pale skin answered him, and he laughed as his mouth found hers. They immersed themselves in the delight of each other, silent moments passing uncounted.

Aurelia pulled away first, passion bowing to a more rational state of curiosity.

"What are you doing here?"

He led her to the chairs in front of the windows, throwing the sash wide before sitting across from her; the breeze was thick with redolence and pollen, cooling their ardor.

"I wanted you to know of Florence from a Florentine." Battista grinned. Word of the revolt would have arrived quickly to the door of the marquess, but he feared what prejudice might have arrived with the report, which side had done the telling. Aurelia deserved to know the truth of those she cared for.

She leaned forward eagerly. "It is good news?"

Battista rolled his eyes gratefully heavenward. "It was amazing, Aurelia, simply amazing," he began his tale, excitement bristling in his deep voice. "By the time I returned, the streets were clogged with people, every street and alley leading to the Medici palace. At first, it looked as if a fight would ensue. Ippolito had sent the guards to surround the palace, a human wall. But . . ." He paused for a breath.

"But . . . ," Aurelia squeaked, hanging on his words.

"But the guards are Florentines, *sì?* As the people began to rush the palace, they parted." Battista laughed merrily. "Like Moses parted the sea, it was miraculous. And then many things happened all at once. Niccolò Capponi, the son of he who once drove out Piero de' Medici, stepped onto the balcony and announced, 'The Republic lives again! The Medici are no more!' Then he called for all citizens to arm themselves and rally to the Piazza della Signoria!"

Aurelia cocked an eye at him. "It could not have gone so easily, surely?"

Battista shook his head. "It did not. At that same moment, Cardinal Passerini arrived at the head of the duke of Urbino's cavalry. So many of them, we stopped counting. To this day, no one knows who opened a gate to them. Then the real fighting began." Battista's recollections doused his joy, his head hung with the heaviness. "So many died. So much bloodshed."

Aurelia reached out and grabbed his hand, squeezing it with all her might.

Battista looked up and began again, hands waving in the air with the riotous story. "But the cardinal wanted to retake the palace and the committee of the people would have none of it. They bolted the doors. The duke and his men attacked them with long pikes, but those inside took to the windows and the roof. They threw everything and anything down upon the marauders, furniture, armor, crockery. It was outrageous. It was all wonderful, except . . ."

She slapped at his hand as he left her hanging once more. "Except . . . ?"

Battista shook his head. "Something struck the Giant. I thought Michelangelo would die. The left arm broke off, just below the elbow." He pitched her a sidelong look. "But you knew that would happen, *sì?*"

Aurelia's mouth stretched into a grim line. "I had a thought of it, nothing more. I had hoped he could stop it."

"He could not. Nothing that day could be stopped."

"Tell me the rest," she urged him from the very edge of her chair.

Battista shrugged. "The fighting continued for days. It was unlike war, Aurelia, it was carnage in the street." He looked up at her, a bright star in his deep brown eyes, the smile returning to his well-formed mouth. "But we took the ground. The Republic indeed lives."

Aurelia jumped up and threw herself in his arms; it was the greatest trophy any warrior ever wished to attain. She pulled back of a sudden, pushing him away.

"And what of the Giant? What of Michelangelo?"

Battista laughed. "You will not believe it. It seems one of Michelangelo's apprentices, Guido, ah, no, Giorgio, Giorgio Vassari, and a friend by the name of Cecchino, I believe . . . it makes no matter, though. In the ruckus, they retrieved all the broken pieces, and in the middle of that first night they went to Michelangelo's house to tell him they were hidden at Rossi's father's house, another of the artist's apprentices. They were all safe."

"And . . . he can repair him?"

Battista nodded. "He does so as we speak."

Aurelia sighed deeply with profound relief.

"We did not save Florence, *cara mia*, but Florence was saved nonetheless." Battista tipped his forehead to hers; his story told, the worst of the past few months over, he found release and care in her arms.

"We may not have saved Florence, but we spared the world a terrible fate, never doubt it," she whispered, safe in their intimacy. "You spared the world."

Battista smiled without opening his eyes, wanting nothing more than to rest in this very spot for the rest of his days. "I have done my best, I can say no more." He laughed. "I think I may give up my plundering and live off my bounty."

Aurelia pulled her head away, piercing him with the intensity of her glare. "Be not at war, Battista, I wish it for you with all my heart. But you must be forever on your guard. You have mixed your lot with mine. You cannot doubt what it may mean."

He kissed her quick and light. "It is where I belong, it is—"

"You must never forget the evil that taints the good in this world," she plunged ahead, allowing him no room to naysay her.

"So many men throughout time have thrown their lot in with the bad. You must always beware. Even I, and those who will come after me, can never know all the powers at work in this world. Dante knew of man's woes, men's darkness. We can never forget." She squeezed his shoulders, her thin fingers digging into his arm, and shook him as she would a mischievous child. "Promise me, Battista."

He looked down at her, convinced by the potency of her warning and the ardency of her emotions. All they had seen and done . . . he could never deny any possibility ever again. "I promise, my lady. To you, I swear it."

Aurelia's smile lifted with reassurance, gaze moving to his mouth, lips opening to him. With a low moan of pleasure, he met her invitation, lips brushing hers before capturing them tenderly.

They barely heard the light knock on the door and, though they both desired to, they did not ignore it.

"Enter," Aurelia called, her soft breath caressing his face.

"*Per favore*, madonna." The young maid opened the door a crack and leaned her head in. "The marquess says it is time for your guest to depart."

"Yes, of course," Aurelia responded, and turned to the maid. "We will be out in just a moment."

The maid dipped a curtsy but not without a waggle of her brows at her mistress; Aurelia giggled like a young girl.

"There are many who care about you here," Battista said grudgingly. "I am glad of it. But there are more who love you back in Florence."

Aurelia stepped away, but he pulled her to him yet again.

"Come with me." It was a last desperate plea, one he knew she must deny, one he had to make regardless.

She reached up, her soft fingertips closing his lips. "For all things there is time and purpose. We must serve our time and our purpose. To be together would change both."

He kissed her fingertips; he would bother her no more. As he had heard her tell the marquess, he would accept the joys of what they had, without dwelling on what they could not have.

"I will walk you out," she said, and, curling her hand in his arm, led him through the palace and out into the courtyard.

Gonzaga waited for them in the sparkling sunshine, the scent of warmed stone sharp in the air. The marquess cast upon him a most particular look, and Battista feared reprisal came at last. But Federico approached with an extended hand. Battista took it with cautionary surprise.

"I come to bid you farewell and safe journey, della Palla." Federico looked up at him with an eye of respect. "I blame you not, not at all. You served my ward well. Nothing else needs to be said."

"She is well worth serving, signore." Battista shook the hand in his. "It was my honor to do so."

From beside him Aurelia yelped with delight, tossing off his hand and running to the near courtyard gate.

Turning, Battista smiled. Aurelia rushed at Frado, who had appeared in the square, his and Battista's horses' reins in hand. Battista's smile turned to laughter as she threw her arms around the startled man, unable to deny the twinge of pain at the sight of these two—two so very dear to him—sharing their mutual affection.

Turning from the marquess with a tip of his head, Battista neared the pair in time to hear Aurelia's decree.

"I leave him to your capable hands, dear fellow," Aurelia said sweetly.

"*Sì, donna mia.*" Frado blushed. "Of course, my lady."

Aurelia turned to Battista, parting no longer deniable.

He bowed, taking her hand and brushing the soft underside of her wrist with his lips. Neither would say the word; they simply smiled as space rose up between them.

"Once a year," Aurelia called out as he approached his horse. He twisted back round in silent question.

"Once a year, I am allowed guests," she said again. "But none have ever called."

His heart trembled in his chest, mouth curling, kissed by a bittersweet grin. "Then perhaps I shall be the first."

Aurelia's lips puffed with air; her eyes glistened. "The first, *sì*. And the only."

Battista's restraint broke. Dropping his reins, he ran back, pulled her to him, and heedless of the eyes upon them—from the courtyard, from the stairs, from the windows of the palazzo above—his mouth lit upon hers, drinking of her with a deep and passionate kiss.

Lifting slightly, he brushed his lips over hers, across her moist cheek, to flutter against her ear, where he whispered the words of Dante:

" 'O lady, you in whom my hope gains strength, you who, for my salvation, have allowed your footsteps to be left in Hell, in all the things that I have seen, I recognize the grace and benefit that I, depending upon your power and goodness, have received.' "

Battista lifted his head just enough to see her face, the glow of her sweet smile.

" 'You drew me out from slavery to freedom by all those paths, by all those means that were within your power. Do, in me, preserve your generosity, so that my soul, which you have healed, when it is set loose from my body, be a soul that you will welcome.' "

Postscript

I saw within Its depth how It conceives all things in a single volume bound by Love, of which the universe is the scattered leaves

—*Paradiso*

Pope Clement VII remained a prisoner in the Castel Sant'Angelo for many months. He exchanged his life for a ransom of 400,000 ducats as well as the cession of many highly coveted territories within the Papal States. Disguised as a peddler, he escaped Rome and took refuge first in Orvieto and then in Viterbo. When he returned to Rome, in the fall of 1528, he was to find a city destroyed and deserted. Clement became a weak, ineffectual man, in many ways the puppet of the emperor, in order to secure the fate of the Medici family. In later years, it appeared Clement would tip his alliance back toward France, but the world was never to know. He died in 1534, after ingesting the death cap mushroom. Only a few days before his demise, Pope Clement VII commissioned Michelangelo to paint the altar wall of the Sistine Chapel.

Historians disagree on the extent of collusion on the part of Charles V, the Holy Roman Emperor, in the sack of Rome. Charles had tried for some time to gain an audience with the pope, only to be turned away. Some theories propound that Charles's men took the matter into their own hands, gaining him access in an unprecedented violent manner. There are, however, an equal number of theories claiming Charles was, at heart, a peaceful man, though his life was occupied by a series of wars, a man committed to opposing and thwarting the Protestant reform. These same speculations claim the emperor was embarrassed by the acts committed in his name, though he suffered no compunction in taking full advantage of their victory.

Most all agree that May 6, 1527, when Rome fell, marks the end of the Renaissance era.

Every year on May 6, new recruits are sworn in to the Swiss Guard in commemoration of the soldiers' bravery on that fateful day.

In 1529, the emperor's forces—with the blessing of the pope—besieged Florence. The citizens of the Republic, including Battista della Palla and Michelangelo Buonarroti, fought bravely for many months, though they fell, in the end, to the emperor's superior military might. When the Republic tumbled in 1530, Charles V restored the power of the Medici, who were to rule until 1737.

Battista della Palla returned to his art acquisition during the siege, hoping to bolster Florence's supplies and allies. For the French king, François I, Battista attempted to acquire the celebrated panels of the *Story of Joseph* painted by a trio of artists, Andrea del Sarto, Jacopo Pontormo, and Il Bacchiacca, from Pierfrancesco Borgherini. Borgherini's wife thrust herself between della Palla and his bounty, castigating him as "a most vile dealer in second-hand goods, a cheap salesman," one determined "to dismantle the furnishings of respectable men's bedrooms."

During his lifetime, della Palla "acquired" many remarkable masterpieces, Pollaiuolo's *Labours of Hercules,* Pontormo's *Raising of Lazarus,* Andrea del Sarto's *Abraham Sacrificing Isaac* and *Charity,* and Rosso Fiorentino's *Moses and the Daughters of Jethro,* to name but a few. Most, if not all, found their way to France and the hands of its king, and many still hang upon the walls of the Louvre. When Florence fell and the Medici returned as ducal rulers, Battista della Palla was imprisoned for life in the fortress of Pisa, where he was murdered in 1532. Though there is no evidence of a marriage, his letters speak of a love that ruled his heart.

Elected to the Nove della Milizia, the Militia Nine, Michelangelo served Florence as Governor General of Fortifications. He designed and engineered the defenses of Florence against the forces of the emperor and the Medici pope. Once the family of despots had been restored to power, Pope Clement eventually pardoned Michelangelo, having earlier dubbed him as an outlaw, and returned his properties to him, those in both Florence and Rome.

At the age of sixty-two, Michelangelo Buonarroti began three years of work on one of the greatest of all his masterpieces, *The Last Judgment.* Essayed upon the altar wall of the Sistine Chapel, it was the largest ever completed in a single fresco at the time. Many say he worked as a man possessed, answering a call from above.

From the description of symptoms Michelangelo presented with in the last days of his life, it seems clear he suffered a series of strokes before dying, at the astounding age of eighty-eight, of a slow fever.

Michelangelo penned many a verse throughout the course of his years. In one, he divulged the sum of his life, and that of this humble author, with but a few short words:

> If I was made for art, from childhood given
> A prey for burning beauty to devour,
> I blame the mistress I was born to serve.

On Dante and The Legend of Zelda

Dante Alighieri wrote his *Commedia* between 1308 and 1321, finishing just months before his passing. The work was dubbed "divine" in 1555. The epic poem has been translated more than 120 times. The seminal translation, and the one used for the basis and creative inspiration of this book, was that done by Henry Wadsworth Longfellow in 1867.

Dante's work was indeed intended as allegory, but in my efforts to pay homage to The Legend of Zelda—to combine the inspiration of both—I took Dante's symbolism and gave it a physical construct, while simultaneously endeavoring to stay faithful to his symbolism; a daunting task. I encourage anyone interested in the *Divine Comedy* to reread the three passages depicted in this book with the *Divine Comedy* as a companion and compare the challenges to the appropriate passages. See how they were translated, and imagine how those not alluded to might have been done. It is an amusing exercise that may lend a greater understanding of this book and the *Divine Comedy*.

There may be many who don't know of The Legend of Zelda, who may scoff when they learn it's a video game. But as pastimes will, this particular game has brought me great joy. I started playing the real-time adventure in its first incarnation in the late 1980s and have since played every version that has appeared on every platform. It has provided me with hours and hours of stimulating escapism in a virtual world where the burdens, difficulties and duties of my own life could not find me. And yet it challenged me and brought me the thrill of conquest. It afforded me a wonderful environment in which to bond with my sons, one that grows ever stronger. I feel no shameful compunction in offering an homage of gratitude to something—video game or not—that has given so much to me.

Throughout the *Divine Comedy*, there is the constant and frequent use of the number three and multiples of three. Dante's intention was to honor the three people who make up the one God: God the Father, God the Son, and God the Holy Spirit. In this book, the number three is equally as dominant, but for my own reasons.

In The Legend of Zelda, the symbol of the triforce—three triangles within a larger triangle—denotes the characteristics of a true hero, characteristics worthy of aspiration: wisdom, strength, and courage. I've used threes not only as symbols of these Zelda traits, but also because of other connotations the number represents for me. Like Dante, I have faith in the concepts of the Father, the Son, and the Holy Ghost. I also believe in the power of Ask, Believe, and Receive. And, most important of all, I am resolute to the compass points of my world, the one formed with my two sons.

The Art:
What Exists and What Does Not

Praxiteles was a sculptor who lived in the fourth century BC. He loved a woman, the Thespian courtesan Phryne, who, it is written, was the inspiration for much of his work, him and many others. Pliny the Elder wrote a great deal about Praxiteles, including the possibility that there were two sculptors of the same name, one possibly the other's grandson. While Praxiteles was the first to sculpt the nude female form in a life-sized sculpture, the relic searched for in this book is a creation of this author alone.

Giotto di Bondone was born in Florence in 1267, the son of a farmer who was discovered by another great Florentine painter, Cimabue. Giotto created hundreds of paintings and frescoes in a style that did change the methodology of painting, evolving it from the crude traditional Byzantine style, and earning him the moniker of the father of the Renaissance movement in painting. He was a contemporary and companion of Dante Alighieri, a friendship that earned Giotto a mention in the *Divine Comedy*. There is no work called *Legatus Praxiteles Canonicus* (The Legend of Praxiteles's Legacy); that, too, is of the author's creation. Giotto died in 1337.

The Madonna with Child and Saint Giovannino (Madonna Col Bambino e San Giovannino) is attributed to Sebastiano Mainardi (1460–1513) and hangs in the Palazzo Vecchio Museum in the Sala d'Ercole. It exists as described in this book, including the "air ship" in the top right corner.

Carlo Crivelli (1435–1495) painted *The Annunciation, with Saint*

Emidius in 1486, a painting that depicts a beam of light sent from a round object in the sky down upon the head of Mary. It hangs in the National Gallery in London.

Rows of round, hovering objects fill the sky in *The Miracle of the Snow: Foundation of Santa Maria Maggiore* by Masolino da Panicale (1383–1447), which hangs in the Museo di Capodimonte in Naples, Italy.

Many, many more paintings that include inexplicable objects in the air exist, most of which were rendered during the Renaissance period.

Bibliography

Books:

Bell, Rudolph. 1999. *How to Do It: Guides to Good Living for Renaissance Italians.* Chicago: University of Chicago Press.

Brucker, Gene. 1998. *Florence: The Golden Age, 1138–1737.* Berkeley: University of California Press.

Castiglione, Baldesar. 1967. *Book of the Courtier.* Trans. G. Bull. Harmondsworth: Penguin Books.

Cohen, Elizabeth, and Thomas V. Cohen. 2001. *Daily Life in Renaissance Italy.* Westport, CT: Greenwood Press.

Michelangelo. 1987. *Michelangelo, Life, Letters, and Poetry.* Trans. George Bull. New York: Oxford University Press.

Ramsden, E. 1963. *The Letters of Michelangelo.* Stanford, CA: Stanford University Press.

Stone, Irving. 1962. *I, Michelangelo, Sculptor.* New York: Doubleday.

Thornton, Peter. 1991. *The Italian Renaissance Interior, 1400–1600.* New York: Abrams.

Vasari, Giorgio. 1991. *Lives of the Artists.* Trans. Julia Conway Bondanella and Peter Bondanella. New York: Oxford University Press.

Von Däniken, Erich. 1970. *Chariots of the Gods.* Trans. Michale Heron. New York: Berkley Books.

Internet Sources:

The National Gallery
http://www.nationalgallery.org.uk

The Palazzo Ducale in Mantua
http://www.fermi.mn.it/ducale/index.htm

Pastena Caves:
http://www.grottepastena.it/

Video Sources:

"Closer Encounters." The History Channel Web site.
http://www.history.com/shows/ancient-aliens/episodes/season-1
(accessed September 2010)

A READING GROUP GUIDE

THE KING'S AGENT

Donna Russo Morin

ABOUT THIS GUIDE

The following questions are intended to enhance your group's reading of THE KING'S AGENT.

Discussion Questions

1. In the first chapter, we are introduced to Battista della Palla and his activities. In the very acts he commits, we are privy to the dichotomy of those actions and of the man himself. Discuss the contradiction, how it is exposed, and what it reveals about Battista's character.

2. In Chapter 3, the relationship between the marquess of Mantua and the Lady Aurelia is established, but with some distinct ambiguities. What are these incongruities and what do they reveal about the characters? What specific instances can be cited to attest to the disparities of their relationship?

3. The political climate of Florence, as well as that between all the Italian states, dictates much of the story. Discuss the most prevalent conditions of the era. What are Battista's opinions and attitudes and how do they shape his actions?

4. When Battista and his men first receive the message from François I, Pompeo describes the sculptor Praxiteles, saying, "It is oft told that he loved the same woman for all his life, modeled many of his works after her in fact, but they never married nor had children." Whose life does this foreshadow? Whom then, can it be assumed, did Praxiteles love?

5. In Chapter 6, Pope Clement says, "When you are trapped in the middle, either way may lead to peril." Between whom is the pope trapped? What actions and decisions have brought him to this perilous position? In addition to these two forces, what other group is the pope encountering with difficulties?

6. Chapter 10 includes detailed descriptions and discussions of artworks containing strange and seemingly inexplicable ob-

jects in the air. In the author's note on The Art are listed the locations of these pieces. After studying the paintings, discuss possible explanations of what these objects are and why they may exist in the artworks.

7. Throughout the book, the Lady Aurelia struggles to serve her duty and her purpose while attempting to experience the joy and fun that life can offer. What are her duty and her purpose? Did they change as the story unfolded? Do people encounter the same struggle in today's world?

8. In their final challenge in the Hell below the palazzo, Battista is confronted by the image of his uncle, whose evil actions brought about his death and that of Battista's father. Discuss some reasons why the task included such a personal challenge. What might Aurelia have meant when she said, "Your love for him has doused his flame. You were the only one who could"?

9. Aurelia's covert visitation in Chapter 15 convinces Battista that her true motive for embarking on the quest with him was not to assist him, but to thwart him. What other actions of hers could be interpreted in a similar manner?

10. Also in Chapter 15, as Battista agonizes over his suspicions about Aurelia his thoughts are described as follows: "Like specters—one by the name of anxiety, the other agitation—two women, though they were one and the same, stood in his mind." Though the narrative speaks of Aurelia, of what else do they serve as a symbolic foreshadowing?

11. In Chapter 17, a reason for the broken relationship between Michelangelo and Leonardo da Vinci is introduced, an argument over what they considered to be the preeminent art form, painting or sculpture. Which artist supported which

medium? Other reasons for the disparaging relationship are suggested. Discuss the validity of each.

12. Discuss the intention of the description of Battista as ". . . a man who stooped to thievery with great frequency he knew little of dishonesty." What of him does it most succinctly describe?

13. Discuss the meaning of the challenge Battista and Aurelia endured in Purgatory, the one explained by Aurelia's words: "Dante tells us, through Virgil, that the value of material possessions decreases with sharing while the value of spiritual possessions increases, but only if of a balanced nature, so that one does not feel beholden to the other."

14. " 'He will delight in your beauty,' Battista told her, then shrugged. 'As he does mine. It is his way.' " Discuss this line about Michelangelo from Chapter 21; what does it reveal about the artist? How does it relate to the line "No talent so vast could overcome the misery of living a life in constant conflict with itself."

15. Discuss what Michelangelo meant when he said, "It was an ascension that felled me, I assure you." How did Michelangelo's complex religious and spiritual beliefs affect his relationship with his art and with the popes and the Vatican? Would it have had any consequence in his relationship with Aurelia?

16. Discuss the ramifications of Aurelia's statement in Chapter 29, at the test of the faithful in front of the renderings of Jesus Christ. "Life puts before each human the tests belonging to each life. Here is one of yours." Why was this challenge so particular a test to Battista? What did his choice

reveal about himself and his faith? What was the implication behind the sentence that read: "It came to him, the truth of all mankind, no more readily apparent as when Jesus hung on the cross."

17. What did Aurelia mean when she said, "It was not meant to be stopped," in Chapter 33, when Battista condemned her for not doing anything to stop the sack of Rome? How does her answer relate back to a previous discussion they had concerning fate and destiny?

18. "Their love was a brutal thing, painful by its very nature, and yet more beautiful than anything they had ever known." Discuss the true meaning of these words, found in Chapter 34.

If you enjoyed *The King's Agent,* treat yourself
to more of Donna Russo Morin's delicious
and distinctive brand of historical fiction.
Read on for a taste of

TO SERVE A KING

A Kensington Trade Paperback
on sale at your favorite bookstore.

One

It is the little victories,
That bring us the big ones.

—Ignatius de Loyola (1491–1556)

1520

Beneath an unmerciful sun, the squire dropped the flag with a flourish. Riders kicked at glistening flanks; horses charged forward with little between them save the narrow wooden poles of the lists. Hooves thundered upon the jousting field; the pounding boomed in the ears. Dirt clumps flew up into the air as if tossed in celebration. Weighted and encased in full armor, plumes on helmets bobbing with every gallop, the combatants raised their lances with steely determination, eyes locked upon the impending opponent as they cradled their weapons in the crook between bicep and chest.

Nobleman, courtier, commoner, and peasant jumped to their feet in the overflowing, banner-festooned stands, holding their breath as the two kings bore down upon each other. The impact, when it came, burst out like two worlds colliding. Lance met armor, snapping with a riotous crash and a splintering of wood, and the air ruptured with gasps and cheers. Each competitor had broken his lance upon the other; yet both had kept their saddle. The match was a draw, again.

François quit his black steed with deft agility, tugging off the cumbersome helmet with agitation. Beneath it, his thick chestnut hair lay matted with sweat to his face and jawbone.

"Well done, Your Majesty," Montmorency called out as he approached, raising his voice above the unabated cheering. Beside him, a slight man brandished a satisfied sneer as he scissored his short legs, hurrying to keep up.

With a sidelong look of annoyance, the young king of France scoffed, struggling to remove his gauntlets.

"Do not patronize me, Monty." Finally relieved of them, François threw the thick, padded leather gloves to the ground, words slithering out between grinding teeth. "Damn it all, I cannot best the man."

"That is true," Philippe de Chabot said as he picked up the gloves and slapped them together to dislodge the fresh mud. "But neither can he best you. There are worse ways to spend a day of sport."

In the bright sunlight, François squinted slanted eyes at his companions, his valued friends since childhood, his closest advisers since becoming king five years ago, and felt the heat of his ire cool. Perhaps there *were* other ways to triumph over this adversary yet.

In Henry VIII, François found everything he detested in a king—a hedonist obsessed with the quest for power and pleasure—and yet a part of him strove to imitate this nemesis whom he would never admit respecting, though respect Henry he did. The faults François railed against in his archrival were ones others attributed to François himself. How disgusted he would be to know it.

"Besides," Chabot continued with a shrug of his small shoulders, "you are much better looking."

Monty barked a laugh as François snickered, cuffing Chabot in the arm.

"You must pay your respects to your opponent." The gruff, aged voice doused the conviviality of the young men. Chancellor Duprat approached, skinny legs waddling under a rotund body. "King Henry awaits your hand, Sire."

"Of course." François accepted the intrusion and instruction without argument. Accompanied by his triumvirate of men, he stalked across the rutted tourney field.

"Well ridden, Your Majesty," he called as he approached his challenger, outstretched hand in the lead.

With a devilish smile upon his plump, freckled face, Henry accepted the hand thus offered. "And you, Your Highness."

Cardinal Wolsey, rotund form looming in red cassock and mozzetta, hovered by Henry's side as always, as did the dukes of Suffolk and Norfolk.

These two rivals politely embraced, between them a pull of genuine affection, more potent after the last few days together, yet sharp with the edge of competition, like two loving brothers forever bent on besting the other.

"A worthy match indeed," François conceded. "One deserving of a hearty toast."

"More than one, I should think," Henry agreed. "I will see you at table?"

"It will be my honor." François accepted the invitation with a sweeping bow.

As the men separated and made to quit the field, the crowd erupted into another burst of applause, colorful banners flourishing. With magnanimity, each sovereign acknowledged the accolades with a wave, a nod, and a smile as they quit the field.

A young man standing along the front rail took his pretty wife by the arm, hoisting his daughter higher in his grasp, and began to lead them through the departing congested throng. "Come, *mes amours*, I must prepare to attend the king at table."

"Of course, my dear," replied the delicate woman at his side, skin flushed from a day in the sun.

The toddler in her father's arms put her head down onto his

strong shoulder, blond curls falling on her face as her eyes grew heavy, then closed. Exhausted from the excitement of the long day, she would sleep peacefully tonight.

The royal combatants retired from the tourney field, entourages in tow, each to his own opulent encampment. These men of power and privilege endured no discomforts; though ensconced in makeshift, temporary lodgings, each camp contrived astounding accommodations for this auspicious meeting.

Months in the making, the summit was unlike any conducted before. Leaders who had been overlooked waited with equal amounts of wonder and fear, because any accord between France and England could only spell trouble. The possibility of orchestrating a great peace enticed the English king. The opportunity to bring another to his cause against his rivalry with Charles V of Spain, newly appointed Holy Roman Emperor—chosen by the new pope over François himself—had inveigled the French king forth. A grand meeting, an opportunity to talk; diplomacy and deal making decorated by a grand festival. And yet the undercurrent of competition between the two young and brash *chevaliers*, the constant quibbling for any modicum of superiority over the other, no matter how miniscule, permeated every facet of this audacious assembly.

In the shallow Val d'Or at the very edge of English-occupied France, near Calais, halfway between the castle ruins of Guînes and Ardres, they had met on an early June afternoon.

Henry would have a castle no matter where he laid his head. In the shadow of the Château de Guînes, the Palace of Illusions had been erected with sections brought from England already assembled. Covering an area of more than two acres, it was a convoluted construction of wood and earth covered with a painted canvas to resemble stone and formed with turrets, parapets, and windows. Within its vast rectangular interior lay a courtyard boasting two magnificent fountains fed by three pipes—one for water, one for hippocras, and one for wine.

In a meadow on the outskirts of Ardres, the French had pitched their tents, almost four hundred of them, some as large as any castle's great hall. Many of the nobles in attendance had forfeited all property, selling their fields, their mills, their forests to attend the event with appropriate honor. Surmounted by pennants of golden apples and emblazoned with their owners' coats of arms, the tents of velvet and cloth of gold spread out across the countryside like wild flowers. The field shimmered as if the gold grew from its earth. But no pavilion rivaled the splendor of François's tent.

Taller than any other and sixty feet on a side, two ship masts lashed together supported the mammoth cloth of gold. Blue velvet lined the interior, decorated with fleurs-de-lis and gold embroideries from Cyprus.

Beyond splendid, yet the kings' accommodations paled in comparison to the events conducted over the course of the summit.

Banquets, dances, and mummings filled the nights; a feat of arms—jousting at the tilt, an open field tournament, a foot combat at the barriers with puncheon spears, swords, and two-handed swords—filled the days. The kings were the most rowdy and jubilant attendants of all. In their company were their nobles, their friends, and their women. François had brought his mother; his wife, Queen Claude; and his mistress, the Comtesse de Chateaubriant. Regal and silent by Henry VIII's side stood Catherine of Aragon, with countless fair maidens waiting to warm his bed. As the kings made merry, their ambassadors and delegates made diplomacy, Wolsey speaking foremost for England, while the Queen Mother, Louise de Savoy, spoke for France. Many words passed between these two equally keen minds, but little of lasting consequence was said.

Henry rubbed at his midsection, a replete, resounding belch coaxed forth from the embroidered brocade–covered protuberance. Attendants scurried around him, cleaning the remnants of the evening's festivities like ants upon an abandoned picnic ground. He watched them from his elevated perch on the velvet chair in the corner of the vast room; watched, but cared little about their performance. The last of the guests had retreated in the early hours of the morning, leaving the king in the company of his most reliant confidants.

"Have we found out who the young women are?" Henry spoke to his men, but his unfocused, bloodshot eyes never strayed from the buzzing workers before him, mesmerized, in his hazy stupor, by their tedious, repetitive movements.

The bearded Charles Brandon, Duke of Suffolk, stepped forward, if a bit unsteadily, wine sloshing in a tightly gripped chalice. "They are Thomas Boleyn's daughters, my lord, Mary and . . . and Anne."

Henry pulled himself up from his slump and whipped round, all at once full of eager attention. "Certainly not?"

" 'Tis true, Your Highness, they have been in the French queen's company for some years and are quite soon preparing to return to our homeland."

With sensual, languid movements at odds with his rugged physique, the king reclined once more. "Be sure to send them a personal invitation to court."

"Of course, Your Highness. As you wish," Suffolk assured him, but not without a roll of his eyes and a salacious smile at the small group of men gathered in duty and imbibing.

"Are we done here, Wolsey? I tire of these games." Sounding like nothing so much as a spoiled, petulant child, Henry's bulbous bottom lip stuck out in a pout.

"I believe we have done all we can here, Your Majesty," the cardinal said with neither enthusiasm nor disappointment. "You have done well to sign the treaty."

Henry snarled at him. To make peace with the posturing François rankled; the hand that wielded the quill itched.

"You will see great results from this, I assure you," Wolsey pacified.

It was the slightest of changes, but the king's pout reformed, a devilish grin blossoming in its stead. In that moment, Henry found the joy of the situation in which he found himself: As the lesser of the three world powers, both France and Spain courted him. A master manipulator, he intended to exploit the state of affairs for all it was worth.

"Send a message then, would you, Wolsey? Tell the emperor I would like to talk. He should know of the ostentatious display we have witnessed here. A man with so much to prove as our François, putting on such a show, must have something to hide."

"Of course, Majesty, but per—"

When the hand of his king flicked in his face, the cardinal's thoughts froze on his tongue. Henry leaned forward, resting his free hand upon one knee, eyes fixed upon the young man rushing toward him. The pale, snaggletoothed youth approached his sovereign, lips forming words aching to launch from his mouth. Henry's quieting hand flicked from Wolsey to the approaching squire, who clamped his mouth shut, eyes bulging in fear at the abrupt command.

"Cease and desist." The king's booming voice pummeled the air. "You are all relieved. Make for your beds."

Every manservant and chambermaid dropped whatever lay in their hands, and took themselves off without thought or question. The small gathering of courtiers drew closer to the king, put on guard at once by the abrupt change in his tone and demeanor.

"Speak," Henry barked the instant the last servant had quit the chamber.

With a twitch and an Adam's apple–bobbing swallow, the young man made his report.

"Your fears have been confirmed, Your Highness. The man in question has indeed been seen in clandestine conversations with members of the French contingent."

"Bastard!" spat the king, pounding a fist on the arm of the chair and spewing upon the floor, as if the word and gesture were not enough to rid him of his venomous rage.

The messenger quaked in his worn leather boots, bulging insect eyes once more protruding from his long face. Only Suffolk remembered him.

"You may leave us, good sir. You have done well. Have no fear." With a calming hand upon the youngster's shoulder, the duke turned him toward the door, helping him away with a firm yet gentle nudge. Turning back, Suffolk met with the king's blazing stare.

"You know what to do?" Henry moved not a bit, his voice low and quiet, yet his rage was there for any to see did they know what to look for.

Suffolk's full lips thinned in a grimace, but he bowed, spun on his heel with determination, and left; not a one questioned his compliance with whatever the king demanded of him.

The screams of human and animal mixed in a grotesque chorus, filling the predawn hours with their horror and revulsion. The monstrous flames rose into the black sky, roaring like cannon blasts in the day's most hushed hours. Men, women, and children fled from the orangey blaze in fright while soldier and guard ran toward it. But it was too powerful, too repulsive, and it was impossible to break through to its heart, to penetrate the barrier and save those trapped within. They stood at the aperture of the tent now fully ablaze in the apex of the English camp, waiting to catch those fortunate enough to escape from the fiery cataclysm.

The pandemonium swirled about the inferno like the oxygen that fed it so splendidly. For within every neighboring tent, the brilliance of the flame appeared alive upon the walls, the nexus of its glow indistinguishable through the pale canvas. In terror they ran out of their tents, into the fray; haphazard, undirected commotion. No matter how removed from danger, they ran and screamed, the sickening scent of burning flesh fueling their fear.

"Help us, please," one foot soldier yelled to a passing nobleman, a young man of strong arm and back, capable of hoisting a bucket of water as well as any. But the pampered gent continued his furious retreat, sparing not a glance at the soldier begging his aid.

Coughing and sputtering, survivors staggered from within, but the child emerged without a sound—without a scratch—as if oblivious to the danger she escaped, her long, curly blond hair wafting upward in the rushing air of the blaze at her back. From behind the soldiers, a woman clad in a silk nightgown flung herself forward, as if waiting for this very moment. Snatching the child in her arms she ran, a silent angel intent on her mission.

"How many billeted here, do you know?" one guard called to another as they stood together before the blaze. Few of them remained, so many of them had already rushed toward the physician's tent, the wounded leaning on their shoulders or cradled in their arms.

"No idea," his companion struggled to answer, the flames devouring all the air in and around the tent. "Can't be many. So many . . . already out."

The first soldier acknowledged him with a squinty-eyed nod, holding up a hand in a vain attempt to block the heat from his face, feeling his eyebrows singeing upon his skin. With a hue and cry, both jumped back. The tent, devoured by fire, pitched toward them, collapsing forward with nothing but ash left at its base. Within the crumbling of the remaining wood frame and disintegrating canvas, a whoosh of flames rose higher as one wrenching, agonizing scream roared above the din.

For one suspended moment, the men stood motionless. In the next instant, they moved. Without word or gesture, each bent his head down and charged.

"Could we not have devised a less overt manner in which to deal with this matter?" Henry hissed into Suffolk's ear.

Outside, the smell of burning rubble clung to the air like the desperate grasp of a scorned lover. Dawn's pale gray light tickled at the edge of the earth. In this broken place, physicians and surgeons attended to the wounded while soldiers and servants trod warily through the charred ruins in hopes of finding other survivors. Inside the king's pavilion, the tension clung to every tendril of smoke that slithered in.

"Be gone." Henry dismissed his attendants and guards with an angry flick of his hand, those who had rushed in at the first burst of flames, and threw himself into the embroidered crimson and wood chair in the corner. Head bent, shoulders curled, Henry pierced Suffolk with a potent stare.

"I do not believe it was intentional, Sire—the fire, I mean." Suffolk shook his head, unsure at this moment of the debacle's details. He rubbed roughly at his forehead, as if to clear the jumble of thoughts in his mind. "He was wounded as well. Certainly it is not in an assassin's plans to be injured while carrying out his duties."

"Not a proficient one, at any rate." Henry bit off the snide words. "Was he at least successful? Did any others perish in this debacle?"

"The initial reports confirm the target has been eliminated. His wife and daughter as well. One other died—no one of consequence—but many are grievously wounded."

Henry shook his head of red and gold curls. "Well, there is something in that, I suppose."

"I will find out more."

"Yes, you will." With agitated impatience, Henry tapped his foot on the wood below his feet as Suffolk hovered by his side. "Now."

"I . . . of course, Your Majesty." With a quick bow, the duke took his leave, fairly running as his sovereign's ire pushed at his back. He stopped short at the door, halted by the apparitions standing in the aperture.

Wrapped in a silk shift and dressing gown, the woman looked no less haughty; her soot-stained chin rose from her chest and she walked toward them with shoulders squared. The child at her feet was nothing less than a saintly specter, dressed in white, blond curls forming a halo about her small face.

"I must speak with the king, *s'il vous plaît,*" the woman decreed, the English words lyrical in her heavy French accent.

"I'm sorry, my lady," Suffolk began, "but I'm afraid . . ."

"Let her pass," Henry barked.

Stepping around a bowing Suffolk—perplexity emblazoned on his handsome face—the woman brought the child with her.

Henry rose from his chair, walking forward to greet her, and the confusion crinkling Suffolk's ruddy face fell to slack-jawed shock.

"Madame de Montlhéry." Henry leaned over her hand as she made her obeisance. "Are you all right?"

"I am well, Your Majesty, *merci.*"

"I am most grateful for all your efforts on our behalf this night," Henry said with a small shake of his head. "I am only sorry it has been botched so atrociously. But I am confident no aspersions will be thrown your way."

The woman's pale eyes strayed not a whit from his face. "I owe you my life. There is nothing you could not ask of me."

Henry smiled benevolently, looking down at the child at their feet.

"And who is this adorable creature you have brought to visit me?" he asked, and began to lower his large frame.

"She is my cousin's daughter."

The king straightened as though struck, head snapping toward Suffolk, accusation sharp in his blue eyes. "His daughter? Are you sure?"

"Yes, Your Majesty," Madame de Montlhéry murmured, shuddering at the blast of her sovereign's fury.

"I thought you said they had all perished?" the king snapped at the man hovering by the door.

"It is what I was guaranteed, Your Majesty," Suffolk defended.

"Well, your assurances are meaningless, as is your control of this situation."

"His wife lives, as well," the woman put forth. "She is . . . her face has been . . . no one will recognize her, I assure you. Nor do I believe, with the extent of her injuries, she will last much longer."

Henry clasped his hands across his muscular chest, his knuckles turning white, the skin straining across the bone, clamping down upon his irritation, though sorely tested.

"Suffolk," the king hissed through bared teeth. "Take thee off and see for yourself that the man is dead. I trust nothing this day."

"Your Majesty." The duke bowed, rushing off, no doubt, with thanks to be gone from his incensed ruler's presence, no longer certain his lifelong friendship could protect him further.

"Mum? See mum?" The tiny voice was no more than a squeak, the tug upon Madame de Montlhéry's gown timid yet insistent.

They looked down upon the child as if seeing her for the first time, her presence all but forgotten in the turmoil of the past few moments.

Madame de Montlhéry looked at Henry expectantly, lips parting with elusive words.

Henry lowered himself on bended knees, making himself as small and unmenacing as possible. His smile spread wide, and it chased away any vestiges of annoyance left upon his features. The little girl shrank back, clutching the woman's legs, taking refuge behind the folds of her gown.

"Would you like a treat, my dear? Are you hungry?"

"She loves plum tarts, Your Highness," Montlhéry informed him.

"Is that true? Would you like a sugary plum tart?" Henry asked the wide-eyed urchin.

Though she offered a halfhearted nod, the child remained in the wake of the woman's skirts, her large eyes growing moist and full with tears.

"Goodness, she is a sweet poppet, isn't she?" Henry's voice eased with tenderness.

"She is that, Sire," Montlhéry responded.

"How old is she?"

"A bit more than two."

Henry stared at the child, the pixie nose that spoke of her English heritage, the exquisitely shaped mouth of her French blood, the rosy cheeks, and the pale yellow ringlets.

Henry squinted. "Her eyes. Are her eyes . . . violet?"

The woman smiled with pride, a smile edged sharply with bitterness. "They are, Sire, like those of her *grand-mère*."

"Do you know what I have learned in my few years as king, madame?" Henry straightened, his gaze anchored on the child at their feet.

"No, Your Majesty, but I long for you to tell me."

"I have learned that weapons take on all forms. I have learned that beauty can be such a weapon."

The woman stared down at the child, a different light glinting in her eye. Where she had looked at the girl as a burden, she now gazed upon her as a blessing.

Henry began to pace, his slipper-shod feet plucking out a soft rhythm as he trod a circle around the woman and the child in the otherwise silent chamber, his hands once more clasped together, the steepled index fingers tapping lightly upon pursed lips.

"With your help, madame, I will make her my most powerful weapon."

Madame de Montlhéry lowered her head of fading blond curls, and made her pledge. "I am yours to command, Your Highness, as always."

Henry stopped before her, smiling with satisfaction. "Take her to your home, madame. Raise her as a proper French woman and as your niece, but teach her to honor me above all, above God. Teach her not only to read and write, but languages as well, especially Italian." Henry grew more and more inspired, moving again, spurred by dawning insights, striding to his chair and back again. The light behind his eyes glowed as his thoughts coalesced. "Teach her to cipher, and to shoot."

Montlhéry's head tilted. "To cipher and . . . and shoot?"

"Yes, my dear, to cipher and shoot." Henry jumped to stand before her, grabbing the woman by her shoulders and leaning in, bringing his face within inches of her own. "We will make her the greatest spy there ever was, madame—not a person who became one in adulthood, but one *reared* as a spy. Is it not brilliant?"

"B . . . brilliant, *oui*," Madame de Montlhéry responded, but with little confidence. She stared at the king with ill-disguised confusion.

"And most important of all, madame"—he lowered his voice to a scheming whisper, conspirators bent over their cauldron of plans—"we must teach her to kill."

The heavy, dreadful words hung in the air between them; the silence hummed with their evil intent.

The child stared up at them, comprehending little of what passed between them, mesmerized by it all nonetheless.

"Can you do this for me, Elaine? Can you?"

She swayed at the sound of her name upon his lips. How well she remembered him speaking it as he saved her from the marauding French soldiers who violated her beside the lifeless body of her dead English husband; and months later, as he took her in the night with tenderness and passion.

"*Certes, oui,* Henry. For you I can do anything."

He pulled her hard against him for a quick moment, only to thrust her back. Eager, he lowered himself again to the child. The small girl stared at the man before her, stepping out of the shadow of the woman, as if longing to bask in the magnetic man's light.

"What is her name?"

Elaine drew in a long draught of air, desperate to gain control, to breathe normally once more. "Geneviève, Geneviève de Hainaut."

"No, she cannot carry her father's name." He spoke with a soothing tone of comfort and kindness, knowing the child would understand this better than any words. With care he reached out a hand to Geneviève, watching for any sign that she might pull away from him.

"Come to me, child," he cajoled, his voice as seductive as if he coaxed a lover to his bed. Their eyes met and he felt the thrill of capture. "You are mine now, and always will be."

The tiny bud-shaped mouth twitched with the slightest of smiles and Geneviève took a step forward, and then another. Henry reached out both hands to take her in his arms, and she surrendered as though capitulating to a beloved parent.

Looking up at the woman he had once known as a lover, Henry beamed, victorious. "Let her be known as Gravois, Geneviève Gravois, for it is indeed from out of the grave I have pulled her."

Elaine curtsied low, knowing she had secured the protection and loyalty of this king forever, yet feeling a tear of heartbreak and jealousy, as if she had lost him as well, lost him eternally to this child.

"As you wish, Your Majesty."

As Henry rose, child firmly in his embrace, curled around his powerful form with head resting upon his shoulder, a squire rushed in, stopping short at the sight before him.

"Yes, what is it?" Henry demanded of the silent page.

"The French king, Your Highness. He is here and wishes to see you."

"Of course. Give me but a moment and send him in." Henry nodded with complete composure and turned to Elaine. "Quickly, madame, behind the screen."

Elaine needed no further prodding; fear had gripped her at the thought of François I finding her in the chamber of Henry VIII. She scampered to the screen and its hidden chamber pot, her heels clicking out a frightened percussion. No sooner had the clacking faded away, than it was replaced by the clanging of armor and swords. Into the room François swept, contingent of fellows, as always, in his shadow.

"*Majesté.*" He rushed to Henry's side, no smile of greeting in his eyes or upon his lips, purposeful with sincere concern. "*Comment allez-vous?* Are you all right? We could see the blaze from our camp. I came as soon as I could."

"Have no fear, I am quite well. Many thanks."

François shrugged off his gratitude. "What has happened here? Do you know?"

"I am looking into it, but already I have been assured it was nothing more than an accident—an overturned andiron, it would seem."

"How dreadful. Have many perished?"

Henry chose his words with great care. "Four are dead, and many more injured."

Henry hefted the child, slipping in his arms, a little higher. Though she grew heavier, she appeared wide awake, watching and listening to the two men with great intent. Henry smiled at her and her attentiveness.

"I have brought my physician and my surgeons." François gestured toward the group behind him. "They are at your disposal."

"Quite generous of you, but there is no need. My people have everything under control, I assure you."

The penetrating eyes of the French king scanned his rival's face with blatant suspicion. In the moment of any catastrophe, a helping hand should be accepted with grace.

Henry recognized the mask of displeasure but cared little. His goal was to keep François from learning much, not to acknowledge his magnanimity.

"But I am deeply grateful, nonetheless," Henry placated. "And I will alert you at once should the need for aid arise. You have my solemn promise."

"*Très bien*. As you wish, of course. You will keep me apprised of the situation, I am sure." François gave a small bow of acquiescence. For the first time, he noticed the child cleaving comfortably to the king's shoulder. "And who is this beauty?"

"This? This is my cousin's child. She seems to have wandered from her family in the ruckus," Henry said.

As if she knew they spoke of her, the little girl plucked her head off her pillow and looked the French king in the eye. François laughed at her charm.

"You will take good care of her, yes?" François gently patted the little girl's slipper-clad foot.

"Rest assured, Your Majesty. It is my greatest mission."

"*Bon, bon*," François nodded. "We will talk soon, Henry."

"Of course, François."

With another bow, the Frenchman turned, and with a gesture to his compatriots, began to exit the makeshift castle.

As the king and the child watched the group quit the chamber, Henry pulled Geneviève closer; the little girl squirmed at the intensity of his grasp.

Leaning down, his mustache prickling her soft, tender skin, Henry whispered in her ear.

"That is the man who killed your parents."

The creature writhed on the cot, her whimpers accompanied by the shushing sound of ragged skin rubbing against rough muslin sheets. The physician and his assistant worked upon her wounds, but there was little effort in their ministrations. The burns covered more than half her body and most of her face, the flesh raging red, raw, and moist.

"Has no one come looking for her?" the physician asked.

"Not a one." The woman beside him shook her wimple-clad head.

"Perhaps there is no one," he clucked pitifully. "Perhaps she had made her way to the tent for the night. Such carousing as took place, who knows who ended up where."

"A paramour?" the woman suggested.

"Perhaps. In any case, she won't last long now. Continue the acanthus and thorn apple until her time comes, which, God willing, should be soon. The least we can do for the poor wretch is keep the worst of her pain at bay."

The physician stepped away, off to administer to someone with a chance of survival, and the woman reached for the crushed herbs and warm water on the small table by the bedside. In the dim light of the tent, she mixed the minced dried leaves with the liquid, stirring as she crooned to her patient.

"This will help you, my dear. I swear it will, you'll see." With the tip of the small wooden spoon, she drizzled the concoction into the wounded woman's mouth whenever she opened it to moan and croon.

"I wish I knew what you were trying to say," the caretaker told her patient, gaze pitiful upon the festering flesh. "I wish I could hold you, but it would only bring you more pain."

She stayed with her patient for a bit longer, stroking the small spot upon the woman's head that remained unscathed, until the dying creature began to drift off to sleep.

"Gen . . . gen . . . viève . . ." Gnarled lips mouthed the words. In her haze-filled mind, the wounded woman reached out her hand to the handsome man and the beautiful, golden-haired child, but neither heard her cry, neither took her hand.